EVERY TIME WE SAY GOODBYE

COLETTE CADDLE

ISIS
LARGE PRINT
Oxford

First published in Great Britain 2012
by
Simon & Schuster UK Ltd

Published in Large Print 2013 by ISIS Publishing Ltd.,
7 Centremead, Osney Mead, Oxford OX2 0ES
by arrangement with
Simon & Schuster UK Ltd., A CBS Company

CIP data is available for this title from the British Library

ISBN 978–0–7531–9190–3 (hb)
ISBN 978–0–7531–9191–0 (pb)

Printed and bound in Great Britain by
T. J. International Ltd., Padstow, Cornwall

This book is dedicated to my Twitter friends, who are habitually irreverent, sometimes irascible, frequently indiscreet, occasionally irrational, often impertinent but . . . always interesting.

Acknowledgements

I was quite sceptical when I joined Twitter. I had a preconceived idea that it was a medium where so-called celebrities tweeted about what they'd had for breakfast. Instead, I found a wealth of articles, stories, art and photos and much humour and I was converted.

A writer's life is a solitary one, but my once one-way relationship with readers is now two-way. Within seconds they can tell me exactly what they think of my books and . . . they do. But my interest is not confined to literary matters. I chat daily with people about many things and I love to follow news stories as they unfold, some of which are most definitely stranger than fiction.

Twitter has also turned out to be a wonderful research tool and I am indebted to all those who helped me when researching this book, though some deserve a special mention.

For guidance on legal issues and unravelling the unnecessary red tape I tangled myself in, my thanks to Gwen Bowen, Tom Baldwin and Eddie Murphy. Any errors are entirely my own.

Thank you to Shirley Feehely for the excellent advice on nutrition and health and Jim Montgomery for the insight into criminal investigations.

I am deeply grateful to Dr Joanna Cannon for patiently answering my many questions on all things medical.

At one stage. I couldn't see the wood for the trees and for her cool, calm, clear mind when I was losing mine, I am grateful to Carol Hunt.

For honest and constructive criticism always delivered with humour, thank you, Mandy James.

My thanks as always to the lovely Suzanne Baboneau and her wonderful team at Simon & Schuster for, yet again, dragging me across the finishing line. Gratitude also to Simon, Declan and Helen of Gill Hess for their support and enthusiasm; it never goes unnoticed or unappreciated. I am very lucky to be represented by Sheila Crowley, an agent in a million who is always there when I need her. Thank you, Sheila.

All the characters in the book, forename or surname, are named for the people I have met through Twitter.

CHAPTER
ONE

Marianne Thomson tossed the handful of earth into the grave, flinching as it hit her husband's coffin. Kate let out a strangled sob and Marianne pulled her daughter closer. Her son had wrapped himself around his grandmother's leg and was crying noisily. Dot gently extricated herself, dipped her hand into the container the priest held out to her and, stepping forward, let the dirt fall from her fingers.

"Oh, Dominic," she whispered, stony-faced.

Andrew stopped crying and lunged at the priest. "I want to do that."

"No," Marianne gasped.

"Let him, love." Dot kept a hold of her grandson's shoulder as he moved nearer the grave, a generous mound of earth in his hand.

The five-year-old balanced precariously on the edge and hurled it in.

Marianne looked down into Kate's dark, solemn eyes; she looked so much older than her nine years. With an almost imperceptible nod her daughter stepped forward to take her turn before shrinking back against her mother. Marianne put her other arm around Dot, Andrew between them, and they stood in a

1

tight huddle as the priest finished the service. Mourners swarmed around them afterwards, murmuring condolences before drifting back across the grass towards the cars.

"Come on, let's go and have a nice cup of tea," Helen Sheridan said.

Marianne looked at Dot who was still staring vacantly at the grave. "You take the children," she told her friend, "we'll be with you in a minute."

"Wanna stay with you," Andrew wailed.

She crouched down to hug her son. "Me and Granny are just going to say one more prayer. You go to the car, sweetheart; I promise we won't be long."

He reluctantly took Helen's outstretched hand and Kate followed them in silence. Marianne's gut twisted as she watched the two forlorn little figures walk away. She turned back to her mother-in-law and linked her arm through Dot's. "Are you okay?" she asked.

"My only son is dead; just threw his life away. No, love, I'm far from okay." Dot wiped her eyes. "Why wasn't I able to help him?"

"There was nothing more you could have done," Marianne replied. She had said the words so many times over the last few days and knew she would say them many times more. She didn't suffer the same torture that Dot did. She had stopped feeling guilty, or feeling anything at all, a long time ago.

"I loved him, in spite of everything."

"Of course you did; Kate and Andrew could do nothing that would stop me loving them."

Dot patted her hand. "This can't be easy for you, everyone feeling sorry for Dominic."

"It's fine."

"If you want to tell them all the truth —"

"No, of course not, Dot, we agreed that the children must come first; it's hard enough that they've lost their dad . . ."

"Oh, I wish this bloody day was over. I don't want to see or talk to anyone; do we have to have them all back?"

"It's all arranged, but don't worry. If ever there was a day you could get away with sitting in a corner and saying nothing, this is it."

Dot nodded and with one last look at her son's grave she let Marianne lead her away. "It's a happy release for you at least, love."

Marianne said nothing. It was true, of course, but still a shocking thing for her to say about her only son. The poor woman; how cruel life was. "It's all over now and hopefully Dominic is at peace. Try to remember the good times; there were plenty of them."

Dot squeezed her hand. "You are such a good girl; what would I do without you?"

"You've done a lot more for me than I've ever done for you so, today, let me take care of everything; let's do this properly."

"Right so," Dot agreed and, arm in arm, they strolled back across the grass to join the other mourners.

The day seemed to drag on and on. Marianne was hugged and kissed, her hand squeezed, her shoulder patted. She smiled, inclined her head, and murmured her thanks but her eyes were constantly seeking out the children and her mother-in-law. Andrew was in the garden with Colm, Helen's son, and some other kids kicking a ball around, but Kate wouldn't join in. Marianne suggested that she and Joanna's daughter, Rachel, go upstairs and listen to music but Kate just shook her head and continued to drift between her mother and grandmother as if frightened that they too would disappear. Dot sat in a corner surrounded by a few close friends, a cup of cold tea untouched in front of her.

"Are you okay?"

Marianne looked around and smiled at the concern on Joanna Buckley's kind face. These last few days Jo and Helen had never been far away, quietly taking care of her and her family. "I'm fine."

"Have you had enough of this lot, love?" Helen asked. "Do you want Johnny to shift them?"

"Just say the word," Helen's husband gave Marianne a small salute.

"No, it's okay, leave them for another while."

"How are the kids holding up?" Jo asked.

"Who knows?" Marianne sighed. "Andrew's at least distracted for the moment but Kate is very quiet; I'm not sure what's going on in her head."

"Why don't I take her home to spend the night with us?" Jo suggested. "Rachel will look after her."

Marianne's initial instinct was to turn down the offer; she didn't want to let either of her children out of her sight. Still, perhaps it would do Kate good to get

4

away from this house for a while. "Okay, thanks, Jo. That would be great."

"I can take Andrew too if you like."

"No," Marianne said quickly, not ready to relinquish her baby. "Dot and I need someone to fuss over."

"You look exhausted, Marianne; go and have a lie down," Helen suggested. "No one will miss you for an hour."

Marianne did feel tired; she'd hardly slept since the night that she'd answered the door to the two policemen who'd told her that her husband had taken ill at a restaurant in the city centre. Although there had been a doctor present, they had been unable to revive him. Dominic was pronounced dead at the scene. The results from the post-mortem confirmed that he had died of a heart attack. There had been traces of drugs and alcohol in his system, which didn't come as a surprise; Dominic drank too much and had been popping pills for years. His job as a stockbroker was fast-paced, risky and stressful and though he'd loved it, he couldn't cope without a little help, or, in hindsight, a *lot* of help. He could have moved on to harder drugs in the end for all Marianne knew; he had become adept at hiding his habit from her. She'd given up trying to figure out what was going on in his head; she had stopped trying to help him; she had ceased to care. The only time she confronted him was if his strange behaviour impinged on the children.

It amazed Marianne that none of their friends appeared to have noticed his erratic moods, or perhaps they had just decided to ignore them. As she moved between the groups today, she'd heard them, one after the other, bemoan the fact that he had died at just thirty-eight of a heart attack, no doubt brought on by the stress of his job. He worked too hard, they all agreed. Their words didn't anger or upset Marianne. She just felt numb.

"Marianne?"

She looked up to see Helen watching her with a worried frown. "Yes, I think I might grab forty winks. Will you keep an eye on the children?"

"Of course."

Leaving her two friends to look after the guests, Marianne went upstairs, kicked off her shoes, stepped out of her black dress and stretched out on the bed. She was shattered but didn't bother closing her eyes as she knew that sleep wouldn't come. Was this the price she would pay for her freedom, she wondered; a lifetime of sleepless nights? Still, it was better than freezing every time she heard the front door close late at night and Dominic's footfall on the stairs.

It was hard to equate that intimidating monster with the handsome, funny and loving Dominic she'd married. Back then she'd had to pinch herself; she couldn't believe how lucky she was. To leave the familiar world of St Anne's had been daunting and she'd continued to live a quiet life in the boarding house, rarely venturing out in search of a social life. But then Dominic had burst into her life, bringing with him a sense of excitement and fun that she hadn't known existed. With him anything seemed possible. She fell head over heels in love with him and cried with

6

happiness the night that he'd asked her to marry him. They'd been penniless back then; Dominic was still at university but Marianne was used to living within a tight budget and just sharing a pizza in Dot's kitchen was a treat. She sighed at the memory of those early days together; Dominic had introduced her to the wonder of being intimate with a man. They had been mad about each other and grown even closer when they became parents. Marianne could still see her husband standing at the bottom of the hospital bed, cradling his baby daughter, tears of happiness rolling down his face.

There was a gentle knock on the door. "Who is it?" she called, quickly pulling the sheet across her body.

Kate's head appeared round the door. "Only me. Can I come in?"

"Of course, darling." Marianne held out her arms and Kate climbed up on the bed and snuggled in against her.

"Aunty Helen said I shouldn't bother you and that you were asleep, but I knew you wouldn't be."

"You were right." Marianne smiled and stroked her daughter's long dark hair. "You're not getting much rest either, are you, darling?"

"I don't want to sleep. When I wake up I've forgotten what's happened and then . . ." Kate's voice trailed off.

"It will get easier, sweetheart," Marianne promised, kissing a tear that rolled down her daughter's cheek. "Aunty Jo's invited you for a sleepover tonight."

A range of emotions crossed the child's face. "I can't leave you —"

"Of course you can. Maybe with Rachel in the bed next to you, waking up will be easier."

"But will you be okay?" Kate's eyes, so like Marianne's own, were full of concern.

Marianne smiled at her tender-hearted daughter. "I'll be grand and if I get really sad I'm sure your little brother will give me a cuddle."

"He gives great cuddles. But don't tell him I said that," Kate warned with a glimmer of a smile.

"Won't breathe a word." Marianne hugged her close. "Everything's going to be okay, Kate."

"But life will never, ever be the same again, Mummy. Never."

"No, darling, it won't," Marianne agreed and finally allowed her eyes to close.

When Marianne woke she realized she had slept for nearly two hours. Amazed and guilt-ridden, she hurried into the bathroom to splash water on her face and returned to don the black dress. She paused with it in her hand and studied her body in the full-length mirror with dispassionate eyes. She had kept it well hidden for a long time now, especially from Dominic; would any man ever see it again? she wondered. Dismissing the thought as inappropriate and pointless, she slipped into the dress, ran a brush through her hair and hurried downstairs to find the house quiet except for muted conversation coming from the dining room. She went in to find Dot, Helen and Johnny sitting at the table and Andrew playing at his granny's feet. "Is everyone gone?" she exclaimed. "You should have woken me; what must people think?"

"Anyone who cares about you will be delighted you got a rest," Dot assured her.

Helen hopped to her feet. "I'll make you some tea."

"No, please don't," Marianne groaned. "I couldn't drink another drop."

"How about something stronger?" Johnny's eyes twinkled.

"Yes, I think I'd quite like a glass of wine," Marianne agreed. "Where's Colm?"

"Gone home to make himself gorgeous for his night out."

"I hope you don't mind, Marianne," Helen said, coming back from the kitchen with the wine. "I didn't really agree with him and Di going dancing tonight of all nights but Dot here insisted."

"Quite right too; there's no point in them sitting around moping. Are you okay, darling?" she added, as Andrew moved over and leaned against her knee.

He nodded.

"Whiskey, Dot?" Johnny said, going to the drinks cabinet.

"Please, and make it a large one."

Helen rolled her eyes dramatically as Johnny poured generous measures for himself and Dot. "Well, it looks as if I'm driving."

"Thanks, sweetheart." Johnny winked at her and then raised his glass. "To Dominic."

"To Dominic," they echoed.

"Wherever he may be," Dot sighed.

"He's in heaven," Andrew said.

"Of course he is, love. Come here and give your oul granny a hug."

Andrew went to her and put sticky hands around her neck. "Are you sad?" he asked, pulling away and touching her wet cheek.

"A bit," she admitted, "but keep giving me hugs like that and I'll be grand."

He smiled and turned back to his mother. "Can I watch *Ice Age*, Mum?"

"Yes, darling." He skipped ahead of her into the living room and after she'd settled him in front of his favourite movie, she returned to them.

"Where's Kate?" Dot frowned.

"She went home with Joanna; we thought some time with Rachel might do her good."

"She thinks too much for a child her age."

"Yes," Marianne agreed, systematically shredding a discarded stained napkin.

"She will probably talk to Rachel, they seem close. As for that little fella," Helen nodded towards where Andrew lay sprawled on the floor in front of the television, "I think he'll be just fine."

"They both will be," Johnny assured them.

"Perhaps you should get away from here for a couple of weeks," Helen suggested. "A holiday would do you all good."

Marianne shook her head. "No, I'd prefer to get the children back into a normal routine; they have to get used to life without their dad."

"I think that you're probably right," Johnny agreed, "and time will do the rest."

"The great thing about being young," Dot said, looking wistful. "You just vomit up your grief and get on with it."

Johnny chuckled. "You have a way with words, Dot."

"You two are exhausted," Helen said, meeting Marianne's eyes. "We'll go and let you get to bed."

"It's been a long day," Marianne said, thinking how Dot seemed to have shrunk before her eyes these last few days.

"I am tired," Dot admitted, "but I doubt I'll sleep."

"Still, my lady wife is right. We'd better make tracks." Johnny kissed Dot's cheek and hugged Marianne. "If you need us, just say the word."

"I will," she promised before turning to embrace her friend. "Helen, I don't know how to thank you for everything. The food, drinks . . ."

"Not another word," Helen said as she bent to embrace Dot. "Goodnight, Dot. I'll call you in the morning, Marianne."

"You're an angel." After she had seen them to the door, Marianne returned and put a hand on Dot's shoulder. "Why don't you go to bed?"

"Soon."

"Bedtime, Andrew."

"But I want to stay up with you and Granny," her son protested.

"We'll be going up soon, darling. Now, say goodnight to Granny."

"Night." He flung himself into Dot's arms.

"Night night, sleep tight and don't let the bedbugs bite."

He sped off and Marianne hesitated as she saw that Dot's eyes were full of tears again. "Oh, Dot . . ." she started.

"I'm fine, Marianne." Dot waved her away and Marianne followed her son upstairs.

"Mummy, Daddy *is* in heaven, isn't he?"

Marianne put the book back on the shelf and stretched out beside her son on the narrow bed. "Yes, darling, of course he is."

"Granny says everyone is happy in heaven but . . ." his eyes clouded over, "I won't be able to see him any more, will I? Not unless I die too and I don't want to die."

His face crumpled, and gulping back her own tears, Marianne pulled him into her arms. "You're not going to die, sweetie, not until you are very, very, very old."

"Daddy wasn't very, very, very old so why did he die?"

Marianne looked into the open, innocent face and wondered how she could explain it in words that would make sense and yet not scare him. "Sometimes Holy God needs more angels," she began slowly, "and when He does, He takes very special people up to heaven a little bit early because they are perfect for the job."

"So Daddy's going to be an angel?" Andrew whispered, his eyes round.

"Yes, sweetie, I think maybe he is."

He considered this for a moment. "I'm still going to miss him."

"Of course you are, but do you remember what Granny says about angels?"

"That they look after us."

"That's right." She smiled, relieved; this was going better than she'd expected.

"Maybe God will make him my Guardian Angel," he said excitedly. "That would be cool!"

"It would be very cool. Now, baby, time you were asleep."

"Will you leave the light on?"

"Of course." She kissed his forehead, tucked him in and turned to leave.

"Mummy?"

"Yes?"

"I think *you're* very special; Holy God isn't going to take you up to be an angel too, is He?" he asked in a small voice.

"Absolutely not," she said firmly. "My job is to stay right here and look after you and Kate."

"Good. I wouldn't like Him any more if He did that, I don't care what Granny says."

"It's not going to happen, Andrew, I promise."

"Okay, night," and, clutching his teddy a little bit tighter, he closed his eyes.

As she came out on to the landing, Dot was climbing the stairs.

"Is he asleep?"

"Yes. He wanted to know why his daddy died so young. I told him God needed an angel." Marianne rolled her eyes.

"You did the right thing, though calling my Dominic an angel is a bit of a stretch," Dot joked, though there was no humour in her eyes. "You did him proud today and that's a lot more than he deserved."

"It was important for the children. I can't believe it's over, that he's gone."

"Well, he is," Dot's voice shook slightly. "I suppose I may as well move out."

Marianne stared at her. "Why on earth would you do that?"

"This is your chance to start a new life, darlin'; you don't want me cramping your style."

Marianne leaned against the banister and crossed her arms. "Let's get one thing straight, Dot: you're part of this family."

"That's a lovely thing to say but —"

"But nothing. Apart from the fact that you're the children's only other relative, don't you realize you are the closest thing I've ever had to a mother?"

"Oh, Marianne, what a lovely thing to say!" Dot grasped her hand and smiled. "I must be honest, I'd hate to go; I'd be lost without the three of you."

"And we'd be lost without you." Marianne hugged her. "Now, let's get some rest; it may be late but that young fella will be jumping on us at dawn."

Marianne lay in bed and thought back over the day. It seemed so surreal and she found it hard to get to grips with the fact that Dominic was gone for good. She felt some guilt at her lack of emotion, but then the man she had loved — the funny guy, the good friend, the doting dad — had died some time ago. Of course Helen and Jo knew the truth. Though the three women were very different, their shared history had resulted in a bond that the years hadn't weakened. So she hadn't been able to hide what was going on from them. They had seen the change in Dominic — and in her, and had wrested the truth from her, although not all of it. Her eyes went to the dent in the bedroom door that fresh paint couldn't quite hide, where he'd thrown her against it. She turned on her side and studied the faded blood stain on the carpet by the bed from the time when Dominic had flown into a rage over some imagined slight and slammed the drawer of the bedside table on her finger; it had poured blood and she'd lost the nail. Sometimes Dominic had been remorseful afterwards but there were occasions when he didn't remember having attacked her, asking in all innocence and with some degree of concern, how she had hurt herself.

She'd hidden as much as she could from her friends. She knew Helen would have urged her to leave him or throw him out but she couldn't have done it no matter how much she'd wanted to. But now it was over. Now he was gone and she was free to live her life without looking over her shoulder. And with that thought in mind, Marianne turned off the lamp and fell into a deep and dreamless sleep.

"Johnny, are you awake?"

"How could I be otherwise? You haven't stopped fidgeting and sighing since we came to bed."

Helen turned over yet again and pushed the duvet down a bit. "I'm sorry but it's hardly surprising; my best friend buried her husband today."

"At least he was dead," Johnny muttered into the pillow.

"That's sick." Helen poked him with her elbow.

"It was a joke. Look, sweetheart, it's been a long day, get some sleep."

Helen turned back around to face him. "I can't stop thinking about Marianne and those poor little kiddies."

He stroked her arm. "They'll be fine and your worrying about them won't help. Whatever lies ahead, won't we be there for her?"

"Yes, we will. You've been great this week, Johnny, I'm really grateful."

"How grateful?" he asked, with a sly grin.

"I thought you were tired . . ." she retorted as he ran his fingers down the curve of her body until they came in contact with the bare skin of her thigh, making her shiver.

"I'm never too tired for you, darling."

CHAPTER
TWO

Kate spooned cereal into her mouth. She wasn't hungry and hated cornflakes but if she didn't eat, Aunty Jo would tell Mummy and then Mummy would worry and try to talk to her again. She was beginning to dread their little chats.

"Why do you think you are so restless at night? Are you having nightmares? Do you want to talk about Daddy?" she would ask.

"No, no, no," Kate felt like screaming. "I don't want to talk about Daddy. I just want everything to go back to the way it was."

She'd been having nightmares ever since that night last week when she'd been woken by voices downstairs. She'd crept halfway down to find her granny in tears in her mother's arms as two policemen told them that Daddy had collapsed in a restaurant and died before the ambulance had arrived. It couldn't be true. Her dad was big and strong, well, except for the headaches and the times when he got angry. It scared her when he got mad — it had scared Andrew a lot — but Granny could usually calm him down. Mummy just left the room or took them out for a walk or a drive and by the time they came home, he was usually okay again or had gone to bed. Granny said he got cross because the headaches really hurt him and only rest made them go away. They had to creep around the house when he was resting but Kate had never minded that because he would be happy and funny again when he woke up and sometimes he even played with them.

But now he was dead and she'd never see him again. Even though she'd seen that horrible box being lowered into the grave with her own eyes, she still couldn't believe it. She'd tried really hard to hold in her tears because it seemed to upset everyone when she cried.

"Are you all right, Kate?"

She smiled and nodded at Aunty Jo who was looking at her with worried eyes. She liked Aunty Jo; she was so kind and gentle.

"Rachel, elbows off the table." Uncle Greg frowned over his glasses at his daughter before returning his attention to the newspaper.

The comment caught Kate's attention; wasn't reading the paper at the table worse manners than having your elbows on it? In her house, the only rule at mealtimes was that you weren't allowed to talk with your mouth full, which was fine with her as she loved to sit and listen to Granny tell her stories. Granny Dot had millions of stories and they were all hilarious. Andrew always wanted the ones about Daddy when he was little but Granny was too sad to tell them now. Kate could always tell when Granny was fed up 'cos she got a line right across the centre of her forehead and the sparkle went out of her eyes. Granny had lovely eyes. They were a strange bluey-green, like the sea in that painting in the principal's office, and shone with mischief when she told them rude stories. Mummy always gave out to her but Kate knew she wasn't really cross as she always ended up laughing too.

But it would all be different now. Still, no matter how much they'd miss Daddy, Kate figured breakfast at her house would always be more fun than at Rachel's.

Di appeared, looking pale and tired and Uncle Greg started on her before she'd even sat down.

"What time did you get in?"

"Ten past one."

"I told you to leave at twelve."

"But you said I wasn't to walk home alone," she reminded him, "and no one else would leave until it was over."

"You shouldn't have gone out at all last night, bloody disrespectful —"

"Dad wouldn't mind," Kate blurted out, feeling sorry for Di.

Uncle Greg ignored her. "And I don't want to see you wearing that muck on your eyes any more or you'll be eighteen before you go out again."

Di opened her mouth to protest but her mother gave her a look as she set a bowl of cornflakes in front of her. "Eat your breakfast, love."

"I thought you looked really pretty last night." Kate figured that if anyone could get away with being cheeky it had to be a kid whose daddy had just died. She smirked inwardly knowing her father would approve. He'd never liked Rachel's daddy, always called him Greg-grudge, or G.G for short.

19

"He hates people being happy; begrudges anyone the slightest bit of good luck," he'd said. Mummy had defended Uncle Greg but Kate had seen her smile at the nickname.

"She looked like a little tart," he muttered now.

"Greg!" Aunty Jo said, looking cross.

"Well, I'm sorry but she did." He folded his newspaper, pushed back his chair and stood up. "Time one of us did some work. Don't forget to leave my suit with the dry-cleaners, Jo; Di, cut the grass, and Rachel," his eyes softened a little when he looked at his youngest daughter, "behave yourself and look after your friend."

He gave Kate an awkward pat on the shoulder as he passed and she felt guilty; maybe he wasn't so bad after all.

"And for God's sake, Jo, try and cook something edible for dinner tonight."

Or maybe he was; wait till she told Daddy — Kate pulled up short as she remembered she wouldn't be able to tell him; she wouldn't be able to talk to him ever again. He was gone. He was dead.

"Kate?"

She looked over to see Rachel staring at her, her eyes wide with shock, and realized that she was crying. Not quietly but in loud, gut-wrenching wails and though Kate really did try, she couldn't seem to stop.

"Go and brush your teeth," Aunty Jo told her daughters before crouching down and gathering her into her arms. Kate bawled like a baby, her whole body shuddering and shaking.

Finally, feeling drained and embarrassed, she pulled away and wiped her eyes on her sleeve. "Sorry."

"Don't be sorry, love; why wouldn't you be sad, you poor thing?"

Kate felt the tears start to well up again. "I need to use the bathroom," she said, pushing back her chair and fleeing upstairs to the loo where she locked the door and let the tears flow. When the shudders had reduced to hiccups she went to the sink and washed her face. She looked in the mirror; her eyes were all puffy and bloodshot. Mummy and Granny would know the minute they saw her that she'd been crying. Feeling even more miserable she opened the door to find Rachel sitting on the ground outside waiting for her.

"You okay?" Her friend scrambled to her feet and looked at her with large anxious eyes.

"Yeah, fine, sorry." Kate sniffed.

"That's okay. Will we go outside?"

Kate shook her head. "No, I think I should go."

"You don't have to. You can stay the whole day if you want to; Mummy said so."

"Sorry, Rachel, but I want to go home."

Rachel hugged her. "I'll go and tell Mummy."

"The poor child was a mess." Jo sat down on the stairs as she talked to Helen and cringed as she noticed the window beside the hall door badly needed cleaning; she'd see to it as soon as she'd finished the call.

"Well, it's hardly surprising," Helen was saying. "Imagine, that was the first funeral those poor children had been to and it was their dad's. Still, maybe they're all better off without him."

"They probably are and I can't help thinking that Marianne is still young; maybe some day she'll meet someone else."

"Do you think she'd want to marry again?" Helen asked. "I'd have thought that the last couple of years would have put her off men for life."

"Still, life is easier if you have a partner," Jo insisted. Despite Greg's shortcomings, being Mrs Buckley made her feel safe. The very thought of being alone in the world again made her shudder.

"I suppose that's true. I know a woman whose husband left her and people just dropped her because she was the odd one out."

"That's terrible!"

"Well, I think they did it for her sake; it was hard for her being surrounded by couples and what's the alternative, set her up with a blind date?"

"Did you drop her?" Jo asked.

"Sometimes," Helen admitted, "but I had more girls-only nights and invited her to them; she seemed to like that."

"You never invited me to girls-only nights," Jo said, feeling left out.

"I gave up inviting you to things a long time ago, Jo," Helen retorted. "The only time you ever say yes to my invitations is if it's the whole family or just you, me and Marianne."

"I know, sorry." It was true, Helen had invited her to plenty of things over the years but Jo just felt uncomfortable around strangers and could never think of a thing to say.

"Anyway, Marianne will be fine. We just need to keep a close eye on her."

"Absolutely," Jo agreed. There was nothing she wouldn't do for Marianne. If it wasn't for her, Jo wasn't sure she'd have made it through her time in St Anne's. "She'll be okay though, won't she, Helen?"

There was a short silence before her friend replied. "Of course she will."

And she would, Helen reassured herself after she'd hung up. Marianne had always had a cool head and there was no reason to believe she would lose it now.

Most of the kids at St Anne's had grown cautious and suspicious the longer they were in the children's home. After you'd been pinched, kicked, had a precious doll broken or sweets stolen, you learned to be on your guard. Not Marianne though. She was only a few months old when she took up residence and a more sweet-tempered baby you couldn't find. At three she was moved from the nursery into a dormitory and eight-year-old Helen was charged with helping her to bathe, dress and brush her teeth. It was the best thing that had ever happened to Helen and she embraced her new responsibility with gusto. She had been four when she came to St Anne's after her mother had died and her father had spiralled into depression and alcoholism and was no longer capable of looking after her. Helen was told he was sick and he would come and collect her when he was better. And so every time she heard the bell announcing a visitor, Helen was convinced it was her daddy coming to reclaim her but he never did. As she got older she grew quieter and spent her time wondering what she had done to upset him and if perhaps it was her fault that her mammy had died and that's why he didn't want her any more.

And then suddenly Marianne was there and it was as if she suddenly had a family again. Being Marianne's carer also gave her a new status and won her respect from the other children, which rebuilt her confidence and gave her a new focus. No little girl was ever looked after as well as Marianne. Helen took her job seriously and went way beyond her brief: reading to her, nursing her when she was poorly and sneaking her treats when they came her way. The adoration in her eyes when Marianne looked at her was her reward, making Helen feel six feet tall.

And then Joanna Duffy had arrived and threatened Helen's position. Jo was almost twelve and it was rare that older children came to the home; the corridors were full of Chinese whispers. She'd been a troublemaker; she'd stabbed her dad; she'd been raped by her brother. Helen had no idea where the stories originated but everyone took against the girl and the bullies set out to make her life hell. But soft-hearted, ten-year-old Marianne had rushed to the rescue and drawn her into their cosy little circle. Helen had felt threatened, afraid that she might be squeezed out given there was only two years between the other girls. But Jo was such a frightened little mouse that before long Helen had found herself mothering her too.

When the time had come for Helen to move out of St Anne's, she was torn between feeling excited about the new life that lay ahead and sadness at leaving Marianne and Jo behind. They had been pretty traumatized at the time, too, though she reassured them that she would visit. And she had, every week without fail, and once a month she'd take them out. She put a lot of thought into their outings. She'd had little money and had to be creative, but there was a lot you could do in Dublin for free. If it was a nice day she would take them up to Phoenix Park or to the Botanical Gardens or to Dollymount to paddle, build sandcastles and play in the dunes. She would pack a picnic of dainty sandwiches, lemonade and crisps — forbidden in St Anne's as they were too messy — and buy ice-cream cones for afters. On wet days she would take them to a museum or the National Art Gallery or window-shopping in the Ilac Shopping Centre off Henry Street where they could marvel at the clothes and stay dry. Sometimes, if she could afford it, Helen would treat them to beans and chips in Fortes café before returning them to St Anne's.

That was the hard part. Walking back through the heavy door that banged shut after them with a depressing finality. The reception area held only a hard sofa covered in garish red leatherette, and a large statue of a rather grim and colourless Saint Anne, a vase of tacky plastic flowers at her feet. On the wall there was a crucifix, a holy water font and a picture of the Pope. When she lived here, Helen had never noticed the plain magnolia walls, the plastic chair covers, the scuffed tiled

25

floor and the pervasive smell of disinfectant. It was only in contrast to the vivid colours of the outside world that she noticed how drab and depressing the home was. Even the boarding house she lived in, though modestly decorated and cheaply furnished, was far cheerier; the walls decorated with posters and photographs of previous tenants on their wedding day or holding new babies. Music rang out from the ancient radio in the kitchen, radiating a cheer and warmth that had been sadly absent in St Anne's.

It was the nun who ran the place who they had all lived in fear of. Sister Ignatius was a cold, hard and angry woman who seemed to think that the only way to get through the pearly gates was by crushing those around her. She used to frown on laughing or singing; the first demonstrated a silly frivolous nature, the second should be reserved for praising the Lord.

"Bitch," Helen muttered now, feeling the familiar taste of bile at the back of her throat at the memory of the woman and her cruelty. But despite Ignatius she was here today and maybe because of her, she truly appreciated her family and her life.

CHAPTER
THREE

"Andrew, you know you're not allowed to play with that clock. Put it back up on the fireplace and do it carefully or you'll break it."

Marianne watched, stunned, as her son deliberately let it slip from his fingers and the crystal smashed into smithereens on the kitchen floor.

"Why on earth did you do that?" she exclaimed in frustration.

"It's only a stupid clock." He kicked at the pieces of glass with his bare foot.

"Stop that; you'll hurt yourself."

"So? You don't care."

"Of course I care."

"You don't, you only love Kate."

Marianne crouched down and put her arms around him. "Now that's just silly. I love you just as much as I love Kate."

"No, you don't." He shrugged her off. "I wish you'd died instead of Daddy!"

Marianne gasped; his words were like a knife through her heart. He stared back from defiant eyes, red-faced and shaking. "That's not a very nice thing to say, Andrew."

"I don't care, it's true. I hate you!"

"What's all this then?" Dot stood in the doorway, taking in the scene with raised eyebrows.

Marianne gave a defeated shrug. "He deliberately broke my clock." She started to pick up the larger pieces of crystal and placed them on a tea cloth.

"I'm glad I broke your stupid clock."

"I beg your pardon?" She heard her own voice rising and knew she was close to losing her temper.

"I think I should take this fella out of your way for a few hours. I was just going to do the shopping; Andrew can help me. Where's Kate?"

"At a birthday party; she'll be dropped home about seven."

"Then why don't you relax and run yourself a nice bath," Dot suggested. "And have a glass of wine while you're at it."

"I might just do that," Marianne said with a grateful smile. There had been many outbursts in the last couple of weeks and they were all beginning to get to her; sometimes she just wanted to scream. A few hours' breather from her angry son and silent daughter would be welcome. "You do what your granny tells you, do you hear me?" she said to Andrew.

"I'm not going —" Andrew started in a furious voice.

"Oh, yes you are," Dot assured him, jamming his Crocs on and frogmarching him down the hall.

"Bye," Marianne called after her son, hating parting from him in anger, but he didn't answer. She sat back on her heels, feeling decidedly sorry for herself.

It was almost five weeks since Dominic had died and she'd thought the children would be over the worst but she'd been kidding herself. She could barely drag a word out of Kate and Andrew was turning into the kid from *The Omen*. This latest tantrum had shocked and hurt her although she knew she shouldn't take it to heart. She was confused by it. Yes, he'd adored his daddy but Dominic had spent so little time with his son that she was surprised he was missing him so much. She certainly hadn't expected it to affect her own relationship with her son. And now Kate seemed to have pulled away from her too. She couldn't understand what she was doing wrong. She had been careful to spend time alone with each of her children and had reassured and encouraged them both to talk about their dad.

"Ouch," she yelped as a shard of glass pierced the soft skin beneath her fingernail and it began to bleed. Tears pricked her eyes and she wondered what else could go wrong today. As she stretched towards the worktop for a piece of kitchen towel to stem the bleeding, the doorbell rang. "Typical," she muttered and picked her way through the glass and out into the hall. If this was a bloody salesman, then he had picked the wrong door. She swung it open with a vengeance and sighed. "Oh."

Johnny smiled. "Well, there's nothing like a warm welcome."

"I'm sorry, Johnny," she grinned.

"Dear God, what happened to your hand?"

"It's nothing." But when she looked down, the paper was soaked red.

Johnny propelled her back down the hallway to the kitchen. "Sit."

"But I have to clean this mess up," Marianne protested as he pressed her into a chair.

"It can wait; let me check your hand." He knelt at her feet, heedless of the glass around them and carefully peeled the tissue from the cut.

"Really, it's nothing. I was cleaning this mess up and a piece of glass went under my nail."

"Let me make sure that it's not still in there."

Marianne winced as he probed around her fingertip.

"No, it seems to be clean. Where will I find a plaster?"

Marianne nodded towards the cupboards. "Top drawer."

"What happened anyway? It looks like Beirut in here. Ah, here we are." Johnny selected a plaster and came back to dress her finger.

"It was Andrew. He broke my crystal clock deliberately, the little demon."

"It's not funny, Johnny," she said when he chuckled, but she couldn't help smiling. "He's an awful handful these days; I don't know what I'm going to do with him. I know he must be missing Dominic and I have to make allowances but the way he looked at me just now, it was as if he really hated me." Marianne felt her eyes fill up.

"Of course he doesn't hate you." Johnny smiled up at her and then stopped as he saw her tears. "Ah, don't, sweetheart." He folded her into his arms and Marianne buried her face in his chest. "This has been a terrible time for you but it will get easier. And you've got me and Helen and Jo and Greg to look after you. Well, okay, maybe not Greg —"

Marianne laughed, then hiccupped and drew back from him. "Oh, look, I've made a mess of your shirt."

"Never mind the bloody shirt. The kids will be grand. Right now I think you need to look after yourself."

"I'm fine."

"I don't think you are. I know that you and Dominic had your problems but his death must have come as a terrible shock and you're so busy fussing over Dot and the kids, I'm not sure you've dealt with your own feelings."

"I'm okay, honest," she insisted. "Now I'd better clean this place up."

"I'll do it."

"You don't have to."

"No, but I'm going to while you make me a nice cup of tea."

"Fair enough." She wiped her eyes and went to fetch a brush and pan from the hall cupboard and a thick plastic bag to empty the debris into.

"Do you want me to have a word with Andrew?" he asked as she put on the kettle.

"Dot took him off for a few hours, perhaps she'll get through to him; he adores her."

"He adores *you*."

"He's hiding it well," she joked but she had to swallow back more tears.

Johnny sighed. "He's only five. You're being too sensitive, sweetheart."

"I know, you're probably right but it's hard not to be. It has been such a strange few weeks. There's so much to take in."

"How are you feeling?"

"I'm honestly not sure."

"Relieved perhaps?"

Marianne looked at him in alarm.

Johnny rested the brush against the table and sighed. "Helen told me all about Dominic."

"I see."

"Don't be cross with her. It was straight after we heard the news and I was saying how sad it was and she said you were probably better off. Well, she obviously had to explain that; she'd never have broken your confidence otherwise."

"I know that, Johnny."

"I tell you, it nearly caused a divorce. I was furious that she hadn't told me. If I'd known that he'd raised his hand to you, Marianne, I'd have throttled him."

"Which is exactly why I didn't want you to know. You hitting him wouldn't have helped; it might have made things worse. He was a sick man, Johnny. I had to deal with it in my own way."

He looked at her in disbelief. "And did you deal with it?"

She looked away. "It's easy to see things differently in hindsight."

32

"I know, love, I know."

He went back to cleaning up the mess and said no more until they were sitting drinking their tea. "Will you tell me about it, Marianne?"

She nodded silently. There was no harm in him knowing now.

"When did it start?"

Marianne stared into her mug. She didn't have to think hard; she remembered every detail about that night right down to the fact that her son was wearing the green Babygro covered in bears. "It was when Andrew was about nine months old. He was teething and miserable and there was no consoling him. Dominic had only just got to sleep and the crying woke him. He went completely ballistic, totally over the top. Well, I was furious with him. His screaming and shouting wasn't doing anything to calm Andrew down, the poor child was terrified. It was after midnight but I strapped Andrew into the car and went for a drive; the car usually settled him. After about an hour I took him home, put him to bed and then came downstairs to make a hot drink. I was stirring in the cocoa when Dominic appeared." She paused, visualizing the scene. "I didn't look up; I was still annoyed. It was one thing shouting at me but at a baby . . ."

"So the shouting happened a lot?"

"By that stage, yes." Marianne sighed. "If I had looked into his eyes, I'd have known to keep my mouth shut but instead I tore into him; I said he should be ashamed of himself."

Johnny studied her intently. "What did he say?"

Marianne bit her lip. "Not a word. He came over to me. I thought he was sorry and coming to hug me, to apologize, but he wasn't. He took the spoon from the mug of cocoa and pressed the bowl of it into my arm." Her fingers went instinctively to the spot on the soft inner skin of her upper arm.

"The fucker," Johnny exclaimed.

"I tried to wriggle free but he held my wrists firm between his other hand and used his body to pin me against the worktop. I couldn't escape. I didn't even scream. I think I was in shock."

"So, what happened then?"

"He let me go, put down the spoon and went back to bed. He never mentioned it again. I actually wondered if he had been sleepwalking."

"And your arm?"

"Oh, I put some ice on it; it was fine," Marianne assured him, then wondered why she was still lying. Why didn't she tell him how it had blistered, kept her awake all night and that it had taken over a week to heal? You could still see a tiny red crescent mark if you knew where to look. She sat back in the chair and hugged her arms tightly around her.

"When was the next time?"

"Months later. The children were in bed and I was watching TV when he arrived home. I could tell as soon as he walked into the room that he wasn't quite right." Marianne frowned as she remembered how disorientated he'd seemed. "You know what Dominic was like, Johnny; he could have a few drinks and not show it at all."

34

"He could hold his drink," Johnny acknowledged.

"He could and sometimes he would drive if he'd a pint or two. But on this particular night I figured he must have had several; his speech was slurred and he was unsteady on his feet. I was disgusted that he'd got behind the wheel in that state and said so. He lost his temper and I knew it was pointless trying to talk to him when he was like that so I said I was going to bed. When I went to walk out of the room, he put out his foot and tripped me." Marianne stopped, and swallowed hard. The memory still upset her. "I fell and whacked my head against the corner of the coffee table."

"Jesus!" Johnny clenched his fist and thumped the table as if it were Dominic's face.

"I was okay," Marianne reassured him. "I just felt a little bit woozy. I expected him to be upset at what he'd done, to rush over to help me." She gave a wry laugh. "But he simply stepped over me saying he'd got work to do. When I came down to the kitchen the next morning, there were scraps of paper all over the table covered with totally illegible writing. That's when I realized that his behaviour was probably down to drugs rather than drink."

Johnny shook his head. "Did he apologize?"

"He never even mentioned it. And when I showed him the pieces of paper, he said he'd just been messing about but I could see he was rattled. I begged him to go and see our doctor and he said he would if it would shut me up. Then I knew he must be scared too and that perhaps we'd reached a turning point."

"Let me guess: he didn't go to the doctor."

Marianne sighed. "No, he went all right but he came home saying everything was fine. I didn't believe it so I called the doctor and told her about his strange behaviour. He hadn't told her he was taking any tablets but she'd suspected as much. She said we needed to find out what he was taking, that he could be putting his health at risk." She paused, remembering the following few days where she'd turned into a private investigator, rummaging through drawers and files, even pulling out the bed and checking under the mattress. "I searched the house from top to bottom but I couldn't find anything," she told Johnny, "so I figured he must be keeping them in the car or his briefcase; I was pretty sure he wouldn't risk keeping them in the office."

"Indeed."

"So, one night after I was sure he was asleep I ransacked the car. I found three different sorts of pills and another two in his briefcase."

"Shit."

"There were no labels on the bottles and the pills were unmarked so I took one of each and brought them down to the doctor. She sent them off to a lab. It turned out he was on sleeping tablets, amphetamines and Valium."

"Amphetamines? But I thought he had a problem sleeping? Why was he taking a stimulant?"

"I know; it didn't make much sense to me either but as he was taking so many things to make him sleep, I guessed he needed them to get him through a day's work."

Johnny shook his head. "Poor bastard. I hate what he did to you, Marianne, but it sounds like he was in a bad way."

"He was."

"Was he hurting you right up until the end? Did it get worse?" His eyes widened. "He didn't —"

"Didn't what?" Marianne frowned, and then realized he was wondering if Dominic had raped her. "Oh, no, nothing like that!"

"Good," Johnny said, looking relieved.

"And no, it didn't continue until the end, although he continued to get worse. He wouldn't get help though and I was afraid that he would start on the kids so I decided to throw him out."

"But you didn't go through with it, did you?"

"No, Dot begged me not to."

"Did she know what was going on?"

"She knew he was taking pills but she knew nothing about his violence. I'd had enough by then so I told her everything."

"That can't have been easy to hear."

Marianne wiped her eyes. "Trust me, it wasn't easy to tell. Dot worshipped Dominic. It was one thing to hear he was a drug addict but to hear he beat up his wife too . . . Anyway, that's when she offered to move in; she said that she'd be the buffer between us and that if he ever harmed the children she would call the guards herself. So," Marianne shrugged, "I agreed and it worked."

"I'm so sorry, Marianne." Johnny gave her hand an awkward squeeze. "I had no idea that any of this was going on. I can't believe Helen didn't tell me —"

"Don't you dare go home and give out to her," Marianne warned him. "I swore her and Jo to secrecy."

He held his hands up. "Okay, I won't say a word."

"Now do you understand why I don't believe we'll get the life assurance money?" It had been a discussion that had been going on for days now. Marianne was convinced that the claim wouldn't be honoured but Johnny maintained that it was not that straightforward.

"Nah, I still think that's defeatist talk."

Marianne laughed. "You don't give up easily, do you?"

"With respect, sweetheart, you're too close to the situation to be objective. Take out the emotion and suffering and examine the facts. Dominic wasn't taking hard drugs. These pills are all available on prescription."

"But they weren't prescribed for him, Johnny," she argued.

"They weren't recreational either," Johnny pointed out. "He was a sick man looking for help. Granted, he looked in the wrong place but he wasn't taking drugs just for the hell of it."

"Maybe," Marianne said, although she still wasn't convinced.

"Did he take out the policy before he started taking the drugs?"

"I think so."

"Excellent. Had he been taking the drugs at the time he completed the application form and not admitted it we wouldn't stand a chance."

"We don't stand a chance anyway, Johnny."

"If you're right, it won't be the end of the world. Dominic had a good job and I'm sure you'll get a generous pension. I assume you own the house."

Marianne shook her head. "No, we have a mortgage." When they had moved from their small terraced house in Santry to the larger semi-detached four-bedroom house in Howth, Dominic refused to buy the house although the idea had greatly appealed to Marianne; she'd have loved it if they'd owned their own home outright. But Dominic had dismissed the idea saying that it made much more sense to invest the money; it would be an excellent nest egg for when he retired. Marianne had bowed to his decision as money was his business and he took care of the family's finances.

"Oh, I'd just assumed . . ." Johnny gave a casual shrug. "Not to worry, what's the monthly repayment?"

"I hate to admit this but I have no idea," Marianne said feeling foolish.

"Well, no reason why you should. You took care of the family and he looked after the bills. If you want me to take a look at your finances, just say the word. I don't want to overstep the mark but —"

"No, please," Marianne said eagerly. "I'd appreciate it; I'm completely out of my depth. He kept all our business papers in two box files upstairs. Hang on and I'll get them."

"Great." Johnny glanced at his watch and stood up.

When she came downstairs he was standing in the hall waiting. "I really appreciate everything you're doing for me, Johnny. It would take me for ever to sort out Dominic's estate alone. I don't know how I'd have coped without you and Helen these last few weeks."

He shot her a look. "Oh, I think you underestimate yourself; you seem to have coped with a lot more than you're letting on. Oh, Marianne, I'd have killed him if I'd known what he was doing —"

She put a hand on his arm. "Don't start all that again."

"Is it okay if I say one more thing?"

"Go ahead," she smiled.

"I never really warmed to the man," Johnny admitted.

"Why?" Marianne asked curiously.

"I'm not sure. I suppose he was a bit too smooth for my liking."

"He wasn't too fond of you either," she confided, laughing.

He looked at her in surprise. "Really? Why?"

"Oh, it wasn't just you. He thought it was a mistake for me to stay in touch with anyone from St Anne's, said I'd be better off forgetting that part of my life."

"But you were quite happy there, weren't you?"

"Absolutely," Marianne agreed. "But he seemed to think that it was something to be ashamed of. I told him that there was no way I would ever give up my friendship with Helen and Jo and he accepted that." She didn't add that Dominic had become more and more scathing of her friends and their husbands as time went on. He'd made less of an effort to hide his feelings and though they hadn't commented on it, she knew they must have noticed; they weren't stupid.

"I'm glad you didn't let him come between you."

"Oh, so am I, Johnny," she assured him, "so am I."

CHAPTER
FOUR

"Will you plait my hair, Mum?" Rachel asked.

"After I've made dinner," Jo told her.

Di looked up from her magazine. "What's for dinner?"

"Pork chops."

The girl wrinkled her nose "Ugh. I hate pork."

"Well, I'm sorry, love, but if I only cooked what you like, we would live on fried chicken and garlic bread."

"And what's wrong with that?" Di grinned.

Rachel giggled.

Her big sister tossed her magazine aside. "Come here, I'll do your hair."

"Really?" Rachel's eyes widened in delight and she immediately sat herself down in the chair Di had pulled out and shook back her long blonde hair.

Jo smiled. It was nice to see the girls getting along. They had been very close when they were younger but these days Di was always either reading magazines or texting her friends and had little time for her sister.

"Ow, that hurt!" Rachel yelped.

"It wouldn't if you held still," Di retorted, brushing her little sister's long hair with sweeping strokes. "Why do you want your hair done anyway?"

"I'm going over to Tracy's house."

"Tracy?" Di met her mother's eyes over her sister's head.

Jo shrugged. Tracy Donovan was the most popular girl in her daughter's class but had always ignored Rachel and never invited her to her flashy birthday parties; Rachel was devastated especially as all of her friends were always there. And now, suddenly, she was part of Tracy's crowd and was spending more and more time at her house. Greg was thrilled that Rachel had been welcomed into the Donovan fold as Tracy's father was some big noise in the city, but Jo wondered about the girl's motives; why the sudden interest in her daughter? The front door slammed announcing Greg's arrival home. "Okay, girls, I'll be serving up in a minute, tidy up, please."

"But I'm not finished," Di protested.

Greg walked into the kitchen and frowned. "What is this? A hairdressers?"

"Hi, Daddy." Rachel smiled, oblivious to his sarcasm. "I'm going over to Tracy's so Di's doing my hair."

"Oh. Well, hurry up. I'm hungry."

Jo smiled. "Pork chops, your favourite."

He came to look over her shoulder. "Make sure you cook them properly."

"I will. Did you have a good day?"

"There's no such thing as a good day any more with the state this country is in," he grumbled.

Jo didn't bother replying, instead lifting the pot of potatoes off the stove and strained them into the sink.

"But, Dad, that's good for you, isn't it? You've never been so busy," Di pointed out.

"Because stupid people spent beyond their means and then come running to me to sort out their problems."

"But you're an accountant. Isn't that your job?"

"Don't be so cheeky, miss," he muttered and left them, scowling.

Jo grinned as she mashed the potatoes. She loved that Di wasn't in the least bit intimidated by her father; she was such a confident sixteen-year-old, although she knew that Greg thought she should be much more respectful. Jo foresaw many more clashes ahead between father and daughter. Di wasn't at all happy with the way her dad talked to her mother and though Jo pretended it didn't bother her, her daughter wasn't fooled. Rachel seemed oblivious to it all but then she was the apple of her daddy's eye, partly because she was the image of his dead mother, whom Jo had detested.

As soon as Jo had met Margaret Buckley she knew she had an enemy. The woman was obviously disgusted that her only son was marrying the product of a dysfunctional family who had ended up in a children's home — or an orphanage as she insisted on calling it. Jo hadn't been wrong; Margaret had done her best to split them up. Thankfully, Greg was unaware of his mother's hostility, or at least he'd pretended to be, and proposed anyway. Jo hadn't hesitated. He was a decent man and he was offering her the chance of a good home; one where she would never brace herself for a slap, step over her father's inert, drunken figure on the stairs or stay out of the house, shivering on the green, until she thought it safe to creep back in. And on the days that Greg irritated or upset her, she would remind herself of the dark days of her childhood and count herself lucky that, never once in their marriage, had he made her feel afraid.

"There!" Di stepped back to admire her handiwork and Rachel turned to her mother, smiling. "Is it nice?"

"Lovely. Now, tidy up and set the table."

When they were sitting around the table, Jo sighed as Di pushed her food round the plate and Greg made a production of sawing his meat. "You did say I should cook it well," she couldn't help saying, after his knife had screeched off the plate for the third time, making her wince.

"Yes, but I didn't say cremate it," he muttered.

"It's lovely, Mummy," Rachel said loyally.

Jo gave her youngest a smile. Her family's attitude towards food often baffled her. Jo had come from a home where meals were hit and miss. If her mother thought of cooking a proper dinner it was usually tasteless and the rest of the time meals were a case of grabbing something when you got the chance; Jo remembered surviving on dry cereal on many an occasion because there was no milk. In St Anne's they'd eaten whatever was put in front of them whether they liked it or not because if they didn't, they went hungry until the next meal.

Now as her family laboured over their food, Jo ate every morsel, excused herself and put the plate and cutlery in the sink. Then she went upstairs to the bathroom and stuck two fingers down her throat. As she cleaned herself up afterwards and reached for her toothbrush, she felt almost happy.

Helen served up the sirloin steaks with baked potatoes, mushrooms and onions and her special gravy.

"Oh, nice one, Ma, this looks great." Colm grinned in delight and went to the fridge for two beers.

"What do you think you're doing?" she asked.

"Leave the lad alone," Johnny said. "A lager won't hurt."

Helen tutted and fetched two glasses of water, setting one down next to Colm's beer. He winked at her and she couldn't help smiling. He was cheeky but irresistible with it and sometimes she thought that she would burst with pride when she watched the way every man, woman and child responded to his charm. "Have you finished your homework?" she asked.

"I just have to revise some poetry and I'm done."

"Poetry." Johnny shook his head as he attacked his steak. "As if that's going to be of any use to you in the building trade."

"An honours degree in English is useful in any walk of life," Helen retorted.

"You're right, love." Johnny smiled. "Your mother's always right, lad, remember that."

"I'll get honours in everything," Colm said confidently between mouthfuls.

"Do you think you'll be able to get out the door with the size of that head?" his father asked.

Colm shrugged. "Just stating the facts."

"You've worked hard, lad, but make no mistake, you'll have to work harder at university."

"Not a problem; it will be worth it when you've popped your clogs and I'm running the show and raking in the cash."

"I'm not planning on shuffling off for a good few years and there isn't much cash to be raked in these days."

"And your father worked round the clock for that money," Helen reminded her son. "We saw so little of him that sometimes you would bawl when he picked you up because you didn't recognize him."

"Nah, I did that because he's ugly."

"Cheeky little bugger," Johnny laughed.

"I don't know why you think that's funny, you're the image of him." And he was, Jo thought, from the shock of black hair to the dark eyes and smile. And though Johnny was over six foot, their seventeen-year-old son was nearly as tall as him. They also had the same quick wit and equally quick temper but neither of them stayed angry for long. The only traits Colm had inherited from his mother was her love of music and obsessive tidiness; Johnny's messy habits drove them both mad.

"Excuse me, I do not have *that* nose!" Colm jabbed the air with his knife in his father's direction.

"What's wrong with my nose?" Johnny pretended to be upset.

"What's right with it?"

"Eat up while it's hot," Helen told him before looking across at her husband. "Are you going over to see Marianne after?"

"I suppose."

Helen sighed at the resigned look on his face. She hadn't expected Dominic's estate to be so complicated, nor had he. Now, when he wasn't looking after his own business he seemed to be wading through the man's papers. She felt guilty for asking him to help Marianne but someone had to. "I can't believe he left her in such a mess."

"I don't suppose he figured he was going to die at thirty-eight."

"How long do you think it will all take?" she asked.

"Honestly? It could go on for years."

Helen put down her knife and fork and stared at him. "But how will she manage?"

"She'll have a good pension and she could always get a job."

"She used to work in a travel agency, didn't she?" Colm said.

"Oh, yes, she practically ran the place, but she gave it up because she wanted to stay home with the children."

"Rubbish, she gave it up because Dominic told her to," Johnny butted in.

"Why?"

"He'd been made a junior partner and he wanted everyone to know that his wife didn't need to work any more," Johnny sneered.

"You don't know that," Helen protested, frowning. Since she'd told him about Dominic's behaviour he could barely mention the man's name without anger creeping into his voice. She'd have to talk to him about that. Colm wasn't stupid and it would be a crying shame if this got out after Dot and Marianne had worked so hard for so long to protect the children. "Marianne hated being away from the children so much," she insisted.

"Perhaps, but she was well in with that firm; I'm sure they would have let her work part-time. It won't be so easy for her to get a job now though."

"No," Helen sighed. The job market in Ireland at the moment was in a sorry state. Her heart ached for Marianne.

"Don't worry, love, I'm sure she'll be fine."

"Yes, but there's the children's education and Dot's not getting any younger . . ."

"Dominic was a stockbroker; you can bet he'll have set up trust funds for the children."

"Don't you know?"

"Not yet; Dominic didn't talk to Marianne about money and I have a lot of papers to trawl through."

"I'm sorry to have landed you in this mess, love, but I'd hate it if she had to deal with all this alone."

"And she doesn't so will you please stop worrying." He wiped his mouth on his napkin. "Now, are there any afters?"

"Brill! Egg and chips!" Andrew's eyes lit up as he clambered into his chair.

Marianne smiled. At least her kids weren't bothered by her economizing.

"Lovely," Dot smiled, taking her seat beside him and squirting some ketchup on the side of his plate.

"More, Granny," he demanded.

"You've enough," she retorted.

Marianne poured milk for him and his sister. "What's wrong, Kate?"

"Nothing." The child sat motionless staring at her plate.

"Aren't you hungry, love?" Dot asked.

"I'm fine," she said, half-heartedly stabbing a chip with her fork and nibbling on it.

Marianne threw Dot a look of exasperation. She was at her wits' end trying to tempt her daughter to eat. The child had always been thin but now she was skin and bone.

"Let's have chip butties," Dot suggested.

"Oh, I'm sorry, there isn't enough bread," Marianne groaned.

"Ah, just as well, I'm getting too big an arse on me anyway," Dot said cheerfully.

Andrew spluttered out his milk. "Granny said a rude word!" He grinned in delight at his mother.

Marianne pretended to look cross. What would she do without Dot? Even Kate was smirking. "I think you meant bottom, Granny."

"Whatever you call it, it's too bloody big," Dot assured her.

Kate and Andrew giggled.

"Did I tell you about the diet I went on before your mummy and daddy's wedding?"

"No." Kate shook her head and ate without thinking as Dot distracted her.

"Well, I had bought this gorgeous suit — it was a lovely shade of green, wasn't it, love?"

"Beautiful," Marianne agreed.

"I got it in a sale about six months before the wedding; oh, it was a great bargain, really great. But then I went to Tenerife with your granda, God rest his soul, on an all-inclusive holiday."

"What's that, Granny?" Andrew wrinkled up his nose.

"It's when you don't have to pay any money once you get there. And they had all of these restaurants and a coffee shop and an ice-cream parlour and lots of lovely bars and so we did nothing but eat and drink for two weeks."

"And the suit didn't fit when you got home?" Kate guessed.

"Wouldn't go edgeways on me!" Dot's face twisted in disgust. "I couldn't even get the skirt over my hips."

"Or your big arse!" her grandson chortled delightedly.

"Andrew!"

"But Granny said it," Andrew protested.

"I did, love, but your mother's right; you wouldn't want to let your teacher hear you talk like that, would you?"

"Miss Maloney, now she really *does* have a fat arse," Kate said, deadpan.

"Kate!" Marianne exclaimed as Andrew collapsed into helpless laughter.

"Sorry, Mum," Kate grinned, "but it's true. So, did you go on a diet, Granny?"

"What's a diet?" Andrew asked.

"It's when you stop eating too much to lose weight, numbskull."

Marianne opened her mouth to tell Kate off again and then decided against it; at least she was talking.

"I went on a few," Dot told them. "First there was this slimming drink that I got in the chemist."

"A drink that makes you thin?" Kate asked.

"That's magic." Andrew's eyes were round.

"Ha! The only magic was it made my money disappear."

"So it didn't work?" Kate said.

"I lost a little bit of weight but only because the drinks were so sickly they put me off food. I gave up on them after a couple of weeks. Then I tried the grapefruit diet."

Marianne raised an eyebrow. "I don't remember that. Please tell me that you weren't living on just grapefruits."

"It would have been simpler if I was. 'Twas a terribly complicated business altogether, I couldn't get the hang of it at all."

"So what did you do then, Granny?" Kate asked before popping another chip into her mouth.

"Well, then I tried the Atkins diet."

"Oh, I remember that one," Marianne said. "That's the protein-only diet, isn't it?"

"That's right."

"No carbohydrates?" Kate frowned. "But that's mad, everyone knows you need carbohydrates for energy."

"I'm very impressed," Marianne told her.

"Mummy, what's carbohiders?"

"Carbohydrates, darling. They're foods like potatoes, rice and pasta."

"So did that one work, Granny?"

"Indeed it did not," Dot said in disgust. "I felt hungry all the time and I had no energy at all so you're right about that, Kate. So then I went on the cabbage soup diet and, yes, that meant eating feckin' cabbage soup morning noon and night."

Andrew screwed up his face in disgust. "Ewwww!"

Dot threw back her head and laughed. "You're right, love, it was awful but a lot more so for those around me; when I farted I could clear a room!"

"What?" Andrew was looking confused again.

"She means they were smelly," Kate said, laughing.

"Granny!" Andrew splurted his milk everywhere.

"But did it work?" Kate asked, wiping her eyes.

"Not at all."

"So did you go on another diet?"

"No, I joined Weightwatchers."

"You should have done that in the first place," Marianne said, mopping up Andrew's milk and refilling his glass.

"I should have, it certainly worked although it would have been even better if I hadn't stopped off at the chippy on the way home." She winked at Kate.

"But you were able to get into the suit in the end," Marianne pointed out.

"I was, although I was wearing one of those awful girdle things that holds everything in. I remember I was afraid of my life to eat in case my jacket burst open and I took someone's eye out with a button."

"Oh, Granny, you are funny," Andrew giggled.

"Tell us about the wedding," Kate begged her mother.

"Oh, darling, you've heard about it a million times —" Marianne started, only to be interrupted by the doorbell. "That will be your uncle Johnny. I'll leave your granny to tell you all about it — again." She hurried out to the door. "Johnny, hi, come on in."

"Hello, love, how are things?"

He kissed her cheek as always, but he seemed tense. "It's not good news, is it?" she said, leading him into the sitting room and closing the door firmly.

"I have no news, really. I can find no policy documents, no records of funds, no details of the mortgage." He sighed. "Are you sure there aren't any other files knocking around the house?"

"I gave you everything," Marianne assured him.

"Perhaps he had a safety deposit box where he kept these things."

"Certainly not at our bank, I've checked. The funds were so low in the deposit and current accounts I thought there must be a third one in just his name but there isn't, at least not in that bank."

Johnny frowned. "You never told me that."

Marianne gave a shrug of embarrassment.

"Don't worry about it. You can bet Dominic has accounts in different banks or building societies; he wouldn't have kept all his eggs in one basket."

"But we've found no details of any other accounts," she reminded him, conscious of the nagging pain in her stomach; an almost constant companion these days.

"Perhaps he kept his papers at work."

"Well, I'll find out soon enough; Dominic's boss asked me to come in and see him next week."

"About time too," he retorted. "In the meantime, Marianne, if you need money, just say the word."

"No it's fine, there's enough to see us through for a couple of months."

"We'll get it sorted, love, try not to worry. Would you like me to come along to that meeting with you?"

Marianne shook her head. "Dominic's boss is rather old-fashioned; I think I'd better see him alone. I'll call you afterwards."

"Make sure you do, I'll be dying to hear all the news."

CHAPTER
FIVE

Jo looked at the invitation in her hand and sighed; she really didn't want to go. An evening at Helen's meant enough food to feed an army, all mouth-watering delicacies that she would find hard — no, impossible — to resist. Helen would look regal in one of her expensive dresses while Marianne, tall and slender with her golden limbs and long dark hair, would look fabulous no matter what she wore. Jo couldn't compete; nothing looked good on her flabby body. She'd have to wear the green dress again. They had all seen it a million times before but Greg would be furious if she bought something new; he was always going on these days about the need to save money but then he had never been the extravagant sort.

He had embarrassed her so many times when they'd gone out with her friends and their husbands. Dominic and Johnny were both generous, Dominic in a rather flashy way, but Greg was always the last to put his hand in his pocket. She was sure that Helen noticed; nothing got past her sharp eyes. It made Jo cringe and she found herself looking for excuses to refuse invitations. But this was Helen and Johnny's twentieth wedding anniversary and short of being at death's door, there was no excuse that would get her off the hook.

At least Dominic wouldn't be there. Jo felt guilty for thinking ill of a dead man but he'd made Marianne so miserable. He had been fun in the past, although Greg never really liked him but hid his feelings because Dominic had contacts. He got on better with Johnny but once he had a few drinks inside him, the snide comments would start to slip into the conversation; when had he developed this nasty, sneering streak? Was it marriage to her that had changed him? Perhaps she had turned out to be a disappointment; that wouldn't surprise her. She'd never been sure what he'd seen in her.

She had been an average student growing up. At sixteen the nuns told her she was best suited to factory work or stacking shelves. When she moved to the boarding house the manager, a kindly, maternal soul, set Jo up with a job in a small supermarket owned by her cousin. It wasn't the most exciting job in the world but Jo was quite content. Her happiness was complete when she met Greg there. The shop was only around the corner from his flat in Ranelagh and he was a regular customer. She had noticed him a few times and, since she wasn't yet trained to work the till, she hadn't spoken to him but she liked his serious face and shy smile.

Then, one day, she'd knocked over a tower of tinned beans. The manager had yelled at her and she was tearfully trying to rebuild it when Greg came to her rescue.

There had been several short, awkward exchanges over the following weeks before he finally worked up the courage to invite her out and they had been together ever since. Jo was so happy and even happier when they married and moved into their tiny home. She'd enjoyed being a housewife and although she wasn't a natural homemaker — her mother hadn't exactly set an example — she'd loved taking care of Greg. When she found out she was pregnant, she was over the moon. The prospect of having her own precious baby to mind and cherish was thrilling.

But it all went downhill from there. She'd piled on the weight, suffered terrible back problems and couldn't sleep. Greg grew less and less sympathetic as the ironing piled up in a corner and dinner was often out of a tin or a carton. It didn't help that Helen had an immaculate house, was an excellent cook and proved quite capable of managing a lively toddler while helping Johnny start up his business. Jo felt completely useless and things didn't improve when Di was born; the responsibility overwhelming her. Sometimes she would catch Greg looking at her, disappointment in his eyes, and she could just imagine the poison his mother poured into his ear.

That sour old woman had been the bane of her life, always criticizing her and looking around in disgust whenever she visited, which was far too often for Jo's liking. Once she'd caught the old battleaxe running her finger along the kitchen shelf, checking for dust, which, of course, she'd found. There was dust on the mantelpiece, Jo noticed now, as she replaced the invitation; her housekeeping skills had not improved with time.

She looked at her reflection in the mirror above it. Her hair was a disgrace and she looked old and drab though she was only thirty-seven. Helen had just turned forty but looked years younger. Then again, she went for facials and manicures and had her hair done at an expensive salon in town every six weeks; it was easier to look good when you put that much time and money into it.

Marianne was different. She was a natural beauty who had changed little over the years. Her hair hung halfway down her back; she'd worn it that way since she'd left St Anne's. Long hair had been vetoed in the home as it made hunting head lice too onerous a task. Marianne had always hated the short, boyish cut. She had never bothered that much with make-up and still didn't. In her skinny jeans and simple T-shirts she looked more like one of Kate's friends than her mother. Jo always felt big and clumsy next to her. She didn't even own a pair of jeans, preferring the comfort and simplicity of tracksuits or leggings; they hid a multitude of sins.

Jo studied her reflection more critically. She really would have to do something with her hair for the party. The last short hairstyle that the girl in the salon had talked her into had looked okay but Jo hadn't been able to recreate "the look" since. She was basically a mess. Was it any wonder that Greg had seemed to lose interest in her?

She had never really enjoyed sex in the way that other women seemed to but the fact that her husband wanted her had always made her feel good. And he had wanted her all the time in the early days. Di's arrival and those first difficult months had put paid to the honeymoon period but then sex had resumed once things had settled down and it had been much the same with Rachel. But in the last couple of years Greg seemed to have lost interest and only ever got frisky after a couple of drinks.

She turned away from the mirror and went into the kitchen to start on the laundry, her thoughts returning to Helen's anniversary and what would be a suitable present. Buying something for the couple who literally had everything was, frankly, impossible and usually expensive. She would have to squirrel away some of the housekeeping and keep her eye out for a bargain. She sorted out the dirty washing, put on the first load and then went to make a coffee. The jar of chocolate cookies that Di adored stared down at her from the shelf and her mouth watered. One wouldn't hurt; then she'd walk to the shops rather than drive to compensate for the indulgence. Feeling better, she settled down with a creamy cup of cappuccino, two cookies — well, she was going to work them off — and a magazine. She was halfway through an article about a soap star in meltdown when the washing machine buzzer went. Startled, she realized that over an hour had passed and she'd now had two coffees and five — or was it six? — cookies. It was too late to walk to the shop now or she'd be late picking up Rachel; she'd screwed up again. Full of self-disgust, she dragged herself slowly up to the bathroom and got rid of the food in the easiest possible way. There was an initial feeling of elation when she flushed the toilet but it was quickly replaced by a sense of shame.

She would get into a proper exercise regime, she promised herself. She knew that making herself vomit was bad for her health and she felt disgusted with herself for doing it; she had to stop. She would check the noticeboard in the supermarket and see if there was a local exercise class she could join. With a little self-control and hard work she would be a few pounds lighter before Helen's party. Feeling pleased with her newly formed plan, Jo ran downstairs, fetched her shopping list and handbag, and grabbed her car keys.

When she got to the supermarket, the car park was packed; was all of Dublin doing their shopping here just to annoy her? She drove around several times before she found a spot. When she went inside it was to discover there were no trolleys and she had to go back out to the car park in search of one. It had started to drizzle and immediately her hair began to frizz. By the time she reached the checkout she was irritable, tired and running late. She only remembered her plan to check the noticeboard when she was loading up the car and the rain was pelting down; there was no way she was going back now. She would ask Di to go online and check slimming classes later. Some of her good humour recovered, Jo drove to the school, but by the time she arrived, the normally sweet-tempered Rachel was scowling and hopping from foot to foot impatiently.

"Mum, the party is in an hour and I have to change," she complained, flinging her bag into the back and climbing in.

Jo looked at her. "Party?"

"Tracy's party!" The child exclaimed. "Did you get her birthday present?"

"No, love, sorry, I forgot."

"Oh, Mum!"

"Don't worry about it, we'll stop off at the newsagent and get a card and give her the money."

"But why can't we get the DVD she wanted? I told her I would."

"There's no time, Rachel," Jo snapped, feeling increasingly frazzled. "She can get it herself with the money."

Rachel said nothing but sighed dramatically to ensure her mother knew that she was not impressed. "Are my pink jeans ironed?" she asked after a moment.

Jo thought of the pile of dirty laundry still sitting by the washing machine. "No, I didn't get a chance."

"Oh, Mum, what am I going to wear?"

"You have plenty of nice clothes. Why on earth is she having a party on a school day, anyway? Don't you have homework?"

"Not much and the party will be over by six, I'll have plenty of time."

"Well, don't expect to watch any TV this evening."

"But, Mum —"

"Not another word," Jo warned, "or you won't be going to the party at all."

She let Rachel go to Tracy's house alone. She didn't have time to change and put on make-up and she wouldn't dream of facing the girl's perfectly coiffed mother looking like this. Rachel skipped off down the road with her card and, looking at her watch, Jo realized that it was time to pick up Di; she hadn't even had a chance to grab lunch yet. She'd buy a coffee at the petrol station and have it in the car on the way. The Crunchie she bought to go with it was a necessity, she reasoned, and quite probably less calories than a sandwich.

Di was also in a strop and barely opened her mouth all the way home. When Jo asked her for help checking out keep-fit websites, she muttered something about a project and disappeared up to her room. Some project, Jo thought, as moments later the ceiling began to vibrate with her daughter's music. She hung the clothes out on the line, reloaded the washing machine and carried the basket of ironing into the living room. After she'd set up the board, plugged in the iron and switched on the TV, she put on the kettle, spooned coffee into a mug, her eyes drifting to the jar of cookies. She was standing watching *Come Dine With Me*, salivating at the creamy dessert they were all tucking into and absently ironing one of Greg's shirts when Di reappeared.

"What's for dinner, Mum?"

It was going to be a nice roast chicken but Jo had forgotten to put it in the oven what with all the running around. "Fish fingers and chips."

Di scrunched up her face. "Again? I really want to cut down on chips, Mum, I'm getting fat."

Jo watched in disbelief as her daughter pinched her tiny waist. "You are not remotely fat!"

"I will be if I keep stuffing my face with chips. Here, Mum, you look tired, let me do that."

Jo's eyes widened in delighted surprise. "Are you sure? Have you finished your homework?"

"Yeah, all done."

"Ah, thanks, darling; you do your daddy's shirts so much better than me, he always says so. I'll see if I can rustle up something a bit healthier although we'll have to wait for Rachel to get back. She's at Tracy's birthday party and I doubt she'll get fed much over there; everything is white in that house."

"Mad, isn't it?" Di grinned and swapped places with her mother. "I'm starving; maybe I'll have a couple of cookies to keep me going."

"Oh, I think Rachel finished them before she went out," Jo lied guiltily. "Anyway, I thought you didn't want to get fat?"

Di pulled a face. "Very funny."

"Sorry. How about I get you a couple of custard creams and make you a nice cup of tea?"

"Yes please, and if you want to, we can check out those slimming clubs after dinner."

"That would be great, thanks." Di was such a good kid when she wasn't in a sulk, Jo thought, smiling as she hurried back upstairs to the bathroom to make room for dinner.

When Greg arrived home, the bolognese sauce was ready and a pot of water was bubbling in preparation for the pasta when Rachel returned.

"Where is she?" he asked irritably, when Jo told him why dinner wasn't ready.

"At Tracy's birthday party; she should be home in ten minutes."

"Oh." His whole attitude changed immediately and he nodded in approval. "I'll go down and collect her."

"There's no need," Jo said, but he was already walking into the hall and she watched as he paused in front of the mirror, smoothed his hair and straightened his tie before he left. She imagined Jools and Jim Donovan's amusement at his obvious attempt to break into their circle and felt a bit sorry for him. Why was he such a social climber? Why did he feel the need to keep up with the Joneses, or, in this case, the Donovans? He was clever and successful too; she couldn't begin to understand why he felt the need to crawl to the likes of them. Still, she couldn't understand Greg much at all these days.

CHAPTER
SIX

Marianne swung her legs out of her car, smoothed the skirt of her suit over her hips before collecting her bag, locking the car and crossing the tree-lined avenue to the imposing premises of Matthews and Baldwin. There was something about this office that had always intimidated her. Whether it was the location in the exclusive south-city neighbourhood, the plush reception area with its floor-to-ceiling oak panelling or the haughty receptionists, she didn't know, but Marianne never felt welcome here and she was quite happy that her ties with the company would soon be cut.

Adrian Matthews kept her waiting for over twenty minutes and by the time she was shown into his office, her smile was strained.

"Thank you for coming in to see me," he said from the other side of his vast oak desk.

Marianne looked at her husband's boss with his solemn gaze, his iron-grey hair and impeccable grey suit; grey seemed to sum the man up. His expression was forbidding and his tone clipped and formal.

"I was on the point of contacting you myself," she told him. "There seems to be a lot of Dominic's personal papers missing; I'm assuming that he kept them here."

His eyes narrowed. "I don't believe that we have anything here of that nature, but I'm afraid, even if we did, I couldn't let you have them."

"Excuse me?" Marianne said, not sure she could believe her ears.

"Mrs Thomson —"

"Marianne, please," she said, surprised at the formal address.

"Since Dominic's death, we have uncovered a number of . . ." he paused, "*discrepancies* in his client accounts."

Marianne looked at him in confusion. Whatever his personal troubles, Dominic was good at his job; he'd achieved the junior partner position at an early age and been entrusted with some of the company's largest accounts, a fact that he'd been very proud of.

"I'm sorry to hear it," she said, making her tone as grave as his, "and obviously I can't comment; he never really discussed his work with me. It is purely papers relating to our own private financial affairs that I want; I'm afraid he left his affairs in somewhat of a mess, but then I suppose he wasn't expecting to die so young."

Matthews' eyes widened. "I don't mean to pry, my dear, but are you facing financial problems?"

Marianne felt herself flush. "Money is tighter than I expected but I'm assuming that Dominic has a bank account or two that I don't know about. I'm embarrassed at how little I actually know about our financial affairs," she confessed, smiling.

Matthews didn't return the smile, instead he simply stared at her from under his heavy grey brows. "I'm afraid, my dear, these discrepancies are quite serious. It seems that Dominic was stealing from the company."

"No." Marianne's voice was barely a whisper.

"Sorry to put it so bluntly." He gave a small, resigned shrug. "If we could have his laptop —"

"What?" she said immediately. "Why?"

"There may be invaluable information on it that would help with our investigation."

"Are you quite sure there isn't some mistake?"

"I'm afraid not. I can see this has come as quite a shock; it was to me too. I must say I never expected to be having this conversation; I had high hopes for Dominic. I find it hard to understand what made him jeopardize his future."

Marianne remained silent for a moment as she considered his words. "Perhaps I can explain it," she said finally. "Dominic loved his job and he worked very hard; becoming a junior partner was his dream."

"He was a hard worker," Matthews acknowledged.

"After his promotion he became very anxious," she continued. "It was important to him that he prove himself and live up to the faith you'd shown in him. When he came home he would stay up until the small hours, working. As a result, by the time he came to bed he couldn't switch off, couldn't sleep. I finally persuaded him to go to the GP who prescribed sleeping tablets, but after a while they didn't work either and he started taking two at a time. When he went back for a new prescription the doctor refused to give it to him;

she was worried Dominic was getting too reliant, which of course he was. Instead she suggested exercise and relaxation techniques and told Dominic to cut down on alcohol and caffeine." Marianne smiled sadly. "There was no chance of that happening. Dominic drank coffee all day long and without the sleeping tablets, he drank more alcohol than ever, hoping it would help him sleep."

Matthews looked perplexed. "He always appeared fine at work. How on earth was he able to function normally?"

"He couldn't," Marianne said, remembering those dark days and how frustrated and helpless she'd felt as her husband fell apart before her eyes. "When he couldn't get the tablets from the GP, he started to buy them online."

Matthews was shocked. "That seems a very risky thing to do — and a very desperate one."

In retrospect Marianne had to agree but it had made some sense at the time. "He was just buying the pills the doctor had prescribed for him; it seemed preferable to him drinking. Dominic wasn't a pleasant drunk; he could become quite aggressive," she explained, thinking that when she'd walked in here today she hadn't expected to be telling Dominic's boss any of this. "All in all, buying sleeping tablets online seemed the lesser of two evils."

"I can understand that," Matthews nodded, his eyes sad.

"It was fine for a while but as time went on the tablets grew less effective and Dominic increased the dose. I begged him not to, I was terrified of the harm he might do himself. In the morning he was bleary-eyed getting into the car and there were days when it was almost impossible to wake him. The only way I finally got through to him was when I pointed out that if I was noticing what a mess he was in the mornings, that you must be too and that he might be jeopardizing his career. Well, that shocked him and had almost an immediate effect; he just seemed to snap out of it. I suppose I should have been suspicious but I was so relieved that he was behaving normally." She paused, wondering if she had really believed everything was okay or had she just wanted it so much that she had closed her eyes to the truth. "But the transformation was due to yet more drugs that he'd started taking in the morning to get him up and going. It's not surprising I didn't notice; he was hardly ever at home. He left for work before we were up and was rarely home before eight, and then with so many business dinners . . ." She stopped at the puzzled look on Matthews' face. "What?"

"Well, my dear, Dominic was a hard worker but he usually left the office by five thirty, six at the latest. As for dinners, given these difficult times we cut the expense accounts of all management eighteen months ago; entertaining clients was vetoed."

"So, where was he?" Marianne wondered aloud.

"I'm afraid I have no idea."

It took a moment for Marianne to twig why he was looking uncomfortable. "You think he was with a woman?" She smiled at the ludicrous idea. Between his

70

erratic moods and heavy workload, Dominic wouldn't have had the time or patience for another woman. But he wasn't working long hours, she reminded herself, and perhaps another woman might account for his ambivalence towards her. She pushed the thought to the back of her mind; she would reflect on it later. "How much did he take from the company?" she asked, thinking of the dwindling current account and their modest deposit account; nothing made sense.

Matthews shook his head. "It's too early to say for sure, but we are talking six figures."

She stared at him, stunned. "I don't know what to say. I had no idea what he was up to, I assure you; he certainly didn't lodge the money in our accounts," she paused and looked at him, "if you want to check —"

Matthews held up a hand, looking embarrassed. "Your openness and honesty makes it even more difficult for me to tell you, Marianne, but I'm afraid there is no possibility of us honouring your pension at this moment in time. Happily, I'm sure that his life assurance will be substantial —"

"They are contesting our claim," she said. "Traces of drugs showed up in the post-mortem results."

Matthews looked at her, his eyes full of pity. "My dear girl, I am so sorry. It seems wrong that you and your family should suffer like this. Let me talk to the other partners about this and see if there is anything we can do."

"Thank you, I appreciate that."

"I'll have a courier pick up the laptop this afternoon if that's okay."

"Of course."

"Thank you. Oh, forgive me for asking but would you mind if we borrowed his phone too?"

"I don't have it; the police suspect it may have been stolen in the restaurant."

"How despicable," Matthews said, glancing surreptitiously at his watch.

"I must go." Marianne stood up. Her legs felt shaky and she steadied herself on the arm of the chair.

"Are you okay to drive?" he asked, looking at her in concern. "I could get someone to drop you and you could collect your car tomorrow."

"I'm fine."

"I doubt that." He shook her hand and sighed. "I am sorry to have been the bearer of such shocking news."

"Will you let me know if there are any developments?"

"Of course."

Marianne drove around the corner and parked before she broke down. As the tears ran down her cheeks, she clenched the steering wheel for support, her whole body trembling; she had never felt as frightened in her life. How was she to manage with no income, no savings and two children and Dot to support? Her breaths came in short, fast gasps and she realized she was having a panic attack. She concentrated on her breathing, willing herself to calm down; she couldn't go home in this state. What the hell was she going to tell Dot? Realizing that she couldn't face her mother-in-law

72

yet, she turned on the ignition, turned the car around and set out for Johnny Sheridan's builders' yard.

She sighed in relief when she saw his distinctive maroon Mercedes and parked rather haphazardly behind it. She wiped her eyes, blew her nose and picked her way through the dirt towards the Portakabin that served as Johnny's office.

"Yeah?"

She opened the door and stood uncertainly in the doorway as he continued to type, his head bent over his keyboard. "Bad time?"

"Marianne." He immediately pushed away from his desk and came around to greet her, his smile faltering when he saw her expression. "You look done in, sweetheart; is everything okay?"

She gave him a watery smile. "Not really."

"Come and sit down." He gestured to a chair and pulled his own around the desk so he could sit beside her. "I'd offer you a cuppa but there's no milk."

"I could do with something a lot stronger."

"Come on then, spit it out, what's up?"

She dropped her bag on the dusty floor and flopped back in the chair; feeling tired and beaten. "I don't know where to start."

"Try the beginning."

She looked into his kind face and took a deep breath. "Dominic was stealing from Matthews and Baldwin, Johnny."

"Are you serious?" He stared at her in astonishment.

"Yes. After he died they were going through his client accounts and apparently there are 'discrepancies'."

"What sort of discrepancies?"

"Adrian Matthews couldn't or wouldn't say; the investigation is ongoing apparently."

Johnny digested the news. "How much are we talking about?"

"They don't know exactly yet but they think it runs to six figures."

"Shit, you're kidding me!"

She shook her head. "I thought Dominic must have done it to pay for the drugs but he couldn't possibly have spent that sort of money, could he?"

"I wouldn't have thought so."

"There's more. All his business dinners, the working late, it was all lies."

"But why? And if he wasn't at work, where was he?"

Marianne shrugged. "You tell me."

"You think he was having an affair? No, Marianne, for all his faults, he loved you; get that silly notion out of your head."

Marianne took a tissue from her sleeve and blew her nose. "Do you honestly think I care, Johnny?"

He looked uncomfortable. No, I suppose not."

"If he wasn't meeting a woman then where was he?"

"He could have belonged to one of these private gambling clubs. That would account for the stealing and his absences, and when he started losing money he dipped into the company coffers."

Marianne wasn't convinced. "He never showed an interest in gambling before; I don't think he ever even backed a horse in the Grand National."

74

"I doubt interest would have anything to do with it; remember he had an addictive personality."

"I suppose," she agreed.

"So, how was Matthews with you?"

"Initially he was quite frosty but he thawed. It helped that I agreed to hand over Dominic's laptop."

"You did?" Johnny frowned.

"It would have looked very suspicious if I hadn't."

"I suppose. You know, Marianne, I think you should take legal advice. We have to make sure that the company can't seize your assets to pay his debts."

"Ha, what is there to seize?"

"Your house, love," he said softly.

"No, they wouldn't take my house!" She looked at him in alarm. "They couldn't . . . could they?"

"Probably not but we should find out."

She shook her head; the nightmare was getting steadily worse. "I'm still trying to get my head around the fact that on top of having no life assurance I now have no pension either."

"He said that?"

"More or less. Why should they cough up for a man who robbed them?"

"But that's not your fault," Johnny protested. "Let me call my solicitor; Eddie's a good guy."

"If you want, but I don't have a leg to stand on and you know it, Johnny."

"We need to find that money, or what's left of it." Johnny drummed his fingers on the desk and frowned in concentration. "Did they have any of his personal papers?"

She shook her head. "Matthews said there weren't any."

"Perhaps we should hire a private investigator."

Marianne raised her eyebrows. "And pay him with what?"

"What a bloody mess. And poor Dot; how do you think she'll take this latest bombshell?"

"I can't tell her," Marianne whispered. Dot had been through enough; she couldn't hit her with this as well.

"But how can you keep it a secret, darling? How are you going to explain the fact that there's no pension?"

"I have no idea but I can't tell her this, Johnny. His addiction was one thing but finding out that her only child was a thief too would break her heart."

He thought for a moment. "The simplest thing to do is tell her that for legal reasons they have to wait until after the inquest before they can pay you any money."

"And what then?" She dragged tired fingers through her long hair.

"Don't worry about that now," he frowned.

"You're right. Lord knows I've more than enough to worry about at the moment." She stood up. "I'd better go."

He gave her a warm hug. "Are you going to be okay?"

"I'm going to have to be, aren't I?" Marianne said, feeling weepy again. But she couldn't give in to tears, she had to go home and convince Dot that everything was fine.

"You'll get through this, love. Helen and I will be with you every step of the way."

She clung to him for a second. "Good, because I have a feeling I'm going to need you."

CHAPTER
SEVEN

When Marianne struggled through the door, laden down with bags, she found Dot standing at the kitchen table, baking.

"Hello, love, how did you get on?"

"Not bad," Marianne said as she put away the groceries. She had decided to do the shopping on the way home to give herself more time to recover her composure. It had worked. As she wandered up and down aisles she counted her blessings. She had two amazing, healthy kids, a wonderful mother-in-law, great friends in Helen, Jo and Johnny, and she knew even Greg would offer support if it was needed. And she no longer had the stormy, threatening cloud in the shape of Dominic hanging over her. Yes, he'd left her a sorry mess to deal with but deal with it she would. "I'm gasping for some tea, want one? I got doughnuts." She reached for the kettle.

"Lovely." Dot put the apple tart in the oven, cleaned up and sat waiting in silence until Marianne had made the tea and joined her.

"So, out with it; what's wrong?"

Marianne met her gaze and smiled. "I can never fool you, can I? Bad news, I'm afraid. It looks like I won't get a penny from Matthews and Baldwin until after the inquest."

"But that could take ages." Dot looked horrified.

"I know." Marianne gave a helpless shrug.

"Have you enough money to last that long?"

"Not really. We're going to have to seriously economize and plan for the worst. I should probably start looking for a job."

"I can't believe it. I thought that Dominic would have plenty of money put by."

"You know Dominic, he didn't really believe in leaving money in bank accounts; he liked to invest." It was true, Marianne thought, and made a mental note to say so to Johnny. Perhaps Dominic had lots of shares that they hadn't discovered yet. Still, if they did, were they hers or would she have to hand them over to Matthews and Baldwin? It all made her head spin.

"I'm sorry, love, you shouldn't have to worry about money on top of everything else."

"Perhaps going back to work is exactly the distraction I need, although I don't imagine getting a job will be easy these days."

"But didn't you have a great job in the travel agency?"

"Yes, but they were different times. Still, I'm sure I'll find something."

"We both will."

"Don't be silly," Marianne laughed.

"Why is it silly?" Dot retorted. "I'm a strong, healthy woman and a hard worker; why shouldn't I get a job?"

"I know you can do it," Marianne quickly reassured her. "I just don't see why you should. Anyway, someone will have to look after the children."

"I should because it's thanks to my son that you're in this mess.

"That doesn't make you responsible."

"Perhaps not, but didn't you say I was part of this family?" Dot challenged.

"Yes, I did —"

"Then let me do my bit."

Marianne smiled though the tears weren't far away. "You know, as mother-in-laws go, you're not the worst."

"Easy, I'll get a big head," Dot laughed. "As for the children, I could still take care of them and get some part-time work in the mornings while they're at school."

"I suppose."

"Don't worry. We've enough grey matter between us to figure something out. I suppose you'll be selling this place?"

Marianne stared at her. "Isn't that a bit drastic?"

"I don't think so. It must cost a fortune to heat and think of what you'd save on the mortgage."

"I suppose," Marianne said, trying to remember exactly what Johnny had said about losing the house.

Would it be better to sell it before Matthews and Baldwin took possession of it? Was she even allowed to? She'd have to make a list of questions to ask Johnny, but she had a feeling that he was right; she needed legal advice. The thought of leaving the large, four-bedroom, red-brick house in Asgard Court didn't upset her that much; she had never really felt at home here. She figured that had more to do with Dominic than the house or its stunning location. He had only bought the property because it was a good investment and a worthy address of a junior partner. Marianne had been so caught up with Andrew's imminent birth that she had gone along with the purchase. It was only months later that she realized how quiet and reserved the neighbourhood was and that there were no women her age and no small children. In recent years she had come to associate the house with the cold, hard, abusive stranger her husband had become.

She knew for a fact that although Dot enjoyed the pretty garden and the lovely walks, she missed the bustling, noisy estate in Kilbarrack where she'd spent her entire married life. It had been hard to leave her home but even after the move to Howth, Dot spent most of her spare time with her old neighbours and friends and couldn't bring herself to sell her home. Instead she rented it out to a couple of student nurses, ignoring Dominic's warning that they would probably wreck the place and she would be better to sell and have a nest egg for her old age. But the nurses were two quiet girls from Roscommon who kept the house immaculate and soon became popular with the neighbours as they were always quick to run errands and dole out medical advice.

"So? What do you think?" Dot was looking at her expectantly.

Marianne looked at her. "Sorry?"

"About selling?"

"It would be madness to do that now with the property market in the state it's in," she said, thinking on her feet while realizing it was true. "The house is probably only worth half what it was when we bought it."

"That's true; I hadn't thought of that. Still . . ." Dot broke off, looking thoughtful.

"Yes?" Marianne prompted.

"Well, I'm just thinking; you could do what I did, you could rent this place out."

"And take somewhere smaller? It's an idea."

"No, we could move into my house and it wouldn't cost us a penny." Dot's eyes danced at the thought of going home. "Nora and Eileen will be moving out in two months."

"They're moving out? I thought they were happy there," Marianne said, playing for time; she didn't know quite how she felt about Dot's brainwave.

"They are, but they miss their families and now that they've qualified they're taking up jobs closer to home. So, what do you think?"

"I don't know, Dot," Marianne hesitated.

Leaving here was one thing; moving into her mother-in-law's three-bedroom terrace house, quite another. Although they got on well, two strong women sharing a small kitchen might be a challenge.

"It would be an awful trek for school every day," she pointed out; it was the first excuse she could think of. Dot didn't respond and she looked over to find the woman watching her, pity in her eyes. "What?"

"Marianne, love, you'll have to take them out of that school. You can't afford to pay those fees any more."

She was right, Marianne realized, the knot in her stomach tightening. The children would have to leave their exclusive private school. It was one of the most expensive in Dublin and the fees would be even higher once Kate moved into the secondary level. Marianne's stiff upper lip deserted her and she felt her eyes well up. Immediately Dot clutched her hand.

"Now, stop that, love. Those kids would thrive anywhere and the little school around the corner from my house has a great reputation. Imagine, we'd be able to walk them there and back instead of sitting in traffic and wasting money on petrol."

Marianne swallowed back her tears and nodded. It did make sense. Life had to change and drastically. She winced as her gut clenched and twisted again.

"So, what do you think?" Dot watched her expectantly.

"It's a lot to take in, Dot. Let me have a think about it and talk to Johnny. I need to find out more about exactly where I stand." Marianne checked her watch and stood up. "I'd better get the kids and you had better rescue your apple tart."

"Damn and blast!" Dot hopped to her feet, grabbed the oven gloves and opened the oven door.

"See you later," Marianne smiled, picking up her keys and bag and going to get her children.

What would they make of all this, she wondered as she popped another indigestion tablet into her mouth and swung the car out onto the main road. She had assured them that life would go on as before. How would she explain these drastic changes to their lives? Moving house and changing school were both unsettling experiences, but the two together so soon after their father's death would be bound to upset them. She would also have to sell Dominic's Mercedes jeep and bring her old Golf back into service. Suddenly Marianne felt scared and vulnerable. Dominic had provided for them all and she'd never had to think, let alone worry, about money. Yet it turned out that he couldn't even do that properly. She felt anger bubble up inside of her at his selfishness. How could a man in his position not make proper provision for the future and what had turned him into a crook? He must have been a lot sicker than she realized, although she knew that if he was here right now she'd quite probably punch him.

But there was no time for self-pity, she had a family to look after, and of course she would cope; she didn't have much choice. She had been a damn good manager at Treacy Travel; looking after four people couldn't be all that difficult. Bringing in some money, though, now that would be a challenge. Marianne wasn't convinced that she'd be able to find a job. Still, she wasn't proud and she could scrub floors as well as the next woman. If that's what it took to put food on the table then she'd do it, she thought, and popped another indigestion tablet into her mouth.

She was hovering near the school gate, keeping a distance from the other mothers — she wasn't up to chit-chat today — and re-playing her conversation with Adrian Matthews, when Kate emerged followed by a furious, red-faced Andrew with the school principal by his side. Marianne sighed as she met the woman's eyes. "Hello, Miss Donohue, is everything okay?"

"I'm afraid not, Mrs Thomson. Andrew bit one of the other children today."

"Andrew!" Marianne looked at her son, horrified. Though he had become a handful at home, her son had always got on well with his school friends; in fact, he was probably the most popular child in the class.

"She started it," Andrew protested.

"She? You bit a girl?" His sister looked at him in disgust.

"Kate, take your brother out to the car, please." Marianne handed over the keys. "Andrew, what do you say to Miss Donohue?"

"It wasn't me —"

"Andrew!"

"Sorry," he muttered, scuffing the ground with his shoe.

"The car," Marianne nodded to Kate before turning back to the principal. "I am so sorry, is the other child all right?"

"She's fine but obviously I had to make it very clear to him that such behaviour was not acceptable."

"You can be sure I will punish him."

"I'm not sure you should."

"Pardon?"

"Of course I'd like you to reiterate that what he did was wrong but I think this is probably a good opportunity to talk to him about the anger he's feeling."

"Anger?"

"It's very common for children, especially in Andrew's age group, to feel angry when they lose a parent, be it through death or divorce. They don't fully understand what's going on but they don't like it and they hit out. Andrew did that literally today. I'm sure it's a one-off; he is usually such a good-natured child. In a way it's good that he's acting out his emotions rather than keeping them all pent up inside."

Marianne gulped. "Like Kate, you mean."

"Yes," the principal acknowledged. "We may need to keep an eye on her but she's an intelligent, sensible child. She will get there but it may take time."

"Is there anything I should be doing? I try to get her to talk but she seems to grow more distant every day." Marianne swallowed back her tears.

Miss Donohue put a hand on her arm. "Right now she's probably watching you like a hawk, terrified that you're going to die too."

"She does seem nervous when I go out alone," Marianne agreed. It hadn't occurred to her that fear might be behind the reason Kate gave her the third degree every time she left the house alone.

"Which makes perfect sense if you think about it. Your husband's death was so sudden; one minute he was there, then he was gone. It's not surprising that she would worry that the same thing could happen to you. We operate the Rainbows and Sunbeams programmes, are you familiar with them?"

"It's therapy for children trying to cope with death and divorce, isn't it? Do you think that's what Kate needs?" The thought scared Marianne; was her daughter really that traumatized? Why couldn't she just talk to her mother?

"No, I really don't. The programme is aimed at children who are still struggling after a year or so. They get to talk and share with other children going through similar experiences. I just wanted you to be aware of it but I think that between you and your mother-in-law, Kate and Andrew will be just fine by then. And do try not to take it personally if Kate doesn't talk to you," she said, putting a hand on Marianne's arm. "She loves you and is probably afraid of upsetting you; you're her whole world now."

"That never occurred to me either," Marianne admitted, shaking her head, "but of course it makes sense."

"Try not to worry. Just spend plenty of time together and I'm sure she will be just fine."

"And Andrew?"

Miss Donohue smiled. "He is attention seeking and using bad behaviour and cursing to get it. I think lots of nice cuddles from his mum should do the trick, and give him time."

"I didn't know he was using bad language in school," Marianne groaned.

"It's under control," the principal assured her. "He's a good boy, we know that and we make allowances."

Marianne smiled. "I'm very grateful."

"It's the least we can do," the woman said, her eyes full of sympathy.

Marianne knew she should say that the children would be leaving school soon, but she was afraid that would tip her over the edge and she didn't want her children to witness her bawling her eyes out. It could wait until another day. She thanked the principal again and hurried back to the car.

"She started it," Andrew said the second she got into the car.

Marianne met his eyes in the rear-view mirror. "I believe you."

Her son's eyes widened in surprise. He looked over at his sister who simply shrugged. "Does that mean I don't get a punishment?"

"No punishment." Marianne pulled into traffic and headed for home.

"That's not fair," Kate complained. "You always punish me if I'm in trouble at school."

"Andrew wasn't in trouble."

"But —"

"Leave it, Kate, please. Do you have much homework to do?"

"No, only a couple of maths questions."

"And you, Andrew?"

"I have two pages to read but I want to do it with Granny."

"In that case, let's go to the playground."

Marianne watched Kate push Andrew on the swing and smiled at his squeals of delight as he climbed higher and higher. For their sake, she decided, she would put her own doubts aside, rent out the house and move to Dot's. Even if she did manage to get a job, she couldn't earn anything like Dominic had and between food, clothes, electricity and trying to put a little by for the future, her income would soon be swallowed up. And though it might take time for her to adjust to living at Dot's, it would be nice for the children to have playmates nearby. Feeling more optimistic, she called to them.

"Come on, kids, let's go and get some fish and chips for dinner and surprise Granny."

The children were happy and chattering when they burst into the kitchen and Dot raised an eyebrow at Marianne who simply smiled. "We decided to treat ourselves; you hadn't started cooking, had you?"

"I was about to put a cottage pie in the oven but it will taste just as good tomorrow, and I must say that smells gorgeous." She sniffed the air. "Is it a nice curry?"

Andrew giggled. "No, Granny! It's your favourite: cod and chips."

"And fresh squishy bread to make butties," Kate said, hurrying to get the cutlery.

"'Tis a feast!" Dot tousled Andrew's hair before going to put on the kettle.

"I thought we deserved a treat," Marianne said as she divided the food onto four plates.

"We do indeed." Dot poured glasses of milk for the children. "Speaking of which, I thought I would take you two over to my house tomorrow."

Kate frowned. "How's that a treat?"

"Kate, don't be cheeky," Marianne said with a frown.

"Sorry."

"It's a treat because there's a street party on."

"What's a street party?" Andrew asked through a mouthful of chips.

"Don't speak with your mouth full," Marianne and Dot said at the same time and laughed.

"Well, all the neighbours get together and set up tables of lovely food and drinks and we have music and dancing and party games."

Andrew's eyes lit up. "Oh, cool, can we go, Mummy?"

Marianne didn't know whether to feel grateful or annoyed with her mother-in-law. It was a good idea to introduce the children to the neighbourhood but she didn't like Dot springing this on her. Was it a sign of what was to come when Dot was back on her own patch?

"Can we, Mum?"

She looked across at her daughter who had cheered up dramatically. "Sure, sounds like it would be fun and I have some errands to run anyway."

Andrew's smile faded and his lips turned down. "But I don't want to go without you."

"Oh, am I not good enough for you, is that it?" Dot feigned a hurt expression.

"Of course you are, Granny." Kate kicked her brother under the table.

"Ow! Bitch!" He stuck his tongue out at her.

"Andrew!" Marianne was about to read her son the riot act when she remembered the principal's words. "I've told you, I don't like you using those words," she said quietly.

"No, only your granny is allowed to use them," Dot said with a wink. "So, are you coming with me or not?"

Andrew giggled. "Okay."

"I'll drop you there and come and join you as soon as I can. How's that?" Marianne told him.

"Great! Is that where Daddy lived, Granny?" he asked.

"Yes, I moved to Kilbarrack with your granda the week after we got married. It was the middle of nowhere in those days, all farmland and only a few houses."

"Where is Kilbawick?" he asked.

"Not far," Marianne said. "You've been there before, sweet-heart, but you were only little."

"I remember it," Kate said. "It's a tiny little house."

Again Marianne was about to tell off her daughter but swallowed her words.

"It was plenty big enough for us, you cheeky monkey," Dot retorted, laughing. "There were six in the family next door and they managed just fine too."

"But haven't you only one bathroom?" Kate's eyes were round with wonder.

"How on earth did we survive?" Dot marvelled with a grin.

"How indeed?" Marianne grinned, remembering the cold, drab bathroom in St Anne's that she'd had to share with eight other girls. She rarely mentioned her childhood to her kids though. She didn't want to be one of those parents constantly harking on about how things were "in my day".

"What?" Kate was looking from her to Dot obviously wondering what she'd said that was so funny.

"They were different times, love, that's all," Dot said. "The house I grew up in didn't even have an indoor toilet; it was in a tiny shed at the end of the garden. I used to hate having to go out there at night."

Now Andrew's eyes were on stalks. "Your toilet was outside? Cool!"

"Bloody freezing most of the time."

Kate laughed.

"Granny said another bad word," Andrew crowed.

"Yes, I think we may have to set up a swear box," Marianne said, delighted to see him smiling and Kate positively animated.

"And there were spiders," Dot continued, "big hairy yokes. One day, a huge fella dropped on my head and I flew back up the path with me drawers round me ankles!"

"Drawers?" Andrew looked puzzled.

"She means pants," Kate said, wiping her eyes. "Oh, Granny, that's funny."

"There was nothing funny about it, believe me," Dot retorted but her eyes twinkled. "Now hurry up and finish your food, it's nearly bath time."

"But it's early," Kate protested.

"Did I say bedtime? I did not. Tonight is bingo night and you have to be shiny and clean and ready for bed in an hour if you want me to read with you before I go."

Hopping to her feet, Kate stuffed the last few chips into her mouth and put her plate in the dishwasher. "I'll have a shower."

"Need any help?" Marianne asked.

"Of course not." Kate threw a look of disdain over her shoulder before disappearing.

"She's growing up, love," Dot patted Marianne's hand.

"I need help," Andrew said reaching over to hug her and leaving a smear of ketchup on her cheek.

"You've got it, sweetie," she told him and planted a noisy kiss on his cheek.

CHAPTER
EIGHT

Once Dot had left for bingo and the children were tucked up in bed asleep, Marianne made herself a coffee. She had just settled at the kitchen table with a pile of Dominic's unopened post in front of her when the doorbell rang. She frowned. This wasn't the sort of road where neighbours stopped by and it was a bit late for a sales call. She went out into the hall, put on the security chain and opened the door.

"Helen!"

"I thought you might fancy some company."

"Oh, I do," Marianne said, as she took off the chain and held her arms out to embrace her best friend.

Helen hugged her tightly. "I am so sorry, pet, as if you haven't gone through enough. Johnny said I should leave you in peace but I knew it was Dot's bingo night and I hated the thought of you being on your own."

"I'm delighted you came; let me make you some coffee."

Helen followed her out to the kitchen. "Are they asleep?" she whispered.

"Yes, all clear."

Helen sat down. "Johnny told me the news; I can't believe it."

"Me neither."

"You haven't told Dot?"

"How could I, Helen? It would kill her."

"She would be devastated," Helen acknowledged. "I find it all so hard to take in. I made Johnny go over it again and again. Is there any way it could be a mistake?"

"I don't know, Helen. The investigation is ongoing but it doesn't look good."

"It could have been somebody who worked for him; he could have been framed. It's easy to blame a dead man." She glanced at the pile of envelopes. "Detective work or just dealing with the bills?"

"A bit of both."

"Can I help?"

Marianne smiled gratefully. "Please. Two heads are better than one."

"I was just thinking on the way over here about Dominic's phone," Helen said as she started to slit envelopes with her fingernail and divide the post into two piles, one for bills and the other for everything else. "Did you ever ring his number?"

Marianne stopped and looked at her. "No. To be honest I hadn't given it a thought until Matthews mentioned it this morning."

"I think you should."

Marianne smiled. "Why's that, Miss Marple?"

"Johnny mentioned that you thought he might have been having an affair."

"No, that never occurred to me. Mattthews jumped to that conclusion because Dominic had lied to me about working late."

"But if he was seeing another woman, her number or messages would be on his phone, wouldn't they?" Helen persisted.

"I suppose so."

"So perhaps if she was with him the night he died, she'd have taken the phone to protect her identity."

Marianne sat back and stared thoughtfully at her friend. "Or he was with someone who was involved in the fraud and they knew their details were on the phone."

"My God, yes!" Helen's eyes widened. "Let's call the number."

"They're hardly likely to answer. Anyway the phone is probably in a bin or at the bottom of a canal by now."

Helen shrugged. "You could contact the service provider and tell them the situation. They'll be able to tell you if the phone has been used since his death."

Marianne clapped a hand to her mouth.

"What?"

Marianne started to laugh. "We are stupid."

"Why?"

"All the information will be on his itemized bill which is probably right here." Marianne patted the heap of bills between them.

"Of course!" Helen started to thumb through them. Halfway through, she found the bill they were looking for and passed it to Marianne. "Here you go."

Marianne flicked to the second page and put it on the table between them.

Helen leaned closer.

Marianne ran her finger down the items. "That's my number and that's Dot's, that's the house phone and that's Matthews and Baldwin."

"What about this one?" Helen pointed to a mobile number that featured regularly.

"I don't recognize it."

"Bingo."

"So, what do we do now?" Marianne asked.

"Call the number and Dominic's and see if the same person answers," Helen suggested. "We don't have to say anything. Oh, come on, what harm can it do?"

Marianne smiled. "Okay, okay."

"I'll call from my phone — they might recognize your number — and put it on loudspeaker so you can hear the voice."

"You're way too good at this."

Helen laughed. "Right. I'll phone Dominic's number first."

Marianne called it out and bit on her knuckle as she watched her friend dial.

"*The number you have dialled is busy*," an automated voice said.

Helen hung up. "Well, that doesn't tell us much."

"Try the other number." Again Marianne called it out and Helen typed it in. They got another automated message.

Helen disconnected and put the phone down. "Oh, well, it was worth a try."

"I suppose we could send a text to Dominic's phone," Marianne mused.

"And say what?"

"No idea."

"Have a think about it; you don't have to do it right now."

"Yes, okay. In the meantime I think I'll send Matthews and Baldwin a copy of this phone bill."

"Yes, and Dominic's credit card bill too; just so they know that you are very firmly in their corner."

"Yes, I'll do that."

"Let's have a look through the rest of his post."

They worked quickly, but apart from an exorbitant gas bill that made Marianne feel nauseous, there was nothing that shone any light on Dominic's behaviour. She yawned and stretched.

"Oh, I'm tired."

"I'm not surprised. You've been lurching from one crisis to another."

"Today was horrible," Marianne agreed.

"I'll go and let you get some sleep. But there was something else I wanted to say . . ."

Marianne braced herself when she saw the solemn expression on Helen's face. "Go on."

"Johnny and I were talking. It could be a long time before you see any cash from either Matthews and Baldwin or the insurance claim —"

"If at all," Marianne grimaced and massaged her stomach.

"Well, perhaps," Helen conceded. "We both think you'll find a job, although you're unlikely to earn as much as Dominic did."

Marianne eyed her friend over her mug. "Are you trying to cheer me up?"

Helen pulled a face. "Sorry, but there's no point sugar-coating it. The good news is that we thought of another way to bring in a little cash."

"Great, I'm all ears."

"It was Johnny's idea. He said you could rent out your house and move into somewhere smaller. That way you would at least be able to pay the mortgage."

Marianne laughed. "Ah, way ahead of you! Dot had the same idea, only she wants us to move into her house, that way we have no rent to pay at all."

"That's a great idea."

Marianne sighed. "It makes sense, although we may well kill each other."

"But you get on so well."

"It's easier in a place this size and I've always been careful to give her some space. But in her house she'll be tripping over me and the kids all the time."

"They'll be at school all morning," Helen reminded her.

"Not during the holidays."

"It's not ideal," Helen agreed, "but sacrifices have to be made. I'm sure she'll be happy to do anything she can to help, given it's her son that got you into this mess."

"Just remember she doesn't know the half of it."

"I won't say a word."

Marianne glanced around the room. "I'm not hugely attached to this place but I can't say I'm keen on renting it to a stranger; you hear such horror stories."

"Johnny will find you someone reliable."

"He's a developer — what does he know about renting property?"

"He's whatever he has to be these days."

"How are things?" Marianne asked, conscious that she had been so wrapped in her own problems she hadn't thought about how hard life must be for a builder at a time when no one could afford to build.

"We're okay. We were blessed to have sold all twelve houses in the Heritage Mews development just before the crash. Johnny was planning to buy more land, so he didn't invest the proceeds. If he had, we'd be bankrupt by now."

"What a frightening thought." Marianne knew no harder working, more intelligent couple than Helen and Johnny and the fact that it was just down to luck that they had survived the property crash was sobering.

Helen's face darkened. "Not everyone was as fortunate. Johnny's friend, Christy Kennedy, got stung badly and it's destroyed him; he's a shadow of his former self."

Marianne sighed. "And I don't suppose he gets much sympathy. Everyone thinks that all builders are loaded and the rest of us are paying for their greed."

"Not poor old Christy. He wasn't much of a businessman and never planned for a rainy day."

"And now every day's a rainy day, poor man. So if Johnny isn't building, what is he doing? He always seems to be busy."

"You know Johnny, he turns his hand to anything and everything. There are still a couple of building projects in the pipeline but he's mainly concentrating on extensions, maintenance and now he's branched into leasing."

"Good for him."

"And he told me to tell you that he knows someone that's looking for a place in Howth."

Marianne stared at her. "No, really?"

Helen nodded. "Yes, just say the word and he'll set up a viewing."

Marianne thought about it for only a moment and then nodded. "Tell him to go ahead; it's not as if I have much choice."

"I'll tell him. Now our next challenge is to find you a job."

"Give me a chance," Marianne groaned. "I'm still coming to terms with the fact that not only was I married to a crook but possibly an adulterer too. Some days I just feel like pulling the duvet over my head and staying there."

"But you won't because you've got two great kids to look after." Helen squeezed her hand. "You're having a rough time, Marianne, no doubt about it but don't start feeling sorry for yourself."

"That's a bit harsh," Marianne bridled.

"Sorry, I'm not having a go at you, honestly, but if I held your hand, made you tea and let you just cry on my shoulder, it wouldn't change things, would it? You have to dig your way out of this mess. Johnny and I will help in any way we can but it's up to you whether you sink or swim."

"I have no intention of sinking!" Marianne protested.

Helen smiled. "Good, I'm glad to hear it because everything's going to be fine."

Marianne stared at her in disbelief. "Fine? I have hardly any money, no job and may lose my house . . ."

"You'll have the rental money from this house, you'll find a job, and there's no point in worrying about the house unless you have to."

Marianne sighed. She knew that Helen meant well and was only trying to help but wasn't she entitled to feel a little bit sorry for herself at the moment? "Yeah, I'm sure you're right; now I really need to get some rest."

Helen looked shamefaced. "Oh, God, I'm badgering you, aren't I? Johnny warned me not to."

Marianne couldn't help laughing. "Everything you say is true, but tonight I'm just not capable of being the optimist you want me to be."

Helen hugged her. "You can give me a smack if you want to."

"Nah, don't have the energy."

"Get to bed, pet." Helen hugged her once more and stood up. "Oh, just one last thing: Johnny wanted to know if the house is in both your names."

"Yes. Why?"

"Well, apparently when a businessman is on the verge of bankruptcy, it's not that uncommon for him to change the deeds of his house into his wife's name so it can't be touched. Johnny and I thought that if Dominic was on the fiddle he might think along the same lines."

"I suppose that makes sense, but if he did change it he never told me."

"You'd have had to sign something."

"Then it must still be in both our names."

"I'll tell Johnny." Helen led the way out towards the hall door. "You know, I do think you're doing the right thing moving, Marianne," she said, turning to look at her friend. "The kids can easily take the train or bus to school."

Marianne clasped her arms tight around herself and shook her head. "They'll be moving to the local school, Helen; I can't afford school fees any more."

For the first time, Helen looked truly shocked. "Oh, of course, sorry, I hadn't thought of that."

"Like you say, it will be fine," Marianne lied, suddenly feeling very alone.

Helen looked at her with sad, worried eyes and kissed her cheek. "Go to bed, pet; everything will look better in the morning."

"Let's face it," Marianne smiled, "it can't look much worse."

CHAPTER
NINE

Rob Lee threw his jacket in a corner, switched on his laptop and hit the button on the answering machine. He scanned his mail as he listened to two messages from clients with problems that would result in him working late again, another from his sister reminding him that there was a family lunch in her house on Sunday — he groaned at the thought — but it was the last message that really caught his attention.

"Rob, hi, Johnny Sheridan here. Listen, I have the perfect house for you; the owner is a good friend of mine and looking to rent it out. Give me a call when you get a chance and I'll fill you in on the details."

"Excellent!" Rob rubbed his hands together and went out to the galley kitchen to make a coffee.

He had first met Johnny when he'd installed a computer system for him nearly three years ago. It was shortly after he'd started his own business and meeting Johnny had been a blessing. He'd sent plenty of other builders and tradesmen to him and Rob hadn't looked back. It was also Johnny who'd pointed out the need for a reliable property website and Rob had taken his advice. The venture had been an overnight success and he'd made a killing when he sold the website only months before the property market crashed. Finally in a position to build a home of his own, he'd turned to Johnny; well, who else? Together they had searched for the perfect site and Johnny had recommended Rus Bowen, a talented and imaginative architect, to design the house. Once the planning came through, he would be able to build his dream home. When he'd said he would like to rent a place near the site where he could both live and work, Johnny had immediately offered to find him a place and Rob was happy to let him. A true entrepreneur, Johnny had survived the crash and seemed to be doing well for himself once more. Rob wasn't surprised; if ever there was a man who was made to bounce, it was Johnny.

Armed with a large mug of strong coffee and a couple of chocolate bars that would suffice as dinner, Rob returned to his desk in the corner of his drab and joyless living room and picked up the phone. Johnny answered on the second ring.

"Hey, Johnny, it's Rob."

"Rob! How are you doing?"

"Great, thanks. You have news for me?"

"I do indeed, sir, good news. Well . . ." he added in more sombre tones, "good for you anyway. I have a friend who needs to rent her house. It's a lovely place, only about eight years old, has exactly the kind of space you were looking for and is in very good condition. And," he added, "it's less than a mile from the site."

"Excellent. When can I move in?"

Johnny laughed. "Don't you want to see it before you make your mind up?"

"I trust you." Rob looked around the cramped room. The only saving grace of this flat, apart from its location in the heart of Dublin, was the large bay window. The busy street below presented him with such a wonderful tapestry of life each day that he rarely bothered switching on the TV set in the corner.

"The bad news is it won't be available for a couple of months, but with the way the planning office drags its heels, we'll be lucky to be breaking earth by then. This house is worth the wait."

Rob sighed. "Okay, then. Why don't you set up a viewing and we'll take it from there?"

"Excellent, I'll do that."

"What's the landlady's name?" he asked, picking up a pen.

"Marianne Thomson."

Rob dropped his pen as Marianne's lovely face swam before his eyes.

"I'll give her a call and get back to you during the week," Johnny continued. "Rob? Are you there?"

"Yeah, I'm here. That's fine, Johnny, appreciate it, take care."

Rob put the phone down and stared out of the window, for once not even seeing the bustling beauty of the city. *Marianne*. He went back in his mind over Johnny's words; he hadn't mentioned Dominic at all. In fact he had specifically said "she"; had she finally left that asshole? He couldn't help feeling a thrill of excitement at the thought of her being single, of seeing her beautiful face again and that gorgeous body. He wondered if she knew that he was her potential tenant and, if so, was she as excited as he was? He wished now that he'd asked Johnny more questions and was sorely tempted to phone him back, but he couldn't think of any legitimate reason for doing so. Frustrated, he realized that he'd just have to bide his time. His coffee grew cold as he sat back in his chair, put his feet up on the cluttered desk and remembered the first time he'd seen Marianne.

His firm had been hired to install a computer system in Treacy Travel, where Marianne worked. Rob was assigned to lead and co-ordinate the project. It had been quite a task; they were using antiquated systems and the small group of staff were resistant to change. Marianne had been the only one excited by the initiative and eager to learn, and Rob had been only too happy to teach her. He'd fancied her straight away. She was a good-looking woman but it was her eyes that had mesmerized him. He could still remember the disappointment he'd felt when he'd looked down and seen the plain gold band on her left hand.

Tom Treacy, Marianne's boss, had made her the project manager and as a result Rob had ended up working with her on an almost daily basis. She was smart, picked things up quickly and was fun to work with, although he remembered that at times she could be quite withdrawn. He'd wondered occasionally if she had health problems as some days she'd arrive looking tired and wan, say she had paperwork to attend to and shut herself in her office. He was fascinated by everything about her in a way that he'd never been before; he was falling in love with a married woman. But whether it had just been wishful thinking, even back then he'd wondered about that marriage. There were photos of her two children on her desk and her walls were covered with her daughter's artwork, but there was no photo of her husband. Rob had overheard some of their calls and they were stilted and Marianne seemed to stiffen when she heard her husband's voice. He'd only met him once. Dominic had come to collect her and Rob had disliked the proprietorial way he'd slid his arm around her waist and noticed too how uncomfortable she'd appeared with it.

Rob figured she knew that he fancied her; she might be married and beyond his reach but he couldn't resist in indulging in some harmless flirting. Then one evening on his way home from the cinema, he'd dropped into the office to check on a job he'd left running and found her slumped at her desk with her head on her arms, crying as if her heart would break. He'd sat on the desk and put an arm around her shaking shoulders and when she'd calmed down he'd made her a mug of strong, sweet tea. He stood over her as she drank it with shaking hands, but she wouldn't tell him what was wrong, dismissing it as something silly. She hadn't been remotely convincing, but he knew better than to pursue the matter. At the end of the day he was only a work colleague although he felt they'd moved beyond that. He was afraid to overstep the mark. It was only when he was lying in bed later thinking about the episode, he'd realized that the expression on her face, the one he hadn't been quite able to fathom, had been fear.

From then on Rob grew more watchful, looking for signs of distress. One day, when there was a group of them standing around the coffee machine laughing, it had struck him that, despite her smile, there was sadness in her eyes. He needed to know the reason and he longed to be the one to take that sorrow away. He wanted to be the one to make her smile with her eyes as well as her mouth. Aware that he was becoming almost obsessive, Rob went on a series of unsuccessful dates but he only ever ended up comparing the women to Marianne and none came close to making him feel the way she did. With the last girl, a curvaceous, bubbly blonde who had a very sexy smile, he'd found himself staring at the various parts of her body while she talked and wondering why he wasn't remotely turned on. A couple of months later, all the staff at Treacy Travel were going for a meal and a few drinks to celebrate someone's thirtieth birthday. He'd had to pass up on it as he'd already agreed to go to a movie with the blonde. He was furious at missing an opportunity to socialize with Marianne; she so rarely joined them for a drink. When he'd broken the news of his date to her, his heart had soared at the obvious disappointment on her face. He remembered nothing about that movie and whenever the blonde had leaned against him, put a hand on his thigh or whispered in his ear, he'd instinctively moved away. When they emerged and she'd suggested he come back to her place, he'd told her he had a headache and went straight to the pub where the birthday party was being held. It was after ten and he expected Marianne to be long gone. But she was still there, obviously a little tipsy, and he had immediately drawn up a stool next to hers. There was much teasing from the gang about his date and he batted the comments away with ease, all the while enjoying the feel of Marianne's bare arm brushing against his. She was a tactile person and more so with alcohol inside her. When she was making a point she would press his hand or touch his arm; he was in heaven. He was probably on his third pint when he turned his head to find her studying him.

"Is she pretty?" she asked in a low voice.

"Yes." He watched her face fall. "But not as pretty as you."

She smiled and then looked away, embarrassed. "I should go."

"I'll walk you to the taxi rank."

Outside she had swayed a little and he'd taken her arm to steady her.

"I don't feel very well," she admitted.

"Do you want to walk for a while? Some fresh air might help."

She nodded and they had wandered in companionable silence through the cobbled streets of Temple Bar. Finally he asked the question he'd wanted to know the answer to for weeks. "Why were you crying that night?"

She said nothing for a moment and neither did he. He willed her to answer, to open up to him.

"I had a row with my husband," she'd said, finally.

"And is everything okay now?" he asked, not sure he wanted to hear the answer.

"No," Marianne replied sadly.

"Do you want to talk about it?"

They had reached an archway and she stopped underneath, rested against the wall and turned her face up to his.

"No, Rob, I don't want to talk."

She was definitely a little bit drunk and he probably shouldn't have taken advantage, but he couldn't resist kissing her. Her lips were sweeter than he'd imagined and her mouth tasted of wine. When he felt her hands go round his neck, he pulled her tight against him and almost groaned at the feel of her lovely body against his. Their kisses grew more passionate and fervent; they were like a couple of teenagers. When he slid his hand inside her blouse and touched one full, soft breast he'd expected her to pull away but instead she'd made a noise deep in her throat and he could feel her nipple harden against his palm. It had taken all of his willpower to pull away from her and lead her towards a taxi rank. If he was ever going to have sex with this woman it would not be in the street when she was drunk.

He jumped as the phone rang again, bringing him back to the present. "Rob Lee. Of course, Mr McGrath, what can I do for you?"

"Thanks, Johnny." Marianne put the phone down and sank into a chair.

Could it really be the same Rob Lee? Was it possible? She felt a twinge in her stomach but it was nothing like the other spasms she had been experiencing lately. Instead it was a delicious warmth accompanied by memories of the most special time in her life; the time when Rob Lee had been her lover.

She hadn't set out to be unfaithful although she figured anyone would forgive her given Dominic's behaviour. By the time she succumbed to Rob's kind, smiling eyes, her husband had gone way beyond reason and bared little resemblance to the man she'd married. She never knew at the end of the day which husband was going to walk through the door: the terrifying tyrant or the happy, horny husband; the doting dad or petrifying parent. Every day was a lottery. If it hadn't been for Rob she'd have gone out of her mind. She wouldn't tell him what was going on; Jo and Helen were the only ones she confided in and even they weren't aware of how bad things had become. She would have liked to tell Rob but it would have crossed a line that she somehow knew would change everything.

There had been no repeat of the night they'd shared that passionate kiss in Crown Alley and neither of them had ever referred to it, but their relationship had changed and she took every opportunity to spend as much time with him as possible, amazed at the peace that descended on her when he was near. At first they would simply dawdle after work and talk. Then they started to go for a quick coffee or a drink on the way home, ending with him dropping her at the train station and her thanking him and kissing his cheek. And then one night he'd stopped her from drawing away, looked into her eyes and kissed her on the lips. It was brief but Marianne had found it intensely erotic and couldn't stop thinking about it. After that, it was a given that if he gave her a lift, they would end up kissing. Marianne was intensely attracted to Rob and she knew he felt the same, but apart from the sexual attraction it was just so good to be around someone so normal, funny and kind. But when he looked at her in a certain way . . . She shivered as she remembered what it was like to drown in those eyes.

It was a cool but bright Saturday the day she finally ended up in Rob's bed. Dot had taken the children to the zoo, Dominic was slumped in front of the TV watching a football match and Marianne was chopping vegetables. He'd shouted out to her but she hadn't heard what he'd said; he was probably just looking for more coffee. Well, he could get it himself. He had been impossible all morning and she was furious when he had roared at Andrew to be quiet, scaring the child witless. The next minute he was in the doorway, frowning, one hand to his head.

"Stop that, I told you my head is splitting."

"Oh, for goodness' sake, don't be such a drama queen. I'm only making a stew," she'd protested, laughing.

"You're laughing at me?"

"No, don't be silly." And then she'd looked up and seen the fury in his face. "Sorry, Dominic, I'm nearly finished."

"Here, let me finish for you," he said, and pulling the knife roughly from her hand he proceeded to hack the vegetables with a vengeance.

"Dominic!"

"What's the problem? You wanted them chopped, didn't you?" He was wielding the knife with such abandon that he was in danger of missing the chopping board and hacking into the polished oak worktop.

"Be careful!"

"Are you afraid I might hurt myself? Is that it, Marianne?"

"Yes, yes, of course I am." Marianne started to gather up all the mutilated vegetables and put them back on the board.

"I won't do that," he assured her and brought the knife down perilously close to her fingers.

Marianne gave a yelp of fear and ran for the door, only pausing to grab her car keys. She drove straight to the office. She didn't know why, though, in hindsight, maybe she did. The weekend was the only time that major changes could be made to the computer systems; there was a good chance that Rob would be there. He was just walking out of the door when she arrived. His face broke into a smile but then he saw her expression and the tears in her eyes.

"What is it?" He put his hands on her shoulders and searched her face. "What's happened? Has he done something? Has he hurt you?"

She shook her head. "No, he was just shouting and screaming; I was frightened."

114

He folded her into his arms. "You're safe now. I was just going home, come with me."

Marianne hesitated. She knew in her heart where this would lead and despite the fact that she was still trembling with fear she also felt excited.

Rob took her silence as reluctance. "You don't have to do anything you don't want to, darling; I just want to hold you."

She slipped her hand into his. "Let's go."

As she'd stood at his window, looking down on the busy shoppers, she'd been conscious of him speeding around the small flat, tidying frantically. Then he'd come and stood beside her, wiping his hands nervously on the back of his jeans. "Tea? Coffee?"

She'd turned to face him. "No, thanks."

He looked down into her eyes, cupped her face in his hands and kissed her. Marianne gave herself up to the moment and when he started to walk her towards the bedroom, she didn't resist. They sank together onto the bed and started to undress each other. When Marianne was down to her bra and pants, Rob drew back to look at her.

"You're beautiful," he told her, and he continued telling her that for the next hour as he made love to her slowly and gently.

She had thought that she and Dominic enjoyed a relatively good love life before he went off the rails, but her opinion changed after that first time with Rob. Sex with Dominic had been fast, furious, frenzied, and largely silent. It was a completely different story with

Rob. For a start he seemed content to just hold and kiss her for the longest time, all the while his eyes feasting on her body, making her feel special and beautiful. And the kisses . . . she sighed at the memory. Rob didn't have one type of kiss, he had a whole collection and she found it hard to decide which she liked best.

That first time he had very slowly kissed and touched her and talked and smiled, and under his gentle hands she had relaxed and opened herself up to him. Afterwards she lay naked in his arms, not at all self-conscious or embarrassed and feeling more at peace than she had in years. It was as if she'd been holding her breath her entire life and could finally exhale.

She'd sworn it wouldn't happen again; her life was complicated enough without this but the more unpredictable Dominic became the more she'd turned to Rob; the more she'd come to depend on him. And now it seemed he was about to come back into her life. And despite her concern for her children and money worries, a small flame of hope stirred within her.

CHAPTER
TEN

Helen knocked on the door before going into the bedroom. As she'd expected, her son was out cold despite the fact that she'd called him three times already.

"It's eight o'clock, you're going to be late. Colm! Move it!" She yanked the duvet off him when he didn't budge.

He groaned. "Okay, okay. I'm coming."

"That boy needs to study more and party less," she said when she returned to the kitchen where Johnny was working his way through a plate of toast, slathered with butter and marmalade.

"Ah, sure, he was only at the cinema and he needs to get a break from the studying." Johnny reached over to switch on the radio.

Helen frowned as she started to make sandwiches for her son's lunch. It was all very well being blasé about Colm's future; yes, he would join the family business, but that wasn't the secure prospect it had once been. If he was forced to look for work elsewhere he would need a good degree under his belt. He was a clever boy, she had no doubts on that score and, like his dad, he oozed confidence, but sometimes she felt he was too sure of himself and underestimated the hard work that lay ahead. Johnny didn't understand what she was worrying about and dismissed her fears, but then he seemed very preoccupied at the moment.

Their usual place for talking through business problems was in bed, after they'd made love and she lay curled up in his arms. It had been a couple of weeks since the last time, she realized; that was unusual. She often felt too tired for sex but Johnny reached for her a couple of times a week, and no matter what mood she was in, once his hands and mouth started to explore her body she soon forgot her tiredness. She was no longer the size ten he had married but when he made love to her she felt beautiful and sexy. Perhaps she would make a special effort for him tonight and when he was relaxed she would find out exactly what it was that was bothering him.

"He's off out again tonight," she said. "It's Fergal Harrison's birthday party. Why don't I make us a nice dinner and we could have an early night."

Johnny looked up absently. "Sorry, love?"

"I said, Colm's going out tonight and we'll have the place to ourselves." She smiled at him.

"Oh, sorry, sweetheart; I've got to go out. I'll arrange to pick Colm up afterwards. I don't like him roaming the streets so late."

"Where are you off to on a Friday evening?" she asked. She couldn't remember him mentioning a meeting; there certainly wasn't anything in the diary.

"I'm going to see Christy."

"Ah, okay." Helen sat down at the table beside him and poured them both more coffee.

"How is he?" she asked.

"Not good," said Johnny. "Bev phoned me yesterday. She thinks he's getting worse; she's asked me to have a word. I don't know how long it will take. Sorry, love."

"It's fine. Of course you must go and see him. Will you come home for something to eat first?"

"No. I'll go straight from work."

"Well, in that case I'll make a shepherd's pie and you can have some whatever time you get in."

"You're a darling." He drained his cup, leaned over to kiss her hard on the mouth and stood up.

As he made to leave, Colm strolled in, yawning and knotting his school tie. Johnny punched him lightly on the arm. "If you get a move on, I'll drop you off."

"Cool." Colm dropped two slices of bread into the toaster and poured a glass of orange juice.

"You should be having something nutritious and filling like cereal," Helen told her gangly son; he was far too thin for her liking.

"He doesn't have time," Johnny protested. "Get your stuff together; you can eat in the car."

"Go on then," Helen sighed. "I'll get the toast."

"Thanks, Ma."

Minutes later she was waving them off, Colm with his bag slung over one shoulder and carrying his toast and the cereal bar she'd pressed into his hand.

"Don't forget to send out the invoice to McNally's," Johnny called back to her.

"It went out in yesterday's post," she told him.

"What a woman!" He winked at her and climbed into the car and drove away.

Helen smiled before hurrying back inside to tidy up. She had promised to drop into Marianne's for coffee at eleven and there was much to do first. Once she'd cleaned up the breakfast things and making the beds, she collected the post from the doormat and took it into the small study to read. Along with the usual bills there was a brief note from the solicitor confirming an appointment with Marianne. She slid it into her friend's file, which seemed to grow thicker every day.

After making some phone calls chasing up money and confirming quotations, Helen turned her attention to her upcoming party. As she scanned her to-do list she was reasonably happy that everything was under control. It was nowhere near as big a production as the parties they'd had in the past but it would still cost a couple of grand. Perhaps that was what was bothering Johnny, she mused. He hadn't said so. In fact he hadn't even asked what it was costing, but maybe he would have preferred something more low-key. Helen felt a pang of guilt. She had always organized their social life and Johnny had always been more than happy to let her. She should have been the one to suggest putting off the party until business improved. After all, they had Colm's eighteenth coming up in a few short months and quite apart from a party, they were planning to present him with a small car and a voucher for driving lessons. Feeling even guiltier at the thought of all that expense, Helen went back through her list, looking for ways to make cuts. She felt happier after she'd reduced the outlay by three hundred euros and quickly getting dressed, she drove the short distance to Howth.

Marianne opened the door looking pale and tired.

"You look terrible." Helen kissed her cheek.

"Thanks very much," Marianne laughed. "And good morning to you too!"

"Well, it's true; aren't you sleeping?" Helen followed her down the hall to the kitchen.

"I am, but Andrew isn't. Three nights in a row he's ended up in bed beside me. I wouldn't mind but he is such a fidget."

Dot looked up from her ironing. "Hello, love, how are you?"

"I'm fine thanks; how are you doing?" Helen went to kiss her noticing that despite Dot's warm smile, there was still some pain in those lovely green eyes. Marianne had been right not to tell her what Dominic had been up to.

"Are you all set for the party?"

"I think so; you're coming, Dot, aren't you?"

"The day I miss a Sheridan do, they'll be carrying me out the door in a box," Dot assured her. "I can't believe that you've been married twenty years."

"It feels like fifty," Helen joked.

"Tea or coffee, Helen?"

"Oh, coffee please, Marianne."

"Dot?"

"Nothing for me," Dot glanced at the clock. "I'm going to pop into town for a while." She lifted the pile of ironing in her arms. "I'll just put these away first.

Cut some of the fruit cake, Marianne; it's lovely, even if I do say so myself."

"How are things? Any more news?" Helen whispered when Dot had left them.

"Nothing. I assume you know Johnny is bringing a guy to see the house tomorrow?" Marianne folded down the ironing board and put it away.

"Oh, Marianne." Helen wasn't sure what to say. If there was one thing she, Marianne and Jo understood it was the value of having a place to call your own. It must be tearing her apart having to give that up. "I'm sure that it will only be temporary."

"Yes." Marianne forced a smile.

"Johnny seems fairly confident that this guy would be a good tenant. Are you definitely going ahead with the move to Kilbarrack?"

"It would be madness not to; it will save us a fortune."

"True. How are you coping?" Helen asked. Marianne seemed to get thinner every time she saw her. "It can't be easy keeping this latest bombshell from Dot."

"It's not," Marianne admitted. "But I have to. I'm also going to actively start looking for a job."

"What would you like to do?"

"Do you think I'll have much choice?" Marianne laughed as she set two mugs of coffee on the table and fetched Dot's fruit cake.

"Maybe not but I think there are always jobs for people with very specific skills, and you did very well managing the installation of that new computer system for Treacy Travel."

"And I really enjoyed it, but how many small companies do you think are installing new systems these days?" Marianne pointed out. "It would be great to get some kind of work in that area but I won't hold my breath; I'm ready to give anything a shot."

"Me too," Dot announced, coming in to collect her handbag.

"Really?" Helen found it hard to hide her surprise; Dot would be collecting her pension soon.

"Absolutely," Dot said, and was slipping on her jacket when the doorbell rang. "That will be Jo; I'll let her in. See you later."

"Bye, Dot," Helen called after her and then turned back to Marianne. "Is she serious?"

"Oh yes, she's determined to do her bit to bring in some extra cash."

"But someone will have to look after the children."

"That's what I said, but she said it won't stop her doing something part-time." Jo came into the kitchen carrying an armful of flowers. "Ah, thanks, Jo, you shouldn't have."

"They're just from the garden, nothing special," Jo assured her with a hug before sitting down and kissing Helen's cheek. "Hello, you. How are the party plans coming along?"

"Fine, Jo, thanks. How's everyone?"

"Not a bother."

"Marianne's going back to work," Helen told her.

"No, really?" Jo looked surprised. "Why?"

Marianne shot Helen a warning look. "It's going to take some time before Dominic's estate is sorted out so I need to earn a living, for the moment anyway."

"That's terrible." Jo frowned. "If you like I could ask Greg if he could help with the estate —"

"Thanks, but there's no need to trouble him, it's just red tape; I'm sure everything will work out in time."

"Of course it will," Helen agreed. She understood why Marianne hadn't confided in Jo. She would tell Greg and then he would probably offer to help sort out her financial problems and then expect to become her full-time accountant. Helen had no real idea of whether he was any good at his job but he was a bit too pushy for her liking and she certainly wouldn't like him to know all her private business.

"So, have you applied for any jobs yet?" Jo asked.

"No, but I'm going to get all the newspapers today and check the Situations Vacant columns."

"You need to put a CV together," Helen said, "and register with some employment agencies. And be sure to put your details up on some of the major employment websites too. Most of the newer companies mainly advertise online."

"Why don't you ask Treacy Travel for a job?" Jo suggested, her eyes lighting up. "They thought the world of you; I'm sure they'd be thrilled to have you back."

Marianne pulled a face. "They went out of business a few months ago."

"Oh, what bad luck." Jo sighed. "So many companies seem to be closing down these days; I suppose it's not a great time to be job hunting."

"There are always opportunities if you know where to look," Helen said with a meaningful look at Jo. "With Marianne's experience she'd be an asset to any small business."

"I didn't mean —" Jo started.

"Think of the people I'll be competing with though," Marianne interrupted. "They'll have degrees coming out their ears."

"Qualifications aren't everything. There are plenty of people about who are academically brilliant but useless when it comes to management," Helen said. "Update your CV and get it out there, Marianne."

Marianne laughed. "Do you know, I haven't a clue how to go about putting a CV together?"

"No problem. Write out all the various positions you held and the responsibilities you have had through the years and I'll do the rest," Helen told her, delighted to be able to help in some small way.

"You don't have to do that," Marianne protested.

"I know but it will make me feel useful and you know me, I love to have a project."

Marianne leaned over to give her a hug. "You're an angel. I'm delighted to be your project."

"Excellent," Helen said, feeling happier. She had felt so helpless lately; there was so little she could do to make her best friend feel any better. Her strength had always been in doing rather than talking. She would not only find Marianne a job, she would find her a damn good one too.

"I'd love a job," Jo said, looking wistful.

Helen smiled. "Will I do a CV for you too then?"

"Sure, what would you put on mine? Second-rate house-keeper, rubbish cook and lethal with an iron. Who'd hire me?"

"I hate it when you put yourself down like that, Jo. You're a lovely, honest, funny, kind and intelligent woman —"

"Ah, please!" Jo waved Marianne's praise away. "I think you're mixing me up with someone else."

"She's not, Jo, you are all those things and more. So," Helen rested her chin in her hand and studied her friend curiously, "what would your ideal job be?"

Jo grinned. "That's easy; I'd like to be a judge on one of those talent shows, you know the ones where they press a buzzer when someone is rubbish? My buzzer would be worn out before the first show was over!"

Marianne laughed. "That would be fun."

"But it's not likely to happen," Helen pointed out, afraid that they were veering away from the subject, and Jo's lack of confidence bothered her. A job might be exactly what she needed to bring her out of herself more. "Come on, Jo, seriously, tell us."

Jo fiddled with her hair self-consciously. "Well, believe it or not, I quite liked working in a shop. I like watching people and I'm fascinated by what they buy." She looked at Helen, reddening. "I suppose you think that's silly."

126

"Not at all; I'm fascinated by that too. When I'm queuing at the checkout I'm always peering into the basket in front. I love the weird ones, you know where there are eight packets of chocolate biscuits and a box of low-cal sweeteners."

Marianne laughed. "I do it too!"

"I wouldn't want to work in a big, anonymous supermarket, though," Jo said, warming to her theme. "I'd prefer one of those small shops where you get to know people."

"I think you would be really good at that," Helen mused. "You are so patient and friendly, you're a shopkeeper's dream employee. Why don't you do it, Jo?" It would be great for her to earn some cash of her own and get out and meet people; her life was much too mundane and solitary.

"Oh, I don't think so. My job is looking after the children and Greg."

"But they're out most of the day," Marianne reminded her. "You could do what Dot's planning to do and work mornings."

"I suppose so," Jo said, "but I still can't see anyone hiring me."

"Rubbish," Helen said. "I'd choose a responsible, mature woman any day over a young girl who simply wanted to finance her social life while she went through college."

"Or who spent their time daydreaming of winning one of those reality shows instead of working," Marianne added with a grin.

Helen studied Jo; she definitely seemed to be considering the idea. It could be the making of her and get her out from under Greg's thumb. Not that Helen felt Greg was entirely to blame; Jo had scurried under that thumb when she got married and stayed there ever since. It wasn't surprising given her traumatic childhood, but sometimes Helen did feel sorry for Greg. He thought he was gaining a life partner but instead he'd taken on a dependant. Now he was a grumpy, self-important bugger and no mistake. Still, he was like a choirboy next to Dominic Thomson. Helen thanked the Lord for Johnny; she had fallen on her feet the day she met that man.

"Let me put together a letter for you, Jo, and you can post it to the shops you'd like to work for."

"Oh, Helen, I don't know . . ."

"Let me write it at least, you don't have to send it if you don't want to."

"And even if you do send it off and get an offer, you don't have to take it," Marianne pointed out.

"Exactly," Helen gave her shy friend an encouraging smile. "Oh, come on, Jo. What have you got to lose?"

"Nothing I suppose." Jo shrugged. "Okay, Helen, write your letter."

"Yes!" Helen gave a triumphant punch in the air and stood up.

Marianne frowned. "Where are you off to?"

"I can't sit around nattering and drinking tea all day," Helen exclaimed with a grin. "I've got work to do!"

CHAPTER
ELEVEN

Rob was a nervous wreck by the time he walked up the drive of number 17 Asgard Court. It was ridiculous, he was behaving like a teenager on a first date, but this would be the first time he'd seen Marianne since the night she'd told him it was all over.

It had been in their usual meeting place, an Italian café in one of the sleazier parts of Dublin. He had always hated taking Marianne there, but she had insisted that it was a safer place to meet as it was unlikely they would bump into anyone they knew. That night, when he'd looked into her eyes, he'd known something was very wrong.

"Has something happened?" he'd asked as soon as they were seated and the waiter was out of earshot.

"Things are a bit difficult at home at the moment."

He'd had no idea what was going on in Marianne's marriage, she had always refused to go into detail, but he'd watched her grow quieter and thinner over the last few months. He'd tried to compensate and had gone to extra lengths to make their time together special, but he wasn't sure that would work today.

"Forget about it for a couple of hours, sweetheart, you're here with me now."

"For the last time, Rob," she said, her eyes full of tears.

"But why?"

"I'm married and I have two babies; I should never have started this. It was wrong of me and unfair to you."

"What's happened, Marianne? Has Dominic said something? Does he suspect you of seeing someone?"

She flinched. "I don't want to talk about him."

"Please. Tell me what's wrong, Marianne, let me help."

"You can't help other than by letting me go, Rob. Please don't make this any harder than it is."

He'd felt gutted by her words. They left the café soon afterwards; neither of them had felt like eating. As they walked back to the car park, side by side, but not touching, Rob wanted to pull her into his arms and beg her to reconsider. But he knew from the determined set of her mouth and the lost look in her eyes that her mind was made up. When he stopped outside the train station, he'd held her tightly in his arms, and kissed her for the last time, and then watched her walk out of his life.

"Rob, good to see you."

Rob did a double-take when Johnny flung open the door and gestured for him to come in. Rob stepped into the hallway, wiped his boots on the mat and glanced around. "Hi. I didn't realize you were going to be here too, Johnny."

"I'm alone. Marianne thought it would be best to let you take a look around the house without her looking over your shoulder."

"Oh, right." Rob swallowed his disappointment. "That was very thoughtful of her."

Johnny clapped his hands together. "Shall we start upstairs?"

"Great."

As Rob followed him from one bedroom to the next, he barely heard the man's comments; he was too busy searching for signs of Marianne. But though there was plenty of evidence of the children in the form of artwork and toys and photos of them at various ages, he could find nothing of her. Even the bright, immaculate main bedroom seemed sterile. He eyed the bed hungrily.

"Is she happy to rent the place furnished?" he asked, thinking how good it would be to lie where she had lain.

"Oh, absolutely. She's moving to a smaller place that's already furnished."

"Can I ask why?" Rob asked.

"There's nothing wrong with the house if that's what's worrying you," Johnny quickly assured him. "The family is just going through a rough patch."

"I see." It was wrong, so wrong, but Rob couldn't help but feel hope bubble up inside him; a rough patch must surely mean a separation. They were in the kitchen and Johnny was explaining the various appliances and waxing lyrical about the garden, from where you could just about glimpse Ireland's Eye, when

131

he saw the photo. It was stuck to the fridge among a mess of photos, Post-its and a colourful magnetic alphabet. It was a shot of Marianne and the children. Her long dark hair hung down over one shoulder and her head was thrown back. She was laughing, showing off the beautiful neck that he'd kissed so many times. She wore a simple white T-shirt and he could see the outline of her small, firm breasts underneath; it made him long to reach out and touch the photograph.

"That's Marianne and her two kids."

Rob started as he realized that Johnny had come over to see what had caught his attention.

Johnny checked his watch. "She should be here any minute."

Rob dragged his eyes away from the photo. "Sorry?"

Johnny turned away and reached for the kettle. "Marianne, she said she'd be back by eleven."

Rob checked his watch. It was a couple of minutes to the hour, a couple of minutes till he saw her again. He wondered how she'd react when they met; if she knew that he was her prospective tenant. "I'd like to take the house," he said quickly.

"We haven't even talked money yet," Johnny chuckled.

"I'm sure the rent will reflect the downturn in the market," Rob grinned. "And I need somewhere close to the site so I can keep an eye on my builder."

Johnny laughed. "It's nice to know that you trust me!"

"So, come on, tell me. What's the story? Why are they moving out?"

"Ah, well, that's a bit delicate —" Johnny broke off as they heard the front door open. "Sorry, it'll have to wait."

As Johnny went to meet Marianne, Rob's eyes returned to the photo. He felt almost afraid to face the door; he really wasn't sure what to expect.

After the night they had parted, he had sent her a couple of texts. He'd just wanted to know that she was okay, and had craved some contact, no matter how small. Marianne responded to them but not immediately and when she did her messages had been formal and brief. He had taken the hint and not contacted her again. He heard murmuring in the hall and their footsteps approaching, and taking a deep breath, he pasted on a smile and turned to face her.

"Marianne, this is Rob Lee. Rob, Marianne Thomson."

He crossed the kitchen, hand outstretched. "Nice to meet you."

"And you," she said with a nervous smile.

"You have a lovely home."

"Thank you." As the kettle clicked off, Marianne moved past him. "Tea, coffee?"

"Tea for me," Johnny replied, sitting down at the table.

"And me." Rob took the diagonal seat so that Marianne would either have to sit next to him or across from him; he wasn't sure which he'd prefer; probably opposite so that he could look into her eyes.

"Have you seen everything?" she asked.

"Except for the garden and the garage," Johnny answered.

"I'll be honest, Marianne, I don't really need to see any more." Rob's voice caught as he said her name aloud. "This house and its location suit me perfectly. I would be happy to go ahead with the rental if you are."

"I think we can trust him not to trash the place, love, and I don't think he has a criminal record."

"Well, there was an allegation of minor fraud, but it was never proven." Rob's grin faded as they stared at him. He turned questioning eyes on Johnny, but the man just shook his head, his eyes clearly saying he should drop it. Rob's heart sank; she'd only walked in the door and he'd already put his foot in it.

Marianne set a plate of biscuits and a jug of milk on the table, slopping it all over the place; some of it splashed on Rob's shirt.

"Oh, I'm so sorry," she said and quickly mopped it up.

Rob's heart flipped when she smiled at him and he resolved there and then that it didn't matter how high the rental was, he was taking this house.

Johnny's phone rang and he pulled it out and looked at the display. "Sorry, do you mind if I take this?"

"Of course not," Marianne said.

He talked briefly, hung up and sighed. "I'm sorry, I have to go. You can iron out the rest of the details between you, can't you?"

Marianne looked up at him, a hint of panic in her eyes. "Well, yes, but —"

He stood up, looking very pleased with himself. "I think this will work out just perfectly."

"I'm happy." Rob looked across at Marianne. He was glad she'd chosen the seat opposite; it gave him an opportunity to study her. Her hair was halfway down her back now and she seemed thinner and more serious, but when she'd smiled he'd seen the glint of humour in her eyes and her mouth was as sensuous as he remembered; the times he'd kissed those lips . . .

"You could move in the first week of June," Johnny said. "€1,400 a month, okay, Rob? With a €1,400 deposit up front?"

Rob saw Marianne's eyes widen at the figure. "Fine," he said instantly.

"Excellent."

Marianne stood up. "I'll see you out."

"Bye, Johnny," Rob called after him, and strained to hear Marianne's frantic whispers in the hallway. The front door opened and closed moments later and he smiled as she walked back into the room. "It's good to see you again."

"And you." She leaned against the counter, crossing her arms in front of her. "Although it feels very odd having you sitting drinking tea in my kitchen."

"I thought you'd prefer it if I pretended we didn't know each other."

She nodded. "Yes, thanks."

"How are you, Marianne?"

She looked at him and gave a shrug. "I'm okay."

His heart sank. He'd assumed that once they were alone that they'd be able to talk just as they used to but he'd been fooling himself.

"Look, if you want to find some excuse not to rent to me, I'll understand." He held his breath as he waited to see if she'd jump at the opportunity to push him out of her life again.

But after a few seconds, she shook her head and sat down again. "No, of course not; I need to rent this place as quickly as possible and I'll feel more comfortable leasing it to a friend."

A friend. Rob stiffened at the word; he had been a lot more than a friend.

"Don't you need to check with your husband first?" he asked, unable to keep the bitterness from his voice.

"Didn't Johnny explain?" Marianne said, her voice barely a whisper.

Rob sat forward. Perhaps he'd been right after all; perhaps Dominic was gone. "He said that you had some problems and were moving to a smaller place. Has Dominic lost his job?"

Marianne shook her head slowly. "No."

"So what is it?" he asked, finding it hard to read her expression.

"Dominic died of a heart attack six weeks ago."

Rob stared at her, stunned. "He's dead?"

"Yes."

He searched for the right words. He hadn't liked the man; he'd hated the fact that he went to bed with Marianne every night; hated that she'd chosen to stay

136

with him, but his heart went out to her; a widow at only thirty-five.

"I'm not sure what to say to you other than I'm sorry. How are Kate and Andrew coping?" He could see surprise on her face that he had remembered their names; as if he could forget anything about her.

"They have their good and bad days."

"And you?" he asked, not entirely sure that he wanted to hear the answer.

"I'm confused, upset, angry. I'm in a bit of a mess, to be honest."

"What do you mean?"

Marianne thought for a moment, as if considering whether or not to go on. "This is strictly confidential, Rob; even Dominic's mother doesn't know."

"You know I wouldn't betray your trust," he said, hurt that she would think otherwise.

"Of course you wouldn't. Sorry, I'm not exactly thinking straight." She took a deep but slightly shaky breath. "I just found out that Dominic was stealing from his employer. I don't know how much he took but it was a lot, and the upshot is that I'm unlikely to get a pension."

Marianne bunched her hair back behind her head in a gesture so familiar it made him smile.

"What?" She frowned.

He shook his head. "Sorry, nothing, go on."

"I probably won't get the life assurance money either. Dominic was taking drugs and they showed up in his bloodstream when they did the post-mortem."

"Drugs? Was he taking them when we were together? Is that what the fights were about?"

"It was a bit more complicated than that, and it's not important now. The bottom line is I can't afford to live here any more." She glanced at her watch. "I'm sorry, but I need to collect the children soon; they have a half-day. Let me show you the garden and the garage."

Rob really didn't care about either, but it meant at least a few minutes longer in Marianne's company. He followed her, watching the seductive sway of her hips and breathing in her perfume. He didn't take in much of what she was saying, he was too busy listening to the music of her voice and reacquainting himself with her expressions. Her proud smile when he commented on Andrew's artwork and how pretty Kate was and her laughter when he tripped over Andrew's scooter and almost went flying. And when she flicked back her hair and some tendrils touched his face he had to dig his hands into his pockets to stop himself grabbing her.

She led him around the side of the house, paused in the driveway, glancing at her watch.

"I'm sorry . . ."

"Yeah, sure, the kids, you'd better get going." Rob reached into his jacket for a business card. "In case you need to get hold of me."

She took the card and read it before looking back up at him. "Did you know that this was my house?"

"Yes." He held his breath as she opened her mouth to say something but then changed her mind. Disappointed, he gave her a reassuring smile. "Don't worry, I'm not stalking you; your house is perfect for me."

She smiled. "Good, I'm glad."

"I really am sorry, Marianne, about everything. If you ever want to talk . . ."

"Thanks, Rob, I appreciate it."

When she didn't meet his eyes he knew that she had no intention of taking him up on the offer. He swallowed his disappointment and with a brief nod, he walked quickly down the drive, steeling himself not to look back.

Later, Marianne went inside and closed the door with shaking hands. She couldn't believe that Rob Lee had been standing here beside her and that he was going to live in her house and maybe even sleep in her bed; the thought sent a shiver down her spine. She had felt embarrassed telling him about Dominic. How many times had Rob told her to leave him, that he was no good? Incredible, given he knew nothing of the physical abuse. Marianne didn't want to tell him about it now. It would only anger and upset him and what was the point? Oh, but it would have been so easy to open up to him. She had been amazed at how, once they were alone, that familiar sense of calm had descended on her. As he had sat at her table, sipping tea, she had drunk him in, every inch; he hadn't changed a bit.

His warm hazel eyes were as clear and direct as ever. His hair, almost the same colour, still touched his collar and there was already a shadow on his jaw despite the fact that it wasn't even lunchtime. She remembered vividly the roughness of that jaw on her cheek; how she would have to pack on concealer before returning home after spending time with him. She shivered at the delicious memory of his skin against hers.

The terrible guilt she would feel after their time together was always worth it. The bittersweet meetings with Rob had been the only thing that kept her going through those dark days, although leaving him had grown harder and harder. Saying goodbye had broken her heart. She had deliberated over it for days, wondered if there any other way out, but she always arrived back at the same conclusion; Rob had to go, for his sake more than hers.

But Dominic was dead now. There was no longer a reason to turn Rob away. And he had come here knowing she was his prospective landlady and client; that had to mean something, didn't it? Afraid to hope and terrified of making a fool of herself, she had tried to remain aloof but she was unable to control the tremor in her hands and voice; she wondered if he'd noticed. In a way she hoped he had. She hoped that he was here because of her and not the house. She hoped that her turn for happiness had finally arrived. And despite the fact that she was leaving her home, was practically penniless and her family's future was so uncertain, Marianne smiled.

CHAPTER
TWELVE

When Marianne finally got round to going to see her doctor about the constant pain in her stomach, Mandy James said it was probably just stress. She wrote out a prescription.

"These should help but you really just need to relax. Are you sleeping?"

"Yes, most nights."

"Try and get some exercise and keep the caffeine and wine to a minimum."

Marianne pulled a face. "Spoilsport."

Mandy laughed. "That's me. How are you doing, Marianne? Really? This has been a difficult time for you."

If only she knew, Marianne thought, but she was reluctant to open up to her lovely GP. If she started to talk she might never shut up. "I'm coping, well, most of the time," she joked.

"Really?" Mandy's eyes were shrewd.

"Really, although I do worry about the children. Andrew is being a little terror in school. He throws tantrums at home for the slightest reason and has turned into a foul-mouth. He's been wetting the bed too."

"All perfectly normal reactions for a five-year-old considering he's just lost his dad. What about Kate?"

Marianne sighed. "I've no idea what's going on in her head. She just won't talk to me about Dominic and she doesn't have much of an appetite."

"Does she talk to anyone else, do you know?"

"A little to Dot, I think, but not much."

"If you think it would help, you can bring them in to see me."

"I'd love your opinion, but if I suggest it Andrew will probably be scared stiff and Kate will clam up if she thinks she's being interviewed."

"Tell them it's just a routine check-up. I'll do all the usual tests and chat to them as I go, how does that sound?"

"Perfect, thank you."

And that's exactly what she did. But having left her daughter alone with Mandy, Marianne couldn't stand the confines of the waiting room and Andrew's whining. Instead, claiming she had a phone call to make, she'd gone outside and paced back and forth in front of the building, head down, hands deep in her pockets. Her attention was caught by the number of butts ground into the pavement; a testament to other nervous patients. She had never been a smoker but had she been offered a cigarette right then she'd have smoked it gratefully. She knew that Dot thought she was being silly bringing the kids down here and maybe she was right, but Marianne couldn't help worrying about them and what harm could it do to get an objective opinion?

Dot sat in the doctor's waiting room not at all sure why the hell they were all there. Since when did you take kids to see a doctor because they were sad? Wouldn't it be strange if they weren't? Still, if it put Marianne's mind at rest she supposed it was worth it. That poor girl seemed to be permanently worried these days. Dot felt ashamed that it was all because of her son. He had put her through so much and now she had money worries too, although Dot hoped that would be short-lived. On the bright side, she was convinced that the move to Kilbarrack would be a step in the right direction. She was stunned by the lack of community in the Howth estate and how isolated Marianne and the children were. Neither was she a fan of the posh private school they went to. The teachers seemed nice enough, it was the parents she wasn't that keen on. They arrived up at the school driving their big cars and dressed in their designer clothes and they didn't seem remotely genuine. As for the gifts, clothes and holidays they showered on their kiddies, well, she thought it was downright madness.

Marianne defended them, she said there were some very nice people, but Dot hadn't seen much evidence of it. Where were they when Dominic died? Not one parent had offered to mind the children for a few hours or even take them to school and allow Marianne and herself time to come to terms with Dominic's loss in privacy. It wouldn't be plain sailing for Kate and

Andrew in their new school, but once they'd settled in and made friends, they'd be grand. She knew that her good neighbours would have their grandchildren primed to keep an eye on the youngsters and make sure they were welcomed into the fold. It would probably be harder for Marianne to adjust. Not only was she leaving a fancy house for her smaller and much simpler one, she would probably feel strange in Dot's house and might be thrown at the way neighbours popped in on a regular basis. But with a bit of luck she'd be out working and that would make the transition easier.

Her thoughts were interrupted by her grandson running a toy car along the window ledge and smashing it into the wall.

"That's not yours, Andrew, stop."

"I'm bored."

"Then find something else to play with." Dot nodded towards the box of toys in the corner of the waiting room. Kate was in with the GP and a tense Marianne had gone outside to make a call. Andrew was not happy, didn't want to be here and wasn't taking any trouble to hide his feelings.

"They're all crap," he retorted.

"That's not a nice word," Dot said and rolled her eyes at the teenage girl tucked tightly into the corner, who simply looked blank and turned away. "Have a look at the books, Andrew."

"Don't want to read a bloody book."

"No bad language."

"You say it, Granny."

"That's different."

"Why?" he demanded.

"I'm a grown-up, that's why."

"When will I be a grown-up?"

"When you're about thirty," Dot told him.

"That's ancient," he exclaimed, and whacked the car against the wall again in disgust.

"It is," Dot agreed, "but it won't be something you have to worry about if you don't learn some manners. Come over here and sit down and we'll read a book together."

"Don't want to read," he grumbled, but nevertheless he dropped the car into the box and clambered up on the chair beside her. "Tell me one of your stories, Granny, not a made-up one."

"Well, let me think." She put her arm around him and planted a kiss on his golden-red hair, so like his father's. "Did I tell you about the time your granda was arrested?"

"What's arrested mean, Granny?"

"It's when the guards come and take you to the police station because they think you've done something wrong."

He turned round eyes up to look at her. "They put Granda in jail?"

Even the girl in the corner looked over at his screech.

"Will you hush. No they didn't put him in jail, they just took him down to the station for questioning."

"But why, Granny, what did he do?"

"Well, you see, he was driving a bit faster than he should have been and the next thing he knew, there was a police siren, flashing blue lights and a copper on a motorbike came tearing up beside him and waved at him to pull over."

"And did he?"

"Well, of course he did; he was a stubborn oul fella be times, your granda, but he wasn't stupid."

"And what happened?"

"Well, the guard climbs off the bike and strides over to the car, a dirty big scowl on him. 'Is it a race you're in, sir?' says he, real sarcastic like.

'Sorry, Garda,' says your granda, as polite as can be.

'And what speed do you think you were doing?'

'No idea, Garda, but I am sure you're going to tell me.'

'Oh, a smart-arse,' says the garda . . .'"

"Granny, that's a bad word!" Andrew giggled.

"It wasn't me that said it," Dot said quickly. "Now do you want to hear the story or not?" Andrew nodded enthusiastically. "Well, Granda says, 'Look, Garda, I'm not trying to be difficult but I really am in a hurry so if you're going to give me a bloody ticket, give me a ticket —' "

Andrew erupted into giggles. "You said it again!"

"Granda was upset," Dot explained.

"So did he give Granda a ticket?"

"Not at all. Sure, that would have been too easy; he was narked and he wanted blood. 'Step out of the car,' says he, and goes off to his bike to get a breathalyser kit. That's a special test where you blow into a bag and it says if you've had too much to drink," she added when Andrew opened his mouth to ask. "'This is ridiculous,' says my Bill, 'I haven't touched a drop.

146

Would you not make yourself useful and go and catch some real criminals?' Well, now, that just made the garda madder, but you see, that was your granda; a good man but he had a terrible short temper. 'Blow into the bag and less of your lip,' says he. So Granda does and of course it's fine, although the fecker took his time about telling him. Well at this stage your granda was fit to be tied. 'I told you I hadn't had a drop, now will you give me a ticket and let me be on my way? My son is sick and I need to get to the late-night chemist for cough medicine.'

'Do you now?' says the garda, obviously not believing a word. 'Can I see your driver's licence, sir?'

Wouldn't you know it? Granda didn't have it with him.

Well, the garda gives him a look and pulls out his little notebook, nice and slow, like. 'Can I have your name, sir?' he says.

"Now Granda knew he was in trouble."

"But why, Granny?"

"Well you see, there was a well-known criminal around in them days and what was his name? Only Bill Thomson, the same as Granda's. So he says, 'The name's Bill Thomson, Garda.'

'Aren't you feckin' hilarious altogether?' says the garda. 'Let's see how funny the lads find you down at the station.'

'Garda, I'm not kidding you, honest, that's me name and I don't have time to go to the station; I told you, I'm on me way to the chemist. Can't I drop you in the licence tomorrow?'

"Well, the garda just fixes him with a glare. 'You can follow me down to the station, sir, or I can call for a squad car to take you there. Now which is it to be?'

So down he went and they kept him there, kicking his heels for a while until another garda that used to play hurling with Granda arrives. Well, sure it was all grand then, the copper was all apologies, even made him a cup of tea and while Granda drank it and had a natter with his friend, your man only went off on his bike down to the chemist for the medicine. Well, they were the best of pals after that. They even went —"

Dot broke off as the door opened and Marianne walked in with a red-eyed Kate.

"Okay, come on, Andrew, your turn, sweetheart."

"I don't want to go to the doctor." Andrew shrank in behind his grandmother. "I'm not sick."

Marianne crouched down in front of him and touched his face. "I know love, but this is just a check-up. Mandy is only going to look in your eyes and ears with her torch and listen to your heart; don't you remember she let you use her stethoscope the last time?"

Kate smiled at her little brother. "And she gave me this." She held up a chocolate lollipop and Andrew's eyes lit up.

"Will she give me one too?" he asked, already climbing down off the chair.

"Of course she will," Marianne said and led him from the room.

148

"So, how did it go, luvvie?" Dot asked, patting the place that Andrew had vacated.

Kate sat down and shot a nervous look at the girl sitting in the corner.

"Don't worry about her," Dot whispered. "She's in a world of her own."

"Mandy says I am the healthiest nine-year-old she's seen this year," Kate said.

"Well, isn't that grand. Did she say anything else?"

"Not much." Kate sighed. "She asked me about Daddy. Everybody wants to talk about Daddy."

Dot squeezed her hand. When Dominic was pumping his body with those bloody drugs, had he even thought of the hurt it would cause? "Don't you want to talk about him, love?"

Kate shook her head. "It just makes me feel sad. Aren't you sad, Granny?"

Dot swallowed back her tears. "Of course I am, but I know he's safe in heaven with your granda."

"But I don't want him to be in heaven, I want him to be back here with us," Kate protested, her eyes filling with tears.

"I know you do but," Dot nudged her granddaughter in the ribs, "at least he won't be working, that'll make a change, won't it?"

Kate smiled and took the tissue Dot held out to her. "He did work an awful lot. I didn't mind weekdays; I was doing my homework and had to go to bed early anyway, but I hated him being out over the weekend. All my friends' dads used to do stuff with them on the weekend. Even G.G. took Rachel and Di swimming."

Dot stroked the child's silky hair and sighed. It said it all that even Greg-grudge Buckley was held up as a better father than her son. But she couldn't let Kate see that she shared her view, the child needed reassurance.

"But your daddy was out working hard so that he could give you and Andrew a lovely home and a good life, not because he didn't want to be at home with you. Sure, he was as proud as punch of the two of you; adored the very ground you walked on. Don't you think he would have loved to have been home with you morning, noon and night?"

"I know he couldn't have done that, Granny," Kate said, looking indignant.

"No, love. All he could do was his best for his family and that's what he did. Now, tell me, what will we have for tea?"

Marianne was standing in the corridor waiting when Andrew emerged, grinning from ear to ear and brandishing a chocolate lollipop.

"Bye, Andrew," Mandy called after him.

"Seeya," he said cheerfully.

"My turn," Marianne smiled. "You go to Granny, darling, I won't be long. Well?" she asked after she'd closed the door. "What's the verdict?"

Mandy waved her into a chair. "I really don't think you have anything to worry about with either of them, Marianne. Andrew is reacting exactly as any child his age would but it's great that he can talk about it. I think to get the aggression out of his system it might be a good idea to organize lots of outdoor exercise and plenty of family time. How is he sleeping?"

"Fitfully."

Mandy nodded. "Yes, I expected that. The exercise should do the trick."

"And the bed-wetting?"

"I'd ignore it as much as possible; I think time will take care of the rest."

"Okay. And Kate?"

"Kate is very mature for her age and a deep thinker."

"Tell me about it," Marianne sighed.

"She didn't say much but I would imagine that she's terrified of all sorts of things, in particular you or Dot getting sick or dying. Could she be worried at all about your financial security?"

Marianne's eyes welled up as she wondered if Kate had overheard any of her conversations with Dot about job hunting. "It's possible," she admitted.

"Don't start guilt-tripping, Marianne," Mandy warned. "This isn't your fault."

"How can I help her?"

"Just reassure her at every opportunity. Hold her and kiss her, even if she doesn't respond. Do things with her without Andrew, even if it's simply going for a walk or baking a cake. And watching a sad movie together can be a perfect opportunity to bring up difficult subjects. Also, don't be afraid to cry in front of them, Marianne. If you let them see your emotions, if you open up and talk about how you feel then they will do the same."

Marianne thought about how she'd always tried to pin on a smile for the children. How she and Dot had talked in hushed tones about Dominic and shut up as soon as the children came into the room. How she'd left them watching cartoons while she ploughed through the bills and bank statements. "I've been handling it all wrong," she told Mandy, horrified.

"Stop that, of course you haven't," Mandy said with a kind smile. "Try not to worry, Marianne. You will all be fine, I promise."

CHAPTER
THIRTEEN

The day of Helen and Johnny's party dawned and Jo dragged herself out of bed, pulled on a dressing gown and went downstairs to make tea. Rachel was sprawled in front of the TV watching cartoons.

"Morning, love." She went over to kiss her daughter.

"Hey, Mum." Rachel jumped up and wrapped her arms around her mother's waist in a tight hug.

"Where's your sister?"

"Still in bed."

Jo's eyes shot up to the clock; Di was due at the hairdressing salon in thirty minutes.

"Go and wake her, Rachel; tell her she's going to be late for work."

Jo poured cereal into two bowls, added milk and set them on the table before putting on the kettle. Rachel was halfway through her breakfast and Jo was sipping her coffee and leafing through a magazine when Di walked in, still buttoning her shirt.

"You should have called me, Mum," she complained. "Maria will kill me if I'm late again."

"You wanted this Saturday job, no one made you do it," Jo reminded her. "And you do know how to set an alarm clock. Now don't waste time moaning, sit down and eat your breakfast."

"I don't have time; I'll grab something on the way."

Jo looked up at her. "It won't take two minutes, love; you need your strength if you're going to be on your feet all day, and remember it's the party this evening."

"You're a fine one to talk; when was the last time you ate a proper breakfast?" Di looked pointedly at her mother's coffee but sat down at the table and started to spoon cornflakes into her mouth.

"We're not talking about me, cheeky."

Di grinned. "Remember, Maria's doing your hair at two. Don't be late."

"I won't," Jo sighed. "Though I doubt she will be able to do much with my mop." Jo hated getting her hair done. She always felt like a guilty child, sitting there, while her hair was picked up in clumps and peered at critically; it was almost as bad as visiting the dentist. "What are you wearing?"

"My black jeans and the silver T-shirt," Di said.

"Oh, love, that's very casual for a party. Would you not wear the purple dress, you look so pretty in that."

"It makes me look fat."

"No it doesn't. You look gorgeous," Rachel looked in adoration at her big sister.

Di smiled as she stood up. "Want me to put your hair up on top for you?"

"Oh, yes please." Rachel's eyes lit up. "And will I wear my pink or orange top with the pink jeans?"

"The orange," her sister pronounced.

Jo looked from one to the other in dismay. "But I've ironed your blue dress."

"Oh, Mum, I look like a dork in that!" Rachel rolled her eyes.

"It is a bit childish, Mum," Di said.

"She's eleven, not sixteen." Jo shot her youngest a reproachful look. "You've only worn it a couple of times."

Why did children, especially little girls, want to grow up so quickly? Her daughters were so different from her; Di full of confidence and attitude and Rachel, though shyer was still much more outgoing that Jo had been at the same age.

"I'm sorry, Mum." Rachel looked at her, large baby-blue eyes full of remorse. "It's just not very cool."

"It's dreadful," the less tactful Di said.

"Well, sorry, I'm sure. Go on then, get down those jeans and I'll press them for you."

"And my top, Mum?" Di said, fluttering her eyelashes.

Jo laughed. "Oh, all right."

"Mwah!" Di planted a kiss on her cheek and patted her sister's head. "Later!"

"Whatever happened to saying goodbye?" Jo asked as the front door slammed.

Rachel giggled. "What are you going to wear, Mum?"

"My green dress."

Rachel pulled a face. "You always wear that, Mum. Why don't you try on the black trousers and that nice lacy pink blouse?"

"Trousers?" Jo frowned. Greg hated her wearing trousers; he'd always liked her legs and used to complain that she didn't show them off nearly enough. It had been a while since he'd said that though.

"They're not really dressy enough for a party," she said to Rachel.

"But Aunty Marianne often wears trousers."

"Well, Aunty Marianne has a fabulous figure and would look gorgeous in a sack."

"I think Aunty Marianne is much too thin," Rachel confided, "and you have bigger boobs; all the guys like that."

"Rachel Buckley!" Jo said, stunned but amused.

"Well, Tracy says they do and that's why her mum puts those padded things in her bra."

Jo bit her lip to stop herself laughing. If Jools Donovan knew the things her daughter told her friends . . . "I tell you what, you go through my wardrobe and see if you can find anything nicer."

"What about Dad?"

Jo almost groaned at her daughter's hushed tone. Greg never got up before ten on a Saturday and woe betide anyone who disturbed him any earlier. "It's okay, Dad went to play golf at seven."

Rachel grinned broadly. "Great, let's have a fashion show!"

"Let me have another coffee first," Jo begged.

"Bring it up with you, oh, come on, Mum, you want to look gorgeous, don't you?"

Jo couldn't remember ever feeling gorgeous, but it was hard to resist Rachel's enthusiasm and it wasn't often they had some fun, just the two of them. "Okay, lead on, Gok!"

Jo sat with her back against the headboard and watched in amusement as her daughter went through the wardrobe with a critical eye. Where had her two daughters' love of fashion come from? Certainly not from her or either grandmother. Greg's mother seemed to have lived in grey, beige or brown, and Jo had only hazy memories of her mother's clothes other than that she took very little care of her appearance. She had been a plain, bitter, bad-tempered woman who rarely smiled. It wasn't surprising, Jo supposed, given the man she'd had to put up with.

Jo's father had been a nasty, abusive piece of work who made them all tremble when they heard his key in the door. He always seemed to be shouting though he was worse when he'd been drinking, and her mother's way of coping was to join him in his drinking. When the two of them had had a few, they tore strips off each other and Jo would either go out or hide in her bedroom, her hands over her ears. It hadn't been as bad when her big brother Chris had lived at home. He'd stay with her and make her laugh and convince her that it was all a big joke. But as soon as he was sixteen, he'd shoved a piece of paper into the eleven-year-old Jo's hand and left for ever. When she had smoothed out the page, she found a name and a number and Chris's almost illegible scrawl: *Call these people when you've had enough.*

It was almost a year before she'd finally rung that number. She'd been at hockey practice and come home to find both parents passed out in the kitchen, a broken bottle on the floor, alcohol and blood pooling on the tiles and a vicious cut on her dad's head. Her mother had warned her time and again to stay away from the neighbours and not to tell their business to all and sundry, but she had to do something. She sometimes wondered what would have happened if she'd dialled 999 instead; would she have ever ended up in St Anne's. She'd never been as happy there as Helen and Marianne, but she'd never have met them otherwise and that would have been a tragedy. She couldn't imagine how lonely her life would have been without them.

"Mum, you're not listening!"

"Sorry, sweetheart." Jo looked up to see her daughter standing over her, holding a silky, royal-blue dress that was years old.

"This is nice."

"I'd forgotten I had that," Jo admitted. "It's quite low cut."

"So?" Rachel grinned. "I already told you that you've great boobs! Try it on."

"Not now."

"Oh, come on, Mum, please?"

"Okay then," Jo sighed.

"I'll go and find shoes that match."

"I'll wear my new sandals. They're comfortable."

"It's not about being comfortable, Mum, it's about being gorgeous." Rachel grinned before hurrying downstairs to the hall closet where all their shoes were kept.

Once alone, Jo quickly changed into bra and pants — she hated anyone seeing her saggy, dumpy body — and pulled the dress over her head. It was a little tight. She hadn't succeeded in losing the weight she'd hoped to, nor had she joined up to any of the classes that Di had found for her. She was eyeing herself critically in the small mirror of her dressing table when Rachel returned.

"Oh, wow, that looks great. Here, put these on."

Jo looked dubiously at the navy high-heeled shoes that she'd hardly ever worn.

"They pinch."

"Oh, Mum!" Rachel rolled her eyes.

"Okay, okay." Obediently, Jo put on the shoes and did a slightly unsteady twirl. "Well?"

"Wow, Mum. You look gorgeous."

Jo smiled. "I'll do. Now go and get dressed and tidy your room and then we'll go and do the shopping." She looked once more at her reflection. She didn't look bad but she was no oil painting. Still the dress was a change from the green one and the high shoes flattered her legs; that should make Greg happy.

Would he fancy her in this dress? she wondered as she hung it up and donned her shirt and leggings. He wasn't the sort of man to dole out compliments but she always knew from the look in his eyes if he approved. When they were at the shopping centre, she'd drop into the menswear shop and buy him a new shirt and tie, he'd like that. Then she'd get a nice card for Helen and

Johnny to go with their present, which she just knew they would love. It was a small, pretty watercolour of the bay at Portmarnock that their house looked out on. Thinking of Helen made her wonder if she should phone to see if her friend needed help but she dismissed the idea. Helen was a wonderful organizer and no doubt had an army of caterers and cleaners beavering away. No, instead she would get the shopping done, buy Rachel lunch and then it would be time for the hairdresser. Perhaps Maria would work miracles and tame her hair and she might not look too bad at all.

"Colm will you please get off the phone and go and pick up the cake?"

"Hang on a sec," her son said to his latest squeeze, a cute little redhead from the Holy Faith School down the road. He put his hand over the mouthpiece. "Will you chill, Mum. What's the rush?"

"Don't tell me to chill," Helen said irritably. "Just do it."

"Gotta go, Jill, I'll see you later. *Ciao*."

Ciao? Really? Helen despaired. "You won't be seeing anyone later, Colm, you are not going out and missing this party."

"You don't want me hanging around all night, especially once Dad starts telling his embarrassing stories, do you?"

Helen turned away to hide her smirk. Johnny did tend to get nostalgic after a few drinks and would often wax lyrical about their first dates. Helen both loved and hated these anecdotes. She loved that he remembered those days so well and with such fondness, even though it was more than twenty years ago but, a private person, she was uncomfortable at the level of detail he went into. "Okay then, but don't you dare leave until after the cake has been cut, and I want you home by one o'clock."

"Mum —"

"One o'clock. Now, go and get the cake."

"Yes, Mother; right away, Mother; going now, Mother."

Helen smiled as he sauntered out of the room. He really was so like his father. Johnny's temperament had been one of his greatest attractions when they first met. He was so calm and self-assured and always smiling; Helen had never met anyone quite like him before. Twenty years, she could hardly believe it. They had been good years, although she and Johnny had had their share of arguments. But in comparison to the rows she'd witnessed between her parents, they were of no consequence and she'd never doubted his love.

She hoped he'd like his present. She had trawled all the antique shops in Dublin before she'd found what she was looking for. They were heavy, gold and diamond period cufflinks in the traditional Irish Claddagh shape: the symbol of love. They hadn't been cheap but given her recent economizing she didn't feel too guilty, and anyway Johnny was worth it. She had given him a lilac linen shirt and flamboyant purple silk tie this morning as his present, but now she'd laid them out on the bed for him to wear tonight with his pale grey suit and she left the cufflinks on top as a surprise.

161

She smiled, wondering what he'd bought her. He had presented her with roses this morning but said she must wait till this evening for her proper gift. She really didn't care what he bought her; every day with him was present enough. She had never dreamed as a frightened child cowering in her room that life could turn out to be as good as this and it was all thanks to him.

CHAPTER
FOURTEEN

Marianne stood in front of the mirror and grimaced at her reflection. Was wearing a red dress tasteless? She'd planned to wear the black, only to discover a tear in the skirt that was very noticeable and even Dot, who was a wizard with a needle and thread, said she wouldn't be able to repair it at such short notice.

"You look lovely," the woman in question said from the doorway.

"Don't you think it's a bit much given —"

"No, I don't. Anyway, you don't have much choice, love. I told you it was a bit hasty taking all those lovely clothes to the second-hand shop."

"I got six hundred euros for that lot and when am I going to get to wear stuff like that now?"

Dot grinned. "Nights like tonight?"

"That's why I kept the black. It's timeless and fits perfectly; I can't believe it's torn and all I'm left with is this thing."

"You have nothing to feel guilty about, Marianne, remember that."

"I just don't want people whispering about me; imagine if one of the children heard."

Dot went to the door. "Kids!"

Kate came in from her bedroom looking pretty in pink, her long dark hair held back with a glittering band. "What's up?"

Andrew came dashing up the stairs, pulling at the stiff collar of his shirt. "This is itchy, Mum," he complained with a scowl.

"Are you wearing a T-shirt?" she asked.

"Yeah."

"So after a while you can take the shirt off."

"But, Mum —"

Dot pressed her finger to his lips. "Shush mister, and tell me, does your mother look nice?"

Andrew looked at Marianne and smiled shyly. "Yes, like a princess."

"Kate?" Dot asked.

Marianne's daughter nodded silently, but her eyes were smiling.

"Your mum wanted to wear her black dress only it's ripped and so she has to wear this but she thinks people won't like her wearing red because your daddy died."

Andrew screwed up his face. "That's dumb."

"Ha!" Dot's laugh was triumphant. "I couldn't agree more; what do you think, Kate?"

"Daddy loved you in that dress, Mum. Wear it for him."

Marianne hugged her. "You know what, you're right; he did love this dress and he absolutely hated me wearing black."

"There you go then. Now, is anyone going to tell me I look nice at all?" Dot twirled, her green floral-print dress flaring out around her.

164

"You're gorgeous," Marianne smiled. And indeed Dot did look elegant. The silky material of her dress flattered her curvy figure and shapely legs, she'd had her hair done in a more glamorous style for the occasion and was wearing a bright-red lipstick that added a touch of fifties chic.

"Gorgeous, Granny," Andrew agreed.

Kate giggled. "We can call you G.G. too!"

"Don't you dare," Dot warned, laughing. "Where's the present?"

"On the hall table." Marianne grimaced. The crystal photo frame seemed a paltry gift but Johnny and Helen would be annoyed if she spent money they knew she didn't have. But she knew they would love the photo she'd put in it; one of them on their wedding day. She'd taken it as the couple were leaving the reception. Helen looked radiant in a vivid blue dress, her eyes shining with happiness, while Johnny wore a broad, proud smile and had a protective arm around her shoulders. It captured the happiness of the day perfectly.

Dot had also made up a stunning floral display from the garden; another personal touch that Helen would appreciate.

"I bet we've got them the best presents," Andrew said, dancing down the stairs ahead of them.

"Of course we have!" Dot said.

Marianne slipped into her red high heels. "Kate, can you manage the bouquet?"

"Yes." Kate gently touched a velvet pink rose. "They really are lovely, Granny."

"I will miss the garden," Dot admitted.

Kate looked up at her in alarm. "What do you mean? Where are you going?"

"You're not going away, Granny, are you?" There was panic in Andrew's voice.

Dot looked at Marianne, her eyes filled with horror and remorse at her gaffe; they had agreed not to tell the children they were moving until the last minute so they wouldn't have time to dwell on it.

Marianne smiled at her to let her know it was okay, but she felt flustered realizing that she would have to tell them now. "Granny's not going anywhere, at least not without us. Come on, we'll be late."

"But, Mum —"

"I'll explain in the car, Kate," Marianne said, her mind racing; what could she say? How could she tell the children that they were broke and about to leave their home and school? She hadn't had time to prepare, hadn't given any thought to how she would explain; she'd thought she had weeks to come up with a plausible reason. But she had no choice but to explain now otherwise their imaginations would run wild. Judging by Andrew's expression, his already was.

"I'm sorry, love." Dot put a hand on her arm as the children climbed into the back of the jeep. "You could tell them that the boiler or something is broken and that's why we're moving to my place for a few months."

"No, Dot, I don't think so. Mandy said it was important to be honest with them and anyway, a busted boiler wouldn't account for them having to move schools."

Dot looked upset. "Me and my bloody big mouth."

166

"It's done now, don't worry about it. Just follow my lead."

"I'm keeping my mouth shut from now on," Dot assured her.

They followed the children to the jeep and Marianne used delaying tactics for as long as she could. Were they all wearing seat belts? She couldn't talk while she was reversing out of the drive, or pulling out into busy traffic for that matter but, finally, when she was cruising out along the coast road towards Portmarnock and the silence was heavy in the car, she knew she had to say something. She decided to follow Mandy James' advice, and taking a deep breath, announced: "We're moving to Granny's house."

Dot shot her a look of alarm but said nothing.

"Cool," said Andrew, "there are loads of kids to play with there."

Marianne exhaled. Taking them to that street party had been inspired. Both children had really enjoyed it.

"But why?" Kate asked.

Marianne took a quick look over her shoulder; Kate didn't look upset so much as puzzled. "We don't have as much money now that Daddy's not here to look after us," she explained. "If we move to Granny's, we can rent out our house and get more money that way."

Kate absorbed this for a moment and then said, "So are we broke?"

"Of course we're not," Dot laughed.

"But we aren't rich either," Marianne added quickly; she didn't want Dot making any promises they wouldn't be able to keep. "We need to make some changes to the way we've been living."

"Like what?" Kate asked.

"Well, I'm going to sell the jeep and I'll probably get a job and," Marianne took another deep breath; this was the cruncher, "you'll be leaving school and going to the one around the corner from Granny's."

"Oh good," Kate said. "I hate my school."

Marianne almost crashed the car. "Don't be silly; you don't hate it."

"I do."

"But why, pet?" Dot asked, turning around to look at her granddaughter.

"There's a gang in my year that are always picking on me, taking my stuff and trying to get me into trouble."

"The little bitches," Dot exclaimed, incensed.

"Granny!" Andrew crowed.

"Well, really!"

Marianne stopped at the level crossing as the lights flashed and the barrier came down announcing the imminent arrival of a train. She turned to look at her daughter. "Why didn't you tell me, darling?"

Kate shrugged. "It hasn't been as bad since Daddy died; most of them feel sorry for me now and if the teachers catch them saying anything bad, they get into trouble."

"I hate school too," Andrew announced.

"Do you, darling?" Marianne took his statement with a pinch of salt; he always copied whatever his big sister said. She would let Kate's comments go for now but

168

they had worried her; she would revisit them another time when they were alone.

"Do you think you'll like going to school in Kilbarrack?" Dot asked them.

"Is it really only around the corner? Will we be able to walk?" Andrew asked.

"You will indeed or go on your bike; young Billy next door goes on one of those strange skate contraptions."

"A flicker? Oh, I'd love to get one of them!"

"Dream on," Marianne told him. "I told you we need to save money, not spend it."

"It's okay," he said. "I'll get one for my birthday."

"Haven't you heard a word Mum's said, dork?" Kate said to him. "We're broke."

"You haven't been listening either then, Kate," Marianne told her. "We're not broke we just need to tighten our belts a little; there won't be any foreign holidays for a while."

"Can we go camping?" Andrew bounced up and down in his seat. "I'd love to go camping."

Marianne exchanged an amused glance with Dot. "I suppose we could afford a tent."

"You can go without me." Dot shuddered. "I don't fancy that at all, I'd lie awake all night worrying about what was crawling over me."

"Just like the hairy spiders in the outside toilet," Andrew giggled.

"We could stay in a caravan," Dot suggested. "We had some great caravan holidays when your daddy was little, although there were a few dodgy ones too."

Marianne frowned as she tried to recall a story that Dominic had told her. "Didn't you get flooded once?"

Dot threw back her head and laughed. "That's a slight exaggeration but we did have a close call right enough; Lord, I'd forgotten all about that!"

"What happened, Granny?" Kate asked.

"Well, we had a caravan when your daddy was little. Oh, it wasn't the fancy mobile homes they have now, it was very small and basic but it meant we could go anywhere at the drop of a hat and it cost next to nothing. It was in June and the weather forecast for the weekend was fantastic, so Granda took a half-day off work on the Friday and we headed down to Clare to a lovely spot we'd heard about on the Shannon River. Your daddy was only four and he hated being stuck in the car for long because he got so bored — there were no computer games in those days — so we would stop along the way for snacks or to let him have a run around. But the closer that we got to Clare, the darker the clouds got and by the time we arrived, it was raining hard, your daddy was tired and irritable and we were dying to get him to bed. But do you think we could find the feckin' caravan park? Not at all. We drove round for nearly an hour before we finally found it and by this time it was dark. It was such a relief and your granda found a grand pitch looking out over the water, nice and close to the bathrooms."

"Bathrooms?" Kate frowned. "Why did you need bathrooms?"

"There was none in the caravan," Dot explained. "I told you it was basic."

Even Marianne was surprised at this. "But you had a loo, right?"

"Ah, yes, we did. Anyway, by the time we were settled, it was lashing rain but we were warm and cosy inside and that's all that mattered. We were all tucked up fast asleep and then I heard a thump and a cry and hadn't your daddy fallen out of bed!"

Andrew giggled. "I do that sometimes."

Dot turned to smile at him. "You do and so did your daddy, only this time it wasn't his fault; wasn't the caravan leaning over to one side. Well, luckily he wasn't really awake and I popped him back into bed and tucked in the bedclothes tight so he wouldn't fall out again, and then I went to get Granda. Well, he was disgusted at me waking him up in the middle of the night, said I was imagining things until he stood up and went flying across the room."

"Oh my God," Kate gasped.

Marianne smiled as she turned off the main road and into the lovely little street where Helen and Johnny lived. The children were completely diverted by Dot's story, her bombshell forgotten, although she knew that she would be inundated with questions tomorrow.

Dot continued with her story. "Granda had parked in a dodgy site that had flooded and we were sinking into the mud on one side and the water was lapping up the steps. There was a warning sign but, sure, we never saw it in the dark."

"So what did you do?" Marianne asked.

"Granda got dressed and went off to find the owner of the site. They had a guesthouse too, and so were able

171

to give us a room for the night. Just as well, by morning the caravan was nearly on its side. But the next day was fine and with the help of a few other men on the site, Granda soon managed to rescue it. We were very lucky, it wasn't damaged at all."

"I don't think I want to go on holiday in a caravan," Andrew said, looking fearful.

"Ah, sure they're all very fancy nowadays, love, with all mod cons."

"What's a mod con?" he asked.

"Modern convenience," Marianne explained. "It means all the things that make life easier like showers, microwaves, TVs, washing machines, that sort of thing."

"But it could still sink," he said, a stubborn look on his face.

"If we went on a holiday like that, we would stay in a place where they provided the caravan and it would be on blocks or cement so it could never sink," Marianne assured him as she pulled into the driveway and parked next to Helen's Audi as Johnny had instructed. "Now, let's go and party!"

CHAPTER
FIFTEEN

A smiling Johnny opened the door as they approached, looking suave in a beautiful grey suit and highly polished black shoes. "Welcome, Thomsons. Come in! You look sensational, Marianne," he said, bending to kiss her cheek before enveloping Dot in a tight hug.

"Don't be doing that," she laughed. "If your wife catches you, she'll have your guts for garters."

"She knows that I can resist anything but a beautiful woman, Dot."

"Get away with you," she said giving him a playful push. "I'm old enough to be your mother."

"Ah, but you're like a fine wine; you get better with age." He turned to smile at Kate. "And yet another beautiful lady! Hello, Kate, what a pretty dress."

"Thanks, Uncle Johnny," she said shyly.

"And how's the man of the house?" Johnny picked Andrew up and tossed him in the air before catching him in his arms and throwing him over his shoulder.

"Stop," the little boy squealed, giggling, kicking his feet and pummelling Johnny's back with his tiny fists.

Johnny set him back down. "Well, aren't you a tough little man? Let me see those muscles."

"Where's Helen?" Marianne asked as her son started to push up his sleeves.

"In the kitchen, go on through. Dot, come, let me get you a drink and kids, wait until you see what's in my garden."

As he led the family through the living room towards the French windows that opened on to their large back garden, Marianne carefully carried the flowers down the hall and nudged the door open with her hip. Helen, elegant in a grey silk dress that complimented her dark hair and buxom figure, was sitting at the island frowning over a list. Marianne smiled. Helen had lists for everything and any event she organized always went off like clockwork.

"You look lovely, Helen."

Her friend hopped up, smiling, and came to hug her friend. "Thanks, Marianne, what beautiful flowers, but you shouldn't have, they must have cost a fortune."

"Not a penny," Marianne laughed. "All Dot's handiwork."

"No!" Helen marvelled. "She has really excelled herself this time. They will look perfect in the centre of the buffet table; the one the caterers brought isn't a patch on this. That's a gorgeous dress, Marianne."

"I hadn't intended to wear it; I feel a bit self-conscious to be honest. It's not really what a new widow should be wearing, is it?"

"Don't be silly, no one expects you to wear black all of the time."

Marianne perched on a stool. "So, what did you get for your anniversary? More diamonds?" Johnny was a

174

generous man and also a thoughtful one; Helen's presents were always carefully chosen. It was something Marianne had always envied. Dominic had been useless at choosing gifts and most of the time had just pressed a few notes into her hand and told her to buy herself something nice. Had he had a mistress, she wondered and, if so, did she get the same treatment or had he showered her with gifts?

"He only just told me, Marianne; he's booked a cruise for us." Helen's eyes shone with excitement. "Fourteen days touring the Caribbean, isn't it wonderful?"

"Fantastic," Marianne smiled thinking of the conversation in the car about caravans.

"I never thought when we were in St Anne's that one day I would end up living a life of luxury."

"You and Johnny have worked damn hard to get where you are today; you deserve it."

"Aw, bless you." Helen beamed. "Come on, we'd better show our faces; the other guests will be arriving soon."

"You are lucky with the weather, it's a lovely day." Marianne followed her outside and stared at the sight that greeted her. A large, white-and-lemon striped marquee took up a third of the garden and a bouncy castle had been set up at the far end where her son was already playing, Dot encouraging him to go higher while Kate looked on. She wished her daughter was up there with him, laughing uproariously. Marianne did wonder about this bullying business; perhaps that was the real reason Kate was so withdrawn.

"Here you are, Marianne."

She looked around to find Johnny at her side, a glass of champagne in his hand. "Oh, no, thank you, Johnny. I'm driving."

"You won't be leaving for hours yet and one glass won't hurt."

She smiled and took the glass. "Okay, thank you. Happy anniversary."

"Cheers. Shouldn't I get a medal for putting up with her for this long?" He nodded towards where Helen was going around the marquee, questioning staff and rearranging cutlery.

"Oh, how you've suffered," Marianne teased him.

"Ah, don't I know it?" he said, eyes twinkling. "You are looking particularly sexy today, sweetheart."

"You behave yourself," she warned him, but couldn't help smiling. Johnny had always been an outrageous flirt.

"You're no fun," he laughed.

"This all looks wonderful, Johnny."

"Ah, sure no one can throw a party quite like Helen," he said, pride in his voice. "Tell me, have you got together with Rob yet?"

Marianne looked at him, startled, caught off guard. It was so strange to hear Rob's name and to think that her ex-lover would now become an acceptable part of her life.

"He said he wanted to drop by and measure up the office so he could buy some extra fittings," Johnny explained.

176

"Oh, that. Yes, he did call but he hasn't had a chance to do it yet; I think he's out of the country at the moment."

In truth, she had been startled to get the phone call, immediately thinking Rob wanted to meet up. Instead he had been cool and businesslike and asked permission to replace her simple office fittings with his own.

"I realize that probably doesn't suit you and that you wanted to lease the house fully furnished, but I need to maximize the space —"

"That's absolutely fine," Marianne had assured him.

There had been a moment's silence and then Rob had simply said that he would be in touch on his return and hung up.

"Did you hear anything more from Matthews and Baldwin?"

Marianne shook her head. "Nothing."

Johnny shook his head in frustration. "They should be keeping you informed."

"Maybe there's nothing to tell. Anyway, why should they, Johnny? Dominic ripped them off; his widow is hardly their concern."

"You're too reasonable and understanding for your own good," he smiled. "Tell me, did you find the deeds to the house?"

"No. The bank doesn't have them and I have looked everywhere I can think of."

"Did you contact the lawyer who handled the purchase? He'll have a copy."

"He's retired and nobody seems to be able to find any of our details; every time I phone they give me the run around."

"That's bloody ridiculous! What's the name? I'll get on to them —"

"It's okay, I can handle it."

"But you've enough to worry about with the children and the move and looking for work."

"Oh, please, don't remind me." She tried to smile.

"If you want to give yourself a head start, you should think about upskilling. Talk to your lodger about it."

Marianne stared at him. "Rob? I didn't realize he was in the training business; I thought he installed computer systems for small businesses."

"Rob's a clever guy; he's got a finger in a few pies. He made a killing when he sold a property website he'd developed and now he's branched into training; I'm sure he'd give you a good deal."

"That's good to know," Marianne laughed. The idea of Rob teaching her was a tantalizing one. "But before I can think about training I need to pack away all our belongings. There's so much stuff that we won't be taking with us; I'll just have to put it all up in the attic."

"If there are any bits and pieces that you want to sell I know a great dealer who would give you a fair price."

She looked at him thoughtfully. She'd sold her good clothes but it hadn't occurred to her to try selling anything else. "What sort of bits and pieces?"

"You name it," he shrugged. "Furniture, art, jewellery. Frank Power will find a home for it and you couldn't meet a fairer man."

Marianne ran through an inventory in her head. She had little expensive jewellery but there were a few items of furniture that had cost a fortune, notably Dominic's desk and the diningroom suite that sat twelve.

"Worth every penny," Dominic had said at the time when she'd gasped at the price. "You wouldn't believe the amount of business done around a dinner table and we'll be entertaining a lot more now than we used to."

They had for a couple of years and then it had tapered off; why had she never realized that before? The only other items worth real money were the crystal, the dinner service and the cutlery and . . . "Oh my God!"

"What?" Johnny frowned.

"The paintings!" Marianne exclaimed. "You must have heard Dominic talk about them, Johnny. He bought art for years as an investment."

"Now you come to mention it, I do remember him showing me a modern piece that he paid a couple of hundred for; it looked more like a child had been let loose with a paint set, just blobs of colour."

Marianne laughed. "I know the one you mean, I didn't think much of it either. There're a lot more like it in the attic."

"They could be worth a few bob. You should at least have them valued, what harm can it do?"

"None at all."

He clinked his glass against hers and smiled. "Great. I'll talk to Frank."

Jo had shrunk into a corner of the marquee with her plate of tasty canapés and glass of wine, feeling self-conscious and surplus to requirements. Di and Rachel were off with the other kids, and Greg was in the centre of the marquee in conversation with a couple of other men. Even at this distance she guessed from his expression that they were discussing the economy; did he ever talk about anything else? She was more than happy that he had left her to her own devices; he'd irritated her the minute they'd got here.

"Some people aren't affected by the recession, are they?" he'd muttered as they stood taking in the splendour of the marquee, the extravagant buffet and the small band playing muted blues music in the corner.

Jo hated the way he said it; he sounded so bitter. Yes, it was a bit ostentatious and Johnny and Helen obviously weren't short of money, but they'd earned every penny; weren't they entitled to spend it however they wanted? And despite the fact that they had gone up in the world, they hadn't changed or forgotten their old friends. Jo might not be the best when it came to socializing but she knew most of the people here even if it was only to nod to. Indeed, Helen and Johnny were the perfect example of a couple who hadn't let success go to their heads and Colm was a grand lad, not in the least spoiled.

"Jo, what are you doing here all alone?"

She looked up to see Helen standing over her and smiled. "Enjoying the lovely food and people watching; it's a wonderful party, Helen."

"Thanks, love. Come and meet my new neighbour, Eleanor. I just know that you two will hit it off; she's originally from Cabra too."

Jo could imagine nothing she'd hate more than to talk to someone who may have lived near her family home. "I'd prefer not to, Helen. I have a bit of a headache. You don't mind, do you?"

"No, of course not. Let me get you some painkillers or would you like to lie down for an hour?"

"No, really, don't worry, I'll be fine."

Helen eyed her worriedly. "You are a little pale, though I must say, I think you look wonderful tonight; that colour really suits you."

"Thanks." Jo smiled. She was quite pleased with how she looked. The make-up and softer hairstyle made the most of her plain features and even Greg had said that the navy dress was very flattering.

"Why don't you go and sit in the garden?" Helen suggested. "It's stuffy in here and the fresh air will help your head."

"I will when I've finished eating," Jo promised.

"Can I get you anything else?"

"I'm fine, go and look after your guests!"

"*You're* my guest," Helen protested.

"No, I'm your friend, you don't have to worry or impress me."

"Bless you!" Helen blew her a kiss and hurried off to check on a group of women sitting nearby.

Moments later Marianne joined her, carrying a plate of food and a glass of water. "Oh, good, a seat; my feet are killing me." She sank into the chair beside Jo and eased off her shoes. "You look great, Jo, that dress is fabulous and your hair really suits you that way."

"Thanks; you look stunning too," Jo said and meant it. The vivid colour accentuated Marianne's dark hair and golden skin and was a pleasant change from the drab clothes she'd been wearing these last few weeks.

"I feel like the merry widow but I'd nothing else to wear, so what could I do?"

"You have nothing to wear?" Jo rolled her eyes. "Oh, please, you have tons of fabulous outfits."

Marianne grimaced. "Not any more, Jo. I had to sell most of them."

"What? Why?"

"Oh, sorry, that sounds melodramatic; I just sold the dressy stuff that I hardly ever wore."

"Is money really that tight?" Jo asked. She'd thought Marianne's financial problems were only temporary and would be sorted after the inquest.

"No, I just don't know how much money we will have to live on or for how long so I'm not taking any chances. I'm renting out the house, we're moving into Dot's and I'm taking the kids out of school; they'll go to the local primary in Kilbarrack."

"Oh, Marianne, I'm so sorry." Jo looked at her, horrified. Other than something happening to the children or Greg, she could think of nothing worse than having to give up her home.

"It's fine, we'll cope," her friend said with a shrug of resignation. "My biggest worry was how the kids would react to changing schools but they seem delighted. All

182

that money wasted on private education. Ironic, isn't it?"

"You were just trying to give them a better start than we had. If you need any help, Marianne, just say so." She wasn't much use at anything in particular but she could and would back up her friend. "School runs or babysitting, anything. All you have to do is ask."

"You are sweet, Jo, but you live in Shankill!"

"Yes, but we're only five minutes from the train station and isn't Dot's house only around the corner from Kilbarrack Station?"

"Oh my God, I hadn't thought of that. How brilliant, Jo. We'll be able to meet up much more often."

"No, we won't."

Marianne frowned. "Why not?"

"Because you'll be off in a fancy office doing a high-powered job."

"Ha, I wish!"

"But it does mean that I can come over and look after the kids or they can come to me; travelling on the DART is so much easier than dealing with traffic jams."

"That really cheers me up, Jo," Marianne said. "We don't see nearly enough of each other."

Jo smiled, warmed by the genuine pleasure on Marianne's face. "Well, that's all going to change."

CHAPTER
SIXTEEN

Dot sat in a deck chair, enjoying the feel of the sun on her face as she watched the children play. Kate sat at her feet, pulling grass; in fact the child had been stuck to her like glue since they got here. That chat with the doctor hadn't seemed to make much difference, not that it surprised Dot.

"Why don't you go and play with the other kiddies, luvvie?"

Kate just shrugged.

"You know, I miss your daddy a lot but when I get down I try to remember the happy times and there were so many." At least that was true, Dot comforted herself, a pity most of them were so long ago.

"Tell me one, Granny."

"Well, let me think." Dot put a hand on her granddaughter's silky head. "Did I tell you about the first time your daddy met your mummy?"

Kate looked up, a spark of interest in her eyes. "It was at a dance, wasn't it?"

"Not just any dance, it was called The Grove and the coolest place to go on the north side of Dublin. It started out in Belgrove School, oh, years ago, but there was a fire and they moved to St Paul's School in

Raheny, that's a boys' school next to St Anne's Park; you've been there a few times, haven't you?"

"Yes, for walks and to play tennis."

"I must take you to the rose garden some time," Dot mused. "It's very pretty."

"What about The Grove, Granny?"

"Aren't you impatient, missus?" Dot teased. "Well, it was nothing special really, I've no idea why they were all so mad about the place; you'd want to ask your mother that. It was held in an ordinary hall every weekend, from nine at night until one in the morning. Your granda wasn't at all impressed at your daddy staying out till that hour and only let him go a couple of times a month. You had to be sixteen to get in although I know lots of the younger kids managed to forge membership cards to get in; I know for a fact your daddy did." She laughed. "He'd say he was off out to play chess with some of the clever young fellas in his class and of course Granda swallowed that, but I knew very well what he was up to."

"How could Granda think he was staying out so late to play chess?" Kate asked, frowning.

"Ah, your daddy wasn't stupid, he came home early on those nights; he loved the place. It ran for years and years and it always had the same DJ, now what was his name?" She paused, frowning, racking her brains.

"It doesn't matter, Granny. Tell me about Daddy meeting Mum."

"That happened much later. Your dad was nineteen; he'd left school and had started university. He probably wouldn't have been going there any more at all, only he was always broke and it was cheaper than the clubs and discos in town. It was only years later that he told me the full story of the night he met your mother. It was her first time there and the bouncer was giving her and her friend a rough time."

Kate frowned. "What's a bouncer?"

"The person who decides who to let in. From what your daddy said, there was one man who was more interested in making the poor kids suffer than anything else. He'd question them, examine their membership cards while everyone queued up behind. Well, your mum was close to tears, terrified of the bully, she was, and didn't your daddy step in to sort it out. He'd been going so long, the bouncer knew him well and as soon as your daddy said that she was a friend, he let her in straight away."

"But she wasn't a friend?"

Dot shook her head and smiled. "No, but she was after that. Your daddy was smitten straight away although your mum refused to go on a date with him for a long time."

Kate looked cross. "Why, didn't she like him?"

"She says she did but she was very young, had only just left the children's home and the rules at the hostel were quite strict. She wasn't supposed to go out in the evening without another girl, and when she did go out she had to be home before twelve. So, for a couple of months, Dominic would only see her there once a week and then she was gone by quarter to twelve. Finally he persuaded her to go out with him. They met up for a burger in town and walked around St Stephen's Green.

Well, the state of him before he went to meet her." Dot smiled at the memory. "He was as nervous and excited as a puppy! After that they met once or twice a week at The Grove or in Bewleys on Grafton Street and when I saw that it was serious, I told him to ask her to tea. Your granda and I loved her immediately."

"Here you go, Dot." A smiling Helen walked towards them with a plate.

"Mother of God, girl, how can I possibly eat all that?" Dot stared at the slice of cheesecake, chocolate cake and generous spoonful of ice cream.

"I'm sure someone could help you."

Kate bent her head and said nothing. Helen raised her eyebrows at Dot who gave a helpless shrug.

"Di and Rachel are making some slush puppies, Kate, why don't you go and help them."

Kate hesitated for a moment and then stood up. "Okay. I won't be long, Granny."

"You go ahead, darling, I'm grand."

When the little girl had run off towards the house, Helen smoothed the skirt of her dress and sat down. "You're not socializing much today, Dot. Is everything okay?"

"Fine, love, I'm just trying to give Marianne a break by looking after the kiddies. Kate wants to be with her all the time yet doesn't say much; it's driving the poor girl mad."

"She has so much on her plate, you both have; I'm worried about you."

"There's no need, we'll be grand. The one thing she was worried most about was telling the kids that they had to leave school. She decided to leave it till the last moment so they wouldn't have time to get anxious about it, but me and my big gob; I let it slip just as we were walking out the door today."

"Oh no, how did they react?"

"Well, that's just it; Marianne explained everything to them on the way over and they don't seem in the least bit bothered. Andrew is delighted that he'll be able to walk to school or go on his bike and the real shocker; it turns out that Kate was being bullied in that feckin' posh school, can you believe that?"

"That's awful. What happened to her?"

"Some gang of kids were teasing her and making her miserable. We haven't got to the bottom of it yet, but we will."

"If there's anything I can do . . ."

"You are doing more than enough, love, and that fella of yours is a diamond; you were lucky to get him."

Helen looked around the garden until her eyes came to rest on her husband, who was now nodding gravely as Greg talked feverishly, hands waving. "I was, and I think I'd better go rescue him now; Greg's on a tangent and Johnny looks like he might thump him."

"Ah, let him," Dot said. "Somebody should knock some sense into the misery guts."

Helen laughed. "You may be right but I'm not having him ruin my party. Why don't you go into the marquee and enjoy a glass of wine with Marianne and Jo? We'll be cutting the cake soon, and no doubt my dear husband will have a few words to say."

Dot looked around for Andrew and saw that he was having a ball playing chasing with some other children. "I will," she agreed.

Helen hurried towards her husband, easily the best-looking man there; Dot was right, she was lucky. As she neared, she could hear Greg holding forth and caught the word "development". Oh great, that old hobby horse. He wasn't the worst in the world but Dot was right, he never seemed to stop moaning and it was clear that he didn't approve of Johnny and was jealous of his success.

"They destroyed the city and ruined our heritage; it was a bloody travesty that the Wood Quay Viking site wasn't preserved," she heard him say as she arrived at their side.

My God, thirty years later and he was still going on about that, despite the fact that they were all children at the time. Johnny's eyes were glazed as he stared into the middle distance. Thank God he wasn't taking the bait today, she thought, and smiled when she saw that he was sipping water.

"Everything okay, Greg? Did you get enough to eat?"

He turned, a flash of irritation crossing his face at the interruption, before he remembered his manners and nodded politely. "A feast fit for a king as always, Helen. Thank you."

From anyone else that would be a compliment but from Greg it sounded like a criticism. "How can you be spending money on fancy parties at a time like this?"

was the underlying message. Helen chose to ignore it and slipped her arm through his.

"Let's go inside and join the others. We have a cake to cut. Darling, organize the champagne, would you?"

"Yes, ma'am!" Johnny saluted and mouthed a thank-you behind Greg's back.

"Di and Rachel are being a great help today, Greg; they're lovely girls," Helen said.

"Rachel is a good girl, but Di has a bit of a wild streak."

"She didn't get that from her mother," Helen retorted.

"No, of course not, but Joanna's parents were nutters."

Helen resisted the urge to punch him and pointed him towards his wife. "Jo and Marianne are sitting over there, Greg. Why don't you grab a couple of chairs for you and Dot?"

Marianne laughed and applauded along with the others as Johnny spoke, regaling them with stories of his courtship with Helen. She was enjoying the party, glad now that the children knew about the move. She still wanted to get to the root of Kate's problems at school but the little girl seemed content for the moment, sitting next to her and playing games on Marianne's phone. Andrew was on her other side, half-asleep after all the action outside. Johnny was just finishing off and had called Helen to join him for the toast when Marianne's phone beeped loudly.

"Sorry!" she exclaimed, snatching it from her daughter and switching it off.

"But Mum —" Kate protested.

"Shush," Marianne hissed and turned her attention back to Johnny.

"So, everyone, please join me in drinking to the health of my lovely wife," he was saying. "Thank you, my darling, for tolerating me for twenty years. I hope you'll be able to live with me for another twenty as I get old and cranky."

"Crankier," Helen joked, turning her face up for his kiss.

After that toast, Johnny's friend, Christy, voice slightly slurred, proposed another toast to the happy couple.

When they had taken their seats once more, the catering staff started to cut up the cake and the band turned up the volume and started to play jazz numbers.

"He spoke well," Dot said.

Joanna smiled. "He always tells such great stories."

"Telling tales comes with the job," Greg muttered.

Marianne saw Jo shoot him an angry look and turned away, loathe to let her friend see that she had noticed. Taking a sip from her champagne flute, she switched her phone back on to make sure that Kate hadn't left a game running. She really shouldn't let the children play with it; the games always seemed to eat up her battery. But there was no game running, just a text message. A text message from Dominic. She knew it couldn't be from him and yet she felt her heart leap in her chest. She hesitated for a moment and then pressed enter to read it.

STOP THIS. PLEASE STOP.

She frowned. What the hell? And then as she ran her eye up the screen and read the messages that had preceded it, the text made sense.

"DADDY, ITS KATE. ARE YOU THERE, DADDY?"
"ARE YOU IN HEAVEN?"
"DADDY, PLEAS ANSER ME AND LET ME NO UR OK."
"I MISS YOU DADDY."

Marianne's glass slipped silently from her fingers, soaking the skirt of her dress.

"Butterfingers," Dot laughed. "Good job it's champers; it shouldn't leave a stain."

Marianne continued to stare in horror at her phone.

"What is it, Marianne? What's wrong?" Jo asked.

Marianne looked up, suddenly conscious of her wet skirt clinging to her legs and Jo, Dot and Greg watching her curiously from the other side of the table.

"Oh, it's nothing. Just a member of the PTA committee giving out to me for not attending a meeting." She summoned up a smile and shoved the phone into her bag. "I'd better go and use Helen's hairdryer on this, I'm a mess."

"I'll come with you." Dot stood up. "I need to powder my nose."

192

After Colm had shown them up to Helen's room and fetched a hairdryer, Dot perched on the edge of the bed and looked expectantly at her daughter-in-law.

"So what was all that about?"

Marianne sank onto the bed with a sigh. "Kate has been sending text messages to Dominic's phone asking him is he okay and if he's in heaven."

"Oh, holy mother of God, the poor love."

"And," Marianne pulled out the phone, "during Johnny's speech, she got an answer."

Dot blinked. "What do you mean?"

"Whoever has the phone seems to have a conscience." Marianne read out the message. "'Stop this. Please stop.' I know it's stupid, but for a second I thought it really was from him."

"Poor Kate."

Marianne's eyes widened. She had been so caught up in wondering who the text was from that she had completely forgotten her daughter. "I must talk to her."

Dot stood up and hugged her. "Dry that dress and I'll keep an eye on her till you get down. What will you tell her?"

"That her daddy isn't talking to her from the grave."

"Oh, bless us and save us," Dot said angrily, and crossed herself. "Are you going to reply to the message?"

Marianne stared at the phone and shook her head. "It can wait."

When Marianne returned to the marquee, the tables had been cleared from the centre of the room and

Johnny was waltzing Helen around the dance floor to one of her favourite Cole Porter songs: "Every Time We Say Goodbye".

Jo was alone at the table.

"Are you okay?" she asked as Marianne took her seat. "That text seemed to really upset you."

"I was just trying to delete it and let the glass fall. Stupid of me; I should have put the bloody thing down first. Isn't it a wonderful party?" She smiled at her friend, knowing she would swallow her story; Helen wouldn't be taken in so easily.

"Lovely," Jo said, sounding wistful.

"Where are the kids?" Marianne looked around anxiously.

"They're outside having ice cream and Slush Puppies. Colm and Di are looking after them."

"I should go and check —"

"Marianne, relax, they're fine."

"I'm worried about Kate."

"Do you remember the day I first came to St Anne's?"

Marianne nodded. "How can I forget it? You looked like a terrified little mouse."

"I was scared stiff. Between the nuns, the teachers, the kids and the noise, I was completely overwhelmed. I was more petrified that day than on my worst with Mam and Dad and I'd have given anything to go home."

"Those first few weeks you hardly opened your mouth; getting you to speak was like pulling teeth."

"I know. I was sure it was only a matter of time before you hurt me too. Sorry," Jo added.

Marianne stared at her. "You're saying Kate's afraid of getting hurt again."

"Maybe."

Marianne stood up. "Thanks, Jo. I think I'll go talk to her."

"Good luck."

Marianne could see Kate shrink into her chair, her face frightened when she saw her mother coming, and her stomach clenched. Why couldn't she reach her daughter?

"Hi guys." She smiled at the children and pulled up a chair.

"Hiya." Colm grinned. "Want a drink?"

"Ugh, no, they look radioactive!"

She nodded at the blue concoction that Kate was drinking. "You realize that you'll probably go blue now, don't you?"

"Don't be silly," Kate said, but she smiled.

"Look at mine!" Rachel held up a fluorescent pink mixture.

"At least it goes with your jeans," Marianne laughed.

"I'm making a multi-coloured one," Andrew announced.

"Does that mean you'll have multi-coloured sheets tonight?" Marianne shuddered.

"Mum, that's disgusting," Kate protested, but she was laughing.

"Well, you're not going to tell me that between the sugar and colouring, this is the healthiest mixture?"

"We went very easy on the sugar," Di promised with a grin.

"She did," Colm added, "but I threw in some more when she wasn't looking."

"You're kidding," Marianne winced.

"Yes, I am," Colm laughed. "Popcorn?"

"I couldn't eat another thing after that feast; I'm surprised you lot can."

"We're growing," Kate reminded her.

"Especially you," Andrew said to his sister. "Soon your arse will be as big as Granny's!"

"Andrew!" Kate and Marianne said together while the other children laughed.

"What? I'm just saying what Granny says."

"Well don't," Marianne warned. "And leave your sister in peace. I was going to get some drinks, Kate, will you come and help me?"

"Okay." Kate eyed her suspiciously but got to her feet and followed her towards the house. "I thought the caterers got all the drinks for people."

"They do," Marianne took her hand and instead of leading her into the kitchen, drew her round the side of the house where it was quiet. "I just wanted a word."

"Oh, Mum," Kate whined.

"You don't have to say anything; you just have to listen. Okay?"

The child nodded but kept her head down.

Marianne wasn't sure this would work; perhaps she was opening a whole new can of worms but she felt she

196

had to try something drastic to get through to her daughter.

"I was a tiny baby when I arrived at St Anne's. Someone, I presume my mum, left me in a holdall in the reception of a busy hospital."

"Really?" Kate's head flew up in horror.

"It was the perfect place to leave me," Marianne reassured her. "As soon as I started bawling I was discovered and handed in to the nurses. Not only was I warmly dressed, but there was a bag of baby clothes tucked in beside me, and a full bottle of formula and a page with all the details about my birth, weight, blood-type and the shots I had. Don't you see, Kate, my mum loved me."

"How can you say that? She gave you away."

"Yes, but we don't know why. She may have been only a child herself; her parents may have made the decision for her. She may have been sick or dying; she may have been really poor." Marianne shrugged. "There are a thousand reasons why she might have done it but, Kate, the point is that she made sure to leave me somewhere that I would be safe; she looked after me. I'm not sure how old I was when I was told but I cried."

Kate's hand found its way into hers and Marianne smiled, touched.

"You know what though?" she went on.

"What?"

"I stopped crying, Kate, because I realized that it didn't change anything. For years I used to look at women in the street and wonder: is that her? You reminded me of that today, sending texts to your dad. I suppose what I'm trying to say is that though he died, you still have tons of wonderful memories and he will always be with you," she placed their joined hands over Kate's heart, "in here."

"You don't have any memories of your mum," Kate pointed out tearfully.

"No, I don't, but how can I miss what I never had? I was a happy child, I had some lovely people mind me so, in a way, I had lots of mums! And I had Aunty Helen who was like a big sister and still is." Marianne gently wiped Kate's wet cheeks. "Now, shall we go home?"

CHAPTER
SEVENTEEN

Rob called Marianne the minute he got back to Dublin, but all he'd got was her answering service. He felt disappointed and frustrated and phoned Johnny in the hope of gleaning more information and getting things moving, but the man had been equally vague and obviously dying to get off the phone. On the plus side, the contract was signed and he would move in to Marianne's house — Marianne's bed — in five weeks.

"Coffee's made. I've got to run, darling."

He turned and smiled as Vanessa Montgomery walked into his arms and turned her mouth up for his kiss. She tasted of toothpaste and her body felt soft and pliant under his fingers, and yet all he could think of was a leaner, harder body that seemed to fit his perfectly.

"Mind my hair," Vanessa warned, stepping back and smoothing her perfect blonde bob. "How do I look?"

He smiled. "Gorgeous." And she did. She was sexy, smart and she had been his girlfriend for almost a year. She spent three or four nights a week here now; he resisted going to her place, it was so feminine he felt an intruder there. Again, he found himself thinking of

Marianne's home and how much he preferred its relaxed and more family-friendly decor.

"I have a meeting after work but I could meet you for dinner in Mel's Bistro about eight."

"I'm not sure, Vanessa. I have a mad day. I'll call you later, okay?"

"Okay sweetheart." She kissed him again and yelped as she turned and collided with the corner of his desk. "I'm so glad you're getting out of this dump; I can't wait to see the new place. The kitchen sounds like heaven and that patio . . ." She sighed. "We'll be able to have barbecues!"

Rob smiled in relief as the phone rang, well aware of where that conversation would lead. He gave her a playful pat on the bottom. "Go to work, you'll be late."

"Oh, crikey, I will! Okay, later, darling." Vanessa blew him a kiss and left.

He dealt with the call swiftly and watched as Vanessa got into her car and drove away. She was dropping very heavy hints about moving in with him lately and though he'd managed to deflect her so far, he knew it was only a matter of time before she confronted him. Vanessa was sweet and funny but she was not the sort of woman to be trifled with. He wasn't sure why he was holding back. Their relationship was easy. He enjoyed her company but moving in together, going to bed with her every night and waking up beside her every morning? That was another story. And then Marianne had walked back into his life, and the thought of moving into her house with Vanessa, of making love in Marianne's bed; he just couldn't get his head around it.

Ridiculous as it seemed, he felt it would be almost adulterous.

After mulling things over for a few days, Marianne finally drove out to see Helen straight after she'd dropped the kids at school. She was delighted to see Johnny's car there too. He was on the phone when he opened the door and he pointed her towards the kitchen.

"That was Rob," he said when he joined the two women. "He's been trying to get hold of you, anxious to measure up the office. Are you avoiding him, Marianne? You're not having second thoughts?"

"No, not at all, I'm a bit distracted, that's all. There has been a development."

Helen looked at her over the rim of her coffee cup. "We only saw you on Saturday."

"It was a great party."

"Glad you enjoyed it," Johnny said. "Now, out with it. What's happened?"

Marianne took a deep breath. "I got a text just after your speech. It was from Dominic's phone."

"No!" Helen lowered her mug and stared. "What did it say?"

"First let me explain." And she told them of the texts that Kate had been sending.

"The poor kid," Johnny rested his chin in his hand. "When she actually got a reply she must have got the fright of her life."

"Yes, I think she did."

"Can I see the message?" he asked.

Marianne fished the phone out of her bag, found the text message and then slid the mobile across to him.

Putting on his glasses, Johnny picked it up and read it. "She sounds spooked."

"We don't know it's a woman."

"It's a woman." He handed the phone to his wife.

"I think he's right," Helen said. "Have you replied?"

"No, I wasn't sure what to say."

"I'm amazed that not only has she kept the phone, but that it's switched on," Johnny remarked.

"Perhaps she's using it."

"No, remember the phone bill; there have been no calls or texts made from it since Dominic died." Helen shot her a worried look. "Which could mean that she's keeping it for sentimental reasons."

"You think this woman was his lover?" Marianne looked at her.

"I'm sorry."

"Nothing to be sorry about, Helen."

"I think you should call her," Johnny said.

Marianne sighed. "I'm not sure I want to. What if she wants to meet?"

"I hope she does," Johnny retorted. "And if she doesn't suggest it, you should."

"But why?"

"She may be our only real lead to what Dominic did with the money. She could have it, for all we know," Johnny pointed out.

"My God, I hadn't thought of that."

"I'll come with you if it makes you feel better."

"Yes please, Johnny; that would be great. I suppose I should tell Matthews and Baldwin."

"Let's talk to her first," Johnny stood up and started to pace. "Remember the firm has its own interests at heart, not yours. If we let them deal with her then we only have their account of what she says."

"You're right," Marianne said, realizing what a vulnerable position she was in. "I don't understand why she replied to Kate's text," she added as Helen handed back her phone.

"The texts spooked her," Helen said. "That's obvious. Perhaps she just reacted without thinking or perhaps she has nothing to hide. She may be as ignorant of Dominic's behaviour as you were; I'd be amazed if she has access to his money. He was a clever man."

"Then what use is she to us? What's the point in meeting her?"

"Because we've got feck all else to go on," Johnny said unhappily. "Think of this as a jigsaw puzzle. You have some of the pieces, Matthews and Baldwin have some of the pieces, and this woman will probably have a lot more. Let's hope that when we put them all together, we can come up with some answers."

"Johnny's right. She may be the difference between you having an easy future or a hard one. Perhaps if you were able to help the company recover at least some of the money they would pay you a pension."

Marianne bit her lip. They were right, of course. She wasn't upset at the thought that Dominic might have been having an affair, but she was furious if he'd squandered his money on this woman and as a result his children were suffering. She had no wish to meet her but she needed answers and Dominic's girlfriend was the most likely one to provide them. It hadn't occurred to her that there might still be a possibility of receiving a pension; that would make a huge difference to their lives.

"I know you said that you and Dominic weren't close but aren't you even a little bit curious as to what she looks like?" Helen asked.

"And wouldn't you like to punch her?" Johnny grinned.

Marianne laughed. "I'm a little curious but I'm more angry with Dominic than with her."

"So . . ." Johnny nodded towards the phone. "Call her."

"No!" Marianne was horrified at the thought. "I'll send a text." She looked from Helen to Johnny. "What will I say?"

"Keep it simple," advised Johnny. "Tell her you want to meet."

Marianne paused. "Where?"

"The middle of the Ha'penny Bridge at midnight?" he grinned.

"Ha, ha, you're hilarious. Seriously, where do you think?"

His brow wrinkled as he considered the options. "Not your place. Here if you like."

"No," Helen shook her head, "that would scare her off. You need to meet on neutral territory — a hotel or pub."

"Somewhere quiet enough that we can talk in private," Marianne agreed.

"I've got it. The Herbert Park in Ballsbridge," Johnny said. "That way you have parking but it's away from the shopping area so no gaggles of gossiping women."

Helen raised her eyebrows "Gaggles of gossiping women — charming!"

He laughed. "Ah, you know what I mean."

"Okay then." Marianne picked up the phone, her hand shaking slightly. "When?"

"Friday at eleven?"

"So soon? She stared at him; that was the day after tomorrow.

"Why wait?"

With a sigh of resignation, Marianne typed in the message, hesitated and then with a wince pressed "send". She watched the display for a few seconds until a delivery notice appeared. "She's got it."

Johnny laughed. "Stop staring at it, she could be in another bloody room or at a meeting or out for the day for all we know. Relax."

Marianne sat back in the chair with a sigh. "You're right."

"Did you tell Dot about this?" Helen asked.

"She knows about the text but nothing else. I told her that perhaps the person who'd stolen Dominic's phone was feeling guilty."

"Why are you protecting her like this?" Johnny said irritably.

"You think I should tell a woman who's just lost her only son that not only was he a drug addict, but a criminal and a womanizer too?"

"You can't protect everyone, sweetheart."

"Johnny's right." Helen shot her a worried look. "You'll make yourself ill if you keep taking so much on yourself."

"Are you sure you're not having second thoughts about this move, or is it Rob you have a problem with?"

"No, honestly, I'm fine with the move and with Rob." Marianne wondered when she'd stop feeling weird saying his name aloud.

"He's a good guy; I wouldn't have recommended him as a tenant if I didn't completely trust him."

"I know that, Johnny," she hurried to assure him.

"So what are you worrying about?" Helen asked. "There's definitely something."

"It's Kate."

"Would you consider sending her for counselling?" Helen asked.

"I've talked to her school principal — a lovely woman, I'm going to miss her — and Mandy James, my GP, and neither of them think that it's necessary. They say she's just displaying the usual signs of a child dealing with grief."

"But you're not convinced, are you?" Helen said.

Marianne sighed. "I was until I heard about this bullying business and that she was sending text messages to her dead father."

"The bullying you do need to check out," Johnny agreed. "But I wouldn't worry about the texts."

206

"Really? Or are you saying that just to make me feel better?"

"No, I mean it. When my mother first passed away I often used to go to her grave and talk to her about my problems; isn't this just the modern version of the same thing?"

"I suppose it is," Marianne agreed with a grudging smile. Johnny always had a reasonable explanation for everything.

"Kate will be just fine. I'm not so sure about you, Marianne; perhaps you're the one who needs help."

Helen groaned. "Johnny! Sorry, darling, he means well, but subtle he isn't."

"I'm just saying she's carrying a weight on her shoulders and it can't be healthy trying to keep all of this from Dot."

Marianne thought of Rob; she was an expert at keeping secrets. "I'm fine but I will be a lot happier once I've got on top of our finances. And, you know, there are other silly things that I'd like to learn; how to change a tyre or check the oil in my car. How to change a fuse —"

"Ah, for God's sake, woman," Johnny laughed.

"It may seem silly to you, but I can't believe I don't know these things."

"I understand," Helen said. "With knowledge comes confidence; you will feel more in control if you don't need to ask for help or advice over every little thing."

Marianne nodded. "Exactly! I can't help feeling that if I had been more proactive in the past, perhaps I wouldn't be in this mess."

"Now that's just rubbish," Johnny said, looking at her in disbelief. "Nothing you did could have stopped Dominic taking drugs or stealing."

"No, but I would have noticed money going missing from our bank accounts. I can't believe that I knew he was taking drugs and that I never considered how much he was spending on them. How stupid was I not to keep an eye on things and siphon some money away?"

"Hindsight is a wonderful thing," Helen said, her eyes full of sympathy.

"I know and I am not going to dwell on it. Instead I am going to make sure that no one ever hoodwinks me again and —" Marianne stopped as her phone chirruped.

"Another text?" Helen asked, sitting forward in her chair.

Marianne nodded.

"Well, go on then, take a look; she can't bite you," Johnny laughed.

Marianne read out the message. "'Fine. See you there.' "

"Great!"

"Great," she echoed, feeling sick.

CHAPTER
EIGHTEEN

The kids had finished dinner and were now playing in the garden. Aware that Marianne seemed preoccupied, Dot announced that she was going to do some weeding and then planned to take the children down to the pier to buy fish.

"So if there's anything you need to do or anywhere you need to go," she told her daughter-in-law, "go ahead, we'll be grand."

"Has Johnny Sheridan been talking to you?" Marianne asked suspiciously.

"No, love, why?"

"Ah, he's nagging me to call Rob Lee, our tenant; he wants to come and check out the office."

"Oh, well do it, love; we can't afford to lose him."

"No."

"Did you tell Johnny about the text?"

"Yes, and Helen. They got a kick out of the fact that Kate spooked the thief."

Dot looked at Marianne's pallor and the dark shadows under her eyes.

"Why don't you have a lie down, love? You look worn out."

"No, I'm fine. I have some emails to check and I'll make that call."

"Well, please yourself; I'll keep this pair busy."

"Thanks, Dot."

Dot pulled on her gardening gloves and went outside. As soon as he spotted her, Andrew abandoned his bike and came running.

"What are you doing, Granny?"

"I'm going to weed the garden, luvvie."

"Can I help?"

"That would be grand." Dot knew he'd probably dig up more flowers than weeds but if it kept him happy, sure, what was the harm? She looked over at where Kate sat on a swing, reading a book. "How about you love, want to give us a hand?"

"No."

"Oh, go on, my back's playing up terrible today; I could really do with some help." As she expected, Kate immediately set down her book. "Good girl, get your mother's gloves."

As his sister went down to the shed at the bottom of the garden, Andrew's face clouded. "I want gloves too, Granny."

"You do not!" Dot pretended to look horrified. "But sure aren't you a man? You're not worried about keeping your nails nice now, are you? Your da never ever wore gloves."

"Daddy never worked in the garden," Andrew protested, as he looked doubtfully down at his fingers.

"Well, that's only because he didn't have time. But he helped me when he was a boy like you; Granda used to give him fifty pence for cutting the grass."

"I could do that," Andrew said immediately, his eyes lighting up.

"Ah, no, love, sorry; I couldn't let you loose with the electric mower, your mother would kill me. Tell you what, why don't you get your spade; these flower beds need digging. Do you think you're strong enough to do that?"

"'Course I am!" He charged off, passing his sister on the way.

"Where will I start, Granny?" she asked.

"Right here beside me, love, we'll have it done in no time."

Andrew returned and started digging wildly. Dot winced as he bisected a hydrangea in the process.

"No, Andrew!" Kate screeched.

"It's okay, love, it doesn't matter. We'll be leaving here soon anyway and I doubt the man that's renting it will be that bothered about the garden."

"Will you miss it?" Kate asked, looking around at the large, pretty garden that Dot had nurtured since she'd moved in.

"A bit, but 'tis only a garden; it will be nice to get back to my own little one. I have some great plants and trees that have been there years. What about you, love? Will you be sad to leave?" Dot kept her voice light and her head bent over her task so the child wouldn't feel she was being questioned.

"I'm not bothered."

"Really? You surprise me. I mean, you've lived here for so long. I missed the strangest things when I first came here."

"Like what?" Kate asked, looking over at her.

"Being able to walk to the supermarket and everyone knowing me when I got there. Bumping into my friends, having a gossip across the back fence with my neighbours . . ." Dot smiled; it was lovely to be going home.

"Why did you move in with us, Granny?" Kate asked.

"Your daddy asked me and I was delighted to be closer to you all, luvvie."

Kate frowned. "But your house isn't that far away. We could have visited you."

Dot sighed. Children could run rings round you, they really could. "Well, because your daddy had to work such long hours, your poor mummy was lonely when you were at school and then at night when you went to bed."

Kate seemed to accept this and went back to her weeding.

"So you won't miss this place at all?"

Kate shook her head. "No."

"Not a thing?" Dot asked. "You know that you will have to share a room with your mummy and it's not even half the size of your bedroom."

"I don't mind."

"And there's no room in my little garden for your trampoline or swings," Dot warned, and then wondered why she was trying to put the child off.

212

"I don't care," Kate said.

"And you won't miss any of your school friends?"

"I don't really have any."

"Ah, now, get away; sure, what about all the parties you've had and this house full of screaming girls?"

"None of them are real friends," Kate said, with little sign of emotion.

"What about Julie and Sarah," Dot racked her brain for the other girl that dropped in from time to time, "and Ellie?"

"They don't really like me."

"Now that's just silly. If they didn't like you, they wouldn't hang around with you now, would they?"

Kate said nothing but continued pulling up weeds, shaking off the earth like Dot had shown her and throwing them onto the scrap heap. Dot looked across the garden at her grandson and was glad to see that, happy and knee-deep in muck, he was oblivious to them.

"Were they the ones that were being nasty to you, luvvie?" Marianne had asked her not to mention the bullying, that she would handle it, but how could Dot *not* say something when faced with an opportunity like this?

"Not really . . ." Kate mumbled.

"Not really?! That's a yes then." Dot sat back on her heels, her heart going out to the child.

"No, honest, it was another girl who was being nasty but they just laughed when she did."

Dot heard the wobble in Kate's voice; if she could get her hands on the kid who'd done this. She took a breath and smiled. "Don't be too hard on your friends, Kate. It's very hard to stand up to someone like that; half the time people don't even know someone's a bully. I bet you this girl is very popular, the centre of a gang even."

Kate turned surprised eyes on her and gave a small nod.

"What does she say or do to you?"

"She says I'm a nerd and that I have froggy eyes and sometimes she pinches me and takes my markers and stuff."

"The little bitch!" Dot clasped a hand to her mouth. Kate's eyes widened and then her lips started to twitch. "One of these days your mother will kill me, won't she?" Dot grinned.

Kate giggled. "No, she only pretends to be cross with you."

Dot raised her eyebrows. "Do you think so? Well, thank God for that. So, tell me, did you talk to the other girls about this little . . ." she pretended to bite her lip, "girl?"

This time Kate's smile was broad. "No."

"And will you tell me something? How can your pals help you if you don't ask them?"

The smile disappeared. "But they know what she's doing, Granny!"

"But do they know how she's making you feel?" Kate looked at her in confusion.

"Have you told them?" Dot said gently.

Kate frowned and thought for a moment. "No."

"And when the girl says these things what do you say?"

"Nothing."

"And what do you do?"

"I try to laugh too or I just ignore her."

"So, let me get this straight in my head. Your friends see you either laughing or turning away; did it occur to you at all that maybe they never realized you were upset? Did you think of that?" Kate stared and Dot smiled at her. "Things aren't always as they seem, are they, pet?"

Kate shook her head silently but Dot could see that her mind was working overtime.

"Put it all out of your mind now, luvvie. In a few weeks she'll be history. You'll make lots of new friends in your new school and some of them will be living near us, no doubt."

"I did meet a couple of nice girls at the street party."

"Well, there you go, and imagine you'll be able to see them whenever you like; none of this mammies phoning each other to arrange play-dates business. But promise me something, darling."

"What, Granny?"

"If anyone upsets you, don't ever hide it; no one can help you if you do that. And remember, your granny is always here if ever you need her."

"I promise, Granny."

Kate actually smiled at her and Dot felt her own eyes fill. "Okay, enough nattering; time to get some work done and then we'll go and buy some nice fresh fish for dinner."

Marianne sat staring at the phone for ages before she worked up the courage to pick it up and call him. She and Rob used to enjoy wonderful, long, loving phone conversations, particularly in the mornings when Kate was at school, Andrew was having his nap and Dominic was at work. She would curl up on the sofa and wait for his call, her heart always leaping when the phone rang. Sometimes they talked about family, about what was going on in the world, about the last time they'd met and how wonderful it had been. They'd chat like excited teenagers as they planned their next rendezvous. Their last phone call, she remembered sadly, was the day she'd arranged to meet him to say goodbye. She could still remember how happy he'd sounded to hear her voice and how she'd had to cut the call short for fear he would guess there was something wrong.

With trembling fingers and butterflies in her stomach, she picked up the phone and dialled the number on the business card.

"Rob Lee."

She gasped at the sound of his voice; it was as if the years just fell away.

"Hello?"

"Rob?" Her voice sounded hoarse and she cleared her throat. "It's Marianne."

"Marianne, hello! How are you?"

There was no doubting the warmth in his voice and she closed her eyes and let its rich familiarity envelope her. "Fine, thanks. Just calling to arrange a time for you to come over and measure up."

"I'm getting a carpenter to do it. I'll give him your number and tell him to call you. But don't worry, he won't be fitting anything to the walls; I'll be able to take it all with me when I leave."

Marianne's heart sank. He wasn't coming over himself. And when he moved in she would have no real need to see him. She was overcome with sadness at the thought that this was just a temporary arrangement. She tried very hard to sound as cool and professional as he did. "Sounds like a good idea; I'm sure it will look better than it does at the moment."

He said nothing. She clung to the phone, her ear pressed tight against it.

"How are you, Marianne? Are the children okay?"

His voice was soft and steady and comforting, and she smiled; he hadn't changed. He wasn't the cool professional, he was just Rob. She had always loved his voice. When she was at her most stressed, simply listening to him talk, regardless of the words, had always had a calming, soothing effect.

"I'm fine and Andrew's okay, but I'm not so sure about Kate. She's been behaving a bit oddly."

"I suppose that's to be expected, especially given her age. My god-daughter, Clodagh, is incredibly bright and quick-witted; they seem to be so much more grown-up at that age than we were."

"I just wish she'd talk to me but she seems happier talking to strangers than to her mother."

"Sometimes it's easier to talk to a stranger. You're talking to me, aren't you?" he joked.

Marianne thought for a moment before answering and then decided to take a risk. "You could never be a stranger, Rob."

He hesitated too but when he answered, his voice was quiet and solemn. "I'm glad you feel that way."

She didn't give herself time to think; she just said it before her courage deserted her. "I'm sorry you're not coming over, Rob. There was something I wanted your advice about."

"Then let's meet," he said immediately.

"Okay." She smiled, feeling warmed by his reaction. "When suits?"

She thought about it for a second. She didn't really want him to come to her house, she wasn't ready to introduce him to Dot or the children. Also, it would be best to leave it until after her meeting with Dominic's girlfriend; she was going to find it hard to concentrate on anything before then. "I have a meeting in Ballsbridge on Friday morning; could we meet up for a sandwich somewhere afterwards?"

"Fine, how about The Den?"

"Perfect." The pub was in the Lansdowne hotel, only five minutes' drive from the Herbert Park Hotel. "I'm not sure of a time yet but probably about twelve thirty?"

"Sounds good. Send me a text if there's a problem."

"Okay, then —"

"This advice," he interrupted her as she was about to say goodbye. "Want to give me a hint?"

She smiled, glad he'd prolonged the call. It was good to talk to him again even if it was just about normal, everyday matters. "I need to get a job and I figured that I should probably update my IT skills. Johnny tells me that you've branched into training."

"That's right, but trust me, it won't take much to bring you up to speed. You're a natural."

"Well, thanks for the vote of confidence but I'm not sure where to start."

"Okay, leave it with me; I'll have a think about it."

"Thanks, Rob."

"I'll look forward to Friday, Marianne."

She waited for a moment and when he didn't hang up she said, "Me too," before ending the call, smiling.

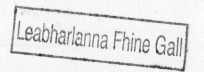

CHAPTER
NINETEEN

Helen had always been able to tell when Johnny was lying to her. If not immediately, then in hindsight; when she replayed a scene in her head she would see all the signs. A man who always looked you straight in the eye was lying when he started shifting through papers, or became engrossed in something on TV or fiddled unnecessarily with his belt or tie. This morning, when she was asking him what jobs he had on for the week he'd been evasive and started re-reading his post. As Helen sipped her tea she wondered what it could be that he was trying to hide. Given that he was in the property game, money was always a worry, but as she did their accounts, she was sure they were in relatively healthy shape despite Johnny's habit of doling out cash to tradesmen so that they wouldn't have to pay tax, a practice she disapproved of.

She'd been taught the importance of honesty in St Anne's and continued to live by the rules of her Catholic upbringing but, Johnny pointed out, wasn't he simply looking after his neighbour the way God intended? Helen found it hard to argue. She didn't really understand the complexities of tax or economics, but she knew she didn't agree with the way poor people always seemed to come off the worst when the going got tough. Still, she felt in her gut that whatever was troubling Johnny, whatever it was he was hiding from her, it didn't have anything to do with the business. More likely he was probably protecting her from something he thought would upset her . . .

"Is there something wrong with Colm?" she blurted out.

He looked up at her, surprise on his face. "Not that I know of. What makes you ask that?"

"You seem preoccupied." She watched him put his glasses back on his nose and return to his reading.

"I'm always preoccupied. Why would you think it's anything to do with Colm?"

"I don't know." She shrugged. "Just a feeling."

"Well, your feeling is wrong. You're never happy unless you've something to worry about, are you?"

"Is there anything bothering you, Johnny?" she asked, ignoring his teasing.

"Plenty!" He gathered up his post, leaned over to kiss her on the mouth and got up from the table. "But nothing I can't deal with. See you later, darling."

"Let me know how you and Marianne get on," she called after him.

"Will do."

Helen continued to sip her tea, still unconvinced by her husband's cheery reassurances. Something was up with him and she would get to the bottom of it. The phone rang and she reached for it, frowning when she saw that it was the woman who'd catered for Saturday's party. She'd been paid and collected all the dishes and glasses, what could she want?

"Hello?"

"Helen? Brenda Flynn here. I hope I haven't got you at a bad time?"

"Not at all, Brenda."

"Oh, good. I wondered if you could help me."

"I'll try."

"Well, I have been having problems with my florist; not only is it an expensive outfit, but they're unreliable, too."

"That's not on, especially with business as it is at the moment," Helen commiserated.

"It can be disastrous," Brenda assured her. "I couldn't help but notice the arrangement on the head table that one of your guests brought; I thought it was very fresh and original."

Helen lowered her cup, delighted. "Yes, I thought so too."

"I don't suppose you could find out who supplied it, could you? I did look for a card but it must have fallen off."

"Are you interested in using them instead of your current florist?" Helen pressed.

"To be honest, I think I'll use a couple of florists from now on but, yes, if the price is right, I am definitely interested."

"Okay, leave it with me, Brenda, and I'll do some detective work."

"I don't know what to say." Dot sat staring at Helen.

222

"Say yes!" Helen exclaimed.

Doubt crossed Dot's face. "But I've only ever done a few classes organized by the ladies' association."

"Does it matter? You're a natural; that's what counts."

"There's not much talent involved in sticking a few flowers in an oasis; Andrew could do that."

"Anyone could do it but not everyone could do it well," Helen corrected. "My caterer, Brenda, has been in the business a long time and she was really impressed with your arrangement. Even if you only ever worked for her, you'd make a nice few bob."

"That's a gas," Dot chuckled. "Imagine getting paid for arranging some flowers?"

"It would be a lot more than that," Helen warned. "Brenda runs a very successful business, one of the few that's weathered the storm in the catering industry; you'd probably need to hire help."

Dot looked alarmed. "Hire someone? Oh, I don't know, Helen —"

"No, you're right, I'm exaggerating," Helen said quickly, realizing she was going way too fast. But she felt excited by the idea of this venture; her gut told her it couldn't fail and her gut rarely let her down. "You can always say that you only ever take on small, select jobs and only the best flowers go into each arrangement."

Dot threw back her head and laughed. "Sure, your one was just a few flowers from the garden."

"But it was stunning. And, who planted the bulbs and tended the flowers as they grew and how much time and energy went into it?"

"But I can't use garden flowers for professional bouquets."

"No, of course not; you'll have to get Marianne to go to the market for them."

Dot stopped laughing and adopted a serious expression. "I suppose it would bring in some extra cash."

"It would and you could do it from home and still be able to look after the children; it's the perfect job for you."

Dot smiled, her eyes twinkling with excitement. "Well, when you put it like that, I suppose there's no harm in giving it a go."

"I'll call Brenda and set up a meeting," Helen said, delighted.

"Not here; the place is a mess," Dot gestured at the chaos.

"No, we'll go to her."

"Won't she be put off that I don't have my own shop?"

"I doubt it. She started her catering business from her own kitchen, Dot, so she knows what it's like to be a small trader starting out. If anything it may be a bonus; without the overheads that come with a premises, you will be cheaper."

"There's another thing: how on earth do I figure out what to charge?"

Helen thought about it. "Good question. I suppose we need to check out what other florists around the city are charging and then decide on a price that's competitive but will be worth the trouble." Helen saw doubt in Dot's face. "Don't worry about it, Dot. Marianne and I can help with all that and once it's done, then all you have to do is arrange flowers."

"Now *that* I can do," Dot beamed. "Lord, who'd have thought it would be so easy to get a job at my age?"

"You haven't got it yet," Helen cautioned.

"No, you're right; I shouldn't be counting my chickens before they're hatched."

"But I'm sure she'll give you a trial run at least; she really loved your arrangement." Helen frowned. "Now, if we could only find Marianne a job. I wonder — did she contact the recruitment companies I told her about? Apart from the cash I think she could really do with the distraction."

"She's gone off to see a consultant this morning," Dot told her.

"No, she's . . ." Helen stopped, suddenly remembering that Dot didn't know where Marianne and Johnny had gone this morning or who they were meeting.

"What?" Dot looked at her.

"I thought she was checking out some sort of training course today but maybe I'm wrong." Helen glanced at her watch. "I'd better get going."

Dot walked her out and gave her a warm hug. "Thanks so much, love."

"For nothing; all I did was pass on a message."

225

"Get away out of that! No wonder Johnny is such a success with you to back him up; you're a great woman!"

Helen smiled. "I really hope this works out; it's about time you had some good luck."

"I won't argue with you there, love."

Johnny had offered to pick Marianne up but as she was meeting Rob afterwards she said she'd take the car.

"I'll meet you at the Lansdowne and we can go and meet the enemy together," he'd joked. But Marianne was glad he'd suggested it; the idea of walking in and meeting her alone made her feel sick. Come to think of it, how was she going to recognize her? And she didn't even have a name. She, on the other hand, would know what Marianne looked like from the photos on Dominic's phone. Suddenly she felt angry. She didn't care if Dominic had been having an affair but it was abhorrent to think of his mistress looking at their family photos.

When she drove into the packed hotel car park, Johnny was already parked. He immediately vacated his spot so that she could take it.

"Morning," she smiled as she sat in beside him.

"Hello, sweetheart, how are you?"

"Scared stiff." She fastened her seat belt and hung on to the sides of the seat as he swung the car out into traffic.

"And what have you to be scared of? She's the one who's in the wrong. I hope she's shaking in her shoes."

226

"We don't know it's a she and it may not be someone who knows Dominic; it could be a thief."

Johnny nodded. "Ah, yeah, right; thieves always love to come and meet their victims."

"Okay, okay, so it's someone who knew Dominic and, yes, it's a woman."

Johnny patted her knee. "Don't worry, love, it will be fine."

Marianne sighed. She had become too dependent on Johnny these last few weeks; she'd have to make a conscious effort in the future not to pick up the phone at the drop of a hat and ask his advice.

The lights changed and Johnny turned right. "I still think you should tell Dot the truth."

"I can't, not now. Perhaps when we have a better idea of what Dominic was up to."

"But if Dominic had lived he would have been dismissed and probably prosecuted. And not only would all of the details have come out about the drugs and the girlfriend, it would have been in the newspapers too and impossible to protect Dot or the kids from the truth."

"I know, and if I have to tell her, I will. Right now I just want to get through this meeting."

Johnny parked the car, switched off the engine and smiled at her. "You're the boss. Come on, let's go and find out exactly what we're dealing with."

As they walked into the lounge area, Marianne's eyes darted around the room but there was no one there who fit her impression of a two-bit thief or a mistress.

"Did you arrange where to meet? Did she tell you what she looks like?" Johnny said, looking around.

"No, but she'll know what I look like from the photos on Dominic's phone."

"Fair enough. Now, tea or coffee?"

"Coffee, please."

Johnny led the way to the bar and Marianne perched on the edge of a stool as he ordered. Her stomach was in a knot and she reached into her bag for an indigestion tablet but had none — typical. She'd expected the woman to be here first, waiting nervously, not keeping her waiting; bloody cheek.

"Marianne?" She looked around as a woman in a smart black suit approached.

"Yes?

"My name is Barbara West. Dominic's . . . friend." The woman offered her hand. Marianne took it, at a loss for words.

Johnny immediately stepped forward to shake hands. "Johnny Sheridan, I'm a friend of Marianne's."

"Pleased to meet you," Barbara said, her voice quiet and polite with little trace of an accent.

"Can I get you some coffee?"

How civilized we're being, thought Marianne; how ludicrous this all was.

"I already have tea, thank you." She pointed to a table in the corner. "I was working while I waited for you."

As they talked, Marianne studied Barbara. She was attractive and stylish and she wouldn't have looked out of place in a courtroom representing the accused. Her black hair was pulled back into a severe chignon that emphasized her high cheekbones, she had a long, straight nose and sharp, dark eyes and she wasn't wearing a scrap of make-up nor any jewellery. Marianne guessed from the telltale wrinkles around her eyes that she was closer to forty than thirty, but she looked good on it. She was the complete opposite to what Marianne had expected. As they followed her back to her table on which sat a sleek laptop, Marianne noticed that Barbara's knee-length skirt and sensible heels didn't disguise a lovely pair of legs. It was strange that she could feel so detached when she was faced with Dominic's mistress but she didn't feel the slightest twinge of jealousy, nor did she harbour regrets. If anything, she was confused as to why a woman like this would have anything to do with her husband.

Marianne looked over at Johnny, willing him to kick off the conversation. He caught her look and obliged.

"Barbara, it's hard to know where to begin. Perhaps you could start by telling us how you knew Dominic and what you're doing with his phone."

"Excuse me?" Barbara's eyes narrowed.

Marianne bridled. "I think they are quite straightforward questions."

"Look, I didn't have to agree to meet you; I did it for Dominic's sake and, I suppose, because I was curious to meet you myself, but if you're going to be like this —"

"Now, just hold on one minute —" Marianne countered, angrily.

"Ladies, let's stay calm. Barbara, I think you need to remember that while you had some sort of relationship with Dominic, you knew that he was a married man and a father, whereas this is the first Marianne's heard of you."

"What are you talking about?" Barbara looked at him in disbelief. "This woman has been making my life miserable for more than a year."

Marianne stared at her. "How on earth have I been doing that? I never even knew you existed."

Barbara folded her arms across her chest. "That's a lie."

"It isn't," Johnny assured her. He glanced at Marianne. "Somehow I get the impression that you're not the only person Dominic was lying to."

Marianne studied Barbara carefully; she seemed upset. "This is all very strange."

The woman managed a brief nod and met Marianne's eyes. "You really didn't know about me?"

Marianne held her gaze. "Not until you sent that text."

Barbara shook her head, bewildered. "I don't understand that. Dominic and I were in love. He said he'd told you all about us and asked you for a divorce but that you refused. He said the house was in your name and you wouldn't sell it and give him his share, and that you threatened to tell Matthews and Baldwin that he took drugs."

"This is laughable," Johnny said, incredulous.

"It's all lies," Marianne said. "Dominic never mentioned your name. I had no idea he was having an affair. Our house is in both names and, while we weren't exactly happy, we never discussed divorce."

"So he lied to me," Barbara said looking stunned.

"It seems that way," Johnny replied, his voice compassionate. "I'm sorry."

Marianne never expected to feel sympathy for this woman but it was hard not to; she was obviously upset. "How did you meet him?" she asked.

"We used to work together a long time ago."

"We've met before," Marianne said. She'd thought there was something familiar about the woman.

"Yes, a couple of times at company functions," Barbara admitted. "But there was nothing going on then. I left Matthews and Baldwin five years ago to take a job in London but my mother got sick and I came home two years ago to look after her. There were no vacancies at Matthews and Baldwin but Dominic put in a good word for me with another firm and I got a great job as a result. We started to meet up after that and as time went on, we became closer." Barbara glanced at Johnny and then back at Marianne. "He told me that the marriage was over but you said if he left that he'd never see the children again."

"The bastard, as if Marianne would ever do something like that." Johnny shook his head in disgust.

"I can't believe he lied to me," Barbara said, almost to herself.

"You knew he was on drugs," Johnny said.

Barbara's expression grew more guarded and she looked away from him. "I knew he dabbled; so did I, occasionally. It's the job. The pressure is intense but so is the buzz when it's going well. When it's not . . ." She shrugged. "I realized that he was probably taking more than he should. He denied it, said he was fine, that he was just having a rough time at home and that once he was separated, everything would be okay. But he said he couldn't talk sense into you. We decided that our only chance of a future was to leave Ireland."

"This is unbelievable," Marianne murmured. It made no sense. None of it. Dominic must have known she'd have been happy to be free of him and that she would have made sure that he had access to the children. It sounded like he'd just strung Barbara along and made promises he'd never intended to keep. For what? Sex?

"I felt very sorry for him. You had the house and his children whereas he had nothing. He was broken-hearted at the thought of leaving Kate and Andrew but he said it was better than them witnessing the constant arguments between you."

Marianne shook her head in disbelief. "We rarely argued and certainly not in front of the children."

Barbara didn't look entirely convinced. "Anyway, I sold my house and handed in my notice; we were all set to leave."

"You gave up your job and your home?" Marianne looked at her aghast. "For Dominic?"

"God love you," Johnny said with a heavy sigh before shooting Marianne an apologetic glance. "Do you have the money from the house sale?"

Barbara shook her head. "My mother had died and I was very upset so Dominic dealt with the estate agent and the solicitor for me. I assume the money is in his account."

"It's not in any of the accounts I know about," Marianne said.

"But it must be!"

Johnny sighed. "By the sound of it Dominic has taken you both for a ride."

Marianne exchanged a look with Johnny, willing him not to reveal anything about the fraud. She felt completely thrown by Barbara's revelations and though it seemed the woman was a victim in all this, Marianne wasn't ready to reveal any more of Dominic's behaviour until she knew exactly where she stood. "How is it that you came to have Dominic's phone?" she asked.

Barbara seemed momentarily flustered. "He left it behind."

"At your house?"

"Yes."

"So, you saw him the night he died?"

"Yes, he dropped by on his way to the restaurant."

"Why was he there?" Johnny had obviously picked up on Marianne's suspicion.

"It was a business dinner."

Marianne looked at her. "He was entertaining clients? Are you sure?"

"Yes."

"Can I have the phone, please?"

Barbara froze. "Why?"

"The police want it," Johnny told her.

"The police?"

"They're hoping it will help them in tracking down where Dominic got the drugs," Johnny explained.

Barbara stood up abruptly. "I'm sorry, you'll have to excuse me for a moment," she said and hurried off in the direction of the ladies.

"That's interesting," Johnny mused. "She's spooked by the idea of the guards being involved."

"Perhaps she knows more than she's letting on."

"About the drugs?"

"Well, it can't be about the fraud; she'd hardly have let him sell her house if she knew about that. By the way, she lied."

Johnny frowned. "About?"

"Dominic wouldn't have been entertaining clients that night. Matthews told me that they curtailed that practice over a year ago."

"He may have lied to her about why he was there or who he was with," Johnny pointed out.

"True." Marianne sighed and dug in her bag for an antacid.

"We need to get our hands on that phone and get the hell out of here. You need to talk to a solicitor, Marianne. I'll set up an appointment with Eddie Madden."

"I think you're right. She's taking an awful long time in there, isn't she?"

"She did seem upset."

"Should I go in and see if she's okay?" Marianne didn't particularly want to go and comfort her husband's mistress but . . .

"It's okay, she's coming."

"Sorry about that," Barbara said, taking her seat.

"No problem." Johnny's smile was affable. "Now about the phone . . ."

"When we get it back from the police you can have it back," Marianne said. "You surprise me though."

Barbara looked at her. "Why?"

"That you want a memento of a man who obviously lied to you."

Barbara said nothing for a moment; she seemed to be considering her words carefully. "I'm not sure why Dominic did what he did but I am sure he loved me. And, the fact is that even though he's gone, he is always going to be a part of my life." She locked eyes with Marianne. "You see, I'm carrying his child."

CHAPTER
TWENTY

"Holy shit."

"That's the third time you've said that," Marianne said, staring at Dominic's phone as they sat in Johnny's car.

"Well, you have to admit, it has been quite a morning." Johnny turned in his seat and looked at her. "How are you holding up?"

"I don't honestly know." Marianne shook her head and laughed. "I'm not sure what to think; this is baffling. Do you believe her, Johnny?"

"About being pregnant?"

She shrugged. "About everything."

"I thought there were inconsistencies but she may simply be protecting herself, as you are."

"True. If we're to believe what she said then she must have thought I was some kind of monster."

"And if she loved Dominic and wanted to feel better about splitting up a marriage then she would want to believe his version of the truth."

"I suppose so."

"You know she may try to recoup her losses from you," Johnny warned her.

Marianne stared at him. "Can she do that?

"I'm not sure, that's why we need to see Eddie."

"I don't believe this." Marianne glanced at her watch. "I've got to go, Johnny, I'm meeting Rob in The Den."

"Oh?"

"I followed your advice and asked him about training," she explained, amused by Johnny's perplexed look; he was so over-protective. "You're welcome to join us if you want."

"Sorry?"

"For a sandwich?"

"Oh, thanks, love, but I've got things to do, places to be." He started the car and reversed out of the parking spot.

"I'm sorry to have dragged you away from your work but I'm very glad you came with me this morning."

"Don't apologize. I wouldn't have missed it for the world! And imagine the money I'll rake in when I write my book."

Marianne smiled. "You'd never sell this story; it's too farfetched. Are you sure you won't join us?" she asked, as he pulled up outside the Lansdowne Hotel.

"I won't; give Rob my best. I'll give you a call as soon as I've set up an appointment with Eddie. I must give Frank a call about those paintings too," he said, and with a wave he was gone.

Rob was at the bar when Marianne arrived. He turned and smiled when he saw her and she felt an old familiar stirring inside.

"Hi. Toasted ham and cheese sandwich and a lager?" he asked when she joined him.

She laughed that he'd remembered. "Water instead of lager, please, although I could do with a drink after the morning I've had."

"Grab a seat while I order and then you can tell me all about it."

She found a table in the busy pub and studied him as he chatted with the barman. It seemed so strange to be here with him and, at the same time, the most natural thing in the world. More than anything, it was a relief to think that she no longer had to worry about being seen with him.

"Sandwiches are on their way," he said, setting down their drinks and lowering himself onto a stool beside her. "Weird not to have to duck and dive, isn't it?"

"I was just thinking the same thing," Marianne smiled.

"So, not a good morning?"

Marianne shook her head, still reeling from Barbara's announcement. "A very, very strange morning. Johnny Sheridan and I just met Dominic's mistress."

Rob choked on a mouthful of lager.

"Oh, sorry, are you okay?" Marianne pulled a tissue from her bag and handed it to him.

Rob dried his mouth and crushed it in his hand. "Dominic had a mistress? Then he was an even bigger fool than I thought; why on earth you stayed with him —"

"I only just found out."

"I told you he didn't deserve you. How long has it being going on? Was she around when we were together?"

Marianne could see that Rob was aghast at the thought that she had ended their relationship at a time when Dominic was off having one of his own. "Does it matter now?"

He looked at her for a moment and then shook his head. "I suppose not. Had you suspected he was seeing someone?"

"Not at all. It was only when I met his boss a few days ago and he told me that Dominic always left work before six, yet he never returned home until very late, that it seemed a possibility. Then on Saturday there was a text from his phone and we suspected it must be from a girlfriend."

"We?"

"Johnny and I," she explained.

"I had no idea you two were so close."

Was that jealousy in his voice? She suppressed a smile. "He's married to Helen, my oldest friend, and he's been helping me sort out Dominic's estate."

"I'm glad you had someone to turn to; it must be a very difficult time for you."

"Finding out that we're broke hasn't helped." She stopped as a waiter arrived with their sandwiches.

"Tell me more about this mistress," said Rob when they were alone again.

Marianne took a nibble of her sandwich before replying. "Her name is Barbara. She is also a stockbroker and used to work with Dominic. He told her that he wanted to divorce me and marry her but that I wouldn't let him go; that I was making all sorts of threats if he left."

"It sounds like he was using her."

"It does. She says they were going to leave the country and start a new life together and she'd given up her job and sold her house; it looks as if he may have pocketed the proceeds."

"Lovely guy your husband," Rob said, sounding bitter. "Or don't you believe her?"

Marianne thought about it. "I'm not sure. I suppose if Dominic was capable of defrauding his company," and beating up his wife, she added privately, "he was capable of stealing from his girlfriend."

He shot her a curious look. "You don't seem upset that he was being unfaithful."

She held his gaze. "I'm not."

"Still, you must be angry with her."

"No. I feel a bit sorry for her; she seems to have loved him."

"You are a very strange woman."

She laughed. "It's just that I'd built her up into a monster in my head; some kind of siren with fake boobs. Instead I met a normal, articulate, intelligent lady, who is attractive in an understated way."

"She sounds just like you," he said, smiling.

"No, not at all!" But when Marianne thought about it, she realized that there were similarities. She frowned. "Well, maybe a little."

Rob finished his sandwich, wiped his mouth and hands and sat back. "It makes sense that he would go for the same type."

"I suppose."

"So, what happens now?"

"Johnny is setting up an appointment for me with his solicitor; he thinks it's important I get legal advice so I know where I stand in relation to Dominic's debts, my pension and now this woman."

"Oh, Marianne; I wish I could help in some way."

She smiled. "You can; tell me what skills I need to get a decent job."

Rob leaned forward on his knees. "What kind of job?"

"One that pays well," she joked but her heart was heavy. Even with Rob's help, she knew the fact that she had been out of the workforce for so long would be a huge drawback, particularly given the number of qualified, experienced people that were out of work. "Seriously, I have no idea, Rob."

"Well, let's start with your skills. You're dependable, intelligent and a hard worker; they are not qualities that are readily available. Trust me, I know."

"I didn't realize you had employees."

"I've had a whole series of them, one more useless than the next. Then finally I found Shay; he was the best. Reliable, creative, easy company, no bad habits."

"So, what happened to him?"

"He fell in love with a Latvian girl, proposed and now they've gone to live in Riga."

She smiled. "Don't worry, I'm sure there's another Shay out there somewhere."

He stared at her for a long moment. "You're right, there is. You."

Marianne laughed. "That's ridiculous."

"It's not. You're the perfect replacement!"

"No, I'm not. I don't know the first thing about website design, Rob."

"Neither did Shay. I hired him to run the training end of the business." His eyes shone with excitement.

"But I'm not a teacher either," she protested, wondering if he wanted to give her the job because he pitied her or wanted to see her more often. "I came to you to get training not give it, remember?"

"Who trained all the Treacy staff on the new system?"

"I did," she admitted, "but that was one system that I knew like the back of my hand."

"You only learned how to use it a couple of weeks ahead of the rest of them but you picked it up much quicker because you're comfortable with software. The latest packages are much simpler to use; you'll have no problems. I can train you and then you can train others; it's all very straightforward. We always made a good team, Marianne, and," he grinned, "you're much easier on the eye than Shay."

"You are completely crazy; it's a ludicrous idea." She popped the last piece of sandwich in her mouth.

"It makes perfect sense. I've witnessed first-hand your skills. The only thing you're lacking at the moment

242

is the technical know-how and you'll nail that in a matter of weeks, trust me."

Marianne looked at him. "I trust you, of course I do, but I'm just not sure it's a good idea."

He frowned. "Look, this is a business proposition, nothing more. I'm not trying to take advantage of you or the situation."

"That thought never occurred to me, Rob," Marianne said, horrified that he would think such a thing. "I just don't want you to jeopardize your business for the sake of doing me a favour."

"Marianne, I'm not doing you a favour. I am delighted to help you out but I'm also a businessman; I wouldn't offer you the job unless I thought you were up to it."

Perhaps he was right, Marianne thought. She had no formal teaching qualifications but she'd had plenty of hands-on experience and she'd enjoyed it too.

"Look, I badly need backup and you need a job. Why don't we give it a go for three months and see how it goes?" he suggested.

Marianne looked at him and smiled. "You're on!"

He grinned. "Excellent."

"So, what exactly is it you want me to teach?"

"Initially, I think I'll let you take over the beginners courses in social networking, word processing and spreadsheets, and we'll see how you get on."

"I've no experience of networking but I'm reasonably comfortable with the other two."

"It would take a day, two tops, to bring you up to speed on Twitter and Facebook," he assured her. "When can you start?"

She thought about the packing that had to be done and all the time-consuming meetings she'd been involved in since Dominic's death, and now there was a mistress to deal with and a solicitor to consult. "I suppose I'd be ready to start training once I've moved house but I can't be precise, Rob; every time I think I'm getting on top of things, something new seems to pop up."

"Well, I'm sure we can work around that; my hours are flexible . . ." He stopped as three young girls squeezed in around the table beside them, chatting and giggling.

Marianne sighed; it would be impossible to talk in privacy now; it would be difficult to be heard over that noise.

Rob smiled. "Why don't we take a walk?"

They chatted easily as they strolled up Baggot and on reaching Mespil Road they crossed, climbed up the bank and stopped by the famous sculpture of the poet, Patrick Kavanagh, sitting on a bench.

"You know this isn't the original," Rob said.

"You told me that before," Marianne said, smiling.

"I did?" He turned from the green statue, surprised.

She nodded. "And that the original is further along the bank and in an awful state; at least it was the last time you told me about it."

"It still is. 'O commemorate me with no hero-courageous Tomb — just a canal-bank seat for the passer-by,' " he quoted.

They turned and started to wander along the bank in silence; it was a grey day, the water was a murky green and people were hurrying past, heads bent against the wind. They paused to watch a swan preen itself, indifferent to their presence and the noise of the traffic. Marianne hugged her arms around her.

"Barbara is pregnant," she told him. It had been going round and round her head and now, as they stood there together, it seemed the most natural thing in the world to confide in him.

He turned to stare at her. "The mistress?"

"Can we not use that word, please. I hate it."

"That must be quite a shock," he said after a moment.

"It is. It adds a whole new dimension to the problem. I thought I'd never have to see the woman again but she's going to be the mother of the children's half-brother or sister; the baby will be Dot's grandchild," she added, the realization shocking her. "Everything will have to come out."

"Barbara may not want it to," Rob pointed out.

"I hope you're right," Marianne said, filled with a feeling of helpless anger. "My family have been traumatized enough without having to deal with this; damn you, Dominic!"

Rob reached out for her hand and squeezed it. "You don't have to let her into your life if you don't want to."

"I'm not sure I'll have a choice. And even if she does disappear, what's to stop the child coming to look for its family in twenty years or so?"

"Will you stop worrying about the future?" Rob shook his head and smiled at her. "Just focus on right now, Marianne. Okay?"

She took a deep breath, realizing that she was on the verge of a panic attack.

"Calm down," he said, looking at her with concern. "You've got this far, Marianne, you're not going to crack up now."

"No." She took some more long, deep breaths and tried to smile. "No, I'm not." They walked on and the feel of Rob's strong hand holding hers calmed her.

"Let's change the subject," he suggested.

"Yes, let's. Tell me about the business. I hadn't even realized that you'd set up on your own."

"Let's say at the time I was in need of distraction."

"Oh, Rob," she sighed.

"Hey, I may never have taken the risk otherwise."

She raised her eyebrows. "Ah, so you're saying that splitting up with me was the making of you."

"I never split up with you, Marianne," he said, holding her gaze.

"No, I'm sorry." She looked away feeling uncomfortable but smiled when his hand tightened around hers. "Go on," she prompted.

"I was working out of a tiny office down in the docklands, long before it became fashionable; I had about four different types of lock on the door. At the beginning there were times when it was a struggle to pay the rent but they're the risks you take when you are self-employed. I started small, just doing what I had always done, installing systems and then maintaining them. After I had a core of regular clients, I set up the website and also branched into training; it was the obvious next step but it only really took off when Shay came on board. Once he left I had to let it slide. I can't afford to do that any more, though; it's the most profitable end of the business these days with the number of people just like you, trying to broaden their skill set so that they can compete in the job market."

"And are you planning to do all that from my house?" Marianne asked, a little unnerved at the thought of people traipsing in and out of her home; she could only imagine what the neighbours would have to say on the subject.

Rob laughed. "No, don't worry. I rent rooms in a hotel in town for any training courses."

"Oh, that's a relief," she admitted with a grin. "I suppose a central location does make more sense."

"I'm actually planning to go down the suburban route, as it happens. I thought some evening classes in schools or community centres would be attractive to stay-at-home mothers or pensioners. We could run much shorter courses giving an introduction to the internet, email and social networking."

"That sounds like fun," Marianne said, impressed, and felt a stir of excitement at being involved in the venture. "I must admit, though, I've never stood up in front of a class of people before; I hope I can do it."

"Of course you can. You'll get used to it very quickly." He stopped short and gestured with his hand. "*Et voila!*"

Marianne looked at the simple wooden bench between stone uprights and felt sad for the poet until she sat down and her eyes rested on the calm waters flowing by. "The seat's not that impressive but it's a lovely location; I'd happily sit here all day," she said with a sigh.

He sat next to her, his arm tight against hers. "Me too."

She closed her eyes and savoured the moment. "Marianne?"

She opened her eyes and turned to look at him, and watched, mesmerized, as his gaze deliberately dropped to her lips and then locked with hers. It was her opportunity to say something to break the spell; she didn't. Rob tipped his head sideways and leaned in to kiss her; she felt a tremor of pleasure ripple through her body at the feel of his mouth on hers. It was a light but tender kiss that brought back memories of the many different kisses they'd shared before and Marianne automatically moved closer to him just as she had so many times in the past. Rob responded by putting his arm around her and his kiss became more insistent.

When they parted, she opened her eyes to find him looking intently into hers. "Oh, Rob."

"Marianne . . ."

She looked down as he took her hand and then gasped as she caught sight of the time on his watch.

"Shit." If she didn't leave right now she'd never make it to the school on time. "I'm sorry but I have to go."

He looked taken aback and immediately withdrew. "I'm sorry, I shouldn't have done that."

"Don't apologize," she told him. "I'm very glad you did. If I didn't have to pick up the children I'd happily stay here all day."

Looking relieved, Rob stood up and held out his hand to her. She took it and standing up she smiled into his eyes. "Would it be okay if I called you later?" he asked. Marianne sighed. "Oh, Rob, it would be very okay."

CHAPTER
TWENTY-ONE

Helen wasn't happy. Johnny and Marianne were supposed to have met that woman at eleven and it was now after two and he still hadn't been in touch. She'd called his mobile and just got his voicemail; she'd called Marianne and got the same. There was no reason for her to be suspicious. This was her husband and her best friend. But her gut had been telling her for weeks now that something wasn't quite right and she'd learned to trust her gut.

When she finally got hold of Marianne, she was in the process of pouring herself a glass of wine; Helen knew it was large from the length of time the glug-glug-glug sound continued.

"Oh, it's like that?"

She could hear Marianne take a sip and then a deep breath before answering. "Her name is Barbara West, she worked with Dominic at Matthews and Baldwin a few years ago."

"So tell me about her," Helen urged, impatient as she heard Marianne paused to have another drink. "What's she like?"

"She looks a little like me only with shorter hair and she seemed quiet but by no means shy."

"Were they having an affair?"

"Yes, although she maintains it was much more than that. She said that Dominic was planning to leave me and marry her."

Helen frowned. "Was he, Marianne? You never said anything."

"I never said anything, Helen, because he never even mentioned her," Marianne said. "He seems to have told her nothing but lies."

"That's incredible." Helen sat with her coffee and listened in silence as Marianne explained about how Dominic had persuaded Barbara to sell her house, dangling the carrot of a life together in a new country. "I almost feel sorry for her," she said at the end of it.

"There's more." She could hear Marianne sigh. "Barbara's pregnant."

"No!" Helen gasped.

"So she says. We left soon after that. I didn't know what to say; I just had to get out of there."

"I can understand that. How long did the meeting go on?" Helen added casually. "Only I tried to call Johnny and couldn't get hold of him."

"Less than an hour but he was rushing off to another meeting."

Helen had to work hard to keep her voice light. "I tried your phone too but no luck there either."

"Oh, did you? I was a bit flustered after all of that and forgot to switch it back on. I never got a message saying you'd called but then Andrew's dropped that phone so many times it's a miracle it works at all."

Helen froze; she knew this woman well and knew when she was telling a lie and she was. She had to take a deep breath before she could manage to reply. "Kids, eh? You sound amazingly calm for a woman who's just met her husband's pregnant girlfriend."

There was a small hesitation. "I'm not upset that he had an affair, Helen, and you know that if he'd asked me for a divorce I'd have happily agreed and wished him luck. But a child; that's knocked me for six, to be honest."

"I can imagine." Helen couldn't continue the conversation a moment longer. "Marianne, sorry, must go; I have scones in the oven. We'll talk again tomorrow. You take care, try not to worry."

"Oh, I need to go myself; there's someone at the door."

"Johnny! What are you doing here? Your wife's just been on; she's been looking for you, you should call her."

"I will, I will." He came in, shooting a quick look around. "Are you alone?"

"The kids are in bed and Dot's gone to visit a friend in hospital. Why? Is something wrong?"

"No, it's just I've been completely distracted all day. I keep going over things in my head and so much of what Barbara said just doesn't make sense."

"You know, I've been the same," Marianne exclaimed, although in her case, her distraction was as much down to Rob. "Cuppa?"

"I'd prefer a real drink but I suppose I'd better behave."

252

Marianne put the kettle on and then turned to face him. "So, tell me, what doesn't make sense?"

Johnny sat down, stretched out his legs and crossed his arms across his chest. "Well, if Barbara thought you knew all about her and she thought that her money was in one of Dominic's accounts, why didn't she come and confront you before now?"

"She didn't confront me at all; she responded to Kate's texts," Marianne reminded him. "But good point."

"And the business about the phone . . ." Johnny shook his head. "I think there's more going on than meets the eye but I can't quite figure out what."

"I know and I agree. Perhaps when we've had a night's sleep things will seem clearer."

"Have you had a chance to check out his phone at all?"

"No, Dot had only walked out the door when Helen phoned and then you arrived. I'll check it out later. I think Barbara was shocked to hear that I knew nothing about her, and that Dominic hadn't asked for a divorce."

"Yes, agreed, and if I were to give her the benefit of the doubt, she has probably been grieving for Dominic and may have only just realized that the money was missing. It would account for why she agreed to meet you so quickly; she was afraid you had got your hands on it."

"And if he'd told her I was a total bitch then she was probably quite worried about that," Marianne agreed.

"I've arranged a meeting with my solicitor for Monday week. Have you heard anything from Matthews and Baldwin?"

"No. I thought about calling Matthews but then I figured that if I seemed anxious, it might make me look guilty," Marianne admitted as she carried two mugs of tea to the table.

Johnny laughed. "I know what you mean, but I think you should set up an appointment with him for that afternoon."

"And deal with both of them on the same day? I'm not sure I could handle that, Johnny."

"I'm afraid you'll have to if you want me to go along; I'm tied up the rest of that week. Besides, the sooner you tell them about the phone and Barbara the better. It will show that you are being proactive in trying to help them recover their money; that's important."

"You're right. I'll call and set it up," Marianne said, feeling panicky at the rate things were moving.

"It will all be clearer after we've had a chat with Eddie."

He yawned and Marianne thought how weary and pasty-faced he looked. "Is everything okay, Johnny?"

"Grand."

"You know if you have too much on your plate, I can see the solicitor alone . . ."

"Not at all; it's no trouble."

"Something's bothering you, though."

"Well, my friend, Christy, isn't the best."

"I'm sorry." Marianne went to the worktop for her packet of antacids.

254

"What are they?" he asked as she popped two in her mouth.

"Indigestion tablets." She pulled a face. "I think Dominic's final parting gift may be an ulcer."

"Give us one."

She handed the packet over. "Why, what's up?"

He shrugged. "Something I ate isn't agreeing with me."

"I thought you didn't look well. Go home to Helen, Johnny."

He drained his mug. "Okay. Do you have the paintings ready?"

"I do, they're in the office."

"Holy God!" Johnny said when he saw the stack of paintings of all shapes and sizes resting against the wall. "I'd no idea he had this many."

"Seventy-four," Marianne told him excitedly. "I know he paid over a thousand for some of them."

"He didn't!"

"If he admitted that to me, then he probably paid more."

"Remember, what he paid and what they're worth now are two completely different things; some of them may well have increased in value but others could be worthless." Johnny held up a small painting and turned it this way and that. "Never been able to make head nor tail of modern art myself; I think the people who pay thousands for it have more money than sense."

"I know nothing about art or its value, so it looks like we are putting our trust completely in your friend's hands."

"I've known Frank since I was a boy and believe me, we can depend on him; a better man you couldn't meet. Dear God, that's ugly!"

Marianne laughed as Johnny grimaced at the abstract he was holding up. "I've always hated that; it's like something from *Crime Scene Investigates*."

He put his head on one side and screwed up his face as he studied the painting that consisted of red and black lines, blotches and a yellow circle. "What the hell is it supposed to be?"

"No idea."

"Don't you just know that's the one that's probably worth the most," Johnny sighed.

"Funny you should say that. Dominic always said to me: if I croak it first, sell the painting but hang on to the frame; it's worth a lot."

"It doesn't look that special to me," Johnny said, looking dubious.

"Still, tell your pal Frank that if he wants he can have the painting but to give me back the frame; I'll put a nice photo of Dominic and the children in it instead."

"I'll take it off now," Johnny said.

"I tried, Johnny, but I couldn't and I was afraid I'd damage the painting."

"Fair enough; I'll leave it to the expert."

They carried the paintings out to the car and then after saying goodbye, Marianne went back inside and closed the door. She took Dominic's phone from her bag and returned to the kitchen. Rob had called and left a message while she was talking to Helen and she was itching to phone him back, but she was also curious to check Dominic's last calls and texts. She'd do that first and then she would be able to relax when she was talking to Rob. She was still in a state of excitement after their special few moments on the canal bank. It had been such a strange day of highs and lows. The thought of Barbara's pregnancy and its repercussions frightened her but the idea that perhaps Rob might still love her filled her with happiness.

She forced herself to concentrate on the phone and put everything else on hold. The first thing she did was to go to his photos; Barbara had said there were some personal ones there. She flicked through a few of Dominic alone. They all seemed quite businesslike; he was in his suit and wearing a formal smile. There were a couple of Barbara but they were slightly blurred and she wasn't as neat and tidy and conservative as she'd appeared this morning in the hotel. And then there were some of Dominic with that telltale look in his eyes. Marianne sighed. She may have stopped loving him but it still hurt to see him so wasted. It was inconceivable that Barbara hadn't noticed it. When it came to the extent of Dominic's addiction she was either lying to them or to herself.

After studying the photos for a few minutes she turned her attention to the text messages. She was disappointed to find they were all quite innocuous but realized that Barbara must have deleted anything personal. She thought for a moment and then searched out Dominic's replies; if she was a woman in love she would find it difficult to delete loving or tender messages. But although Marianne found funny and flirty texts, there were none that could be described as romantic or loving. Feeling slightly deflated, she skimmed the other messages and went through the phone history but could find nothing of note. There was nothing much to tell Rob but . . .

She picked up her phone and called, smiling when he picked up on the first ring. "Hi, it's me."

"Hello, you."

She could hear the joy in his voice and imagined him stretching back in the chair, hands behind his head and the phone tucked under his chin. "I enjoyed our lunch."

"Me too, although I enjoyed the afters more."

She grinned. "The walk was nice."

"Oh, yes," he said. "I enjoyed that too."

"You haven't changed."

"Neither have you."

Marianne clutched the phone closer. She couldn't believe she was talking to Rob again; it was as if they'd never been apart. "I've checked Dominic's phone but there's nothing much of interest."

"That doesn't surprise me; she would have deleted it all first."

"But she wasn't expecting us to ask for it . . . oh, damn it."

"What?"

"I knew something was bothering me all day. She went into the loo just after we asked for it and was gone for a while."

"There you go, then."

Marianne sighed. "I may as well give it to Dominic's boss; he might recognize some contacts that I don't."

"Good idea. Give it to him and put it out of your head for the moment; there's nothing more that you can do."

"You're right."

"I'm always right — had you forgotten that?"

"I had, silly me. So, let's talk about you for a change. Is there a Mrs Lee?" she asked, keeping her tone light but anxious to hear his answer.

"No Mrs Lee," he confirmed.

She could hear that he was pleased she'd asked. "Tell me about your life."

"Not much to tell. I've been concentrating on work and the last few months I've been engrossed in designing the house with the architects; I've really enjoyed that."

"You were always creative."

"Was I?"

"Yes. Do you still listen to jazz?"

He laughed. "I do. Do you still go to those depressing musicals?"

"They're not depressing!"

"They bloody are," he retorted. "It was the one plus about not being able to go out together in public; you couldn't drag me along to one."

"I must check out what's on at the moment," Marianne laughed.

He was silent for a moment. "So, you wouldn't mind being seen with me?"

"Not at all," she said.

"That's nice to know."

"Are you sure you want me working for you, Rob? Is it a good idea?"

"I'm very sure and it's an excellent idea; I never have bad ones."

"Ah, I'd forgotten how modest you were," Marianne smiled.

"I'll send you over the job offer and contract tomorrow."

"Great. I'll get it back to you as soon as I've read it."

"Marianne?"

"Yes?"

"I enjoyed today."

It had been one hell of a morning, Marianne was still in shock at the thought of Barbara having Dominic's child but her overriding memory of today would be sitting on Patrick Kavanagh's bench kissing Rob Lee.

"Me too. Goodnight, Rob."

"Goodnight, Marianne; sweet dreams."

Helen was in bed when Johnny got in. She wondered whether she should pretend to be asleep, sit up and interrogate him or just carry on as if everything was okay. The decision was taken from her hands; Johnny didn't come looking for her. She could hear him move around, the clink of a glass as he poured himself a whiskey and a squeak as the door to the study closed. They never closed doors in this house, there was no need to; or there hadn't been. Feeling miserable and worried, Helen lay thinking, her eyes tight shut, long after Johnny had climbed into bed next to her.

CHAPTER
TWENTY-TWO

Jo finished tidying the kitchen and decided to change all of the bed linen. It was after eleven on Sunday morning; Greg was off golfing, Rachel had gone to dance class and Di, having made a mountain of French toast, was back lazing in bed, texting her friends and listening to music. It was time she got up; Greg went mad when he came home and saw her still wandering around in skimpy pyjamas. And there was a party on tonight that she had been talking about for weeks; Greg would be delighted to have an excuse to ground her. Joanna sometimes tried to pinpoint when her husband had turned into such a killjoy. He had always been conservative and serious but they had still had laughs. Now with every day that passed he seemed to grow more and more like his bitter, sour-faced mother.

With a resigned sigh, Jo went upstairs and tapped on the door of her daughter's room. "Di, you've got five minutes to get up. I want to change the —" She stopped as she pushed open the door and saw the tousled bed was empty. She ducked out again and paused outside the bathroom. "Di?" There was no answer but she heard the distinct sound of retching and she immediately went in and groaned when she saw her daughter on her knees in front of the toilet. "Oh, my poor love!" She quickly moved to Di's side and held her hair back out of the way.

Eyes watering, Di sat back on her heels. Jo rinsed a face cloth, rung it out and handed it to her daughter.

"Thanks." Di smiled and cleaned around her mouth.

Jo put a hand on her daughter's forehead but she didn't seem unduly warm. "What's brought this on, I wonder? Did you eat anything when you were over at Sarah's last night?"

"No, Mum, I'm fine. It's just I'm wearing that thin cream top tonight and I didn't want to look bloated. I really should cut out white bread; it always has that effect, doesn't it?" she added thoughtfully.

Jo stared at her. "You made yourself sick deliberately?"

"Yeah."

"But that's ridiculous, darling; you should never do that!"

"But why not?" Di asked, looking confused. "You do it."

That evening after Di had left for the party and Greg and Rachel were watching a wildlife documentary, Jo sat pretending to read a magazine, still reeling at her daughter's words. She hadn't known what to say, how to handle it and ended up just telling Di not to be silly and to get washed and dressed before her father got home. There was a commercial break in the programme and Greg looked across at her. "Make a cuppa, love; are there any of those brownies left?"

262

She stared at him for a moment and then stood up. "You'll have to get it yourself, I have to go out."

"At this hour? Where?"

She searched her scrambled brain for a reasonable excuse. "I completely forgot that I promised to help Marianne and Dot with the packing. I should have been there hours ago."

"There's no point going all the way to Howth now, it's almost nine," he protested.

"I'm sure there'll still be plenty to do and it would be rude not to." She dropped a kiss on Rachel's hair. "See you later," she said and slipped out the door before Greg came up with any more arguments.

Jo didn't really have any idea where she was going; she just knew she had to get out of the house. Without thinking she turned north and drove along the coast, Di still uppermost in her mind. Her daughter had not understood why her mother was upset; vomiting up food that would make her bloated or fat made perfect sense to her. She'd seen her mother do it so it must be okay. Jo felt consumed with guilt.

By the time she started to pay attention to where she was going, Jo was in Sandymount. She thought of stopping and going for a walk across the beach but it was dark, starting to rain and she'd left without a coat. And so with a sigh she decided to head on out to Howth; it would be hard to explain if Greg found out she'd lied.

Marianne opened the door and smiled. "Jo, what a nice surprise and great timing too."

"Why's that?" Jo asked, stepping inside, grateful for her friend's warm welcome.

"I'm by myself, I've just made a coffee and there's some Pavlova in the fridge just begging to be eaten."

Jo groaned inwardly. "Oh, no, I shouldn't . . ."

"Me neither," Marianne said cheerfully, "but I will and because you're so well mannered, you'll join me."

"Well, when you put it like that . . ." Jo grinned and followed her out to the kitchen. "Where is everyone?"

"Dot took them to the cinema. It doesn't matter if the film is rubbish, Andrew is all excited at just being out at night."

"It's a lovely age," Jo said, thinking wistfully of how sweet Rachel had been at five, although Di had been strong-willed even then.

Marianne cut two slices of Pavlova and put the largest in front of Jo.

"There must be a thousand calories there," Jo protested in dismay.

"Ah, a little of what you fancy does you good," Marianne grinned, tucking into her cake with relish. "If we don't treat ourselves who will? Jo?"

Jo sat staring at her dish, unable to move. She was barely aware of Marianne talking to her until she felt an arm around her shoulders.

"What is it, Jo? What on earth's wrong?"

"I'm so stupid, so bloody stupid. My mother always said so and she was right."

"Stop that; if she said that then she was the stupid one."

"But you don't know what I've done."

264

"Tell me. Did you murder someone? Now that would be bad but not necessarily stupid; the world would be a better place if some of the nutters in it were six feet under."

"I've met a few of them." Jo couldn't help smiling.

"That's better." Marianne handed her a piece of kitchen towel. "Now, why don't you tell me what all this is about?"

"I feel so ashamed; you'll be disgusted with me."

"Why don't you let me be the judge of that?"

Jo dabbed at her eyes and then stared at the sodden paper in her hands, too embarrassed and ashamed to look Marianne in the eye. "You know that I've always had problems managing my weight. I think it was once I left St Anne's I just couldn't believe that I could eat whatever I wanted, whenever I wanted; it went to my head."

Marianne smiled. "For me it was the luxury of being able to have a long, hot bath full of bubbles."

"That's why you're still nice and slim."

"For goodness' sake, you talk as if you are enormous and you are not remotely," her friend protested.

Jo ignored the remark; Marianne was always kind. "When I got pregnant with Di, well, I didn't eat for two but for quads; I found it impossible to shift the weight afterwards and I knew Greg hated it. That just depressed me more."

"Lots of women can't lose the weight and get the baby blues; added to the lack of sleep that's a hell of a combination."

"That's true. I felt big, ugly and depressed but the more miserable I became, the more I ate."

"That's human nature. I keep telling myself that I should cut down on wine but the more I think about it, the more I want it!"

Jo knew Marianne was trying to lift her spirits. Would she when she knew the truth? She twisted the tissue round and round her finger until the tip turned white. "That's not why I'm upset now."

"Go on."

Jo swallowed. "I found a solution to my weight issue but not a healthy one."

Marianne groaned. "Not slimming tablets or laxatives, Jo?"

She shook her head and looked away from those kind, concerned eyes. "I started to make myself sick straight after eating. It sounds disgusting but it did the trick. I didn't put on any weight and I felt back in control again."

"Jo!" Marianne's eyes filled with horror.

"I'm disgusting, I know."

"You are not," Marianne grasped her hand. "Please stop saying that."

"I thought I was discreet, I didn't think anyone knew . . ." Jo put a hand to her mouth, as she recalled the image of her daughter bent over the loo.

"Tell me."

"This morning," Jo started, her voice barely more than a croak, "I found Di doing exactly the same thing."

"Oh my God, poor Jo." Marianne took both of her hands between hers and stroked them.

Jo looked up at her. "And do you know the worst part, Marianne? She didn't think there was anything wrong with it. She smiled at me and just said she wanted to look good for the party tonight. That's what she's learned from me, Marianne. That's what I have taught my daughter, God help me."

Marianne gathered her into her arms as if she was a child and Jo sobbed.

"It's okay, love, everything will be fine. It's not the end of the world. Have a good cry; we all need to from time to time."

Jo felt devastated and a failure as a mother, but it was a relief to have told someone. She pulled back and dabbed at her eyes with the fresh piece of kitchen towel her friend held out.

"Better?"

"No," Jo smiled. "Well, a little. What should I do, Marianne?"

"How did you leave things with Di?"

"I told her if she did it again she was grounded until she was twenty-one. I know I should have talked to her but I was so shocked and upset, Marianne, and I didn't want to treat it as a big issue."

"I think you did exactly the right thing."

"You do?" Jo said, not believing her for a minute.

"Yes, really. If you had sat her down for a heart-to-heart you would probably have scared the living daylights out of her and she'd have started to worry about you and why you were doing it."

"That's true, I hadn't thought of that." Despite Di's confident exterior, she was soft inside and she would worry. Still, Jo doubted Helen would be so forgiving or Greg for that matter. She sighed heavily.

"Stop that," Marianne told her.

"What?"

"Torturing yourself. It won't help. What's done is done. Now you must concentrate on what to do next." Marianne looked up at the clock. "Damn, Dot and the kids will be back any minute. Once Andrew and Kate are in bed we can have a glass of wine and figure it all out."

"Oh no," Jo grabbed her keys and stood up. "I don't want them to see me; I look a mess. Anyway, I'm driving and Greg will be wondering where I am . . ."

Marianne waved her back into the chair. "Phone Greg and tell him you're staying over."

"But I can't." There was the sound of a key in the door and then Andrew's excited shouts. Jo groaned.

"Wait here, I'll head them off at the pass."

Marianne had a quick word with Dot, explaining that Jo needed to talk, and helped get her children ready for bed, smiling at their excited chatter. It was good to see Kate so full of beans. When she went back downstairs, Dot was there. "I'm on the last few chapters of my thriller and I can't wait to see how it ends so I'll say goodnight," she said.

Marianne smiled gratefully and closed the door after her. "Did you call Greg?"

268

"Yes, he said fine; Rachel wasn't impressed, though. She's not used to me being out for a few hours, never mind overnight."

"We need to remedy that," Marianne said, pouring two glasses of wine, "and once I'm in Kilbarrack and we can get to each other easily on the DART, there's no excuse."

She was glad to see that though Jo looked pale and a bit miserable, she seemed calmer; offloading her burden of guilt must have helped. It occurred to her how rarely Jo opened up, especially about herself; why hadn't she noticed that before? She was so caught up in her own problems she hadn't realized that her friend was in trouble. She wondered if Helen had.

"I want to be home before Di wakes, although that's unlikely to be before midday."

"We'll have you out of here by ten at the latest," Marianne promised. "It would have been a mistake for you to go home upset; I'd have been worried sick about you driving and Greg would have known something was up. Are you going to tell him?"

"About me or Di?"

"Both."

Jo closed her eyes and gave a helpless shrug. "I don't know."

"I think you should; it will be better if it's all out in the open and you have his support."

"I wish I could be sure I'd have it but I'm afraid he will just be disgusted with me."

"I'm sure you're wrong," Marianne said, although she wasn't; Greg did have a tendency to be judgemental. "You should talk to your doctor too."

Jo shook her head. "Why would I? It really isn't a big deal, Marianne, I'm not anorexic."

"Bulimic; anorexia is when you just don't eat."

"I definitely eat," Jo laughed but it was a resigned, defeated sound.

"Tell me something, Jo, do you think you're fat right now?"

"Not really. I'm heavier than I'd like to be but if I wasn't puking, I'd be twenty stone; I just can't seem to resist food, Marianne."

"Perhaps acupuncture or hypnosis would help; apparently they can be quite effective for people with eating disorders."

"I don't have a disorder," Jo said, looking at her in dismay.

"No, of course you don't," Marianne agreed hurriedly, "but you're not going to conquer this without help, you must realize that."

Jo nodded. "I know that. I was going to join Weightwatchers. I could take Di along."

"Do you really think that's a good idea?" Marianne asked; it certainly didn't seem so to her.

"I was looking at their website last week and they're not just about losing weight but about exercise, fitness and changing the whole way that you think about food."

"That does sound good," Marianne admitted.

"Only I'd hate to run into any of my neighbours or some of the school mums at a class; I'd die of embarrassment."

"You don't have to go to a class in your area. Oh, I know, you can go to Dot's class!" Marianne was thrilled with her idea.

"I live in Shankill," Jo protested.

"As you keep pointing out to me, that's no distance on the DART and the community centre is right beside the station."

"I'm not sure," Jo dithered.

Marianne sensed her friend's discomfort and realized she couldn't push her too hard. "It's just a thought. Dot seems to have a great time and there are women of all ages."

"I'll think about it but right now I'm more concerned about Di. What will I say to her, Marianne?"

Marianne took a sip of wine as she tried to imagine herself in the same position; what would she say to Kate? "I think you need to be completely honest with her. Tell her what you did was silly, stupid and that you want to get fit and healthy and start to eat better; you could even ask her to help. It would be an indirect way of bringing home to her the importance of a balanced diet and exercise. If she's already worrying about how she looks, then it would be good to nip it in the bud."

"You may be right," Jo said, looking thoughtful. "Di would love the idea of her mother coming to her for help."

"Then why not give it a go?" Marianne topped up their glasses.

"Okay, I will," Jo said, and there was a more determined look in her eye.

"Does that make you feel any better?"

"Yes, but I'm still disgusted with myself."

"We all make mistakes, Jo, we're all fallible. The last few weeks I have got it so wrong with Kate and Andrew."

"That's not true, Marianne, they're fine; I think you've coped brilliantly."

"I haven't coped as much as muddled through." Marianne thought of her children, Barbara, her baby, the missing money . . . She felt exhausted as she listed the things on her mind. But she felt better now, thanks to Rob. She still couldn't believe that he was back in her life. She looked over at Jo and smiled. "You'll muddle through too and I will help in any way I can."

"Thanks, Marianne, you already have. And I will do something, I promise. Not just for Di's sake, I have to think of Rachel too. Imagine if she saw her big sister making herself sick? My God, how could I live with myself if she went the same way?"

"She won't and Di will be fine too; she wasn't doing it because she hated her body, remember, she just wanted to look nice for the party. Once you get her onside, she will become a great role model for Rachel. You said yourself what a strong person she is."

Jo actually smiled. "Yes, she is."

"And you really should tell Greg; it seems wrong to exclude him."

"I know," Jo said, looking guilty, "but I dread how he'll react."

"He may be angry or upset at first but once he gets over the initial shock, he'll be fine. He'd do anything for you and the girls."

Jo didn't answer for a moment but then, with a less than convincing smile, she sat up straight and nodded. "Yes, of course he would."

CHAPTER
TWENTY-THREE

Helen watched Johnny leave and wondered for a moment if she should follow him, but she dismissed the thought as quickly as it had entered her head. What was the point? If he was seeing someone and that someone was Marianne, she wasn't sure she wanted to know. The thought of him kissing another woman's lips and caressing her body made her feel sick. The fact that it might be Marianne was just unbearable. Perhaps it was all just her imagination. Maybe the relationship was completely innocent. It made sense that Johnny was spending a lot of time with Marianne given all that was going on. She had been the one to ask him to look after her friend, she reminded herself. But she had watched him grow more and more preoccupied as the days passed and though he was as affectionate as ever, it was in an absent sort of way; his mind elsewhere. He was also coming home late some evenings or had his phone off when he was out, and his explanations were often vague and didn't ring true. He still made love to her with passion but not as often, and instead of the long chats afterwards that she loved, he would plead tiredness and turn over.

She paced the house anxiously wondering how she could distract herself. She had already introduced Dot to Brenda and the meeting had gone really well. Dot's apprehension about becoming a businesswoman was receding.

She could go and check on Jo but when Marianne had called to deliver the latest news, with Jo's blessing, she'd suggested Helen gave her some space for the moment. "She's very upset and terrified of telling Greg," she'd said. Helen wasn't surprised on either count. Finding your daughter with her head down a toilet would upset any mother and Greg would undoubtedly be furious.

Neither was it a surprise that Jo had driven to Howth rather than Portmarnock that night; she had always been closer to Marianne — wasn't everyone? Tears filled Helen's eyes and she dashed them away. She was relieved that she didn't have to stick to her promise of finding her friend a job at least; she just wouldn't be up to that. She was stunned to hear that Marianne had secured herself a position so easily and that she'd be working for her tenant; had he fallen under her spell too?

"Stop!" she said aloud.

She knew nothing for sure and she was driving herself around the bend imagining various scenarios and all of them based on a hunch and no more. She decided to do what she usually did when she had a lot on her mind: she'd cook. Colm was working hard now in the run-up to his exams and usually only emerged from his room in search of food, so she would cook up a storm for him. That at least would make her feel useful and keep her occupied for a while, and with her hands covered in flour and food cooking on the hob, she wouldn't be able to give in to the temptation of jumping in the car and going in search of her husband.

Marianne and Johnny sat on a bench in St Stephen's Green, the sun streaming down on them through the trees, and prepared for their meeting with Eddie Madden. She popped an antacid and automatically passed him one. He chewed on it as he scanned through Dominic's list of contacts, commenting on some, asking questions on others. She was finding it hard to concentrate as she'd started the day with a phone call from Rob, again. She let her hair curtain her smile; she was finding it hard to stop smiling these days. There had been no opportunity to meet since that lovely day on the canal bank but they'd had several phone conversations and each one was better and longer than the last. Rob was impatient to meet but between packing, meetings with the children's schools and keeping tabs on Jo, Marianne just hadn't had time. Her few free moments had been spent with Kate and Andrew trying to rebuild their confidence and reassure them that life would go on as normal, and that there were many exciting times ahead even if Daddy wouldn't be a part of them.

She'd had a very positive chat with Jane Hunt, the principal of the children's new school, who had suggested the children come in for a couple of hours during the week; the visit had been a huge success. But she itched, yearned and longed to see Rob and to feel his arms around her once more and his mouth . . .

"Marianne?"

"Sorry?"

"That last number that Dominic dialled, can you call it out again?"

Marianne looked down at Dominic's mobile phone bill and read it out.

"No, it definitely isn't here."

"Another one Barbara deleted," Marianne remarked. "Or maybe it was Dominic."

"Either way, there must be a reason. Let's phone them. We'll do it from my phone; these could be people who know you."

"You and your wife should go into the detective business," Marianne laughed. "She said the exact same thing when we were calling Dominic and Barbara's numbers."

"She taught me everything I know."

"What are you going to say if they answer?"

"I'll say, 'Is that Bono?' "

She laughed. "What if a woman answers?"

"I'll say, 'Is that Mrs Bono?' "

"You're hilarious. Go on then, get on with it. Our meeting starts in twenty minutes."

He made the five calls. On two he got an automated message and two people answered stating their names. "Wrong number," he said in both cases and wrote down the names; the fifth turned out to be another brokerage. "We never asked Barbara who she worked for," he said when he told Marianne the name.

"There're a lot of things we didn't ask her; perhaps we should set up another meeting."

"We can decide that after we've talked to Eddie and Dominic's boss."

"It will be interesting to see if Adrian Matthews knows these people," Marianne took the page he handed her, folded it and put it into the side pocket of her bag.

"He probably won't say. You can bet he'll be playing his cards close to his chest. Right, let's go and see what my esteemed solicitor has to say."

"Thanks for coming with me today, Johnny," she said as they stood waiting for the pedestrian light to change. "I'd hate to be facing all of this alone."

"No problem, sweetheart; doesn't it keep me out of trouble?" He laughed and putting his hand under her arm, guided her across the road in the direction of Baggot Street.

Eddie Madden came across as a serious and rather dull man, until Johnny made a derogatory comment about the soccer team he supported and instantly the man came back with a sharper and wittier retort, winking at Marianne. Immediately she felt more comfortable. Once they were seated in his small office, he sat at his desk and listened as they brought him up to speed, making notes in a hardback notebook with an old-fashioned but rather beautiful fountain pen.

"So?" said Johnny when they finally reached the end of their story.

Eddie sat back in his chair. "That's quite a tale, and a poignant one too." He looked over at Marianne. "I'm sorry for your troubles."

"Thank you."

"I wish I could give you some good news, God knows you deserve it, but I'm afraid this could be quite serious. As Dominic's widow, you do inherit his debts."

Marianne felt sick. If Dominic had defrauded his company and stolen from his employer and his girlfriend, who else was going to crawl out of the woodwork looking for money and how could she possibly pay them?

"Having said that," he said, "your initial meeting with your husband's employer will have gone a long way to reassuring them that you were an innocent party in this matter. Your immediate offer to assist them and handing over the laptop on the same day — these gestures will have strengthened your position considerably, so well done on that."

Johnny beamed at Marianne. "I always said you were smart!"

"If they do decide to pursue you, however," Eddie continued, "you could argue that you are not responsible for your husband's criminality. That would bring the whole matter into the public domain —"

"Oh, no, I really don't want that," Marianne gasped.

Eddie held up a finger. "Trust me, they won't either. It would be hugely embarrassing for them and, not only would they come out looking inept, but the press would tear them apart for trying to recoup their losses from a grieving widow who is already suffering as a result of her husband's scandalous behaviour."

Johnny rubbed his hands together. "That sounds encouraging."

"But . . ."

Marianne gave a resigned sigh.

He gave her an apologetic smile. "The but is simply to remind you of the unknowns. For example, this woman, Barbara West, may try to recoup her losses from his estate."

"Marianne couldn't be expected to compensate her husband's mistress, could she?" Johnny said, shaking his head in disgust.

"It's a complicated business. The way she tells the story she allowed him to be her agent and yet the plan was for them to use the proceeds of the house to start a new life together, so it's not exactly theft. Still, she could probably claim at least half of it. It's open to debate. There would need to be a strong paper trail; for example, she would need to provide proof of the house sale."

"She hasn't actually asked for anything . . . yet," Marianne said.

"It doesn't mean that she won't," Eddie replied.

Johnny grunted. "She will; it's only a matter of time. So, what do you think Marianne should do, Eddie?"

The solicitor looked directly at her. "I think you should throw yourself on the mercies of Matthews and Baldwin. Are you taking Johnny along to this meeting?"

"Yes."

280

"That's good. I would be more than happy to accompany you, but taking along a legal adviser at this stage might just raise their hackles. Johnny, keep that temper in check and let Marianne do the talking, but perhaps throw in a comment on how hard a situation this is on everyone involved and what a catastrophe it would be if it ever got out."

"A shot across the bow, so to speak?"

"Exactly so."

"Consider it done." Johnny's eyes twinkled.

"What about Barbara?" Marianne asked. "Do you think I should call her?"

Eddie looked at his notes and frowned. "How did you leave things with her?"

"We made no arrangements but we did promise to return the phone when the police were finished with it," Johnny said.

Eddie chuckled. "Mentioning the police was an interesting idea. If you ever get fed up with the property game you could always become a private investigator."

"I may have to," Johnny retorted.

"So, to be clear, you never mentioned the fraud to her at all?"

Marianne shook her head. "Not a word."

"Good. If she is somehow involved then there's a good chance that she'll think the fraud hasn't been discovered yet and she's safe."

"I just thought of something." Johnny frowned in annoyance. "She never asked about his laptop."

"So?" Marianne said, not following his train of thought.

"Well, if she was guilty of anything, wouldn't she want to get her hands on it? Wouldn't she have at least asked about it?"

"If she did, wouldn't you have been immediately suspicious of her?" Eddie countered.

"Definitely," Marianne agreed; he was good.

"I think you should let her make the next move," Eddie counselled. "What she says or does could be very telling. Let me know how you get on with Matthews and Baldwin."

Johnny smiled at Marianne and stood up. "Shall we?"

"Pleased to meet you," Adrian Matthews said when Marianne introduced Johnny, but he looked far from happy.

"I hope you don't mind me asking Johnny to join us," she said when they were sitting in front of him, "but he's been helping me sort out Dominic's estate. I have told him everything that you told me and we have been working together to see if we can come up with any information that might be of help to you."

Matthews seemed to relax a little at that. "I see, thank you." He inclined his head in Johnny's direction. "Did you have any success?"

"We're not really sure," Marianne admitted. "You may be the best judge of that but we certainly have plenty to tell you."

"Oh, well, that's a good start," Matthews said, looking much happier. "Coffee?"

282

Marianne smiled across at Johnny as Matthews went to the door to talk to his secretary. Their conversation was going exactly as planned. As agreed, she brought Adrian up to date on how Barbara had made contact, emphasizing Kate's part in the process and how much her daughter was grieving for her father.

"Barbara!" Adrian looked startled.

"Do you remember her?"

"But of course. She was one of our rising stars; we were sorry to lose her."

"Why did she leave?"

"She was highly ambitious and took a job in London."

"That's what she told us." Marianne was disappointed to hear that not only was Barbara good at her job but that her story was checking out. She continued, telling Dominic's boss how she and Johnny had met with Barbara and the subsequent conversation.

When she had finished he shook his head in disbelief. "I am so sorry, Marianne. As if you haven't had enough shocks."

"Do you think this woman can be trusted? Johnny asked.

"I couldn't answer that. I didn't really know her that well — we never worked together directly — but I will ask my partner, Tom; she was part of his team."

"We managed to get Dominic's phone back from her and we've checked out the calls and texts but they all seem relatively innocuous," Marianne told him. "But then we compared the log to the phone bill and there were texts and calls to five numbers that had been deleted. We called them and came up with three names." She took out the page and handed it across to him. She watched him as he read and was conscious of Johnny sitting forward in his seat too, but Matthews' face gave nothing away.

"Do the names mean anything to you?" Marianne asked.

"I can't say that they do."

"And the company?"

"It's a small brokerage in Cork. Would you mind if we took a look at the phone and the bill? There may be numbers that would mean something to Dominic's colleagues."

"I can do better than that." Marianne reached into her bag and produced the phone and an envelope. "If you go into the network's website, these are the codes that you need in order to access Dominic's statements over the last year."

Adrian looked taken aback and then he smiled warmly at her. "That is a very generous and considerate gesture; I do appreciate it."

"Marianne is deeply ashamed of Dominic's duplicity and although she is in no way responsible for it she is eager to help in any way that she can. Naturally, her priority is to shield the children. The very last thing she wants is for this matter to end up in the public domain and to add to their grief. And, of course, there is Dominic's mother to consider too."

"Indeed."

"I have tried to reassure Marianne that it is in the company's interests as much as hers to keep this matter

284

a private one. It's not exactly the sort of publicity you want or need, is it?"

Matthews' eyes narrowed and he inclined his head ever so slightly. "No, it most certainly isn't." He looked at Marianne. "We do appreciate your co-operation and I will personally try to ensure this matter is dealt with internally. I will keep you fully informed of our investigations and return the phone to you as soon as possible."

Realizing that the meeting was at an end, Marianne stood up and held out her hand. "I hope you find what you're looking for."

"As do I," he said, then shook Johnny's hand. "Nice to meet you, Mr Sheridan; I'm glad that Marianne has someone she can depend on at this difficult time."

Johnny looked him straight in the eye. "I can promise you I will do whatever is necessary to ensure that Marianne and her family don't suffer any further because of her husband's actions."

Matthews' smile was strained. "That's good to know."

Marianne waited until they were safely in his car before bursting out laughing. "Oh, Eddie would be proud of you!"

"What do you mean?" he said, but he was grinning.

"You were brilliant, Johnny. Thank you so much."

"You did a pretty good job yourself. Now, I'm starving. Let's go and grab some lunch."

CHAPTER
TWENTY-FOUR

Jo couldn't decide what to do. The thought of telling Greg everything filled her with a dread that she hadn't experienced since leaving St Anne's. Talking to Di wouldn't be much easier. Her daughter would have a lot of questions, and God only knew where that chat would lead. But she had to do it, she had to be strong. Her own mother had let her down at every turn; she would not do the same to Di. As she made herself a black coffee and kept her eyes averted from the biscuit tin, she pondered her dilemma. Marianne was right, she couldn't exclude Greg. She couldn't tell Di all about her problem without telling her father and she should really tell him first. She tried to imagine his reaction. He wouldn't roar or shout at her, he never had. He knew that shouting made Jo tremble but it wasn't his style anyway. Greg was more likely to seethe with silent fury, look at her with disappointed eyes and cut her down to size with cruel sarcasm. She hated those looks and found his silences intimidating. Sometimes she thought that shouting might be preferable but not often.

It was crucial that she get the timing right for this conversation. He usually mellowed after a couple of drinks so perhaps she would order in Chinese — her cooking wouldn't help his mood — open a bottle of wine and tell him then. She could settle Rachel in front of a movie and slip Di some money to go out with her friends, then they could talk uninterrupted.

She was a nervous wreck all day and, for once, eating held little attraction. Then Greg called.

"I'll be home late, I'm meeting a client; don't worry about dinner, I'll pick up a sandwich."

"But —" Jo started but he'd already said goodbye and hung up. Feeling deflated she put down the phone and went into the kitchen where Rachel was making a collage as part of her homework. "That's really good, darling."

"Thanks, Mum. Should I use the pink or purple glitter for Di's dress?"

"Purple I think." Jo looked over her shoulder to find her daughter making a colourful interpretation of the Buckley family. "Is that me?" she asked, pointing at a glamorous figure in a blue dress.

"Yes, that's you in the dress you wore to Aunty Helen's party. It's not very good, is it? You looked much prettier."

Jo laughed. "Are you kidding me? I'd love to look that pretty." She noticed they were all wearing broad smiles except for Greg. "How come Daddy is looking sad?"

"That's because he's an accountant and he's always worried about other people's money."

Jo stared down at the top of her daughter's head and then back at the grim image of her husband. "He's not really worried, darling; it's just hard work trying to sort out other people's problems."

"But he works very hard, doesn't he? Poor Daddy."

Jo continued to stare at the image. "Yes, poor Daddy."

The girls were both asleep and Jo was sitting in the dark, sipping her second glass of wine when Greg arrived home. She heard him drop his briefcase in the hall, walk into the kitchen, open the fridge and then he came into the living room and turned on the light.

"Jo! You gave me a fright; what on earth are you doing sitting here in the dark?" He flopped into his armchair and reached for the remote control.

"Please don't turn the TV on; I want to talk to you."

He yawned. "Do we have to do it now? I've had a hell of a day."

"Tell me."

"What?"

"Tell me about your day," she said.

"Jo, what is this? What's going on?"

"Nothing, it just occurred to me that I never ask; so I'm asking now. How is work?"

"It's lousy if you really want to know. I've never had as many clients. I've never worked so hard but getting them to pay their bills is like getting blood out of a stone."

Jo felt a moment of panic as she took in the worried crease in his brow. "Are we in trouble?" she whispered. She had been nervous when Greg made the decision to go out on his own but he claimed that he would make

288

more money and have more control than if he continued to work with the accountancy firm he'd been with since he left university. They were raking it in, he maintained, but he was seeing little of their profits in his pay cheque and it annoyed him that he was working harder and harder to line the pockets of the board.

"No, of course we're not in trouble," he snapped. "At least, we wouldn't be if you were more careful with money."

"But I hardly spend any money except on groceries," Jo retorted.

"And clothes," he shot back.

She looked down at her ancient tracksuit. "Are you serious?"

"Not on yourself, more's the pity; it's all on the girls. You spoil them rotten, Jo; every Saturday Di arrives home with shopping bags and you spend a fortune on designer wear for Rachel on that damned fashion website."

Jo squirmed; she'd forgotten that he saw all of those purchases coming through on her credit card bills. "You're the one who wants her hanging around with Tracy Donovan; you can hardly expect her to wear chain-store trainers when the other kids are dressed head to toe in labels."

"Listen to yourself," he sighed. "Did you have any fancy clothes when you were growing up?"

"No, but then I didn't have any posh friends either."

"We can't afford it, Jo; it's that simple. You need to make cuts."

"Okay, I will, I promise."

"So, why the interest in my job and our finances all of a sudden?" His expression darkened. "You haven't gone and bought something ridiculously expensive, have you?"

"No, of course not."

"Then what?"

She stood up, shaking her head. "Nothing; it doesn't matter. Would you like me to make you something to eat?"

"No, I had a kebab on my way home," he said, turning on the TV and the news channel.

"I'll go to bed, so." She stopped and turned in the doorway. "Greg?"

"Yeah?" He didn't look up.

"I'm sorry. I will try to be more careful."

He looked up then, his expression softer. "Great, thanks love. Goodnight."

Helen was wandering along Grafton Street, window-shopping, although she was paying little attention. Johnny had called to say he was going to be late again and so, leaving Colm to his books and a fridge full of food, her itchy feet and overactive imagination had taken her into town. Her phone rang and she scrambled around in her bag for it. "Hello?"

"Helen?"

"Yes, Jo, is that you? I can hardly hear you; I'm in town."

"Oh, okay, I was hoping we could have a chat but it can wait; enjoy your shopping."

"No, don't go," Helen said. "I was just finishing up; are you at home?"

"Yes." Jo sounded brighter. "Shall I put the kettle on?"

"Do. I'll be there as quick as I can."

Helen hurried back to her car, smiling. She was thrilled that her friend had finally called. She'd been dying to talk to her but she knew there was no point in calling; Jo wouldn't talk until she felt ready. Helen could have called Marianne to see how Jo was doing but she was avoiding her oldest friend at the moment, deliberately timing her visits to Dot for when she knew Marianne wouldn't be around. She was no actress and she wouldn't be able to disguise her feelings. Talking on the phone was a little easier, though Helen kept calls to a minimum and always found a reason to cut them short. It was easy enough at the moment as there was so much going on in the Thomson household, but once they'd settled in to Kilbarrack it would be harder and she would have to come to a decision as to whether to confront her husband or her friend.

Jo looked pale and nervous when she opened the door. "Hi, Helen. Thanks for coming."

"Are you kidding? I was delighted to. Colm is like the antichrist; I only went into town to get a break."

"Is he studying hard?"

"He is," Helen admitted, setting her bag on the table and sitting down. "Where are the girls?"

"Rachel's at her friend Tracy's house and Di has hockey practice. Coffee?"

"Lovely. So, how are you doing, Jo?"

"Grand."

Helen looked at her. Now, did she go along with this or speak her mind? She decided on the latter. Jo had picked up the phone so she must want to talk. "You don't look it."

"Do I ever?" Jo waved in disgust at her own appearance.

Helen ignored that. "Marianne filled me in."

Jo concentrated on spooning instant coffee into mugs. "And you're still talking to me?" she joked.

"Of course I am; why wouldn't I be?" Jo's hands shook as she lifted the kettle and Helen stood up and took it from her. "Sit down, Jo." She quickly made the coffees and waited as Jo struggled to compose herself.

When she finally spoke it was just one word. "Di."

"What about Di?"

"What she did; it was because of me."

"Yes," Helen agreed. "That must have been awful for you, but at least you know now."

"She'd never have done it if she hadn't seen me do the same."

"Maybe, maybe not. But tell me, have you done it since?"

Jo shook her head.

"That's great, well done."

"I've been tempted."

"I'd be surprised if you hadn't, but the point is that you didn't give in to temptation. How long has it been going on?"

Jo wouldn't look at her. "A few years."

"What weight are you?"

"No idea." Jo shuddered. "I haven't stood on the scales in ages; I'd be afraid to."

"I think you would be pleasantly surprised."

"Oh, please." Jo's eyes flashed.

"Do you think I'm overweight?"

"No, of course not."

Helen raised her eyebrows. "I thought we were being honest."

Jo smiled. "You're not skinny, you're curvy."

"I'm plump," Helen retorted. "I could and would happily lose a stone but it's not the end of the world."

"No, and you look gorgeous."

"Jesus, Jo, will you listen to yourself!"

"What?" Jo looked cross.

Helen jumped to her feet and dragged her out to the mirror in the hall. "Look," she said as they stood side by side. "Will you bloody look!"

Jo grinned at her in the mirror. "You don't curse, Helen."

"If you don't start talking sense I'll turn the air blue, believe me. Now answer me; what do you see?"

Jo's smile disappeared and she sighed. "I see a gorgeous, well-groomed woman and a frump."

Helen smiled happily. "Excellent."

Jo's eyes met hers in surprise. "Pardon?"

"Don't you see? There's very little difference between us. If anything you're probably a few pounds lighter; I'm just better at hiding it."

"No way, I'm much heavier than you!"

"Let's go down to the shopping centre; there's bound to be a weighing scale there. If not, we'll buy one."

"This is silly; I'm not going anywhere, Helen." Jo marched back into the kitchen and sat down.

Helen sighed and followed her. "I'm sorry. I'm not trying to upset you."

"I know that. You have to understand, though, that the only reason I'm not enormous is because I was making myself sick."

"So, what's the plan, Jo?"

"The plan was that I would tell Greg last night but he seems to be preoccupied with work at the moment and I didn't want to add to his worries. I must talk to Di, though."

"I thought you had."

"I told her it was silly and that she shouldn't do it but I think I need to confess to her. I'm also going to join Weightwatchers, and Marianne said I should ask Di for her support in sticking to the diet and keeping to the exercise plan.

"That's a good idea," Helen said, trying not to flinch at the mention of Marianne's name. "It's all very well us giving you advice, Jo, but don't you think you should discuss this with your doctor?"

"There's no need for that."

"If you won't do it for yourself, do it for Di," Helen said, knowing it was the only button she could push that might work. "And fine, yes, join Weightwatchers too. The exercise, the company and just getting out and meeting people who are in the same boat will do you good. In fact, maybe I should join you."

Jo looked at her in surprise. "Would you?"

Helen had meant it as a joke but when she saw the expression on Jo's face she realized it was exactly the support she needed. "Yes, what the hell. Why not?"

CHAPTER
TWENTY-FIVE

"So tomorrow is the big day. Isn't it exciting? I can take the day off to help you move if you like," Vanessa offered as she dumped the takeaway cartons from their dinner into the bin.

"Not at all, there isn't exactly much to do." Rob grinned and gestured to his few belongings stacked by the door of his flat.

"It will be nice to have a place where you can cook food without worrying about catching something." She threw a scathing look at the ancient cooker in the corner. "Why you've stayed here so long is beyond me."

"You know why," he protested, looking out of the large fifth-floor window. It was late but the streets were busy with groups of giggling girls heading out for the evening; tourists still rambling, cameras slung around their necks; workers hurrying home, phones pressed to their ears; and entangled couples wandering along oblivious to the world around them.

She came to stand behind him and slipped her arms around his waist. "Perhaps we should mark your last night properly."

Rob felt her breasts press into his back as her hands moved down to caress his crotch. His treacherous body responded and he felt like a total bastard. He had been avoiding her as much as possible since he'd kissed Marianne. Being with Vanessa wasn't right any more and he would have to end it. He turned within her embrace and kissed her lightly on the lips. "I have an early start, Van."

She looked up at him, her lovely eyes full of concern. "Is everything okay, honey?"

"Everything is fine," he lied, smiling. She was so pretty and sexy and so bloody understanding and patient; she deserved much better than him. He kissed her soundly, out of guilt more than anything, and she responded eagerly. He pulled away. "I'm just tired; it's been a busy time."

"I understand, only . . ." She trailed off and looked down.

"Only?"

"This may be our last opportunity to spend the night together for a while, Rob; I'm going away."

"Really? Where?"

"A girl in the head office in London is going on maternity leave and they've asked me to take over. She's an assistant editor, Rob; it's a great opportunity for me."

"That's terrific, Van," he hugged her, delighted; becoming an editor was her dream. "London, wow! I'm thrilled for you; when do you leave?"

She bit her lip. "The day after tomorrow."

"Crikey, they didn't give you much notice!"

"I've known about it for a while but I was afraid to tell you." She disengaged herself and went to sit down on the sofa.

He sat in the armchair opposite, leaning forward on his knees. "I don't understand."

She studied her hands. "It's simple really. If you had asked me not to go then I wouldn't have."

"I wouldn't have done that!"

"That's what I thought."

Rob massaged the bridge of his nose. "You'll have to help me out here, Vanessa. I have a feeling I'm saying all the wrong things."

"You are." She smiled but her eyes looked anything but happy.

"Please explain."

She sighed. "We've been together for nearly a year, Rob, and I think it's time we made some sort of commitment to each other."

"Commitment?" He wondered if the panic showed in his eyes.

"I'm talking about moving in together but I'm not sure it's what you want. I'm not sure you know what you want."

He stared at her, at a loss for words, and saw the pain in her eyes that his silence caused. "Vanessa . . ."

She gave him a brave smile. "Perhaps being apart for a while is a good thing; it will give you time to think."

"I'm a lousy boyfriend, aren't I?" he said, feeling like a total shit. He found it hard to lie to her; he knew he couldn't say the things that she so obviously wanted to hear. He knew he should end it here and now but that would be like a kick in the teeth. "How long will you be gone for?" he said instead.

"I'm not certain. About six months, but I'll be back for weekends," she assured him. "And you could come over and visit."

"Sure."

"Are you annoyed with me, Rob?"

"No, of course not; this is exactly the kind of lucky break you need."

"And what about you?" She searched his face. "What do you need?"

One word, one name, immediately came to his mind and he closed his eyes briefly for fear that she would somehow read his thoughts. "Right now I need sleep," he joked but when he looked at her there was a reproachful look in her eyes. "I'm sorry, Vanessa, that sounded facetious. It's just there is so much going on at the moment between work, moving, dealing with the planning office and meeting with the architects, that I find it hard to think beyond getting this damn house built."

"Of course, I understand."

But it was clear from her expression that she was hurt. He moved over to the sofa and pulled her into his arms. As they kissed, he felt her hand unzip his trousers and knew that she would be staying the night. When she pushed him back on the sofa and climbed onto his lap, he closed his eyes and tried very hard not to wish she was Marianne.

Rob slept fitfully that night. When he woke, light was creeping through the crack in the curtains. This time tomorrow he would waken in Marianne's room, in her bed; though she wouldn't be with him, the thought still excited him. He turned on his side and watched Vanessa as she slept. Why couldn't he love this woman, he wondered. She was stunning; he could picture the smiling, green-eyed, golden-haired babies she would produce. She was sleeping like an innocent, a slight smile on her lips and one arm thrown over her head exposing a large, full, beautiful breast. He studied it dispassionately, wondering why it didn't stir him the way a simple photo of a woman in a white T-shirt had.

Sitting close to Marianne on that bench, the touch of her bare arm and the scent of her hair had been enough to arouse him. When he'd kissed her and she'd returned the kiss, he had got completely carried away, moulding her against him, not giving a damn that they were in a public place and behaving like teenagers. He was getting aroused all over again now just remembering the moment. Vanessa stirred and he hurriedly slipped out of bed and headed for the shower; the one plus about this flat was that it was guaranteed to be a cold one.

Marianne stood amidst all the boxes in the narrow hallway and felt like crying. She had been stringent in her packing but still her family's belongings dwarfed the small house and there was yet another vanload to come. She noticed Dot was looking shell-shocked too.

"I'll send some of it back," she reassured her mother-in-law.

"You'll do no such thing, don't be silly. Once we've arranged everything it will be grand; the bedrooms are practically bare, waiting for you."

Marianne resolved to put as much stuff as possible in the bedrooms and sneak some of the rest back to Howth; it simply wasn't right to take over the house like this.

"It will be grand," Dot said again. "We'll be sorted in no time at all, and once the children are settled into school we'll be able to concentrate on our new jobs; I'm quite looking forward to being a working woman!"

"I'm a bit nervous to be honest," Marianne admitted.

"Ah, sure, what have you to be nervous about?"

"It's okay for you," Marianne retorted. "You'll be working from home. I'll be all over the city, teaching total strangers things I've only just learned myself."

"I think you'll make a great teacher. You're very patient and calm and that's what it's all about."

"We'll see. Rob has a manual for me to refer to if I forget anything. It's very comprehensive, every lesson for every course is covered in detail."

"Well then, how can you go wrong? I think those internet classes sound interesting; I might go to them myself."

"Planning to cruise the dating websites, eh?" Marianne teased.

"I might," she laughed. "Bridie next door is always on that Facebook thing. Is it very difficult?"

"No, from what I hear it's very straightforward; you would pick it up in no time at all. I could teach you but you would probably enjoy the classes; I think they'll be fun. Rob's going to start me off with them to introduce me slowly."

"When do I get to meet this fella?" Dot opened a box marked "Kitchen" and started to unpack it.

Marianne kept her head bent as a smile came to her lips. "I'm sure you'll meet him soon enough but I don't want to become the landlady from hell, always dropping in and out, checking up on him." She felt a tingle of excitement at the thought. They would not be working on any training courses together but Marianne just knew that she and Rob would find plenty of excuses to meet.

"No, of course not. But what if he has any problems and you're not around? I'll have to deal with him."

"I'll introduce you as soon as we've all settled in," Marianne promised, though she felt a bit uncomfortable at the thought of her ex-lover meeting her mother-in-law. Dot was such a perceptive woman too; would she pick up on the connection between them? "So when is your first job, Dot?" she asked, anxious to change the subject.

"Like your Rob, Brenda's breaking me in gently."

Marianne felt her cheeks redden at the term but Dot was too busy in her task to notice.

"She's asked me to do a couple of centrepieces for a family dinner next week and then there's a wedding the week after, though I'll just be doing the church flowers for that."

Marianne smiled at the excitement in Dot's voice. "I can't believe how well things are turning out; we're working such different hours we'll easily be able to manage the kids between us."

"No problem at all, and anytime we are stuck there are plenty of good neighbours around who would be glad to pitch in and help. You're part of a real community now, love."

Marianne wasn't sure she liked the sound of that; she valued her privacy, and although the neighbours she'd met so far seemed nice, she didn't want to be swallowed up by them. "I wouldn't be happy leaving the children with anyone else for the moment."

"They've come a long way in the last couple of weeks and starting school will be the making of them."

"I'm not so sure. Moving house and school is a big upheaval."

"Children take these things in their stride," Dot assured her. "I was thinking, perhaps we should have a little housewarming party; it would give you and them a chance to get to know everyone better."

"Don't you think we have enough to do?"

Dot chuckled. "Oh, not for a week or so and just a small do; I'd only invite a couple of neighbours and their families. I thought Andrew and Kate would feel more comfortable on their first day at school if they already had made some pals."

"That's a great idea, thanks." Not only was Dot right, she was thinking of the children's best interests whilst Marianne was getting bogged down in stupid details. She felt her eyes fill up and then Dot's hand was on her shoulder pushing her gently into a chair. "Let's have a cup of tea."

"But there's so much to do . . ."

"A few minutes won't make a bit of difference."

"I don't even know why I'm crying," Marianne said as the tears streamed down her cheeks.

"I think you have plenty of reasons," Dot said, her own eyes suspiciously bright.

"You too," Marianne said, pulling out a tissue.

"Oh, don't you worry. I've shed my fair share."

"Do you cry for Dominic?" Marianne asked.

"Of course I do, and for you and the kiddies. I can't help feeling that I let you all down."

"That's rubbish." Poor Dot, she was so brave and strong it was easy to forget that she had just lost her son and was grieving for him.

"No, I persuaded you to stay with him and to turn a blind eye to his problems. That was wrong. And now when you should finally be able to get some peace, he's still causing trouble. I tell you, if he was alive, I'd kill him!"

Marianne smiled through her tears. She was so glad that she hadn't told Dot about Barbara and the whole fraud business; it would surely destroy her. "It's history, forget it. Aren't we doing just fine, anyway?"

"We are." Dot wiped her eyes and stood up.

Marianne stood too. "We never made the tea."

"To hell with the tea. Let's get stuck in and have this place looking half-decent before the children get home.

Then when they're tucked up in bed, we'll have a glass of wine and put the world to rights."

"I think that may take more than one glass," Marianne laughed.

CHAPTER
TWENTY-SIX

Jo couldn't believe how much she was enjoying looking after Kate and Andrew while Dot and Marianne unpacked.

"I want to send most of it back to Howth but she insists we keep it," Marianne had told her that first night when she had come to collect the children, looking exhausted. "It's like trying to fit Gulliver's things into Lilliput but she insists that the children have all their possessions around them."

"Perhaps she's right," Jo had said, and then offered to look after the children for the full week.

Every day she and Rachel would take the DART to Kilbarrack to collect them and by the time they returned, Di was home from school. Her girls loved having the children around and though Greg complained about the noise levels in the house, he was always smiling when he said it.

Right now, Di was finishing a project in her room, Rachel and Kate were sprawled on the floor working on a jigsaw puzzle, and Andrew was helping Jo make brownies. There was more chocolate on the child than in the bowl but she didn't mind; he was having a ball. Marianne had warned her of his tantrums but there hadn't been one so far. Not that the child had been given a chance; her daughters had kept him so busy. Di, in particular, got a real kick out of mothering Andrew and he was wallowing in the attention.

Jo had been watching her daughter like a hawk but Di seemed to be eating normally. She'd taken them all out for an enormous lunch in the local pizzeria yesterday; Di had tucked in eagerly and there had been no trip to the ladies afterwards. Though Jo was still finding it a struggle herself, she had willed herself to eat sensibly and actually held on tight to her chair afterwards, determined to be strong.

It had taken every ounce of courage she possessed but she had finally sat down to talk to her daughter, deciding to go ahead without Greg. There was no need to involve him at this stage, she reasoned; he had enough worries and she had the situation in hand. She felt quite proud of herself for doing this alone, although she knew she wouldn't be as strong without Marianne and Helen's support.

She had waited until Greg was out one evening and Rachel had gone to bed before broaching the subject. "I want to talk to you, love, about being sick."

"I'm not sick — oh, you mean . . ." Di groaned and rolled her eyes. "Mum, I told you it's no big deal and it was the only time that I did it."

"I know and I believe you." Jo took a deep breath. "It's me I want to talk about."

Di eyed her curiously "You?"

Jo nodded. "I wanted to explain why I did it. I'll be honest, I find this embarrassing, but I just want you to understand how easy it is to develop bad and even dangerous habits."

Di said nothing but Jo could see she had her daughter's full attention. "What you have to realize is that growing up in St Anne's we were fed boring and sometimes downright awful food. What's more, we had no choice; we had to eat it whether we liked it or not."

"That's child abuse!"

Jo laughed. "That's a slight exaggeration; they had two hundred kids to feed on a very tight budget. Anyway, you can imagine how exciting it was when I left the home to be able to decide what I wanted to eat and when."

"What was your first meal?" Di grinned.

Jo didn't even have to think about it. "Fish and chips. Helen used to take Marianne and me out to tea sometimes but she could only afford beans and chips. I remember watching people digging into huge platefuls of cod in crispy batter and how my mouth would water. We got fish in St Anne's but there was no batter and it was usually slimy and tasteless."

"Yuck." Di shuddered.

"Enough to put you off for life," Jo agreed. "Having had such a plain diet, I started eating foods full of sugar and salt; I just couldn't get enough flavour."

"Did you get fat?"

"No, not immediately. I didn't have much money so I couldn't afford too many treats. After I got married I put on a little weight but it wasn't until I was pregnant with you that I started to stuff myself."

"Oh, that's right, blame me," Di said dramatically.

"Naturally." Jo smiled. "Then after you were born I was too tired to cook so we ate lots of takeaways and TV dinners; I got heavier without ever really noticing."

"So, you started to make yourself sick?"

Jo was both ashamed and relieved by her daughter's candour. "No, that started much later. I got a bad tummy bug; I was sick for a couple of weeks and just lived on water and dry crackers. I lost nearly a stone, I couldn't believe it. I had tried dieting but I had no willpower and never managed to lose more than a few pounds and then I just stumbled on this really easy way to control my weight." Jo sighed. "I owe you a lot, Di."

Her daughter looked puzzled. "Why?"

"Seeing you that day brought me to my senses, darling."

Di gave her a hug. "I'm glad, Mum."

"I've decided to join Dot's Weightwatchers class and Auntie Helen says she will too."

"That's a brilliant idea; it should be fun."

"I don't know about that. I was never one for exercise and I hate the thought of being weighed in front of everyone."

"But, Mum, everyone must feel that way."

Jo smiled; she had such a clever daughter. "You're right, and apparently, apart from the exercises, there are talks and they give you healthy recipes."

"Eating a balanced diet is the key to everything," Di informed her with a serious face. "We learned all about that in Home Economics."

"Yet you made yourself sick," Jo reminded her.

"But I didn't do it to lose weight. I did it so I wouldn't look bloated in that top."

"Promise me you'll never do it again."

"I will if you will," her daughter retorted cheekily.

Jo held her gaze and nodded. "You've got a deal. Will you help me stick to the diet and exercise plan, love?"

Jo smiled at the determined look in her daughter's eyes, that she knew so well; Di loved a challenge.

"No problem, Mum. Consider me your personal trainer!"

Jo had dreaded that first Weightwatchers class but Dot had been great. She had introduced her and Helen to a few people and to Shirley, the instructor, but kept it all very low-key, which Jo had been grateful for; she hated being the centre of attention. The weigh-in, the moment she'd dreaded, had passed in the blink of an eye and no one had paid a blind bit of notice. Shirley had given her a warm welcome and made a note of her details. Jo hadn't exactly enjoyed the exercises but they hadn't been too bad, and the talk on the dangers of eating on the go and the tricks to help you stick to the plan were very useful. She was amazed at how much she learned. The evening had flown by and she had felt much happier walking out of the hall than she had going in, and was actually looking forward to her next session.

"Aunty Jo, these are going to be the best brownies ever," Andrew told her.

"I don't doubt it," Jo smiled, not caring that there was chocolate and flour on every surface and smeared down the front of his jumper.

Di bounced into the kitchen and pulled up short at the sight that greeted her. "Wait till Dad sees this," she said, grinning broadly.

Jo glanced at the clock and groaned; it was almost six o'clock.

"Di, help Andrew finish up, love, and I'll get dinner started."

"Okay, my man, let's get these onto a baking tray and then you can stand on a chair and help me wash up."

By the time Greg walked through the door, the kitchen was spotless, the table set and a scrubbed Andrew was sitting watching *Sponge Bob* in his vest while his jumper hung on the line. Greg came straight into the kitchen, his heavy sigh making it clear he was not in a good mood.

"I thought you were on a diet?" he said to his wife when he saw her check on the oven chips.

"Hello, Dad. We're fine, Dad. Had a great day, Dad, thanks for asking," Di said, from where she was pouring milk into beakers for the three younger children.

"Don't you be so cheeky, miss."

"Mum's not on a diet, she's on a healthy-eating plan," Di told him.

"I'm not having chips," Jo told him. "I've made a salad for myself." She would eat the fried chicken she'd prepared for them but she'd soak up the grease with kitchen paper and remove the skin; one of Shirley's tips.

"You don't have to eat different meals from the family all of the time," Shirley assured them. "It's hard enough for most of us to cook one dinner a night. Eat the same meal but adapt it and always have some healthy options in the cupboard that you can dip into if necessary. But if you're caught short, simply trim all the fat off any meat, do without the sauce or gravy and reduce the portion size. And don't worry when you do fall off the wagon; it's not the end of the world. Be a little more careful the next day or increase your exercise or miss a treat. We don't believe in rigid rules and regulations, ladies; that's the sure route to failure and that's not a word we ever use here."

Jo served up the food and called the children. Andrew whooped with delight when he saw the dinner, making Greg smile. Di sat him beside her and was trying to persuade him to eat some peas, much to Jo's amusement, but she was touched by the girl's mothering instinct and relieved to see her tucking into her food. Jo didn't think she herself was out of the woods yet though. Sometimes she had to fight the urge to rush to the bathroom. She tucked into her healthy salad but found herself eyeing Kate's chips longingly. The child was sitting to her right, saying nothing and pushing the food around her plate.

"Do you not like it, love?"

"I'm just not hungry," the little girl mumbled.

"There's brownies for afters with ice cream and chocolate sauce," Di smiled at her.

"But only if you've cleared your plate," Greg said.

"It's okay, I don't want afters."

"It's fine, sweetheart, you don't have to finish if you don't want to," Jo said, shooting Greg a reproachful look. The nuns had always told her to clear her plate and much good it had done her. "Are you sick, love?" She put a hand to Kate's forehead. She was quite pale.

"She's always like this, Aunty Jo. It's 'cos Daddy's dead," Andrew said cheerfully, popping a chip covered in ketchup into his mouth.

"Shut up," Kate scowled at him.

"Don't talk to your brother like that," Greg told her.

"And she shouts and cries in her sleep," Andrew taunted.

"You little shit," Kate retorted with angry tears in her eyes.

"Kate!" Jo said as Rachel's eyes stood out on stalks and Di smothered a giggle.

"Apologize to your brother," Greg ordered.

"But he started it . . ."

"It doesn't matter. You don't call him things like that, at least not in this house."

Jo glared at him; was he implying that Marianne would tolerate such language? She put a hand on Kate's arm. "Kate, please say you're sorry. Andrew's only a baby, he doesn't know what he's saying."

"I'm not a baby!" he shouted. "I'm not!"

"Then why do you wet the bed like a baby?" Kate screamed back.

"Kate, leave the table at once," Greg ordered.

The girl jumped up and ran from the room; Rachel went to follow.

"Stay where you are and finish your dinner," Greg told her.

"I'll go," Jo said, and leaving the room and her half-eaten dinner, went in search of Kate. She found her huddled in a corner of Rachel's bedroom, crying. Jo sat down on the edge of the bed and put her hand on her silky head. "Andrew didn't mean it, darling."

"He did. I hate him." Kate hiccuped, crying noisily now.

"I know you're still sad, but your little brother is sad too."

"No, he isn't. He just pretends to be, to get toys and he does wet the bed!"

"But I bet that only started after your daddy died, didn't it?"

Kate nodded silently.

"You see, we all react in different ways, sweetheart. Your little brother is naughty sometimes because he misses your daddy. Sometimes when we're upset and we try to hide it, our bodies show it in other ways. I'll bet you anything that when Andrew starts to feel better, he will stop having accidents and being naughty. It's hard to believe right now but you will be happy again."

"You think I'll forget Daddy? I'll never ever forget Daddy, never!" Kate scrambled to her feet, ran into the bathroom and slammed the door.

Jo didn't know whether to be relieved or worried when the doorbell went. She hurried downstairs as

Rachel was about to open it. "It's okay, darling. You go and look after Kate; she's in the bathroom."

Rachel tore up the stairs as Jo opened the door.

"Hi, Jo," Marianne smiled.

Jo pushed her back out the front door and closed it. "There was a small . . . incident."

Marianne sighed. "Andrew? What's he done now?"

"Nothing much; he and Kate were squabbling and it got a little out of hand. She's a bit upset."

Marianne rested against the garden wall. "I'm told that this is all normal behaviour and I do prefer anger to silence; that makes me feel so helpless. Tomorrow I'll take her out just the two of us. Perhaps we could visit the grave."

"Is that a good idea?"

"Apparently so, and maybe it will help her to talk. It's late; I'd better take them home."

Just then, Rachel and Kate appeared in the doorway. Marianne opened her arms and her daughter rushed into them and buried her face in her mother's breast.

Jo swallowed back tears. "I'll go and get Andrew," she said, and steered Rachel back inside.

CHAPTER
TWENTY-SEVEN

Helen was ironing Johnny's shirt when Colm walked in. He was wearing only boxers and made straight for the fridge. "Where's Dad?" he asked, before putting the carton of orange juice to his lips.

Where indeed, Helen thought. "No idea. I wish you wouldn't do that."

"He hasn't forgotten, has he?" Colm said, looking over at her and frowning.

"I'm sure he hasn't." Helen forced a smile. It was only the Charity Dinner at the golf club; not that important in the scheme of things but yet more evidence that Johnny's thoughts were elsewhere. He would never have forgotten such a date before . . .

"Did you phone him, Mum?"

When Colm looked cross he was the image of his father. "It doesn't start for an hour," she reminded him. "I'm sure he's on his way."

"One way to find out." Colm reached for the phone.

"Leave it."

"No." He grunted in annoyance. "It's gone straight to voicemail. Dad, have you forgotten it's the Charity Dinner? You need to get a move on, okay? Cheers." He hung up. "You're right, he's probably on his way and is just on a call."

"That will be it. So, what are you doing tonight?"

"Studying. What else?" He grinned. "And then Fergal's coming over to watch the Leinster game with me."

"Fine, but I don't want to come home and find you passed out drunk," she said only half-joking. Colm liked a beer and she didn't object to the odd one or two; better to let him drink at home than on a deserted beach or a street corner where he could get into real trouble. She was careful never to have too much of it in the house and thankfully, like his father, it would never really occur to Colm to actually go out and buy his own. Fergal, though, would probably arrive with a six-pack.

"Of course not, mother darling . . ." Colm broke off as they heard a key in the door.

"Sorry I'm late," Johnny breezed in, smiling. "You look lovely, Helen. I'll take a shower and be ready in twenty minutes."

She held his shirt out to him. "Here."

"You are the perfect wife," he said, kissing her cheek, and as he ran upstairs Helen felt quite tearful.

"Mum? Are you okay?"

"Absolutely fine," Helen said, quickly unplugging the iron and setting it on the worktop. "Put the board away for me, Colm, would you? I need to do something."

As she'd expected, Johnny had left his phone with his keys on the hall table; she took it and went into the study, then closed the door and started to scroll through his text messages. Nothing incriminating at all, and yet she knew in her heart that there was something going on. He forgot that she knew his schedule better than he did and there were too many gaps that he hadn't been able — or hadn't bothered — to explain, and most damning of all, the day he'd said he was going to see Christy Kennedy, it had been a downright lie. She'd never have known, only Bev, Christy's wife, had called that vey night for a heart-to-heart, worried about her husband and had ended the call asking if Johnny would call in when he had a chance. Helen had let a couple of days go by before leaving a note for Johnny passing on Bev's message. He hadn't commented on it since and neither had she.

She went out into the hall, put the phone back with the keys, and went upstairs to finish getting ready. Johnny was fumbling with his cufflinks as she walked into the bedroom. "Here, let me do that."

"Thanks, darling. I do love these; they were a wonderful present."

"I'm glad you like them."

"You should wear red more often," he smiled down at her. "Why do women wear so much black?"

"No idea." She crossed to the dressing table, opened her jewellery box and took out her thick gold choker.

Johnny took it from her and fastened it around her throat before kissing her neck. Helen shivered as she always did.

"Don't be long," he said, heading for the door, and she listened as he went downstairs whistling.

318

She stared at her poised reflection in the mirror, wondered if anyone else would notice her misery. She put a hand to the nape of her neck where he'd kissed her and closed her eyes. It never ceased to amaze her that, after all these years, a kiss or even a look from Johnny could send tingles down her spine. Right now she resented it. How could he smile at her and kiss her and behave as if everything was fine when he was seeing someone else? She had gone over it and over it until she'd nearly lost her mind, and it was the only thing that made sense. Marianne. The woman he was spending most of his time with at the moment; her best friend. She'd thought fleetingly of letting Jo in on her suspicions but it went against every fibre of her being to run to others with her problems; everyone turned to her. She was the sensible, practical and dependable one. And she was happy to play a supporting role because while her friends depended on her, she depended on Johnny; he was her rock. What would she do if she couldn't trust him any more? What would she do if he said he didn't love her any more?

"Helen, come on, we'll be late."

She looked up to see him standing in the doorway and forced a smile. "Coming."

"This is nice." Marianne smiled at her daughter as they strolled along the beach at Dollymount. "We used to take you here all the time when you were little. Do you remember?"

Kate nodded.

"Daddy used to chase you up and down the sand dunes and then the two of you would come sliding down them; I used to give out hell because the sand would get in your socks and shorts, even in your pants; there would be sand all over the house for days."

Kate wrinkled her nose. "Yuck, I wouldn't do that now; sand makes me itchy."

They walked in silence for a moment and then Kate bent to pick up a shell. "I wish he'd never got that job. Everything got bad after that."

Marianne was startled by the remark. "That's not true, darling. We moved to a nice new house, you started school and Andrew was born."

"Duh, exactly." Kate rolled her eyes like a sullen teenager. "The house was cool but there were no kids to play with, Andrew just bawled all the time and Dad was never around."

Marianne was about to tackle each point and then she realized that the last was the only one that counted; she had to draw Kate out about her father. Her GP, Mandy, had said it was important to talk frankly and not to avoid the issue.

"Don't dress it up, don't romanticize it and, above all, don't avoid answering questions," the doctor had told her. "Whatever you say will be much less frightening than what Kate is probably imagining right now."

Feeling that this might be one of the most important conversations she ever had with her daughter, Marianne paused for a moment, choosing her words carefully. "Let me explain about promotion, Kate," she

320

explained. "That's when you get a more important job and get paid more money for doing it. You only get promoted if you are really good at your job. The problem is that, although it's a reward for your hard work, it usually means you have to work even harder. It was probably silly of me, but I thought that because Daddy spent so much time at the office, you wouldn't miss him as much now."

"But I always knew he was coming home, Mum."

Marianne looked down into the dark eyes that held an expression too old for a nine-year-old. How she had underestimated the depth of her daughter's pain. It really didn't matter how much Dominic had hurt her, as far as Kate was concerned, he was her daddy. "Are you cross that he's never coming back?"

Kate glanced at her. "Do you mean cross with God?"

Marianne shrugged, yet again struck by her daughter's maturity. "With anyone, I suppose."

Kate thought about it for a moment. "I think I'm cross with everyone, but with God most of all. You said he took Daddy to heaven early because he was special but that doesn't make sense; there are lots of seriously special people in the world. Why didn't he take Nelson Mandela? He's super-special and seriously old."

"You are clever," Marianne smiled.

"So you don't think that's why he died?"

Marianne looked into her daughter's eyes and, with Mandy's words ringing in her ears, she shook her head. "No, darling. I think he died because he worked too hard and didn't look after himself properly."

"I bet he ate lots of rubbish when he was out," Kate said, "and drank too much beer."

"I think you're probably right."

"Then I'm cross with him too," Kate scowled. They walked in silence for a moment then Kate bent to pick up a stone and skipped it across the water. "Mum?"

"Yes?"

"I'm angry at my friends as well."

Marianne looked at her in alarm. Surely not more bullying? "Why, sweetheart?"

Kate turned her miserable eyes up to meet Marianne's. "Because they have dads."

"Oh, darling." Marianne hugged her close and stroked her long, beautiful hair. "That makes perfect sense to me." They stayed like that for a moment and then Kate pulled back and looked up at her.

"Are you cross, Mum?"

"I'm a little cross with Daddy," Marianne answered honestly, "and for much the same reasons as you, but I try to remember the good times we had together." She waved a hand towards the sand dunes. "Like the fun we had here."

"I loved our last holiday in Spain."

Marianne smiled. That had been a good holiday; Dominic had seemed calmer and, always a good swimmer, had spent a lot of time playing with the children in the pool or dodging waves with them in the sea. She could still remember their excited squeals. "Remember when you were flying the kite and it fell into the water?"

"Oh, yes!" Kate grinned. "It got all tangled up in that man's feet on the airbed and he was snoring his brains out; Daddy was trying to get it back without waking him but Andrew couldn't stop giggling and I had to drag him away."

"What about when Daddy insisted that Andrew try some squid?" Marianne groaned.

"Eww, yes!" Kate screwed up her face in disgust. "He spat it out all over the table. He really is a little monster."

"Yeah, but he's *our* little monster." Marianne put her arm around her daughter's shoulders as they walked on. "He misses Daddy too."

"That's what Aunty Jo said." Kate stopped and looked guiltily up at her mother. "I told everyone about him wetting the bed yesterday."

"So I heard."

"Sorry."

"I think it's him you should say sorry to. I know he was winding you up, and I realize he is annoying, darling, but will you try to be more patient? We have to look after each other now."

"Okay."

"You know, I think we should do something really fun this weekend."

Kate looked at her. "Like what?"

Oh, I don't know. Maybe something we used to do with Daddy."

"Let's go to a carnival!"

Marianne pretended to look horrified. "Oh no, you know I'm scared stiff of those rides!"

"Oh, go on, Mum, please?" Kate begged.

"Oh, okay, then," Marianne agreed with an exaggerated groan. "But I refuse to go on a rollercoaster; you can go on that with your granny."

Kate grinned. "Yeah, Granny loves all the scary stuff."

"I'm so glad that Andrew is scared of heights too. I can stay with my feet firmly on the ground with him while you and Granny go and scare yourselves silly!"

"You're such a wimp, Mummy."

"I am," Marianne laughed. "Now let's go home. I don't know about you but I'm bloody freezing."

"Mummy!" Kate giggled.

"That just slipped out," Marianne said with a complicit grin. "Don't you dare tell your brother."

As they headed back to the car, Kate's arm tight around her waist, Marianne felt a sense of peace now that her daughter was finally talking openly and honestly with her. She could cope with any financial fallout once her children were okay, no problem at all.

CHAPTER
TWENTY-EIGHT

Rob wandered around the house, too nervous to sit down. Although they had talked on the phone and exchanged emails and texts, this would be the first time that Marianne had visited him since he'd moved in; the first time he'd seen her since that kiss by the canal. He couldn't help feeling excited. His eyes went involuntarily to the fridge where her picture had been; God, he wished she'd left that behind. Still, she would be here, in the flesh, today. The thought of taking her in his arms and kissing her again thrilled him. He felt sure she would respond. But was he moving too fast? If he rushed her she might decide not to work for him and think he'd only offered her the job in order to get his hands on her. Which was true but in a much deeper way. It wasn't just Marianne's body he wanted, it was the whole package.

Which reminded him of Vanessa, who he hardly even thought of these days. They talked a couple of times a week and she sent him regular messages on Facebook, but his responses were brief and infrequent.

When they had first got together, Rob had found it very sexy to have a woman phone him from her bedroom and tell him what she was or wasn't wearing, but now it just made him uncomfortable. Now when she did it he made some excuse to get off the phone and called her back when she was in the office. She hadn't commented on this which he took as a good sign; hopefully she was enjoying herself too much to notice. With a bit of luck, she'd become completely immersed in her new life and soon forget him. It was the coward's way out but he really didn't want to be the one to end the relationship and hurt her.

The doorbell rang and he hurried to let Marianne in.

"Hello!" She smiled shyly.

"Hi." He stood back to let her in, struck as always by her elegance though she was simply dressed in a white shirt, jeans and flat shoes. Her dark hair was loose and almost to her waist; he had to clench his fists to stop himself reaching out to touch it. "It must feel strange coming back to your own house as a visitor."

"A little."

"You can use your key if you want . . ."

"Oh, no, that would be wrong." She seemed horrified by the idea.

"Tea?" he asked.

"Please."

He led the way into the kitchen. So much for things being more relaxed. They were behaving like strangers. "So, are you settling in okay?" He filled the kettle, glad to have something to do with his hands.

"Yes, we're getting there. I have a few boxes in the car that I'd like to store in the garage — if that's all right with you, of course."

"I already told you, it's fine." They were speaking regularly, having some lovely long chats, catching up on the last couple of years and yet now she seemed so formal; was she regretting letting him get close again?

"Thanks. Dot's house is so much smaller and I hate taking over the place."

"Do you think she minds?" He had never met Dot Thomson and knew little about her; Marianne had only ever really talked about the children.

"No, she's just so glad to be home again she could cope with anything."

"And the children? Didn't they mind leaving all this?" he gestured around the large airy kitchen and the enormous garden beyond it.

"No." She walked over to the window and stared out. "I thought the last day here would be hard but they walked out without a backwards glance. It just goes to show that we attach more importance to these things than kids do."

To hell with this, he thought, and went to stand behind her. "I'm so glad you're here." He ran a finger lightly down her arm. Marianne didn't turn around, didn't even say a word, she simply leaned back into him and let her head rest against his shoulder. He wrapped his arms around her waist and felt her tremble.

"Oh, Rob." She turned her head to look up at him.

He almost gasped at the warmth in her eyes and with a groan he bent his head to kiss her. She turned and wrapped her arms around his neck. He pulled away, and when she opened her eyes she seemed dazed for a moment and then she smiled. "I've missed you, Marianne. I've missed you so much."

"I've missed you too," she whispered before guiding his mouth back to hers and kissing him hungrily. Rob let his hands run over her body, reacquainting himself with its contours as she seemed to melt into him; it was as if they had never been apart. He stepped back and looked into her eyes. "I want you, Marianne."

"I want you too," she said, sounding slightly breathless.

He took her hand, led her out of the room and towards the stairs, pausing to take her in his arms for another kiss.

"There's something I have to tell —" She froze as the doorbell rang.

"Ignore it," he murmured, but looking over her head he saw Vanessa's distinctive outline through the mottled glass. "Oh shit, sorry. I have to answer that."

"That's okay. Why don't I wait in the office? I am supposed to be here to work," she joked.

"Yes, good idea. I won't be long."

The doorbell rang again and Vanessa called out. "Rob? Are you in there? This is a fine welcome home!"

He could have cried as he watched Marianne's smile disappear and a shutter come down. "Look, Marianne —"

"I think you should let her in, don't you?" she said, and pushing past him, went into the office and closed the door.

"Fuck," Rob muttered and straightening his clothes he opened the door. "Vanessa!"

328

"About time too. What on earth were you doing?" She dropped her rather large overnight bag at his feet and stood on tiptoes to kiss him.

"Sorry, I was on a call."

"I thought I heard voices."

"Yes, my new IT instructor is here. He nodded towards the office door. "We're actually in the middle of a meeting."

"Go and finish your meeting; I can wait." She kissed him again. "Upstairs if you like."

He tried to smile though he felt more like crying. "Sorry, that's not possible; there's a class due in an hour," he lied.

She looked at him. "Are you throwing me out?"

"No, of course not, I've got time for a quick coffee." He led the way through to the kitchen. "You should have let me know that you were coming."

"It was a last-minute thing. I was supposed to be at a conference today but it was postponed so I decided to come to Dublin for a long weekend. Wow, this is nice!" She ran her fingers along the shiny, black granite worktop and then left it to go to the window. "Very nice."

He said nothing as he made her coffee, wondering how to get rid of her; there was no way she was staying the night let alone for the full weekend. He carried the mug over to her and then went back to lean on the counter to drink his own, anxious to keep some distance between them. In the unlikely event of Marianne walking in, he didn't want her to see Vanessa hanging off him. "How's your mum? She must be delighted you're home."

"I haven't told her I'm here," Vanessa admitted. "I only have a couple of days and I wanted to spend them with you."

"I'm sorry, Vanessa, that's impossible; I'm completely tied up."

"You don't work twenty-four hours a day," she protested. "Anyway, I'm tired so I'll be quite content to relax and enjoy your gorgeous new pad and be here waiting for you when you get home."

"That's just the thing; I'm running a weekend training course right here," he said, surprised at how easily the lies came to him. "You'll have to stay with your mum. I'll take you out to dinner tomorrow night if you like."

"I've come all the way from London to see you, and all I get is one lousy dinner?" She looked at him, incredulous.

"It's hardly my fault. You should have given me some notice," he said, hearing the edge in his voice and hating himself for it.

Vanessa reddened. "I'm sorry, I didn't think it would be a big deal." She stood up and made for the door.

"Vanessa, wait. I'm sorry for being so abrupt; you just took me by surprise, that's all." Well, that was at least the truth!

Immediately she turned and smiled, relief in her eyes. "It's okay, I should have called and let you know I was coming. Have you got time to at least give me a tour?"

"Sure." As he took her around the house, he rehearsed how he'd introduce her to Marianne. It would be obvious that Vanessa was his girlfriend but so what? He was thirty-one years old; wouldn't it be odd if he didn't have a partner? Only he knew, in his heart, that what would bother Marianne was that he hadn't told her. He needed to stay calm, get rid of Vanessa as quickly as possible and reassure Marianne that Vanessa wasn't important. In fact no woman he'd ever been with was important. They all paled into insignificance next to Marianne. She was the only woman he'd ever loved, the woman he still loved. And now that he'd found her again he had no intention of letting her go a second time.

Feeling decidedly uncomfortable showing Vanessa around Marianne's house, especially with the woman herself sitting in the office, he breezed from room to room, hesitating at the door of the master bedroom. If Vanessa had arrived ten or fifteen minutes later, he wouldn't have heard the door, never mind have answered it, and he'd be making love to Marianne right now.

He left the office until last and, pausing outside the door, he turned to Vanessa. "I should explain: Marianne, my new instructor, is the woman who owns this house. It turns out she needed a job and she's a perfect replacement for Shay."

"That was lucky," Vanessa said, but her eyes had clouded over.

"Yes, let me introduce you," he said with forced cheeriness, and with a brief knock on the door, led her into the room. Marianne was sitting at his desk, reading through the course notes on Facebook. "Hi, Marianne, how are you getting on?"

She looked up and smiled politely. "Okay, thanks."

"Sorry I've kept you waiting . . ."

"No problem."

"This is Vanessa; Vanessa this is Marianne Thomson, my landlady."

Marianne stood up and stretched out her hand to shake Vanessa's. "Pleased to meet you."

"And you."

Vanessa smiled but Rob could see her sizing up Marianne. His mobile rang and he looked at the display and could have screamed. It was the planning officer that he'd been chasing for days; he couldn't afford not to take the call. "Sorry, excuse me for a minute." With a huge sense of foreboding, he stepped outside, dreading the thought of what might be said in his absence.

Vanessa perched on the arm of a chair. "It must seem odd to have left your home and now be working in it."

"Yes, a little," Marianne agreed, feeling sick with jealousy at the sight of the girl's pretty face, voluptuous figure and gorgeous legs.

"I'm delighted that Rob has finally found a replacement for Shay; it will allow us to spend more time together."

"That's nice," Marianne croaked.

"You have a fabulous home."

"Thank you."

"I want to reassure you that we will take care of it." Vanessa gave a conspiratorial smile. "Rob's reasonably well house-trained."

Marianne struggled to return the smile. "Good to know."

"It's great for us to be so near the site; I am really excited at the thought of watching our home being built brick by brick."

"I'm sure that will be a wonderful experience," Marianne said, tempted to punch her smug face.

"Rob wanted to get married this year but I said it was madness. Just imagine trying to plan a wedding as well. Much better to concentrate on getting the house of our dreams built first."

"Makes sense," Marianne agreed, feeling positively sick.

Rob returned to the room. "Sorry about that."

"No problem, I should go anyway and let you two get back to work." Vanessa kissed him and smiled into his eyes. "See you later, darling."

When Rob came back into the office and sat on the edge of the desk next to her, Marianne immediately moved her chair as far away as possible.

"That was terrible timing, although I suppose it could have been worse," he grinned.

"Oh, I think it was perfect timing," she said.

"What do you mean?"

"We were about to do something and for all the wrong reasons."

"Wrong reasons?"

"It's natural, I suppose, that we should remember our past with fondness and it would be easy to slip back into an affair but it would be very wrong and make it impossible for us to work together."

He stared at her. "So, did I imagine that kiss, the way you looked at me, the way you said 'oh, Rob' just like you used to?"

Marianne shrugged and managed to produce what she hoped was a nonchalant smile. "No, but, hey, I'm only human. Seriously, though, Rob, it's not possible to turn back the clock and I don't honestly think I'd want to." She got some pleasure from the stunned look on his face. How could he have strung her along like this?

"I hope you're not saying this because of Vanessa. She is my girlfriend but only because I've been too cowardly to finish it. She's a lovely girl —"

"Yes, she is and you would be mad to give her up, especially for me."

He reached out and gently pulled Marianne's chair closer until her face was only inches from his. "It's over with Vanessa regardless of what you decide, Marianne."

She steeled herself to hold his gaze and tried desperately not to inhale the scent of him. "I think that's a shame."

"I don't believe you. I think you would find it hard to see me with another woman."

"Probably," she admitted, realizing it was pointless to lie. "But I'd get over it. Things have changed, Rob. I'm a different person now. I have two children to look after; two children who are grieving for their dad and

334

completely dependent on me. They are all that's important to me now."

"You don't have to do it alone, Marianne." He threaded his fingers through hers and stared at their hands entwined before looking back up into her eyes. "I've missed you so much."

Marianne felt herself weaken and then she remembered the lovely Vanessa. "It's too late, Rob." He was building a home with the girl, he'd proposed to her; how could he dismiss her so easily and why, in all their chats, had he never even mentioned her? She tried to pull away from him but he wouldn't release her hand.

"You came here today knowing that we would end up in bed together, and that's where we'd be right now if it hadn't been for the interruption."

"How can you call your girlfriend an interruption?" she said, disgusted with him.

"Stop reading things into my words," he protested. "You know I didn't mean it like that. I don't understand why you're being like this. You're saying we shouldn't be together because of my soon-to-be-ex-girlfriend, yet you were happy to have an affair when you were a married woman."

"It's not the same at all and if you can't see that then you're blind." She pulled her hand free and got up to leave.

"Marianne?"

She paused and turned slightly, but she couldn't look into his eyes, afraid her resolve would weaken.

"Fine." He sighed. "If it's what you really want, I'll be your tenant, you can be my employee and we'll leave it at that."

"That's what I want." It was completely irrational but she felt gutted that he was ready to give up on her so easily.

"Then that's the way it will be." He led the way out to the front door and held it open for her. "See you here at nine o'clock on Monday morning."

"I'll be here. Bye, Rob."

CHAPTER
TWENTY-NINE

Jo was about to leave the community centre after the Weight-watchers class when Shirley beckoned her over.

"I'll be out in a minute," Jo told Dot and Helen and crossed to the instructor.

"I won't keep you, Joanna, I was just wondering how you got on this week? You sounded very down when you phoned me."

"I was, and there were a few times when I weakened and ate more than I should and went into the bathroom fully intending to . . . well, you know." Jo had baulked when Marianne suggested she should come clean and tell the fitness instructor everything, but it had been the best thing she could have done. Now whenever she felt weak or panicky, Shirley was just a phone call or a text away. She'd only contacted her twice but the woman's soothing voice and common sense were enough to give her the strength to go on.

"But you didn't." Shirley smiled.

"No, whenever I walk into that bathroom I think of my daughter and that's enough to stop me."

"How is Di?"

"She seems fantastic and since we've started seeing more of Dot's grandchildren she's blossomed."

"Do you think she's eating properly?"

"She is, and she's determined to make us all eat healthier and get fitter too. I get interrogated every day: have I done my exercises? What have I eaten? And she is always dragging me out for walks and now she is even pestering her father to give up salt."

Shirley laughed. "Good for her. Are you finding it hard to keep to the exercise programme?"

"I must admit, it is a little boring," Jo said, "but I enjoy the walks."

"Good. Make sure they're brisk ones. What about swimming?"

"Doing lengths is so dull," Jo complained.

"Forget lengths," Shirley told her. "Take the children with you and perhaps a beach ball and simply have fun; that way you're all getting exercise and the kids will love it."

Jo knew she was right. If she told Rachel that they were going swimming together, she'd be over the moon; she could even take along Kate and Andrew and make it a proper outing. "That's a great idea, Shirley. I'll definitely do that."

"Good. I'll see you next week and remember, any problems just call me."

"Thanks a million."

"Swimming?" Marianne said when she'd doled out sparkling water to Dot and Jo. Yet again Helen had only popped her head in for a minute and then had to rush off; she seemed to be very busy these days. "I think that's a great idea; Andrew and Kate would love it."

338

"So where will we take them?"

"You could go to the National Aquatic centre in Blanchardstown; it's supposed to be a wonderful place for the kiddies," Dot said.

"Will you come?" Jo asked.

"I will not! Getting into a bath is the nearest I ever get to swimming."

"We can arrange other outings," Jo said. "It doesn't have to be just swimming."

"That would be great but we can't go too mad," Marianne cautioned. "We're far from rich."

"There are plenty of things to do in Dublin that cost little or nothing if you use your imagination," Dot assured her. "If the weather is good you can go to the beach or the Botanic Gardens or take a picnic up to Newbridge or Ardgillan House — the playgrounds there are wonderful and the grounds are perfect for a nice walk."

"We could even take a barbecue," Jo said. "Every time the sun comes out, one of my neighbours meets up with all the aunties, uncles and cousins and they spend the day together."

"And during the summer we could go to the festivals in the city centre," Dot said.

"What festivals?" Marianne asked her.

"There are lots. In June there's one with street performers. I went with Bridie last year; it was great fun and the children would love it."

"And we can take them on the train to Greystones or up to Donabate," Jo said, warming to the idea.

"We could go lots of places on the train," Dot said. "it's not that expensive."

"And when the weather is bad I suppose there are always the museums," Marianne mused.

"And the morning movies in the cinemas are quite cheap so we could go mad and do that from time to time," Jo said.

"It all sounds great," Marianne said. "We must ask Helen to come along."

Dot's eyes lit up. "Do you know what? If we all got together we could take a house somewhere in the summer months for a week or two and it wouldn't cost much at all."

"Oh, that's a great idea," Jo said. "Greg was only just saying that he'll probably be too busy to take time off for a holiday."

"He could join us at weekends," Marianne said. "Wow, it looks like we're in for a full summer!"

"I would love us to spend more time together," Jo said. She just knew that it would be easier sticking to her new regime with her friends around her. "I don't know why we haven't, to be honest."

"It will be a challenge to arrange holidays with us both working," Marianne said to Dot.

"True but if we book a place near a train station we could commute if and when we needed to. Do you know what sort of hours you'll be working yet?"

"At first I'll be only working in the evenings. Rob is still putting together the summer schedule but I should know the dates in a week or so and he says if there's a problem he can usually step in once I give him some notice."

"That's decent of him. What's he like?" Jo asked. She felt a little jealous of Marianne becoming part of the workforce.

"He's very nice, easy to get along with and tidy thankfully, so the house should be in safe hands."

Jo rolled her eyes. "But what does he look like?"

"She is rubbish on the detail, isn't she?" Dot agreed, eyes twinkling.

Marianne laughed. "He's around my age, probably a little taller than Greg, quite athletic and he has brown hair and eyes."

"He sounds like perfect toy-boy material," Dot winked at Jo.

"Hard luck, Dot — he's getting married next year and I met his fiancée. She's gorgeous."

"Ah, but he hasn't met *me* yet," her mother-in-law pointed out. "Younger men like me." Dot settled back in her chair and gave a wistful sigh. "I'll always remember the Pope's visit in 1979 . . . I met the most gorgeous man."

Marianne frowned. "Eh, weren't you were a married woman in 1979?"

"So? Just because you're on a diet doesn't mean you can't look at the menu, does it?"

Jo laughed. "True enough. So, what happened?"

"A few neighbours got together and arranged a minibus to take us into Phoenix Park for the Mass. There were so many people going that we had to get up at the crack of dawn to get to our places in time. Well, the driver was a fine specimen altogether. And as I was climbing up into the bus he was eyeing up my legs. Excuse me," she added when she saw Marianne's look of disbelief, "I was only thirty-one and I had great legs!"

"You still do," Jo assured her.

"Thank you, pet. Well, anyway, he stuck with us for the day and I shared our picnic with him. I'll always remember him saying he'd never tasted scones as nice as mine."

"Sounds like it was more than your scones he was after," Marianne laughed.

"I'm telling you! He spent the day making eyes at me and flirting. Bill never even noticed. And then it was time for the Pope to go around between the corrals to give us his blessing. Well, naturally, we were all pushing closer to the barrier to get a better look at the Holy Father and the next thing I know, this fella is behind me and pressing right into me."

"Oh my God. What did you do?" Jo asked.

Dot smiled. "Well, just for a few minutes, I settled back and enjoyed it."

"Dot!" Marianne looked at her mother-in-law in astonishment.

"Oh, for goodness' sake, it was just a bit of innocent fun," Dot protested.

"So . . . what happened?" Jo asked.

"Well . . ."

"Yes?" Marianne prompted.

342

"When he helped me back into the minibus he squeezed my hand and I squeezed his back. There, I've admitted it. Now I'm going to hell," Dot grinned.

"I think you're safe," Jo laughed. "I love that story. It's nice to be made to feel attractive from time to time."

"That sounds like the voice of experience," Marianne teased her friend. "Have you any stories you want to share?"

"Unfortunately not. I don't think any man has ever flirted with me."

"Oh, I'm sure they have; you probably just didn't notice," Dot told her with a kind smile.

"Perhaps." Jo said, but she knew it wasn't true. Greg was the only man who'd ever shown any interest in her and she had a feeling lately that he probably regretted it. "So," she said brightly, "where will we go for our first outing?"

Helen sat in the sitting room staring blankly at the TV, her mind upstairs with her husband. After all the strange behaviour and unexplained absences there had been yet another development. She had hurried home from Weightwatchers, reheated the curry she'd made earlier and opened a bottle of wine. While the food warmed she took a shower and then put on the silk pyjamas that Johnny loved so much; he was a very tactile sort of man. With Colm out studying with his friend, she planned to drag Johnny straight up to bed once they'd eaten and after they made love she would ask him outright what was going on.

But when Johnny arrived home he hadn't commented on her appearance. In fact, he hadn't even seemed to notice. He ate sparingly, refused a drink and then had indeed gone straight to bed but pleading a headache. She wasn't sure whether to feel worried, angry or rejected but there was most definitely something wrong, and she was sure it had something to do with Marianne Thomson.

CHAPTER
THIRTY

Dot pulled up outside the school in Howth to collect the children. She was just getting out of the car when her mobile phone rang. She looked at the display but didn't recognize the number. "Hello?"

"Hello, Mrs Thomson?"

"Yes."

"This is Rob Lee. I hope I haven't got you at a bad time."

"Oh, hello! No, not at all, it's fine. Nice to talk to you at last."

"And you," he said. "I have a problem, I'm afraid. I tried to get hold of Marianne and Johnny Sheridan but both of their phones are switched off and so I'm bothering you."

"Don't worry about it; how can I help?"

"Well, the thing is — I'm outside the house and I've locked the car keys and the house keys in the car so I'm a bit stuck. I was hoping you might have a spare set."

"I do, of course, right here on my key ring." Dot looked at it and smiled as she talked to him. "I'll drop them in to you as soon as I've collected the children from school."

"Oh, no, please don't go to any trouble. I'll get a taxi to Kilbarrack."

"No need, love. I'm just down the road."

"Well, that is good news, thank you so much."

"I'll be with you in ten to fifteen minutes at the most."

When Dot told the children there was an errand of mercy to run, their interest was immediately piqued.

"How did he lock himself out of the house and his car, Granny?" Kate asked, her expression clearly showing that she thought he must be an eejit.

"No idea, luvvie. You can ask him that yourself."

Minutes later she pulled up outside the house to see a handsome young man sitting on the garden wall, a sheepish smile on his face. He immediately hopped down and came to meet her.

"Hello, Mrs Thomson. I'm so sorry for dragging you up here."

"You didn't drag me anywhere; didn't I tell you I was just down the road? And, please, call me Dot."

"Well, Dot, thank you. I really appreciate it."

Andrew scrambled out of the car. "What's your name?" he demanded.

Rob hunkered down and smiled. "My name's Rob and you're Kate, right?"

"No!" Andrew giggled. "That's Kate." He pointed as his sister climbed out of the car, a reluctant smile on her lips.

"Ah, of course, silly me. In that case you must be Andrew."

"I am."

346

"How did you lock yourself out of your car and the house?" Kate asked.

"Well, I was putting my fishing gear in the boot and I put down my keys inside. I had closed the boot before I realized my mistake. Stupid, wasn't I?"

"Yep," Andrew agreed.

"Don't be so rude, young man," Dot told him.

Andrew ignored her. "Are you going fishing now?"

"I am. Are you a fisherman, Andrew?" The little boy shook his head. "You should try it sometime; it's great craic."

Dot handed Rob her bunch of keys. "Well, this gets you into the house but what about the car?"

"I've a spare set inside."

"Ah, grand."

He opened the door and handed her back the keys. "I can't thank you enough, will you come in and have a drink? Or how about an ice cream?"

"Not at all. You go and enjoy your fishing."

"Ah, sure the fish aren't going anywhere and I fancy an ice cream."

"Please, Granny?" Andrew put on his sweetest, most plaintive expression.

"Ah, well, go on then," she agreed.

"Do you have kids?" Kate asked.

"No, why?" Rob asked.

Kate gestured at the three flavours of ice cream, chocolate sauce, strawberry syrup, wafers and cones.

He grinned. "My sister's two boys come to visit and they love ice cream, but to be honest, I'm a bit of an addict myself."

"Can I make my own?" Andrew asked.

"Sure, let's get you set up here." Rob lifted him on to a stool and arranged everything around him.

"He'll make an awful mess," Kate told him.

"He always does."

"Do not," Andrew protested.

"I'll help," Rob smiled at her. "What would you like?"

"Just a vanilla cone, please."

"Ah, you have simple tastes. What about your granny? I'm guessing she's a strawberry and chocolate fan."

Kate's eyes widened. "How did you know that?"

He tapped the side of his nose and whispered, "I could tell you but then I'd have to *keeel* you."

Kate giggled.

"He knows from looking at the size of me that I eat anything put in front of me," Dot laughed.

"Get out of that," Rob retorted. "You're no size at all."

"In that case, make mine a large one with all the trimmings," Dot smiled, enjoying the man's easy company and his relaxed manner with the children.

"How old are your nephews?" Andrew asked.

"Christopher is eight and Jonathan is four. They will be up to visit me next week; you can come and play with them if you want."

"Cool. Then we can play on the trampoline and swings again," Andrew said with a delighted grin.

"Why don't you talk to your sister about it first?" Dot suggested. The woman might not want two strange kids visiting and she didn't want Andrew and Kate to end up disappointed. "Now, we should make a move and let you go fishing."

"But I'm not finished yet," Kate protested.

"Don't worry, I'm in no rush; there's more chance of catching a fish if the sun is going down."

"Do you have a boat?" Andrew asked.

"No, I fish from the pier or the rocks."

"What do you catch in Howth?" Dot asked.

"Pollack or whiting usually. It's a bit early in the season, but as it's the first free time I've had in a while, I thought I'd give it a go."

"My husband, God rest him, used to take my son."

"Daddy went fishing?" Andrew scowled. "He never took us."

"Well, it was when he was little," Dot explained. "He'd probably forgotten how."

"No, he was just too busy; he was always too busy," Kate mumbled, her face dark.

"I'm afraid that's what happens when you grow up," Rob told her. "I hardly ever get a chance to do the things I'd like."

"Have you brought your nephews fishing?" Kate demanded.

"A couple of times," Rob admitted, shooting Dot an apologetic look.

She shook her head. "It is sad that you didn't get to do more with your daddy, love, but we have a grand summer planned; you won't have time to turn around you're going to be so busy."

"But will we be going fishing?" Andrew asked.

"Well, I don't know how to fish myself," Dot admitted, "but I suppose I could learn."

"If you want, you can come down with me now and I can give the three of you a quick lesson," Rob offered.

"Ah, no, love. It's very kind of you but we won't intrude on your nice peaceful afternoon."

"Honestly, I'd enjoy the company."

"Can we?" Kate asked eagerly.

"Please, Granny," Andrew begged.

She looked at the eager faces of the children. It was really unfair to this poor lad; he was probably just being polite but she found it hard to resist the kiddies. "Okay, but just for a little while and you'll only be able to watch; if I take you home soaking your mother will murder me."

"Ah, I think I can help there." Rob stood up. "Come on." He led them through the connecting door to the garage and after checking in a couple of boxes, found what he was looking for. "Here we go." He drew out two sets of red wellies and two nets.

"Cool!" Andrew's eyes lit up in delight.

Kate sighed. "They won't fit me; I'm almost ten."

"Try them on; Christopher's a big lad."

The children tugged off their shoes and put on the wellies.

"They fit," Kate said, her eyes lighting up in delight. "But what about our uniforms?"

"You're not going swimming, are you?" Dot said. "Anyway, one more day and you won't need them any more."

350

"Wait." Rob rummaged in the box again and pulled out two windcheaters. "These will keep you reasonably clean and dry."

"I don't suppose you have anything in my size?" Dot joked.

He grinned. "I'm afraid not."

"Ah, so your fiancée isn't a fan of fishing?"

Rob frowned. "I don't have a fiancée."

"Oh, sorry, I just assumed you were engaged; Marianne mentioned that you were getting married next year."

"I don't know why —" Rob started.

"Come on, let's go," Andrew urged, all kitted out and impatient to get moving.

"Okay, okay, mister, we're coming," Dot laughed and hurried out of the garage after the children.

Dot had been nervous at the thought of the children standing on the high wall of Howth Pier; a strong wind would take Andrew away, and although she was four years older, Kate wasn't that much bigger than him. But Rob took them to a quieter spot where the water was shallower and the children would be safer, and so Dot found a flat rock to sit on and watch. It was odd to be here in the company of a total stranger but he seemed a lovely and very patient lad. Andrew was on his best behaviour while Kate listened intently as Rob explained everything that he was doing. He allowed each of the children a turn with the rod and showed them how to reel in the line, but the rod was too heavy for either of them to be able to cast off. She smiled, amused that she even remembered the term; Bill would be impressed. She had some very fond memories of their fishing expeditions. They had been happy days; there was something very calming about the sport. She must ask Rob where she could get some smaller rods and she would make a point of bringing the kids here on a regular basis.

They both seemed happy and carefree today and there was a definite improvement in Kate's mood. Marianne's chat with her had helped and mother and daughter seemed much closer. Dot was happy for her daughter-in-law. The poor girl deserved some happiness in her life. But though things did seem to be looking up, Marianne had seemed very low in the last week. Dot had said as much but she'd insisted she was fine. Maybe she was finding it hard to settle into her little house. That thought made Dot frown. She wished Marianne would go out more but except for outings with the children or the occasional drink with Helen and Jo, she went nowhere. Dot wondered if perhaps she was grieving for Dominic, but dismissed the idea immediately as idiotic given what he'd put her through.

"Granny, Granny," Kate squealed, her voice louder and more excited than Dot had heard it in months. "I've caught something!"

"Steady now," Rob said calmly, taking the weight of the rod while allowing the little girl to reel in the fish. "Slowly, Kate, take your time, there's no rush. Andrew, my man, do you think you can handle catching the fish in the net once Kate gets it out of the water?"

Andrew nodded and then, his face a picture of concentration, grasped the handle of the net tightly between his two little hands and trained his eyes on the water rippling around the fishing line.

Dot had to smother a laugh but stepped forward to see what Kate had caught, praying furiously that the bloody fish wouldn't get away.

"That's it, Kate, you're doing great." Rob's voice was quiet and steady. "Can you see it?"

"Yes!" the child gasped, excitement lighting up her face.

Dot swallowed the lump in her throat and gripped Andrew's shoulder as he edged closer to the water to catch a glimpse of the flash of silver as the fish wriggled frantically on the end of the line. And then it was out of the water and Rob hoisted it high for them to see. "Well, would you look at that!" Dot clapped her hands. "Well done, love!"

"Okay, Andrew, are you ready?" Rob asked. "He's a lively little fella so you'll need to keep a tight hold of the net."

"Will I help?" Dot asked, knowing that Kate would brain her brother if he dropped the bloody thing.

"No, I can do it," Andrew insisted.

As Rob lowered the squirming fish into the net, Andrew hung on as if his life depended on it. Rob quickly set down the rod and came over to release the hook from the fish's mouth.

"Now," he looked from one child to the other, "do we keep it and cook it or just take a couple of photos and throw it back?"

Kate didn't hesitate. "Throw it back."

"But take a photo of it first," Andrew said.

"Okay." Dot pulled out her phone. "Say cheese."

CHAPTER
THIRTY-ONE

Marianne emerged from the meeting room and switched on her phone. There was a voice message from Dot, and finding a quiet corner, she played it back. Immediately she heard Kate's voice. "Mum, Mum! I caught a fish! It's huge, it's called a polk —"

"Pollack."

She froze at the distinctive voice that had corrected her daughter.

"A pollack and —"

"It's my turn," she heard Andrew wail. There was a scuffle and then her youngest said, "Mum, I caught it in my net, all on my own. It was really heavy, even Rob said so, but I didn't drop it."

"Say bye, love," she heard Dot say.

"Bye, Mum," her two children chorused happily and then there was silence. Conscious that she was late, Marianne moved out onto the steps in front of the hotel but there was no sign of Johnny. She quickly checked her other messages and found a multimedia one from Dot. She pressed enter and waited for the photo to load. And then there it was: her two kids grinning broadly, a fish between them held by none other than Rob Lee. A horn blared and she looked up to see Johnny's car stop on the other side of the road. She quickly shoved the phone into her bag and ran across to him, almost relieved that she didn't have time to wonder how or why her children were out fishing with her mother-in-law and ex-lover.

She'd got a call first thing this morning from Adrian Matthews asking if she and Johnny would like to drop in later. There had been some developments.

"Nothing to get excited about," he'd warned her, "but I'd prefer not to go into it over the phone." And so Marianne arranged a meeting for after her course finished and called Johnny to see if he was free to join her.

She sensed him hesitate. "If you're too busy . . ."

"No, no it's fine," he said, but he sounded tired and distracted and once they'd agreed a meeting place, he hung up.

"Hi, Johnny," she said breathlessly, climbing in beside him. "Thanks for this."

"No problem, sweetheart. How did it go today?"

"Great, I enjoyed myself," Marianne said, pleased that Rob had been proven right and she was having no problem mastering the technology.

"When do you start?"

"Next week. I'm teaching pensioners how to use email, Twitter and Facebook over three evenings. I'm a bit nervous to be honest."

"You'll be grand. So, any idea what Matthews has to tell us?"

"Not a clue but I don't think it's anything earth-shattering."

356

Johnny guided the car through the heavy afternoon traffic towards Donnybrook. "Still, it's good that he's keeping in touch."

"Why wouldn't he?" Marianne couldn't help retorting. "I've bent over backwards to help him, despite the fact that I'll probably get nothing out of it."

"Hey, what has made you so pessimistic all of a sudden?" Johnny glanced at her.

"Sorry. I suppose I'm feeling a bit stressed." She pulled out a tissue and dabbed the corner of her eyes; she didn't want to go into the office looking like a panda.

"I'm not surprised. When you go home, have a nice hot bath and an early night and you'll be right as rain in the morning."

Marianne thought of Dot's small bathroom and smaller boiler; by the time the children had been bathed, it would take at least two hours for the water to heat again and even then there would be barely enough to cover her legs and she would emerge shivering. "Yes, that's what I'll do." She smiled at Johnny.

He pulled into a parking spot straight across the road from Matthews and Baldwin. "Now, let's go and find out what the man has to tell us."

"Marianne." Adrian Matthews walked into reception, his hand outstretched.

"Hello." Marianne shook his hand and tried to hide her surprise that he'd come to greet them personally.

"Mr Sheridan, good to see you again." Matthews offered him the same firm handshake.

"Please, call me Johnny."

"And I'm Adrian," he replied.

Marianne and Johnny exchanged bemused looks as they followed him down the corridor to his office. He paused at his secretary's desk. "Would you like tea or coffee?" he asked them.

"Tea please," Marianne said.

Johnny smiled. "Me too."

"Tea all round, please, Kara." He stood back to let Marianne precede him into his office and when she went to sit at the desk he stopped her. "Let's sit over here, we'll be more comfortable."

Marianne glanced at Johnny who just shrugged. She figured that Matthews had either very good or very bad news to break. While they waited for the tea, Johnny and Adrian made small talk but she couldn't bring herself to join in. Since that day in her house with Rob when Vanessa had arrived, she had found herself becoming increasingly depressed.

The few times she'd seen or talked to Rob since, he'd been pleasant. He'd said he was too busy to train her himself but she didn't believe that. He was keeping his distance and he was probably right. She found herself wishing that Vanessa hadn't shown up that day and that he had taken her to bed. If he had, she was sure that they would be together now, despite the fact that he was engaged to be married.

Kara brought the tea and once they all had cups in hand, Adrian got straight to the point. "My apologies for dragging you in here but I feel this matter is too sensitive to discuss on the phone. There has been a small development. It would appear that Dominic was not working alone."

Marianne stared at him, too stunned to speak.

"And do you know who else was involved?" Johnny asked.

"Let's say there is a very strong case against one person but we have no hard evidence yet." He looked at Marianne. "It may help you to know though that Dominic seems to have been just a pawn in the operation. He may only have been involved because he was being blackmailed by someone aware of his drug habit."

"Well, that's a turn up for the books," Johnny said, shaking his head in wonder. "No wonder the poor guy had a heart attack; he must have been under terrible pressure. Is the mastermind of the operation one of your other employees?"

Marianne finally found her voice. "Barbara."

Matthews nodded. "You are quite right, although as I said, we can't prove it yet."

"We thought there were discrepancies in her story." Johnny looked from Marianne to Adrian. "But I'd never have guessed this."

"Well, thanks to some of the leads we got through the phone contacts, we found out quite a lot about Ms West. For one thing, she didn't give up her job for Dominic; she was advised that it would be in her best interests to leave."

"Why's that?" Johnny asked, leaning forward.

"For behaviour that, though not quite criminal, was less than ethical, shall we say . . . As for her house, yes she sold it and there is no paper trail but neither is there any evidence that Dominic was involved in the transaction."

Marianne felt as if her head was going to explode; nothing made sense. "But the baby . . ."

Matthews raised his eyebrows. "Ah, yes, the baby. I talked to one of my staff who used to be quite a close friend of Barbara's. When I mentioned Barbara might be pregnant, she laughed and said something to the effect that before even taking a pregnancy test, Barbara would have been on the phone making an appointment for a termination."

"So you think she lied to us?" Marianne hoped, if nothing else, that at least this was true. She'd spent many sleepless nights worrying about Dot and the children finding out about Dominic's other child.

"It's looking that way."

"But why would she? And how could she blackmail him? She loved him." Marianne looked at Johnny. "You saw her face when I told her that Dominic had no plans to divorce me."

"She did seem devastated," Johnny agreed.

"Yes, well, my colleagues and I have discussed that at length. We think her stories about the house and baby must have been to gain your sympathy and put you off the scent. Think about it: in telling you he'd stolen her money and that she was jobless and pregnant, it never occurred to you that she had anything to do with the fraud, did it?"

"No," Marianne agreed.

"I thought she might know more than she was letting on but I certainly didn't think she was the one pulling the strings," Johnny admitted.

"But blackmailing him?" Marianne frowned. "I find that hard to believe."

"Perhaps he'd finished with her," Johnny mused. "Perhaps he'd had enough and was ready to tell all and take the consequences and she had to do something to stop him."

Marianne's thoughts flashed back to an evening only a few weeks before Dominic had died. He had come home looking much more alert than usual and had been very sombre and contrite and promised that things were going to change, that he was going to be a better husband. He seemed so genuine that she had thought there was hope, but very quickly things had returned to the way they'd been before. Had he tried to break free from Barbara and she'd turned nasty?

"Why are you so sure she is behind the whole fraud though?" Johnny asked. "And, if you are, why can't you get her for it?"

"Well, that's just it — we're not completely sure. But it's clear from Dominic's laptop and phone records that he was more of a runner than anything else. As she is the person he seemed to be in contact with the most and she already has a history of unethical behaviour, she seems the likely ringleader. We believe there's at least one other person involved; someone from the company she worked for. They are currently investigating that."

"So you have nothing really on her?" Marianne said, feeling deflated.

"We know that she lied to you about the sale of her house."

"What about it?" she asked.

She told you that he handled it and that he had the money, isn't that right?"

"Yes."

"That's a total fabrication. The house sale didn't go through until after Dominic's death."

"So that's why she never made contact with you before, Marianne," Johnny said. "She didn't need anything from you."

"And then she told us that story so that she would look like a victim rather than a crook," Marianne realized. "Can't we go after her for that?"

"For what, telling a lie?" Johnny sighed. "Remember, love, she never asked you for anything; she hasn't made any demands."

"She knows that it's only a matter of time before we discover the fraud. Right now she's probably planning to leave the country," Matthews said.

"If she hasn't already," Johnny pointed out.

"She hasn't. We've got a PI following her but if she leaves before we've got some hard evidence then there's not a lot we can do about it."

"It's so bloody frustrating that she could get away with this." Johnny looked at Marianne. "I wonder if she has the deeds of your house?"

"No, she couldn't have. She thought the deeds were in my name," Marianne reminded him.

"That's true. So, he lied. That doesn't sound like a man in love, does it?"

"He must have been afraid and trying to break free from her." Marianne actually felt sorry for her husband.

"Given that Dominic wasn't quite the villain you thought he was, does it mean you will give Marianne his pension?" Johnny asked.

"I can't answer that yet."

"But you wouldn't have found out about any of this without her help," Johnny protested.

"Believe me, I am well aware of that." Adrian looked Marianne straight in the eye. "I will be fighting hard for you and I don't give up easily."

"Thank you." Marianne smiled at him. "That's good to know."

Outside, Johnny put his hand on her arm and guided her back to the car, but she stopped halfway. "You go on, Johnny. I think I'll take the train."

"Then I'll drop you at the station on Lansdowne Road."

"No, I'll walk."

"But it's a good twenty minutes away and you can't walk in those." He glanced down at her heels.

"Really, I'll be fine. I just need some time alone before I face the family."

He sighed and gave her a hug. "Call me anytime, okay?"

"I will, thanks."

"Oh, and Frank says that he should have a valuation for us tomorrow."

"Great. I'll order the yacht and the sports car," she joked.

"Take care, love."

He drove off and she started walking down the road in the opposite direction, but within moments became aware of a car slowing beside her and the passenger window lowering.

"Get in, Marianne," Helen said, not even looking at her.

CHAPTER
THIRTY-TWO

"Helen, hi! This is a nice surprise."

Helen couldn't bring herself to even look at her friend. "We need to talk."

"Okay. You seem upset; what's happened?"

"It can wait until we get to the house," Helen said.

Dot and Jo were ready to leave when they got home.

"Why aren't you in your tracksuit?" Jo asked.

"I'm not coming tonight, I have a dreadful headache."

"Ah, you poor thing." Dot gave her a sympathetic smile. "Get an early night, love."

"Yes, I think I will," Helen said, although she had no intention of leaving until she'd said her piece.

Once Dot and Jo had left, Marianne excused herself to go and check on the children. "Put on the kettle, Helen," she said as she disappeared upstairs. Helen ignored the instruction and instead paced the kitchen as she waited to hear what Marianne would say. How could she be so pleasant, so brazen? If Helen hadn't just seen the two of them together for herself, Johnny's smile, the protective hand on her back, she'd begin to doubt herself.

"I'm so sorry about that." Marianne came in almost half an hour later and shut the door. "Andrew is completely hyper this evening."

"Is he okay?" Helen asked.

"Absolutely fine, just excited because he went fishing for the first time today and he's finding it hard to settle. Tea? Coffee?"

"Nothing." Helen continued to pace.

"Please sit down, you're making me dizzy. What is it? What's wrong?"

Helen stopped in front of her. "I saw you with Johnny."

"Yes, we were at Matthews and Baldwin —"

"Are you having an affair?" Helen blurted out.

"Are you serious?" Marianne laughed. "Of course we aren't!"

"Look at me and say that," Helen demanded.

Marianne's expression changed from one of amusement to hurt as she looked Helen straight in the eye. "There is nothing going on between me and Johnny, Helen, and to be honest I'm stunned you could think otherwise."

Helen groaned. She'd known Marianne a long time and would see through her in an instant if she was lying. "I'm sorry, Marianne, but I'm sure he's having an affair with someone."

"Well, it's not me."

Helen sank into a chair and rested her arms on the small table. "I've been going mad; he's being behaving so strangely and you two were spending a lot of time together."

"We're not —"

"I know, I know, I believe you. But if it's not you, who is it?"

"Why are you so convinced he's being unfaithful?"

"His habits have changed, he's preoccupied, he's staying out late and I've caught him lying."

"About what?"

"He says he's going somewhere and doesn't."

Marianne frowned. "I don't understand how he'd have time for an affair; he's practically living with us."

"So you can see why I jumped to conclusions."

"Yes, Helen, I can, but I promise you're wrong."

"I know. I'm sorry."

"It's okay. Have you said anything to him?"

"No, I wanted to talk to you first."

"So, what are you going to do now?"

"I suppose I'll go home and talk to him."

Marianne pressed Helen back into her chair with a gentle hand. "Hang on, if you go in there accusing him the way you just did me, this could get completely out of hand. Let me make some coffee; let's talk this through."

"What's there to talk about? What other reason could there be for him sneaking around?"

"It could be anything." Marianne went to make the coffee. "Perhaps there's a problem at work or he has money worries —"

"You forget I work with him and I look after all of our accounts," Helen pointed out.

Marianne glanced back at her. "I think if Johnny wanted to keep something to himself he could; maybe there's a problem of some sort that he just doesn't want to worry you with."

"We've always been a team; why would that suddenly change?"

"Oh, I don't know, Helen, but I find it very hard to believe that he's being unfaithful."

"You didn't suspect Dominic of being unfaithful but he was."

"Only because he was never around anyway," Marianne carried two coffees to the table and sat down. "And I didn't care enough to wonder. Don't look so shocked, Helen; you can't think I still loved him after all he put me through, and you certainly can't compare our marriages."

"Not at the end, no, but in the early days you were mad about each other," Helen reminded her.

"That seems like a lifetime ago," Marianne admitted, "and he was a different man. Drugs turned him into someone I didn't recognize, someone I didn't even like."

"Poor Marianne."

"There's no reason to pity me; it's all over now and I finally have some peace."

"I did feel that you were more serene recently but today you seem sad."

"I'm fine. There's been so much to take in that I suppose I'm just exhausted."

"You never talk about this woman Dominic was seeing or how you feel about this baby."

"I've tried but you weren't returning my calls," Marianne retorted.

"I'm so sorry." Helen felt dreadful for thinking Marianne was capable of betraying her and abandoning her when she most needed a friend.

"It's okay," Marianne squeezed her hand. "I can understand why now but I still think you're wrong about Johnny."

"Let's forget about him. Tell me all about Barbara. I'm glad you're not upset about her but it still must have come as quite a shock that Dominic was having an affair."

"Of course it did, and when I met her I couldn't see what the woman had seen in him. Oh, that sounds awful but towards the end, Dominic was in such a dreadful mess and could be downright horrible a lot of the time. It was a relief that he was out so much and made it easier to shield the children."

"Johnny described her as posh totty."

"A good description," Marianne grinned. "She's attractive, classy and, it seems, very clever."

"Do you think she loved him? Do you think he loved her?"

"I'm not sure what I think after everything I heard today."

Helen forgot her own worries momentarily as Marianne told her about the meeting with Dominic's boss that afternoon. "No wonder you're exhausted," she said when Marianne paused for breath. "This is all very dramatic and strange."

"And incredibly complicated; I'd have been lost without Johnny. I come out of these meetings and my head is spinning, but he remembers everything."

"I'm glad," Helen said grudgingly. She was grateful that Johnny was looking out for her friend but that didn't absolve him from whatever else he was up to. "So what happens now?" She stopped as the front door banged. "They're back already?"

Marianne glanced at the clock. "Doesn't time fly . . ."

Dot breezed in. "Helen, you're still here!"

"I made her a cup of tea and she took her tablets and felt a bit better, so she stayed for a chat," Marianne said smoothly.

"Yes, I'm fine," Helen nodded, glad that Marianne was thinking straight at least.

"Tea, Dot?" Marianne asked.

"No, thanks, I'm off out again."

"Out?" Marianne raised an eyebrow.

"Just to the pub for a quick drink. It's Shirley's birthday so it's gin and slimline tonic all round," Dot joked.

"Is Jo going?"

"No, she said she'd prefer to have a cuppa with you. She'll be here in a sec; Rachel just called to say goodnight. See ya!"

"Does she ever stop?" Helen asked when they were alone again.

"Not often," Marianne grinned.

"Does she know anything about what's going on?"

Marianne shook her head. "Nothing."

"How do you think she'll take the news that she's going to be a grandparent again?"

"You're pregnant?"

370

Helen looked up to see Jo standing in the doorway looking shocked.

"No!" Marianne assured her.

Jo looked at Helen. "But you said —"

"Come and sit down. I'll open a bottle of wine. I think we could all do with a drink."

"Should you be drinking if —"

"I'm not pregnant, Jo!" Marianne said as she rooted in the cupboard for a bottle of wine.

Jo flopped into a chair. "I don't understand."

"It's complicated," Marianne said, wrestling with the cork.

"Here, let me." Helen took the bottle and prized off the cork with ease and poured some into two glasses.

"Join us," Marianne said.

"I'm driving."

"You don't have to; you could always leave the car here tonight and get the last train home." Marianne's eyes twinkled. "Let Johnny wonder where you are for a change."

"Good thinking." Helen smiled and poured some wine for herself.

"Cheers." Marianne raised her glass to her two friends.

"Will one of you please tell me what's going on?" Jo looked from one to the other, frowning.

"I suppose I should start at the beginning," Marianne said. "You know I told you there would be a hold up with the insurance money and Dominic's pension, Jo?"

"Yes, because of the inquest."

371

"I lied; it was nothing to do with the inquest."

Helen sat in silence as Marianne told Jo the whole sorry saga. "Helen and Johnny are the only ones who know about this, Jo, so please don't let this slip to Dot."

"Of course I won't."

Helen could see that Jo was hurt that she had been in on the secret. "I only know what's been going on because Johnny was helping Marianne sort out Dominic's estate."

"I'd have told you, Jo," Marianne said, "but you've had your own problems lately."

"It's okay, I understand. But will you be able to keep it quiet now if this woman is going to have Dominic's baby?"

"Ah, well, that's what I was just about to tell Helen; there may not be a baby."

"What?" Helen exclaimed, now totally confused. "I don't understand."

"Adrian Matthews thinks that it was all just a story to win our sympathy."

"It should be easy enough to tell," Jo said. "It's two months since Dominic died so she'd be showing by now, wouldn't she?"

Helen looked at Marianne. "Did she say when she was due?"

"No, but she spent ages in the bathroom; she said she was suffering very badly with morning sickness and had been for weeks."

"Then she definitely should have been showing," Jo said.

Marianne stared at her and then at Helen. "She was wearing a suit with the jacket closed, but no, she didn't look pregnant; how stupid of me. Why didn't I realize that before?"

"You've had enough to think about and why would you doubt her? What a conniving bitch; imagine lying about something like that," Helen marvelled. "She must be guilty."

"She must have cared for him, though," Marianne insisted. "She looked distraught when she found out that he'd lied to her about the divorce."

"And if he did that, then he can't have really loved her, can he?" Helen pointed out.

Marianne sighed. "I'm not sure what to think any more."

"Forget about her, and him for that matter," Helen said. "You and the children and Dot are more important, and at least you're not going to get landed with Dominic's debts and may even get your pension."

"Well, I don't know that for sure yet," Marianne cautioned. "Johnny said he'd call Eddie Madden — that's the solicitor — but," she said turning to Jo, "it certainly looks more hopeful."

"I can't believe how strong you're being." Jo shook her head in wonder. "And I thought I had problems!"

"It's been a bit of a nightmare," Marianne admitted.

Helen looked at her. "Are you going to tell Dot about all this?"

"Dot doesn't know?" Jo said.

"Not about the fraud or Barbara. How could I tell her, Jo? He's caused her so much pain already, and though she puts on a brave face, she misses him terribly. And why tell her now? What's the point?"

"There is none," Helen agreed. "As long as Barbara doesn't land on your doorstep one day with Dot's grandchild and the whole fraud business doesn't end up in the papers."

Marianne groaned. "Are you trying to cheer me up?"

"Sorry," Helen said, realizing that she shouldn't be trying to bring her friend down on the one day that she'd finally had some good news.

"It's okay. I suppose there is always a risk of it coming out, but I think I'll take that risk and deal with it if it happens."

"But it must be a terrible strain keeping all of this from her, Marianne," Jo said, looking worried.

Marianne smiled at her and then at Helen. "As long as I've got you two to talk to I will cope with whatever happens."

"You've got us," Helen assured her, "though I'm surprised that you want anything to do with me after today."

"Why, what happened today?" Jo asked looking from one to the other.

Helen looked at Marianne who rolled her eyes and stood up. "I think I'd better find more wine."

CHAPTER
THIRTY-THREE

"I don't believe it for a second." Jo waved her glass around precariously. "Johnny would never ever be unfaithful."

Marianne ducked out of the way as it almost collided with her nose. "I agree with Jo."

"I wish I could believe that, but he's been lying to me," Helen said, visibly upset now that the wine was taking effect and her guard was down.

"I'm sure there's a very good reason," Jo insisted.

"Like?" Helen sniffed.

"Perhaps he's in some kind of trouble."

"You're not helping, Jo," Marianne groaned as Helen's eyes widened in alarm.

"And exactly what kind of trouble could he be in?" She moved the wine bottle out of Jo's reach.

"Maybe he's being threatened," Jo said. "I've heard that's happened to some developers."

"Jo!"

"Oh, my God, you're right!" Helen gasped. "Some of Johnny's friends have left the country because of it."

"Oh, really; I'm making you both some coffee." Marianne stood up and put on the kettle.

"Not that instant stuff, it disagrees with me," Helen complained.

"Tough, I'm on the breadline."

"Tea. But Jo is right; it would make sense."

"It would." Jo nodded so hard Marianne thought she wouldn't look out of place in the back window of a car.

"This is complete rubbish. Stop hypothesizing." Marianne grinned. "I've always wanted an excuse to use that word; Sister Rose Catherine would be proud of me."

"You were always her favourite," Jo said of their English teacher.

"It's not rubbish," Helen insisted. "It makes perfect sense."

"You're listening to Jo's speculations after half a bottle of wine and saying it makes sense?" Marianne said as she spooned coffee into mugs. "No offence, Jo."

"None taken." Jo drained her glass and reached for the bottle.

"It has to be something really bad or he wouldn't keep it from me."

"Oh, for pity's sake, will you just ask the man," Marianne said, plonking down the coffee a bit more forcefully than she'd intended. Perhaps she should have some too.

"Marianne's right; ask him."

Helen looked at them but said nothing.

"What?" Marianne said, alarmed to see the normally composed Helen in tears.

"I'm afraid to. What if there is someone else?"

Jo threw her arms around her, almost strangling her in a hug. "Ah, don't worry, darling. I'm sure everything's going to be fine."

Marianne laid a hand on Helen's shoulder. "Of course it is."

Jo sat back in her chair with a sigh. "I'm a terrible friend; if I wasn't so caught up in my own problems I'd have noticed that you two weren't happy."

"Drink your coffee and don't talk rubbish," Marianne teased.

Helen pulled out a tissue and wiped her eyes. "I'm glad your problems are sorted at least."

"What's wrong?" Marianne asked when Jo didn't reply.

"Nothing."

"Oh, come on, Jo, tell us what's wrong," Helen said. "It's your turn."

"Is it the diet? You're not making yourself sick again, are you?" Marianne asked.

"No, I'm not, honest."

Marianne exchanged a look of relief with Helen. "Good woman."

"Why did you do it, Jo?" Helen asked.

"I told you; it was the easiest way to lose weight."

"I think there's more to it than that."

Marianne wondered why Helen was being so pushy, and then she realized that with Jo more than a little drunk, this was a good opportunity to get to the root of her problems. However, she still hadn't responded. Marianne nudged her. "Have you gone to sleep?"

Jo shook her head.

"Please talk to us, Jo," Marianne begged. "How many times in St Anne's did we promise each other that we'd be friends for ever? Don't you know that you can tell us anything?"

"Anything," Helen agreed.

"It was fear," Jo said, not looking at them.

"Fear?" Marianne said, almost afraid herself of what was coming. Jo seemed suddenly vulnerable, just like the child who arrived at St Anne's all those years ago, looking wary and suspicious and silent.

"I was afraid of losing Greg, of losing everything."

"But why would you ever think that might happen?" Helen asked, looking baffled.

Jo finally looked up and met Helen's eyes. "For the first time in my life I had someone who wanted me, who looked after me and who gave me a home. I was so happy, but at the same time I kept waiting for something bad to happen."

"Like what?" Marianne asked.

"I've no idea but I just couldn't believe that it would last. And then I started to put on weight and I just knew Greg was disgusted with me."

"I'm sure he wasn't," Helen said.

"He was; I could see it in his eyes when he looked at me. And the more I saw that, the more depressed I got and the more depressed I got, the more I ate."

"But now you've taken control," Marianne pointed out, her heart aching for her friend. "The Weightwatchers classes are helping, aren't they?"

"Oh, yes, and the instructor, Shirley, has been so kind."

"So what's the problem, Jo? Helen asked.

"There is none, not really. It's just that the fear doesn't go away, it never goes away."

Marianne thought for a moment before speaking. "You know what, Jo? In all the time we've known each other, you've never really talked about your childhood; I don't mean your time in St Anne's, but before that."

Jo shrugged. "Sister Ignatius said the best thing I could do was to just forget about it."

"Typical," Marianne groaned.

"Do you and your brother ever talk about it?" Helen asked.

"We hardly talk at all, really," Jo admitted. "And we've only met up a handful of times in recent years, and two of those were Mam and Dad's funerals. We're like strangers really. He looks a bit like Dad now." She shivered.

"Perhaps you're better off avoiding him altogether; you need to look after yourself," Helen suggested.

"You know what, Jo? I think you need to talk to your doctor about all of this," Marianne said gently. "You've been keeping everything locked up inside for so many years, it's a wonder you didn't go mad."

Jo smiled. "Ah, sure I did."

"Well, for a crazy woman you've done a damn good job of raising a family," Helen retorted.

Jo smiled. "They're good girls; I am lucky."

"Have you ever told Greg any of this?" Marianne asked.

"No." Jo looked aghast at the thought. "If he knew I felt like this it would really worry him."

"But you need to talk about it," Marianne insisted.

"Why do I? You and Helen are fine." Jo's sigh said that it was her own fault that she was in this state.

"But we came from entirely different backgrounds," Marianne protested. "I was in St Anne's since I was a couple of weeks old; I never knew any other life. And though Ignatius was a bitch and the place wasn't exactly the Ritz, it was my home and I have lots of good memories."

"And I'm no different, Jo. I don't remember life before St Anne's," Helen reminded her. "But you came from a violent home, you were just going into puberty and some of the kids gave you hell; you can't possibly compare us."

Marianne could see doubt and worry in Jo's eyes. "I could come with you if you like, or I'll take you to see my doctor. Mandy is so easy to talk to and I'm sure she could send you to someone who could help."

Jo's eyes lit up. "Oh, yes, I'd much prefer that. My doctor is a nice man but he plays golf with Greg and, well, I just wouldn't feel comfortable talking to him."

"You tell me when suits and I'll set up an appointment with Mandy. We can see her while Greg's at work and he need never know if you don't want him to."

"Thank you," Jo said tearfully. "You're very good."

"Why don't you stay the night?" Marianne asked. "I could put Kate in with Andrew and you could have her bed."

"No." Jo glanced anxiously at the clock. "I should go; Greg will be wondering where I am."

"Johnny too." Helen stood up and stretched.

"Good! It will keep them both on their toes," Marianne laughed.

Marianne was washing their glasses when her phone buzzed. Drying her hands, she went to check it just as she heard Dot come in. It was a picture from Rob of Kate proudly holding the net with the fish in it, and Andrew and Dot either side of her. She smiled as Dot walked into the room. "Look," she said, handing the phone over.

Dot laughed. "Ah, that's a lovely one! Isn't it great to see Kate smiling like that?

"So, tell me: how come you were out fishing with my tenant?" Marianne asked, trying not to sound too curious.

"Rob locked himself out of the house and he couldn't get hold of you . . ."

Marianne closed her eyes briefly; how she'd love Rob to get a hold of her.

". . . so he phoned me. Well, I was only down at the school so we were able to go straight up and let him in. And then when we were eating ice cream —"

"Ice cream?"

"Yes, Rob insisted we go in and have some to thank us; ah, he's a lovely man altogether."

"He is," Marianne agreed. "And the fishing?"

"Well, he was on his way down to a place not far from the harbour and the children were fascinated, wanted to know every last detail, so he asked us to come along."

Marianne felt a warm glow at the idea of Rob spending time with her children, although she'd have been even happier if she'd been there too.

"And you don't have to worry about their uniforms; Rob kitted them out with wellies and jackets." Dot pointed at the phone.

Marianne noticed for the first time that the children were wearing rainproof gear. Of course, she remembered now, he had nephews around the same age. "It looks like you had fun."

"It was a great afternoon; he's a lovely fella."

"Do you fancy him?" Marianne teased.

"Don't you? A fine-looking man like him?"

"This is a very strange conversation to be having with my mother-in-law."

"Yeah, well, we're a strange family," Dot grinned. "But I hope you know that I would never mind you taking up with another man, although I'd probably want to interview him and send him for a medical first, mind."

Marianne had to laugh at that. "You don't have to worry, Dot. I'm not interested in going out with anyone." Well, she was, but he was taken and that was an end to it.

"Ah, you're young, love. You'll meet someone one day, of course you will."

"Perhaps," Marianne said, though she doubted she would ever love anyone the way she loved Rob. She took up the phone and flicked back to the earlier photo of him with Kate and Andrew; how right they looked together, so right that it hurt.

"In the meantime, it will be nice for the children to have a good male influence about the place."

"They're not going to see him that often," Marianne reminded her.

"I wouldn't be so sure; he invited them over next week to meet the nephews."

"Did he?"

"He did, and he struck me as the kind of man who keeps his promises."

"You only met him today, how are you so sure?" Marianne asked, curious as to why Rob had made such an impression on Dot in a few short hours.

"Ah, when you see the way a man is around children you just know."

"I suppose you do," Marianne said. She was touched that Rob had been so kind to her children, but then he'd always loved kids and had probably enjoyed meeting Kate and Andrew having heard so much about them. It made it even harder to accept that he could never be hers. He must really love Vanessa if he'd asked her to marry him; Rob wasn't the kind of man to enter into marriage lightly. And yet, he'd been ready to throw that away for her. The thought thrilled her but she couldn't let him do it. The only reason he'd said those things was because of their history and their sexual chemistry that seemed as strong as ever. When he touched her, an electric shock ran through her body. She couldn't believe that, despite having had no contact for so long, when he held and kissed her it was if they'd never been apart. But she was the past and Vanessa was his present and his future.

"Sorry, what was that?" she said, realizing that Dot had said something.

"Nothing important, love," Dot chuckled. "I was just saying that I think he's basically a good man."

"Yes, Dot, I think you're right."

CHAPTER
THIRTY-FOUR

Rob saved the document and then emailed it to Marianne. He thought for a moment about how to phrase the covering note; should it be light or businesslike? He opted for businesslike. He hadn't heard a word from her since spending the evening with her children, which surprised and hurt him. He thought he would reach her and that she would realize he was serious, but perhaps she had changed and it was too late for them. With a heavy sigh he started to type.

Hi Marianne,
Enclosed are some notes about the course next week, though I'm confident you won't need them. I'll be in London for a few days but still available on the mobile if you need me.

He paused, willing her to need him.

Can you come over on Friday evening so we can review how it's gone?
Good luck!
Rob

The phone rang, and looking at the display, he saw Vanessa's lovely smiling face flash up. "Hi, Vanessa."

"Hello, darling, how are you?"

"Fine but busy; I've a lot to do before I head to the airport."

"I can't believe you're finally coming. We'll have a great time, Rob."

"I'm looking forward to the break," he said, though he found it hard to inject any enthusiasm into his voice.

"I thought we'd go straight to dinner and then we could meet up with some of my friends at a club later."

"Sounds good."

"You'll like them, Rob, they're fun."

"I'm sure I will."

"Okay, then. I'll see you at the airport. Text me if there are any delays."

"I will," he promised.

"Later, darling."

"See you later, Vanessa."

Helen had given Colm fifty euros to make himself scarce for the evening. She made a lovely dinner of Dover sole followed by banoffi pie, two of Johnny's favourites, and opened a bottle of the Australian white wine he liked. When everything was ready to serve, she put on some music, dimmed the lights and lit some candles. Finally, she hurried upstairs, put on a silky red dress that Johnny loved, some lipstick, combed her hair and sprayed on the perfume he'd bought her for Christmas. If there was another woman, she was going to make damn sure that he realized exactly what he was giving up. Feeling sick with nerves, she went downstairs and was just bending down to the oven to check on the fish, when he walked in.

"Well, now, there's a sight to raise any man's spirits after a hard day's work."

She stood up and turned to see him leaning against the door-jamb, watching her with appreciative eyes.

"Do we have someone coming for dinner?" he asked.

"No one."

"Well, that is good news." He crossed the room, took her into his arms and kissed her. "Can I have you for dinner?" he asked as he ran his hands all over her body.

"Later, darling. I need to talk to you."

He groaned. "Ah, I should have known there was an agenda. I don't give a damn if you've spent our life savings on a coat, Helen, I want you."

She smiled, revelling in his excitement and thinking how could he possibly be like this with her if he was having an affair; perhaps Jo and Marianne were right.

He pulled back slightly and studied her. "What are you smiling about?"

"Nothing. Go and pour the wine, dinner is ready."

Johnny chatted easily throughout the meal and when he finished his dessert he sat back contentedly with his wine and smiled at her. "Okay, out with it, woman."

Helen took a sip of water before she answered, suddenly feeling both guilty and foolish. "I followed you on Friday, Johnny. I saw you with Marianne and I jumped to the wrong conclusion."

He looked at her, puzzled for a moment, and then realization dawned. "You thought I was screwing around with Marianne?"

Helen squirmed at his crudity. "Is it so surprising? You've been spending so much time with her and she's so pretty and you seemed so cosy together. And you've been acting very strangely; lying about where you were going —"

"Have you been following me? Checking up on me?" He looked at her in disbelief.

"No, but only because I was afraid that if I confronted you that you would grasp the opportunity to confess and tell me you were leaving me."

"Oh, Helen."

"Don't laugh at me," she snapped, seeing the amusement in his eyes.

He was around the table in a flash and pulled her out of her chair and into his arms. "I'm not, sweetheart. I'm just amused that you could think there is a woman alive who would ever measure up to you."

"Oh, Johnny." She stared into his eyes, mesmerized by the love and tenderness she saw there. "Do you really mean that, after twenty years together? I'm not the easiest person to live with and I know, by times, I drive you mad."

"We drive each other mad; in good ways as well as bad," he said with a grin.

She smiled. "Mmm, yes, we do, don't we?"

He kissed her long and hard. "Let's go and do that right now."

"First tell me what's been going on."

388

"No," he kissed her. "First I'm going to convince you that you're the only woman for me."

Later, Helen lay back in his arms feeling happy and sated. "I'm convinced."

He chuckled. "Glad to hear it."

"I've missed this."

"What, darling?" He kissed her neck.

"We've always had lovely long chats after sex but in the last few weeks you've just gone straight to sleep."

"Ah, well," he sighed, "that's because if we'd talked, you'd soon have got the truth out of me."

Helen turned around to face him. "So there is something."

"There was, but it's all sorted now." He stroked her cheek and smiled into her eyes. "I didn't want to worry you, darling."

"Well, that didn't work, did it? I've been imagining all sorts of things. Is someone threatening you?"

Johnny looked baffled. "No, of course not; why would you think that?"

"You name it, I've thought it. Now, please tell me."

"Okay." He propped himself up on the pillows. "I found a lump under my arm a couple of months ago. It started to get bigger so I went to the doctor."

"Oh my God." Helen sat up, feeling sick. Johnny's mother had died of breast cancer.

"Now don't panic, it's okay."

Helen nodded, willing herself to be calm. "Are they going to do a biopsy?" She sat back to look at him, running her hands over his chest. "I can't see anything; where is it?"

Johnny turned on his side and raised his arm to reveal a small plaster. "They've already done the biopsy, love. I've been in and out of hospital for every feckin' test under the sun in the last few weeks."

Helen searched his face. "And?"

"I got the all-clear on Friday," he smiled.

"Really? Now you're not just saying that, Johnny, because if you are . . ."

"It's true, honestly," he protested.

"Thank God. But if it wasn't cancer, what was it?"

"Just some harmless cyst; they drained it and I'm fine. They only dragged me in for tests because of the family history."

"It was the first thing I thought of."

"Which is why I didn't tell you."

Helen snuggled into him, kissing the plaster gently. "You shouldn't have gone through this alone; you must have got a scare."

"I did," he admitted. "I had to wait a week for the results of the biopsy and all sorts of things were running through my head. After what happened to Dominic, well, it makes you think."

"Promise me you'll check yourself on a regular basis; not just your chest but," she nodded downwards, "everywhere."

He tumbled her over onto her back, laughing. "I tell you what, my love, I'll make a deal with you: I'll check you if you check me."

She laughed. "Oh, really?"

"Yes, now let's get started."

The Aer Lingus 737 made a smooth landing in Heathrow and within minutes Rob was striding through the terminal towards the arrivals hall and Vanessa. He couldn't help wishing that it was Marianne who was waiting for him but he quickly banished the thought. He would speak to her on Friday. Right now he would concentrate on Vanessa. He threaded his way through the passengers in the baggage area and emerged into the arrivals hall. It was swarming with people waiting to greet colleagues, friends, family and lovers. He scanned the crowd for Vanessa. And then there she was, pushing through the crowd, smiling, her arms outstretched.

"Hello," he said, giving her a brief hug. "You look well." And she did; there was a bounce in her step and a confident tilt to her head. "This new job must be agreeing with you."

"It is," she said, looking up at him with a shy smile. "I'm so glad you're here, Rob. I wasn't sure you would come."

"I had to," he said as she linked her arm through his and they made their way towards the exit.

They went to a restaurant in Chinatown. A fabulous place, Vanessa assured him; everyone who was anyone knew it was the *only* place to eat. He listened with interest as she talked about her job and her authors; she was obviously loving every minute. Again he was struck by the change in her. She had always been bubbly and chatty but she usually wanted to talk about them as a couple.

"You're not with me."

"Sorry," he said with an apologetic smile. "My mind wandered there for a second. I was just thinking how happy you seem here. You've changed."

"No, I haven't," she protested. "It's just the job, I love it."

"I think it's more than that. London obviously agrees with you."

"Are you trying to tell me I should stay here?" she joked, but her eyes were guarded.

"Do you have that option? I thought the girl you replaced was only on maternity leave?"

"She is but another position has come up and I've been invited to apply for it."

"That's very flattering; they must think highly of you."

"Do you think I should go for it, Rob?"

He looked at her. "That has to be your decision."

She stared down at her plate for a moment and then raised her eyes to meet his. "Is there any reason why I should return to Dublin?"

"Well, there's your mother . . ."

She gave an impatient toss of her head. "Rob, please, you know what I mean."

He nodded slowly. "I think I do. So, reasons you should come back to Dublin, let me think. Well, there's our wedding to plan; that's next year after we've moved into our house, right?"

She reddened. "She told you?"

"No, actually, her mother-in-law just mentioned it in passing."

Vanessa's eyes widened. "She's married?"

"She's a widow."

She looked slightly shamefaced. "I didn't know that."

"Why did you lie, Vanessa?"

"I didn't like the fact that you were working with such a pretty woman. I wanted her to know that you were taken. You should be flattered," she gave him an awkward smile.

He couldn't return the smile. "I'm not. I don't like being manipulated. You must have realized that the truth would come out sooner or later."

"I'm sorry. I was wrong. Did you come here to tell me off for embarrassing you, Rob, or is there more?" she asked, fidgeting with the chopsticks with nervous fingers.

He looked at her, feeling a bit of a heel for humiliating her, but what she'd done was wrong and it had angered him. He knew that she'd only done it because she loved him and felt threatened, and that is when he knew that he had to tell her straight. "No, you're right, there's more. I'm sorry, Vanessa —"

"Please don't go on," she begged. "I get it."

He sighed, genuinely miserable now for causing her pain, but he knew that she would soon get over him; she had a new focus in her life. "I'm just saying sorry if you feel I messed you about; it wasn't intentional and I did enjoy our time together."

"I enjoyed it too, Rob. Don't feel bad. I was kidding myself. I knew I cared more about you than you did about me. I suppose I thought that if I loved you enough, you would come to feel the same way about me." She gave a small, sad shrug. "But it doesn't work that way. If I was still in Dublin perhaps I'd be begging you now not to end it — that is what you're doing, isn't it?" Her voice wavered but her chin was up and she looked him straight in the eye.

"Yes. I'm sorry, Vanessa." It was a pathetic reply but there was no point in dressing it up. Rob knew that if he talked at length he would give her some hope when there was none.

There were tears in her eyes but she smiled. "Don't worry, darling, it's okay. You're right. I am happy here and I will definitely survive."

"I think you'll do a lot more than that; I think you've found your niche and you are going to make a brilliant editor."

"Thank you."

"You are a wonderful girl," he said and meant it. "And you deserve a guy who worships you."

"Yes, Rob, I do. Would you mind if we went home now? I don't feel much like clubbing."

"Perhaps I should spend the night in a hotel . . ."

"No, darling, let's say goodbye properly; it shouldn't end here like this."

He stared at her, stunned; he couldn't do it.

She recoiled at his expression. "It is her, isn't it, Rob? It's Marianne. My instincts were right; you've fallen for her."

Rob couldn't bring himself to deny it. "There's nothing going on; she has absolutely no interest in me in that way, Vanessa. She's a widow with two little kids and she needs a job; she's not interested in boyfriends."

"You do love her," she gasped.

"Vanessa —"

She sat up straight in her chair and smiled. "I hope it works out for you, Rob, I really do."

"Oh, Vanessa." He put out his hand to take hers. "You are a very special woman."

She smiled but her eyes were bright with unshed tears. "I sure am! You know what? I think it would be best if you stayed in a hotel tonight, after all."

CHAPTER
THIRTY-FIVE

Marianne looked around the room of people Tweeting merrily and felt a buzz of exhilaration. The antacids she'd popped before the class started had been unnecessary. Not only had she managed to teach these people the basics of social networking, they were obviously enjoying themselves and she was having a ball. Who knew that teaching could be so much fun?

"Pat Feeny, you ought to be ashamed of yourself," one woman called across to the man sitting opposite.

"You're not supposed to talk to me, Sandra, you're supposed to Tweet me. Isn't that right, Marianne?" He winked at her.

"That's right, Pat."

"You see?" He sent another message.

"Pat!" Sandra said when another Tweet popped up in front of her, but she was smiling broadly as she carefully typed her reply.

"Ah, me heart is broke," he said with an exaggerated sigh when he'd read it.

"Shush, you're supposed to Tweet," Sandra retorted.

Marianne, who could follow all of her students' conversations on her laptop, was delighted to see that although there were some stilted conversations about the weather, there were also some lively chats going on about grandchildren, holidays and gardening, and Pat Feeny wasn't the only one flirting. It had been a great idea of Rob's to get into this end of the business; she could just imagine the fun it would be when she did the course with Dot's ladies club.

It had been unnerving at the beginning when they'd filed into the room and sat looking at her expectantly, but as soon as she'd kicked off with a few jokes to lighten the mood, as Rob had suggested, everyone relaxed.

She moved around the room now, answering questions and showing more advanced techniques to those who had picked up the basics quickly. Perhaps Rob wouldn't like her going outside of the course material — he also ran an advanced course in networking — but the way she looked at it, the more enthusiastic they became, the more they would want to learn. They would also spread the word about the classes to their friends.

As they filed past her to leave, she handed out information leaflets about upcoming courses.

"You can teach me anything, anytime," Pat told her.

"Dirty oul' divil." Sandra rolled her eyes at Marianne. "Night, love. Thank you, that was very interesting. My grandchildren will be in shock when they start to get emails and Tweets from their nana. Although, now I come to think of it, they might block me!"

"I'll never block you," Pat assured her over his shoulder.

"Shut up and go home to your wife. How she's put up with you all these years I'll never know."

Marianne laughed. "Goodnight, and thanks for coming." After switching off all the computers, she went down to the school caretaker to let him know she was finished and then went out to her car. She was just about to drive off when her phone rang. "Hello?"

"Marianne, it's Johnny."

"Hi, how are you?" she asked. It was the first time she'd talked to him since Helen had confronted him. While she was thrilled to hear that there was no other woman and that his health scare had turned out to be just that, she still felt embarrassed that Helen had thought they were having an affair.

"Grand, not a bother, love. How's my favourite mistress?"

"Oh, Johnny, can you believe it?" she laughed. Trust him to tackle the awkward situation head-on.

"Of course I can. Sure I'm a great catch; all the women are mad for me."

"Or just mad," she heard a voice say in the background.

"Is that Dot?"

"It is. I just dropped in hoping for a quick word; will you be long?"

"I'll be there in fifteen minutes."

"Excellent. Put the kettle on, Dot."

When she walked in, Andrew was sitting on Johnny's knee munching a biscuit and Kate was by his side colouring.

398

"I believe that we're all set for free fish from now on," Johnny said in greeting.

"Ah, yes, thanks to my two budding anglers."

"Three," Dot told her. "I fancy having a go myself."

"So, how did the class go, Teacher?" Johnny asked.

"Really well. I'm not sure how proficient they are but they certainly seemed to have fun."

"Will you come and teach at our school, Mummy?" Andrew asked.

"I wouldn't be allowed, darling. Teachers have to go to college for a long time to be good enough to do that job. Now, you should be in bed."

"I just want to show Uncle Johnny the photos of my fish."

"Another day, pal," Johnny told him. "I need to talk to your mum and then I'm off home to bed too."

Andrew's eyes widened. "You go to bed at the same time as me?"

"Every chance I get," Johnny assured him.

Dot laughed. "Come on, Andrew, if you're quick I'll tell you a story."

"Not out of a book, Granny. I want to hear one of yours."

"Don't we all?" said Johnny. "Maybe I'll stay the night."

"Don't be silly," Andrew giggled. "You wouldn't fit in my bed."

"I'd better go home so and see if your aunty Helen has any tales to tell."

"Bed," Marianne hugged her son. "I'll come up later and say goodnight."

"Mum, can I watch a video?" Kate asked.

"Just for thirty minutes."

"They're both in great form, Marianne," Johnny said when they were alone.

"Yes, they are settling in very well. They love the fact that they can walk to school and play on the green with their friends." Marianne poured a cup of tea for herself. "So, have you news for me?"

No, I just wanted to arrange our next date."

"Oh, stop," Marianne laughed.

He grinned. "Actually, I do have news. Frank came back to me about your paintings."

"Oh? Am I going to be rich?"

"I wouldn't go that far," he chuckled, "but you should do quite well."

"Oh, Johnny, give me more than that," she pleaded. "Are we talking a new toaster, a fridge, a car or a country estate?"

"There are no guarantees, Marianne, but Frank says about forty of them are worth auctioning and he would expect them to fetch at least a hundred grand."

Marianne stared at him, stunned. "You're kidding?"

"Knowing Frank, I'd say that's a conservative estimate; he knows your circumstances and he would never give you false hope. That said, these are difficult times, Marianne," Johnny cautioned. "I find it hard to believe that people are paying the same kind of money for art that they used to."

"I'm sure you're right."

"But he says that because people are afraid of trusting the institutions they are more inclined to invest

400

in something that they can actually see and, I must admit, I trust his judgement, so," he shrugged, "who knows?"

"Johnny, if I got half of that amount I would be thrilled. This is fantastic news."

"So, will I let him go ahead and put them up for auction?"

"Absolutely! Please thank him for me."

"Come along on the day and do it yourself. I think you might like him; all the ladies seem to."

"If he pulls this off I will be his willing slave for life," Marianne assured him.

He laughed and stood up. "I'll go and get the others out of the car. A few he thought were worthless but the rest he says may increase in value over time. It seems Dominic knew more about art than we gave him credit for. Oh, but I nearly forgot! That ugly one that you hate so much? Frank says it's not worth a whole lot and neither is the frame. He figured that perhaps it was the contents that Dominic wanted you to hold on to."

"The contents?"

Johnny produced an envelope from his inside pocket and handed it to her. "He found this."

Marianne looked at it and saw her name written in Dominic's distinctive, flamboyant hand. "I wonder what it is."

"Well, there's only one way to find out," Johnny sighed. "Open it, woman!"

Marianne's hand shook as she tore open the envelope. There were two A4 pages inside; one was a handwritten letter, the other a typewritten page.

Johnny drummed the table with impatient fingers as she read Dominic's letter first.

"Oh my God," she breathed.

"What?" Johnny searched her face.

"He was a clever son of a bitch." She put a hand to her mouth and swallowed back her tears. "It seems he did still care about us, after all."

"Oh, Marianne, tell me, for God's sake."

She handed him the letter. "See for yourself."

Dear Marianne,
If you're reading this then I've disappeared or I'm dead; either way you're probably better off.

I'm sorry for everything. I hope you know that I never set out to hurt you in any way. I always thought I would stay in control, I certainly never believed that I would end up being controlled — but then I was always a conceited bastard, wasn't I?

But I didn't forget you, the kids or my mother; whatever happened I was determined to protect and support you. I paid off the mortgage and the house has been transferred into your name only; the deeds are with a new solicitor, his card is enclosed. Set up a meeting with him as soon as possible, Marianne, and give him the enclosed document. You may or may not know, but I've been involved in a fraud. Reading that back I feel very ashamed but it wasn't premeditated, Marianne, I was simply stupid. Anyway, my solicitor will talk to Adrian and I hope, as a result of the information I've provided, they should be able to recover at least some of the money. My solicitor will explain everything and will look after your interests.

Give Mam a hug, tell her I'm sorry for giving her so much grief. Keep looking after our wonderful kids as well as you always have; tell them I loved them. You must decide how much or how little to tell them about me, Marianne. I know whatever you decide it will be with their best interests in mind.

Love,

Dominic

Johnny set the letter down. "Well, that's a turn up for the books." He took off his glasses then sighed when he saw the tears roll down Marianne's cheeks. "Ah, why are you crying, love? This is good news."

"I know. I suppose I just feel guilty for being so ready to think the worst of him."

"He gave you no reason to think otherwise." Johnny's expression was cold and unforgiving. "He deserves no accolades for finally doing the right thing. Now dry those tears, love. What's on the other page?"

Marianne wiped her eyes and picked it up. "Just some company names and addresses and what look like policy numbers."

"Excellent!"

"He says that I've to bring a copy of our marriage certificate to the meeting."

"Okay, phone the guy first thing and set up an appointment. Adrian Matthews will be serving us champagne instead of tea when he hears this news."

"Will you come with me?" Marianne asked.

"Are you kidding?" He rubbed his hands together in glee. "I wouldn't miss this for the world. Do you know you may end up a wealthy woman before we're through?"

"Perhaps I won't have to work, after all," Marianne said. The thought made her sad. She'd had a wonderful time taking the class this evening, but the thought of watching Rob and Vanessa building their dream home and then possibly even having to attend his wedding . . .

"You'd be mad not to work." Johnny looked at her as if she'd lost her senses.

"But the children need me," was the only reply she could think of.

"The children need a healthy, happy and confident role model, not a self-sacrificing mother who turns into a bitter, disappointed old woman."

"What a pretty picture you paint, Johnny," she said with a wry smile.

"It's the truth and you know it." He stood up. "Get a good night's sleep, sweetheart; I've a feeling tomorrow's going to be quite a day."

"Johnny?"

"Yes?"

"Thanks for everything."

"Ah, sure, don't I have to look after my girlfriend?" He laughed. "See you in the morning, love."

CHAPTER
THIRTY-SIX

First thing the following morning, Marianne called Dominic's solicitor. After an initially frosty reaction when she asked for an immediate appointment, the receptionist came back just moments later telling her to come in at ten thirty. Adrian Matthews agreed to see her at two when she told him that she had new information. She hoped that meeting wouldn't take too long; she was taking Jo to see Mandy at five and she really didn't want to have to cancel — it was a miracle Jo had agreed to see the doctor at all. Straight after that she would be going to take another class. Marianne was also very conscious that the housewarming party was planned for Saturday night and she hadn't been around to help Dot prepare for it at all.

"Perhaps we should put it off," she suggested when she told her mother-in-law of her busy schedule. Thankfully Dot wasn't remotely curious about all the meetings she'd been going to with Johnny, accepting that it was a necessary part of sorting out her son's finances.

"We will do no such thing; the children are looking forward to it. Anyway, all we have to do is tidy the house and make a few sandwiches. Bridie is bringing a cheesecake, Jo and Di are making buns, and Helen said she'd supply a meringue. As for booze, no one will walk in here without at least one bottle. The party's going ahead, okay?"

Marianne met Dot's determined look and saluted. "Yes, ma'am!"

Philip Kenny was a thin, smooth character with incredibly cold, expressionless eyes. Marianne took an immediate dislike to him but within minutes could see why Dominic had chosen him for the job. He was razor sharp and, she imagined, ruthless.

After he'd examined the marriage certificate and asked her a couple of personal questions that only Dominic's spouse would be able to answer, he opened the single file on his desk and took out an envelope. "Your husband instructed me not to open and read this except in your presence, so you must bear with me."

As the man read, Marianne glanced nervously at Johnny who rolled his eyes.

Kenny took his time, re-reading parts and, after what seemed like an eternity, set down the letter and looked across at her. "It seems your husband was involved in a fraud."

"Yes, I know that. His employer discovered it after his death."

"Have they got to the bottom of it yet?"

She shook her head. "They believe they know who was ultimately behind it but they have no proof."

"They do now," Kenny assured her. "Is Barbara West their suspect?"

"Yes!" Marianne sat forward. "So they're right?"

"It would seem so. Your husband has left a very detailed and damning statement and, more importantly, account numbers where various monies have been deposited."

"That's great news," Johnny smiled and squeezed Marianne's hand.

"How has your relationship been with them?" Kenny asked.

"Excellent. Marianne has co-operated fully; they wouldn't have progressed this far with their investigation without her help."

Kenny ignored the comment and addressed Marianne. He hadn't wanted Johnny at the meeting but Marianne had insisted. "Speed is imperative now. I suggest you phone this man," he glanced down, "Matthews, and arrange for us to go straight over there."

"Us?"

"Yes, from now on I will be attending any meetings you have with your husband's employer."

Marianne looked slightly alarmed. "I'm not sure I can afford —"

"My fees have been taken care of."

"Oh, I see," Marianne said, although she didn't really. Dominic must have paid the man up front or perhaps one of the account numbers was to cover the solicitor's bill. She looked over at Johnny for his reaction but he just shrugged and smiled. "I've arranged a meeting for two o'clock."

"I'd prefer to do it now; I'm playing golf this afternoon and I have a feeling that Mr Matthews will be happy to accommodate us. Now, will you phone him or shall I?"

The rest of the day went by in a whirl and when Marianne finally sank down on to Helen's comfortable sofa to enjoy a glass of wine, she felt exhausted. Jo had said little about her session with Mandy but when she emerged from the doctor's office she gave Marianne a tight hug that spoke volumes. Tonight she seemed very relaxed and sat next to Helen as Johnny told them of their meetings with Kenny and Matthews in a typically theatrical and entertaining fashion.

"And there you have it," he said in conclusion. "Barbara West is not pregnant, she is definitely still in the country and it's only a matter of time before she's brought to justice."

Helen frowned. "But won't that mean the whole business will be in the papers?"

"That seems to be where Rottweiler Kenny comes in. He and Dominic seem to have gone to great lengths to prevent that, but only time will tell."

"If it comes out, it comes out," Marianne said with a resigned shrug.

Johnny raised his eyebrows. "That's a remarkably laid-back reaction from you."

"I was just thinking the same thing," Helen said. "You've gone to such lengths all along to protect Dot and the children."

"And I'm glad I did, but its different now. Dot would have been so ashamed and devastated before but now she would take great comfort from the fact that, in the end, Dominic did the right thing. I think I should tell her everything. As for the children, perhaps it would be no bad thing for them to know first-hand how drugs can ruin a life."

"Whoa, slow down, girl, don't rush into anything."

"Helen's right," Johnny said. "It could be months, even years, before anything comes to light; there is no need to make such enormous decisions right now."

"Yes, of course, that's true," Marianne agreed.

"How is the job going?" Jo asked.

"It's only day two but I have to say, I love it. I went in there this evening hardly able to think straight but within minutes I was completely engrossed."

"I'm glad everything is finally working out for you," Jo said. "It's wonderful that you own the house outright; that must be such a relief."

"It is," Marianne said with feeling and yawned. "Oh, I'm so sorry."

Johnny laughed. "Come on, I'll drop you home."

"Don't be silly, you can drop me to the train station along with Jo."

"If you need anything done on Saturday just call," Helen said, hugging her friend.

"Thanks."

"You'll sleep well tonight, I think." Johnny smiled as they walked out to the car.

"Yes," Marianne lied. The thought of seeing Rob tomorrow evening already had her stomach in a knot; she'd be lucky if she slept at all.

Jo crept into the house, slipped off her shoes so she wouldn't wake anyone, and went into the kitchen for some water. She pulled up short when she saw Greg sitting at the table drinking a beer. "Oh, hi, I thought you'd be asleep."

"You mean you hoped I would be."

"What does that mean?" she said, fetching a glass and going to the tap.

"You're hardly here these days. When you're not with Helen or Marianne or going to a class, you're out walking with the girls; anything, basically, to avoid me." He drained his can and crushed it.

She looked at him in astonishment. "I'm just trying to get my weight under control; I thought you'd be happy."

"There's nothing wrong with your weight," he said in frustration. "Why are you always going on about it?"

"But you don't like me fat."

"When have I ever said that? In fact, when have I ever said that you're fat?"

"Well . . ." Jo faltered, at a loss to come up with an example. "You don't have to say anything; I can see it in your eyes."

"What can you see?" he demanded.

She couldn't look at him. "Disappointment."

He sat back in his chair with a sigh. "You're right, I am disappointed."

She looked up, hurt and surprised by his bluntness, but then she saw the despondent look on his face.

"Disappointed that I can't afford to give you the life that Johnny gives Helen or Dominic gave Marianne.

Disappointed that despite working my arse off at a job I hate, it's still a struggle. Disappointed that I have a lovely family but instead of enjoying them I snap at them; instead of doing things with them, I spend my time looking for ways of earning more money or schmoozing up to the likes of Tracy Donovan's dad at the golf club hoping to get more business. Did you know that the reason that little bitch has got so chummy is because Rachel has been doing some of her maths homework for her?"

"No! How did you find that out?"

"When I was taking Rachel to school this morning, she dropped her bag and Tracy's copy book fell out."

"What did you do?" Jo asked, half-afraid to ask.

"Nothing. I could see immediately from her expression that there was something going on, so I pretended not to notice. I thought it would be better if we both sat down and talked to her over the weekend."

Jo looked at him, surprised that he'd shown such sensitivity. "The poor kid; she was buying friendship."

"I suppose we all do that at one time or another," Greg said, looking tired and fed up.

Jo sank into the chair beside him. "I didn't know you hated your job."

"Detest it. I hate fucking golf too." He raised his eyebrows when Jo giggled. "Are you laughing at my misery?"

"No, love, I'm laughing because that was funny. I'm sorry you're miserable. I always thought you were doing exactly what you wanted and knew exactly where you were going."

"Well, if I'm honest I suppose that's what I wanted you to think. You were so insecure when we met, Jo; such a frightened little thing. I wanted to make you feel safe."

"Oh, Greg; you're a good man."

"You don't really believe that; you think I'm a grumpy bastard and as for Di, I'm just a waste of space, an embarrassment."

"She's a teenager who thinks she knows it all; hating us is her job." She smiled at him.

"You were supposed to say I'm not a grumpy bastard," he grumbled.

"You have your moments," Jo smiled. "Oh, Greg, Why haven't we talked like this before?"

"I don't know. I suppose neither of us were exactly brought up to share. My mother always told me to 'be a man', which basically meant put up and shut up."

"Then let's make a deal that we'll talk more, okay?"

"Okay."

"As for not being able to give me things, I have everything I want and need, and don't ever compare yourself to Dominic; he gave Marianne a terrible life."

Greg's eyes narrowed. "What do you mean?"

"It's too long a story to go into tonight, but he was seriously messed up and he was far from a good husband."

"Wow. Please tell me Johnny Sheridan's an asshole too."

"No, sorry," Jo laughed. "He's a good guy, but like everyone else he has his problems."

"Why have you been going out so much lately," Greg said, "if it's not to get away from me?"

"I told you, I'm trying to get my diet under control."

"And I told you that you're not fat."

"I know, and you've no idea how good it is to hear you say that. I thought that if I didn't get back in shape, you might leave me."

"What? That's ridiculous."

Jo could have cried in relief at the look of total disbelief on his face. "I've been very stupid, Greg. Trust me, you may well want rid of me when I tell you everything."

He took her hand. "Look, Jo, I may not be the sort of husband who brings home flowers or takes you out for slap-up dinners, but I love you and I doubt there's anything you could do or say that would change the way I feel about you."

"Do you really love me, Greg?" she asked, looking at him intently.

"Bloody stupid question, 'course I do." His expression softened. "Now just tell me."

CHAPTER
THIRTY-SEVEN

Marianne had applied some make-up in an unsuccessful effort to disguise the dark circles under her eyes as a result of the sleepless night. But even though she was tired, it had been a nice day. She had helped Dot clean the house that morning while the children played on the green and then she'd taken the two of them to Portmarnock with their newly purchased nets to mess about in the rock pools. Afterwards, as they sat on a wall licking ice-cream cones, she asked them if they missed Howth.

"Only the trampoline," Andrew said, "and I'll get to play on that next week."

"We'll have to see about that; they may have other plans," Marianne warned him.

"No, Rob said he'd arrange it and he will," Kate said confidently. "He's our friend."

"Wish he was mine," Marianne muttered now as she parked in front of her house — her house! It was such a relief to know that she actually owned something. Even if she never got a pension, with no mortgage to pay, the proceeds from the sale of her paintings and a regular salary, the future seemed so much more secure. She was glad that finally Dominic had done something that showed he still cared about his family. She would heed Helen and Johnny's advice and not tell Dot just yet but it was good to know that if the time came, she could assure her that Dominic had done the honourable thing in the end.

She checked her reflection and groaned at the washed-out face that looked back at her. An image of the pretty, vibrant Vanessa came to mind but she dismissed it, reminding herself that she wasn't in competition with Rob's fiancée. She popped an antacid, stepped out of the car and went to the boot to collect her bag and business folder. As she walked up the path she prayed that her voice would be steadier than her nerves and she didn't make a complete eejit of herself.

It was some moments before the door opened and a distracted Rob, his phone clamped to his ear, waved her in. "Go on into the kitchen and grab a cuppa, I'll be with you in a minute," he whispered before retreating into the office and shutting the door in her face.

Marianne's heart sank as she realized he must be talking to Vanessa, and then anger took over when she thought of the intimate phone conversations they'd shared in the days before his fiancée walked in on them; how could he have behaved like that?

She was sorely tempted to leave but that would seem childish and then he would be in no doubt of her feelings and, if nothing else, she still had her pride. She had agreed to a working relationship so she would just have to grin and bear it. She continued down the hall and pushed open the kitchen door, pulling up short at the sight that greeted her. The kitchen had been transformed into a café, a rather grubby and vaguely familiar one at that.

Rob had recreated Mario's, their old haunt. Marianne's smile broadened as she took in all the detail. Two lamps with red shades spread a brothel-like glow across the room. The table was covered in a cheap, synthetic, red-checked tablecloth. In the centre stood a Chianti bottle complete with a red candle dripping wax down the sides, and beside it a jar holding a plastic red rose. She started to laugh when she noticed the fake crystal glasses that were almost identical to the ones in Mario's. The unmistakable smell of lasagne and garlic bread drew her attention to the glass door of the oven. Marianne peered in, wondering if Rob had cooked it. She certainly hoped not — she had experienced a couple of his disastrous efforts in the past. And then she was distracted from the food by the sight of the fridge door covered in photos. As she moved closer she saw that they were all of her, taken by Rob on his phone either when they were in the café, his car or at his flat. One photo made her gasp as she remembered he'd taken it just after they'd made love. It seemed abundantly clear too as her hair was tossed, her eyes shining and her lips parted in a languid smile. She closed her eyes briefly, savouring the memory of the afternoon that had resulted in that smile. There was only one photo of Rob and it was right in the centre of the display. It was the one of him with her children.

416

"They look happy, don't they?" Rob murmured in her ear, making her jump.

"I don't know what to say," she whispered.

"Tell me you love me." He turned her to face him and rested his hands on her hips.

"No." She pushed him away and walked around the other side of the table; it was easier to be strong if there was something between them.

"Why? Because of Vanessa?"

She looked at him in disbelief. "Yes, because of Vanessa!"

"She lied to you, Marianne."

"What do you mean?"

"We're not engaged, we never were."

Marianne searched his face, trying to take in his words. "But she said you were getting married next year."

"So I heard. The truth is that she felt threatened by you and wanted to make it clear that I was unavailable."

"Which you are; she's still your girlfriend," Marianne pointed out. "Tell me, did she know when she walked in on us that day that we'd been talking almost daily on the phone?"

He shook his head. "No, she didn't. But it doesn't matter now, Marianne. The reason I went to London was to tell her it was over."

Marianne's heart lifted, though she felt almost afraid to believe him; she couldn't take much more of a battering. "Why did you finish with her? Was it because of me?"

"Yes and no. We've been together about a year and it was fine; she was lovely."

Marianne flinched, amazed at how much his words hurt.

"Then she started to make noises about moving in together and I knew I couldn't do it, that it wasn't what I wanted. I was about to end it when she was offered a temporary job in London. It seemed the perfect out. I figured she would soon forget me and the relationship would just die a natural death."

"You wimp." Marianne tried to sound disapproving but couldn't prevent a smirk.

"A total wimp, but don't I get brownie points for flying to London and ending it face to face?" He walked around the table and stopped just inches away.

"You should have done it sooner."

He put his arms around her. "I know."

Marianne looked up at him, drinking him in and yet still nervous. She was thrilled he had finished with Vanessa, but couldn't help feeling sorry for the girl. If she cared so much about him to lie, how devastated she must feel now. "How did she take the news?"

He looked slightly uncomfortable. "She was okay. She loves it over there and the job seems to be working out well. So . . ." he looked into her eyes, cupped her cheek and ran his thumb along her lips, "am I forgiven?"

"No," she said, wondering if he could hear the tremor in her voice; a dead giveaway that his touch was having the same effect it always had.

"Why not?"

418

She scowled, not ready to let him off the hook despite the fact that her heart was thumping simply because he was so close. "Because you never told me about her, of course. You were taking me to bed, Rob, and she walked in on us. And if she hadn't, would you have even mentioned her?"

"You know I would have," he looked reproachful. "Yes, I admit, I put it off because I was just enjoying getting to know you again and I didn't want to do anything to spoil that. But she was never the one, Marianne. My biggest sin was staying with her for so long. Do you believe me?"

"I believe you," Marianne said, spellbound by the look of love in his eyes.

"Does that mean I'm forgiven?" He kissed her.

She felt her whole body melt. "It does," she said, and kissed him back, losing herself in the taste of him.

"Can I interest you in some lasagne?" he murmured.

"No." She moved closer so that she could feel the length of his body against hers.

He groaned. "In that case, let's go upstairs and work up an appetite."

"No!" Marianne drew back; how could she have forgotten?

His smile faded. "What is it, what's wrong?"

Marianne sighed. "We need to talk."

"We can talk upstairs, darling . . ."

"No, here. Can I have a drink, please?" She sat down at the table.

"You're worrying me now." He produced a bottle of Saint Emilion and filled the glasses.

"That's not what we used to drink." She picked at the wax on the bottle, wondering how he'd react to what she had to say.

"No, but serving you the vinegar that Mario used to stock would be taking the illusion just a little too far." He raised his glass to her. "Cheers."

"Cheers," she said without enthusiasm, and took a sip.

"What is it, darling, what's wrong?"

"I need to tell you why I ended things between us."

"It doesn't matter . . ."

"Please, Rob, just listen," she begged.

"Okay, go ahead." He settled back in his chair, his eyes on her face.

She took another drink. "I told you that Dominic used to lose his temper and scare me. What I didn't tell you is that sometimes it went a bit further than that."

Rob's expression froze. "Are you saying the fucker hit you?"

She nodded.

"Marianne!"

She held up her hand. "He hurt me a few times, though, to be fair, I don't think he realized what he was doing; sometimes he didn't even remember."

"You told me he took a lot of pills but I had no idea he was violent; why didn't you tell me?"

She looked at the reproachful and frustrated expression on his face and sighed. "What was the point? You couldn't have done anything."

"You should have left him; I would have given you a home and protected you and the children."

"He never hurt the children."

"He just knocked his wife around; that's okay then." He crossed his arms and shook his head in helpless fury. "What did he do to you?"

"Rob —"

"Just tell me, Marianne. Please?"

She sat in silence for a moment. She didn't see how it would help but she knew that they would never be able to move on if she wasn't completely honest with him. "Okay." As Marianne told him of the various episodes, she watched the fury build up in him and wondered if she should continue.

"Go on, it's okay," he said, and she smiled at how easily he could still read her after all this time.

"I realized that my period was late and I thought I might be pregnant. I bought a test and waited until the children were asleep that night before I used it. I was in the bathroom just opening the box when Andrew let out a scream so I dropped it and ran to him. It turned out to be just a night terror but it took me a while to calm him." She pause and massaged her stomach, wishing she hadn't left the antacids in the car. "When I came back into the bathroom Dominic was sitting on the side of the bath with the test in his hand. I could see that not only was he high, he was mad too."

"But why?" Rob asked.

She met his eyes. "We hadn't had sex in months so he knew it meant that I was seeing someone else."

"Oh, Marianne," he shook his head in anguish. "What happened?"

She stopped for a moment as she remembered that terrifying night. It was amazing how clear each detail was.

"There was a heavy glass jar of bath oil beside him and he just picked it up and threw it at me. It missed but smashed against the wall; there was glass and oil everywhere. I turned to run but he was too quick for me. He swung me around, held me against the wall and . . ." she swallowed, "he punched me in the mouth."

"Jesus!"

"He never said one word during the whole thing, and then he just left afterwards, the way he always did. I wasn't sure what damage he'd done but blood poured out of my mouth and my whole face throbbed. I went to get some toilet paper to clean myself up but I slipped in the oil and fell hard. I felt something stick into me but I didn't pay much attention. All I wanted to do was get everything cleaned up in case one of the children saw it or me. I dragged myself up onto the toilet seat and was mopping up my mouth when I saw a shard of glass sticking out of my stomach."

"I don't believe this." He stared at her in shock. "Why didn't you call me?"

"Oh, Rob, you were the very last person I could call," she said, half-laughing, half-crying. "Though I felt dazed, something told me that it would be a bad idea to pull out the glass. So I tied a towel around me and went into the bedroom and phoned Helen. She stopped off on the way over to collect Dot, When she saw the state of me she was furious; I've never seen her so angry. She

422

wanted to call the guards. 'Now do you see what your precious son is capable of?' she said to Dot. Anyway, she carted me off to A&E. It looked worse than it was, though. I only had a chipped tooth and a cut lip but I was right not to pull out the glass; it had gone in very deep and they said if I had, I could have bled to death. Anyway they sewed me up and sent me home."

He looked at her. "Were you pregnant, Marianne?"

She shook her head and felt a tear trickle down her cheek. "No, Rob, I wasn't."

"Did you report him?"

"No."

"He hurled a glass jar at you," Rob exclaimed. "If his aim had been better he could have killed you; how could you protect him?"

"Because he's the father of my children, because I'd been unfaithful and because I realized that night what a very sick man he must be. I did decide, though, to throw him out."

"And did you?"

Marianne sighed. "No."

Rob looked at her, his eyes full of frustration. "I just don't understand."

She looked at him wondering how she could possibly explain the situation; how she could make him realize how little choice she had. "Dot begged me not to," she told him. "She was convinced that he would end up in the gutter if he didn't have his family around him and I thought she was right. Instead, she offered to move in. She said she'd protect me and the children and that she'd shop him herself if he got violent again. So I agreed." Even though Rob was here with her again, silent tears rolled down her face as she remembered how distraught she'd felt at that moment. "I knew that I would have to finish with you. I wouldn't have been able to hide the scar from you and I knew when you saw it you'd want to kill him. There was no way out, Rob. I had to protect you and the only way I could do that was by saying goodbye." Her voice was barely a whisper by the time she'd finished and she had given up trying to stem her tears.

He came around the table and kneeling in front of her, lifted her shirt and examined the red scar that curved around her naval. He kissed it. "I wish you'd told me; I wish you'd trusted me to figure out a solution. We could have been together, Marianne."

She cradled him against her breast, luxuriating in the feel of his lips on her skin. "You're here now; that's all that matters."

He drew back and looked at her. "I want to make love to you."

She looked into his eyes. "I want you to make love to me too."

He stood up and held out his hand to her, and in silence she took it and allowed him to lead her upstairs.

Marianne lay in her old bed, her limbs tangled with Rob's, his fingers tracing the crescent-shaped scar on her stomach. Despite their long, languorous love-making, she still trembled at his touch.

"What are you thinking?" he asked, propping himself up on one elbow and looking down at her.

"I thought only women asked that question." She closed her eyes so that he couldn't read her thoughts.

"I'm getting in touch with my feminine side. Hey, are you crying?"

"No,"

"You are." He kissed her eyes with infinite gentleness. "Why, darling?"

"I can't stop thinking of you in bed with her," she admitted, and then she opened her eyes and looked at him in horror. "Oh, God, you didn't make love to her here, did you?"

"No." He pulled her close. "Forget Vanessa," he said, and kissed her.

"That's easier said than done." She believed him when he said he loved her but he'd still spent almost a year with a very beautiful woman, and the thought of him doing the things to Vanessa that he had just done to her made her feel sick with jealousy.

"How do you think I felt every time you left me to go home to Dominic?"

"It's not the same," she protested.

"Why isn't it?"

"It just isn't."

"Look at me," he demanded. "Talk to me."

Reluctantly, Marianne turned to face him, immediately feeling exposed. Those eyes, those gorgeous eyes always seemed to be able to see right into her very soul.

"Tell me," he ran one finger down the length of her spine, making her shiver.

"I can't think, never mind talk if you do things like that!"

He stopped and smiled. "Okay. I'm waiting."

She sighed. She felt vulnerable but she wanted to be honest with him; knew it couldn't be any other way. "Okay then. Do you remember the first time we made love?"

He snuggled closer, smiling. "Oh yes."

"Well . . ."

"Well?"

"I never slept with Dominic after that."

His eyes widened. "Really?"

"Really."

"Why not, Marianne?"

She held his gaze. "Because it would have felt wrong. I just couldn't do it."

He was silent for a moment, a faraway look in his eyes. She studied him closely trying to figure out what was going on in his head. "Rob?"

He looked at her. "Remember the day we kissed on Patrick Kavanagh's bench on the canal?"

She smiled. "Yes."

"I haven't had sex with Vanessa since then."

"Really?" Her eyes searched his.

"Really. I admit there was an attempt on her part the night before she left for London but," he sighed, "let's say, I couldn't rise to the occasion."

She tried to suppress a grin. "Really?"

He rolled his eyes. "Really."

"Why not?" she pressed, still finding it hard to banish the image of the lovely Vanessa from her mind.

He looked at her in silence for a moment and then traced her lips with his finger. "Because she wasn't you."

"Oh, Rob." She cupped his face in her hands and kissed him.

"I'm glad you weren't pregnant," he said when they broke apart.

"Are you?" she asked, surprised and a little upset. It had never occurred to her that Rob wouldn't have wanted their child.

"Yes, because if he'd killed our baby, Marianne, I think I would have killed him."

She threw her arms around his neck and clung to him. "Oh, my love, if he had I'd have killed him myself."

His eyes widened in surprise. "You wanted the baby?"

Again Marianne's thoughts returned to that fateful day. "I remember when I realized my period was late. I remember going in to buy the test. And I remember thinking that Dominic would know instantly that it wasn't his and that he would go berserk. But . . ."

"But?"

She looked into his eyes. "I didn't care, Rob. I was on cloud nine at the thought that I might be carrying your baby. When they did a test in the hospital and told me it was negative, I cried."

"Oh, my darling." He pulled her tight against him and held her there in silence for a long time.

Marianne relaxed into him, giving herself to him, allowing him to feel through her body what no words could possibly say; she had finally come home.

"How do you think Kate and Andrew would feel if we gave them a brother or sister?" he asked.

Marianne smiled at the tenderness in his eyes and thought she would die of happiness. "They might find it hard to accept if it happened too soon," she said and kissed him. "But, given time, I'm sure they'd love it. They already love you."

He rolled her over onto her back and looked down at her. "So we should just practise for the moment, is that what you're saying?"

She looked up at him, laughing. "Yes, darling, that's what I'm saying."

"You do know I'm serious?"

Marianne frowned. "Serious about having a child?

"Serious about everything, Marianne. I'd love you to have my child. Hell, I'd love you to have several but if it wasn't what you wanted, if Kate and Andrew were enough for you, then they'd be enough for me too. I just want you back."

"Oh, Rob, I love you," Marianne said and clung to him, shaken by the sincerity of his words.

"Then I have just one more question to ask."

"What's that?" she drew back to look at him.

"Once life has settled down for you and the children are back on an even keel, will you marry me?"

She stared at him. "Marry you?"

His eyes held hers. "Yes, marry me. I know you can't begin to think about it now, I know it's far too soon for

428

Dot and the kids to even know about us, and I'm sure you probably have doubts about ever going down the aisle again . . ."

Marianne put her fingers over his lips and smiled. "I have no doubts at all when it comes to you, my darling. Of course I'll marry you. Now, I have a question for you. If I take my hand away, will you please kiss me?"

His eyes smiled and he nodded and Marianne took her hand away. As she lost herself in his kiss, she thought of the days, the months and the years ahead and knew, with total certainty, that if she put her trust and faith in this wonderful man, it didn't matter what shocks or surprises life had in store, she would never ever feel lonely or afraid again.

ISIS publish a wide range of books in large print, from fiction to biography. Any suggestions for books you would like to see in large print or audio are always welcome. Please send to the Editorial Department at:

ISIS Publishing Limited
7 Centremead
Osney Mead
Oxford OX2 0ES

A full list of titles is available free of charge from:

Ulverscroft Large Print Books Limited

(UK)
The Green
Bradgate Road, Anstey
Leicester LE7 7FU
Tel: (0116) 236 4325

(Australia)
P.O. Box 314
St Leonards
NSW 1590
Tel: (02) 9436 2622

(USA)
P.O. Box 1230
West Seneca
N.Y. 14224-1230
Tel: (716) 674 4270

(Canada)
P.O. Box 80038
Burlington
Ontario L7L 6B1
Tel: (905) 637 8734

(New Zealand)
P.O. Box 456
Feilding
Tel: (06) 323 6828

Details of **ISIS** complete and unabridged audio books are also available from these offices. Alternatively, contact your local library for details of their collection of **ISIS** large print and unabridged audio books